Quentin Cundick and The Web of Machinations

ALASTAIR PACK

ISBN-13: 978-1500856151
ISBN-10: 1500856150

DEDICATION

For Fiona, who'll never read it,
and James, who one day may.

CONTENTS

ACKNOWLEDGEMENTS

I've nothing but gratitude to Andrea Orlic of Artrocity for her tireless efforts designing the wonderful cover. Thanks are also due to Morven Pack, Edward Lee and Pab Roberts for their input prior to publication and to my dad John for all his support. And, of course, I'd also like to add a special thanks to my wife Emma for her love and forbearance throughout.

CHAPTER 1: WEDNESDAY

Alone in his office, Quentin was the master of all he surveyed. He sat behind his oh-so-grand mahogany desk and basked in a warm feeling of self-importance. He leant back in his brass-studded, burgundy leather chair and admired his workspace for the sixteenth time that day. He perused the many impressive-looking legal tomes filling the sagging shelves that lined the walls from floor to ceiling. With a smile of satisfaction, he appreciated the ubiquitous 'fake yucca in oversized terracotta plant pot' which resided in the corner of the room. A nice touch, he thought, especially next to the white, horizontal blinds which broke up the sunlight and laid a shadowy cattle-grid across the carpet. He clasped his hands behind the back of his head and let out a gratified sigh. Overall, he felt contentment. He felt that he was a man who had made good.

"You see, my dear chap," explained Quentin, patiently, "there arc two types of people in this world. Those who talk out loud to themselves, and those w-" He stopped as he saw the door to his office open. His legal secretary popped her head around the door. "Yes?" he enquired.

Mavis beamed a toothy smile as radiant as the pearl necklace overlaying her red blouse. "Client to see you, sir."

He cleared his throat. "Seat them and I'll be out in a

minute."

Mavis cleared her throat. "Perhaps I should just send him in, since we haven't had a client in three weeks and you're not exactly doing anything?"

Quentin considered the proposition and nodded perfunctorily. Mavis was replaced by a shabby-looking man, about forty, sporting a tatty suit not this side of fifteen years old. His receding hair was slicked back and his smart silk tie did nothing to make him look more respectable. His hands were calloused and his fingernails dirty. Quentin scoffed inwardly and adjusted the crisp, white, shirt cuffs emerging from the sleeves of his pristine, pin-striped suit.

"Please, take a seat." He gestured with an open palm over his oh-so-grand mahogany desk toward the uninviting straight-backed seat awaiting his client. Normally he would shake hands, but today he decided 'hygiene' featured a shade above 'customer relations' on his priority list. "Any trouble finding us?"

"Not really. No, I didn't," replied his client in a tremulous Welsh accent. "I'm Bryn Jones, I am. A farmer. I've come from Wrexham, I have."

After some quick mental syntax-shuffling, the lawyer nodded his understanding. "It's a pleasure to meet you, Mr Jones. I'm Quentin Cundick and I'll be handling your case through to completion. Now, perhaps you could begin by summarising for me – just quickly – just skimming the surface - what I can do for you?" Quentin made sure the inflection in his voice ensured he wouldn't receive a rambling life story. He had attempted to perfect this technique over the last twenty four years of his career as a solicitor. It rarely worked.

The farmer wrung his hands. "A touchy matter, it is. I was hoping, well, thinking that maybe you could help me with it. Concerns a deal that went sour. A deal that... crossed the border." The farmer gave him a sheepish look.

"That's my specialty," Quentin assured him, lying.

"Da iawn," said the Welshman in his birth tongue. "Da iawn."

"That's your father is it?" Quentin received a curious look and so decided to start afresh. "Perhaps you could take it from the top?"

"Well, it all started a month ago, it did, when some sheep…"

Quentin heard no more. He was already bored. Whatever this man's problem was, it was surely not going to prove to be the intellectual challenge that Quentin craved. As his eyes glazed over, he could hear the man droning on with his erratic phraseology. Slowly, tentatively, he stole a glance at his watch. He did it as carefully as possible, to ensure the farmer wouldn't – couldn't – notice.

"Oh, I'm sorry, have you got another appointment?"

"No, no. Please continue. You were saying..."

He should have known he would be spotted. These Welsh farmers could spot a lost leek in a snowstorm from five thousand paces. Quentin struggled to bring his attention back to the farmer's story, but managed just in time.

Mr Jones cracked his knuckles with inappropriate gusto and launched into his tale afresh. "I was asked to transport livestock to Wrexham from my farm in Rhosllanerchrugog." Quentin controlled the impulse to offer him a tissue. "I have a brother who lives in Wrexham and he put me up. But something unusual happened." He paused, for what appeared to be no better reason than dramatic effect. "Late in the evening a man came knocking. We looked at each other funny, we did. We got up and answered the door, we did."

"Sorry, who answered the door?" interjected Quentin.

"My brother and me. We opened the door and found a man standing there. Never got a name from him, we didn't."

"Could you describe him?"

"Well, he wasn't an old man but I wouldn't say young, either. Not tall, not short. I wouldn't say he was fat, but I would have to say that he wasn't thin."

Quentin knew futility when he saw it. "Not to worry. What happened next?"

"Well, first we thought to shoo him off the doorstep. But

he produced a piece of paper, he did, with an offer from a slaughterhouse in England that was frankly too good to refuse. Very odd, the whole thing was."

"What did you and your brother make of it?"

"Well, we thought it was very odd, we did."

"I see. Please continue." Quentin kept his gaze level. As a general rule, clients didn't like to see their solicitor roll his eyes.

"So, the next day I took the sheep on to Ellesmere where, right enough, the man was waiting. He had a suitcase full of cash with him." He grimaced, remembering how events unfolded. "The police had been informed. They're very strict about livestock crossing the Welsh border. Before I knew it, sirens were wailing and blue lights were flashing all over the place. I don't know if they caught him, but I scarpered. Leapt over a fence and pegged it fast as my two legs could carry me!" The farmer sighed. "I lost my sheep and I didn't get a penny of that cash."

Quentin immediately reflected on how his client intended to cover his fees.

"Anyway, that's not the worst of it. I returned to Wrexham and found my brother... missing!"

Quentin looked puzzled. "Sorry, did you find your brother, or was he missing?"

"He was missing. That's what I'm telling you." He paused, a mixture of emotions flickering across his face.

"And..." prompted Quentin.

"I need to report it, but can't very well go to the police - they'll do me for smuggling."

"Indeed, much has changed since Wales declared war on us. Tell me why you chose this particular firm, Mr Jones."

"Well, I was told you were very good, I was!"

Quentin tried not to show his surprise. "And who told you this?"

"Well, that's the strange thing. It was my brother. He told me before I left Wrexham. He told me there's a Mr Cundick in Chester who is very good if you get into trouble moving those sheep across the border. I remember it clearly, I do, because it seemed so strange at the time. He said you were good at two things: moving sheep and helping missing people. I thought it was a bit of an odd combination. But that's why I remember it, see?" There was a twinkle in the farmer's eye and Quentin thought that was a bit odd too.

"Most peculiar, it is." A second too late Quentin realised what he'd said, and before he could stop himself he corrected it. "I mean: it is most peculiar." Fortunately, the farmer didn't notice. Quentin pressed on. "Was your brother trying to warn you he was in danger?"

"Well, of course, it didn't occur to me at the time, but since I come to think about it, well, no, I don't know, but... that he just might have been!"

Quentin struggled to rearrange the last sentence in his mind, and decided it probably didn't matter anyway. "May I take your brother's full name?"

"He's called Bryn Jones as well."

"You're both called Bryn Jones?" asked Quentin in a bemused tone and, indeed, a slightly bemused frame of mind.

"We have different fathers, see, and they both wanted a son named after them, a 'junior', so to speak, and they were both called Bryn, themselves, see? It's a very popular name where I come from, is Bryn."

"Tell me, Mr Jones, is your, ah, half-brother a client of mine?"

"I don't think so. He never mentioned you before the other day."

"How very peculiar." This was shaping up to be a bit more interesting than he had anticipated. "So, you want me to report him missing?"

"Poor Bryn." The farmer sniffed.

"The problem is, of course, that you were the last person to see him. Your best option is still to go to the police and get them to search for him."

"Mr Cundick, I'm a wanted man, I am. I'm sure they'd help, but not before locking me up. And you know how it is. A man can languish in prison for a long time before anyone hears his case."

"Not necessarily. I've heard prison conditions have become lax due to the civil war. Especially down South. I heard some of the Belmarsh inmates run a Sunday barbecue and poker session for the locals. By all accounts, it's very popular. They lose a few 'lifers' every time there's a beer run. Perhaps not such a worrying thought if it ensures your brother's safe return?" Quentin didn't often encourage a client to hand himself in. These days, it wasn't often he had a client, come to think of it, but considering his hefty hourly rate, and the pervasive lawlessness sweeping the land, he felt it was his professional duty to at least suggest the possibility.

"I can't help you escape the police, Mr Jones. I don't quite know why your brother recommended me, but I suggest you go to the police and tell them everything. I will come and vouch for the earnestness of your declaration, if you want. I'm well acquainted with the inside of the local police station – and for the right reasons, I assure you." He chuckled at the only joke he knew related to the legal profession and then, in a motion he'd practiced many times in the mirror, steepled his hands as if he was very wise.

"I understand, Mr Cundick. I get it. I do. But it's not that simple. It's not just the police I'm worried about." He looked nervously around the room, as if someone might hear what he was about to say. His gaze paused briefly on Quentin's computer and he muttered something like, "Don't like the way your computer is staring at me." Quentin suspected there was something more to this story but he was darned if he knew what. "Mr Cundick," announced the farmer, "you've got to remember what started all this in the first place!"

"Which was?" asked Quentin, using just one carefully selected set-piece from the vast repertoire of interrogation techniques he had mastered over the years, to draw his client to the much sought after and most appropriate answer.

The farmer paused for a moment. He cracked his knuckles. He stood. "I've said too much. I have to go."

"Surely you haven't told me anything you didn't intend

to?" asked Quentin, feeling somewhat short-changed and automatically beginning to rise as he watched his client head for the door.

"I'll be in touch, Mr Cundick." A moment later, he was gone. Quentin heard the front door close as the farmer – his client – left. He sat back down in his office chair and tapped his fingers on the desk. It had all ended a bit abruptly. What had he said? "You've got to remember what started all this in the first place."

Quentin had the niggling feeling he should do something. There was definitely something he was supposed to do. Clients were few and far between these days. Too many problems were being settled by other, quicker, means like kidnapping, lynching and beating. The world was becoming less civilised. He considered the situation for a moment. He definitely remembered having a client three or four weeks ago. What was it he had done then? Ah, yes. Write up his notes.

Quentin turned to face the computer on his desk and pulled the keyboard forward an inch. A web page delivering a shocking headline popped up. He had forgotten until that moment that he'd been reading the news earlier. He looked at the date on the screen. It was two days ago. It must have been that long since he last used the computer. In truth, he did his level best not to use it at all. He avoided online communication at all costs and had deliberately misspelled his email address on his business cards.

He refreshed the screen and the day's news appeared. It informed him that another member of the English royal family had been kidnapped. Further down the page he learnt that the plague had now taken one hundred victims in London. And, apparently, a drunk teenager in Luton had attempted to resuscitate a sodden aardvark using a laundrette's tumble dryer.

"Another typical day," he mused with fascinated distaste.

Quentin started typing. He began by writing the client's name at the top of the document. Underneath, lest he should forget, he wrote: YOU'VE GOT TO REMEMBER WHAT STARTED ALL THIS IN THE FIRST PLACE.

CHAPTER 2

Morning sunlight punched through the three stained-glass windows of the Grand Hall of the Royal Court of King Gruffydd II. The hall was all a-bustle with activity and awash with bright colours as courtiers and tradesmen began preparations for the approaching celebration. The King was absent, but his large golden throne was perched at the head of the room and imposed itself on all and sundry, creating the impression that, even while not present, the King still watched over his loyal subjects and approved their efforts. The hall was decorated with a myriad of colourful decorations and a multitude of vases that would soon contain bouffant flower arrangements. Streams of bunting burst from the rafters and swung across the top of the walls bringing a blast of colour to the drab, worn interior which had long needed a revamp. Stretched tables begging to be piled high with every kind of local and foreign delicacy lined each side of the room and busy servants struggled to lay lengthy, thickly-starched tablecloths along them. The light streaming in through the three stained-glass windows tattooed bright human figures and criss-cross patterns across their white expanses.

On closer inspection, however, it was evident the tables were battered, old, fold-away ones intended for wallpapering.

There should have been a fourth stained glass window at the end of the hall, but it had been substituted with plain glass due to some unfortunate vandalism. Below it, some tables still stood without tablecloths. They would likely remain that way until the very last minute because the local laundrette owner, being no fool, was withholding them as bargaining chips until he got paid.

It didn't take a genius to see that this was a time of hardship for the Royal Court. Truth be told, there had not yet been a time of easyship. The King had only been crowned three years ago and had not yet had time to devise a sensible way of collecting taxes, nor raise funds through other means. Although it was widely accepted as a matter of popular opinion that King Gruffydd II was king, and that Wales was now an independent country which had declared war on its neighbour England, there were still a few people – up and down the country – here and there - who had trouble either adapting to the new regime or, worse, taking it seriously.

The lack of financial backing soon became obvious to anyone involved with the Royal Court. On closer inspection it was more than quite apparent that the King's throne had been bought from a Swedish flat-packed furniture retailer - probably from last year's Otäck range - and had recently had all its exposed wooden areas painted a gaudy gold colour. Up in the rafters, where the pied bunting hung decoratively, every fifth colourful triangle had the words "Cardiff Brownies" printed on it and a careful observer might also notice a lone yellow woggle tucked between two of the flags hanging near the fake chandelier.

Although the servants worked long hours and with quite some enthusiasm, it was probably more accurate to call them volunteers on account of their receiving no wages and only working in their spare time. They were fuelled by a righteous inner fire known as nationalism. The flurry and commotion of their activity filled the Grand Hall; instructions got barked at apprentices, advice got passed between caterers, rumours got spread amongst cleaners, speculation got invented by old men wandering in off the street in search of a public loo, and orders got passed quietly by the King's advisor to the main organisers who obeyed his word like it was gospel, except on those occasions when they ignored him, insulted him or pointed and laughed at him instead.

The advisor, who everyone just called Ivor, at his own magnanimous insistence, was looking down on the room from a balcony. He stood on a footstool to give himself the height he needed to get an ideal vantage point to oversee the preparations. He shouted something down to a tradesman at floor level about the angle of the heraldic tapestry on the far wall, and the man shot off like a misfired firework, tripped over his feet on a rolled up carpet, skipped awkwardly until he was back into an upright position, staggered to a halt by the boy holding the strings attached to the wall-hanging of King Gruffydd II's coat of arms and slapped him across the back of the head. Ivor saw him point up at the tapestry and start signalling that one corner was lower than the other. Neither knew the designer was a friend of the brother of one of the cooks and had knocked it up on a quiet Sunday afternoon, at the behest of the organisers, without bothering to make sure all the edges were straight. The King's advisor nodded sagely from his lofty lookout on the balcony as the tapestry was moved, inch by inch, into an equally crooked position.

He turned his attentions to the red carpet which was being rolled from the main doorway along the wooden floorboards of the hall right up to the foot of the dais. Except it wasn't a dais. It was a stage. The whole palace was really nothing but a hastily converted theatre that had narrowly escaped demolition. Standing on his balcony, Ivor stroked his goatee and mused on the efficiency of the carpet rollers. He couldn't really get too worked up about shoddy workmanship because, in all honesty, he was lucky to have found people eager enough to support a monarchy that they would put unpaid hours into getting this accursed anniversary celebration up and running in the first place. However, as far as these things went, it was up to him to ensure everything went according to plan. He wasn't alone in organising the event, but he knew it would be him who would bear the brunt of the blame if things collapsed at the end of the week.

He left what had once been the theatre's Royal Box and made his way down to the floor of the Grand Hall to see what he could do to help. One of the helpers was holding out a blue vase to him with a questioning look in his eyes. Ivor nodded approval. He was not a tall man and so everyone he nodded to, when at ground level, was somewhere slightly above him. It made it hard for him to assume the metaphorical stature his position in the Royal Court afforded him. That was why he had brought the footstool downstairs with him; not to give him a better vantage point, so much as to give him a fighting chance of being noticed.

"Move it Shorty, we need past," barked an ogre-like teenager with a shaven head, golden nose ring and a white sticker, positioned over one bulging pectoral, that declared his name to be Bazza.

Ivor didn't raise a complaint. He took himself aside and allowed Bazza to move past him carrying the heavy-looking piece of technical equipment that probably belonged to the public address system they were planning to install in the plaza outside. Ivor reminded himself that respect had to be earned. But then again, revenge was free. He'd make sure Bazza was put on the late shift tonight and then would see that the discourtesy was repaid tenfold. Ivor climbed back on his footstool and stroked his goatee. After a while he chuckled, in the way that some evil people do when they think of something that amuses them.

CHAPTER 3

Quentin felt exhausted from typing up his interview notes - a process that had involved three cups of tea, two chocolate digestives, a trip to the loo, a quick scan of the day's news again, and seven minutes of actual work. It had also taken him a good few minutes to remember where to then file the notes. He decided to call Mavis and request another nice, strong cup of tea. Before he could even inhale the required breath to call her name, she stormed into his office looking significantly less than pleased. "Mavis!" he gasped. "You'll have the door off its hinges! Two sugars, white, as usual. Thank you."

"Two men to see you." She proffered an outstretched arm to the door. "They let themselves in, although I did warn them not to and, yes, I explained it would be a breach of the unspoken solicitor-client pact of mutual trust." Her bottom lip quivered. "They confiscated my computer and put it in their van."

"They did what?"

Two men stood in the doorway. Neither man looked like he would break a sweat wrestling a rabid panda into submission, should such a requirement ever occur locally. They were dressed all in black and each held an aluminium brief case. The briefcases looked more like weapons than some weapons did. It struck Quentin that they were certainly more immediately worrying than a flick-knife cunningly disguised as a Pritt Stick would have been.

Quentin's outrage finally brought him to his feet, spluttering. "And who exactly do you think you are?" He was furious that they'd stolen a computer and absolutely livid that his afternoon tea was being delayed.

The men looked at each other and shrugged. The man on the right looked back at Quentin, answering him in a dense, matter-of-fact tone. "Bailiffs, Mr Cundick. Your firm is insolvent." He threw a wad of papers on Quentin's desk. They landed with an oh-so-grand mahogany thud. "We took the computer as payment for delivery of these documents. We'll be back tomorrow for the rest."

The second bailiff looked, if anything, more frightening than the first. A blacksmith could have made a living hammering out iron on his chin. When he spoke, his voice was as deep and dense as a black hole. "Mr Cundick, it will go easier on you if you're not here when we return."

Quentin was utterly lost for words. In the absence of any further conversation, the two men turned on their heels in unison and marched out of his office. On the edge of hearing, Quentin just made out the first complaining to the second. "I've told you before! Don't turn at the same time as me. It makes us look like bloody ballerinas and *that* erodes our threatening *je ne sais quoi*."

The second voice was thick as treacle. "What does that mean?"

"I don't know what," scoffed his partner.

"Then what did you say it for?"

The door slammed shut behind them, mercifully cutting off an increasingly banal conversation that could only upset Quentin further. He slumped down in his seat and mindlessly studied the dark grain that wove through the surface of his oh-so-repossessed mahogany desk. He looked up and realised Mavis was standing by the door, watching him. She was crying.

CHAPTER 4

Fairly satisfied that everything was going to plan, as best as could be expected anyway, Ivor departed the Grand Hall (or the Widow Twankey room as it had been known in its thespian days) and went in search of the King.

"IVOR!"

It sounded like the King was also searching for him. The King's method of searching involved shouting louder and louder; a method that didn't require him to burn a single calorie. His hollering persisted as Ivor tramped his way along the narrow corridor.

Ivor's wasn't a particularly Welsh name, all told, and he accepted that. Actually, no one had brought up the issue of his *first* name at all in recent months. He had thought that as advisor he might have been expected to take a name like Owain Amerawdwr Heilyn, or something, but he retained his own full name, which was quite different. Ivor convinced himself that being the King's advisor carried no small amount of respect. Hardly a surprise, then, that no one had confronted him about his *last* name not being of proper Welsh origin either. It certainly didn't seem to have held him back during his ambitious rise up the ranks of the newly established Welsh court.

The King bellowed again. "Ivor Munchkinhead!"

It bothered Ivor. Why did the King so frequently call him by both his first and last name? Did they just sound good together? Or was it something else? Perhaps some childish, malicious pleasure derived from using both names together? Ivor hoped it wasn't that. He'd known children at school who did that.

At school, there were the ones who taunted you outright. And the ones that just plain bullied you. But then there were those bright, sneaky ones who managed to twist the knife in while you were passing and you'd have walked twenty yards down the corridor before realising that not only had they been making fun of you but that all their friends had been in on the joke and you hadn't. And you'd stop. You'd stop in the corridor and replay it in your mind. Only then would you realise that you'd been watching a comedy and you were the fall guy.

"I can hear footsteps! Are you there? This is your King calling you. King Gruffydd, the second. Remember me? Where in the name of Beddgelert are you?"

Ivor thought it was a silly name for the King to have chosen. There had once been a King of Wales. At least, there had once been someone that came as close to being the King of Wales that anyone who wasn't the English king could claim to be, and that man was called Gruffydd ap Llywelyn. So, of course, the new king had brazenly decided to take that name for all the connotations it boasted, and ostentatiously called himself King Gruffydd II. Disturbingly, it had actually proved quite popular with the plebs. Ivor thought it was a silly, pretentious and affected thing to do. What kind of person would adopt such a name?

"Ivor Munchkinhead! Are you there?" He was nothing if not persistent.

"Right here, sire!" yelled Ivor, a little louder than was strictly necessary.

It wasn't his fault that his parents weren't Welsh. Or that they got drunk and changed his name by deed poll for a laugh when he was only seven years old. Or, for that matter, the unfortunate events that mysteriously befell them a few years later; what he nowadays liked to call, "the accident".

Ivor entered the King's chamber. "Sire!"

The King didn't look up. He was sitting at his desk, pouring over a piece of paper. His podgy hands were smudged with black ink. His cheeks were smeared with black marks where he'd scratched himself. He seemed almost studious as he reread the speech he was composing for the anniversary celebrations. Having spent so long shouting for his advisor one might assume that he would be pleased to see him, but instead, to Ivor's utter annoyance, he made him wait. It was a power play. One Ivor just had to endure. The King was more important than him, so therefore he had to wait. That was how it worked.

After a moment or two had passed, the King deigned to speak to him. As he spoke, Ivor watched the fat bastard's jowls wobble under his strangely numerous chins. "It's not right. A king should not have to write his own speeches."

"I absolutely agree, sire. I'm actually quite skilled in the art of writing oratory. Perhaps I could take what you've written and produce a redraft for you?"

"Don't be so presumptuous. I've almost got it cracked. I just need a new pen. This one's run out."

"A new pen, sire?"

"Yes. Why do you think I called you here? Fetch me a new pen, man."

That wasn't in his job description, but there was no one else to do it. Servants were expensive and not entirely approved of by certain human rights groups. Of course, that being the case, it wouldn't have hurt His Esteemed Majesty to find a bloody pen for himself. Ivor remembered something.

"I believe there may be one of those black gel pens you like - the ones you ordered specifically for this desk - in the drawer to the left, sire, where you asked for them to be stored, if you remember, sire." Hardly a nuance of upset was apparent in his voice, although one of his hands trembled slightly as if he was fighting against balling it into a fist.

"Ah, it's alright. I seem to have got this one working again. Panic over." The King chuckled vacuously to himself and his chins quivered.

"I'll get back to the preparations then, sire." Ivor bowed, and was ashamed of doing so.

"Yes, that will be all." The King still hadn't actually looked up.

Ivor stepped out of the room. He let out a weary but silent sigh and trotted off along a worn carpet that had once seen thousands of actors and actresses anxiously pace up and down before their scenes.

"Ivor Munchkinhead!"

Ivor turned on his heel and returned to the King's chamber. "Sire?"

This time the King fixed him with his good eye. The other one stared at the corner of the room, which it sometimes did when the King was tired and always did when he was drunk. "Any news about the uprising in Cardigan Bay?"

Ivor sighed inwardly. This was another power play. The King didn't care about that petty skirmish. He knew it. Ivor knew it. But nothing could be done about it. "I was going to debrief you this evening, sire. Apparently the small uprising has been quelled. It turned out it was really only a man in a pub who had said something unpleasant about Your Royal Highness and then got into a fight with a man and his dog."

"You mean a man with a dog."

"Not exactly."

"Oh?"

"The outspoken miscreant went for his opponent, missed, tripped, punched the dog then fell and knocked himself unconscious on the corner of a table. He was arrested and, when he woke up, apologised and swore allegiance to Your Majesty."

"Another victory for the crown! Very good indeed. Thank you. That will be all, Ivor Munchkinhead."

Ivor bowed graciously and left the room. He could hear

the clamour of the preparations still taking place as he got farther down the corridor. A sudden dramatic increase in noise and shouting told him things were starting to go awry without him.

It was proving to be a long day and there was still much to be done. The chandelier needed refitted as it was only held on by one screw and a wad of chewing gum. There were other problems too, but the big problem was that the whole court system was a bit of a mess. It lacked a proper figure of authority at the top, which shouldn't be the case with a monarchy, when you thought about it. The problem was pervasive and slithered through every part of the new regime like a slow-working alcohol.

The war on England was a prime example. No one took that seriously. The Welsh knew they didn't have the money, manpower or, indeed, firepower to make good on their idle threats and the English had barely even noticed it. They were too busy trying to quash the republican uprising. No, there was definitely something wrong with the present regime - something soft, or even rotten, at its core.

"Oh! Ivor Munchkinhead!"

Ivor turned back.

"Sire?"

"Oh, nothing. Sorry."

"That's quite alright, sire."

It was no wonder that in his slightly-lower-than-shoulder-height head Ivor could feel a malignant thought forming. In fact, it wasn't so much a thought yet as just the inchoate stirrings of a pre-thought. It was, to a thought, what an acorn was to an oak, or a cub to a lion, or a curry to a damn good fart. Although he couldn't have described the exact nature of the thought just yet, it had a name. It was a dangerous name. It was a name that dare not speak its name.

CHAPTER 5

Quentin was alone with his thoughts as he drove home at the end of what he optimistically called a working day. The early evening was grim. The sky was thick with dark clouds and rain battered down with depressing relentlessness.

Mavis had left him. She had upped and gone. Technically she had quit, but being the only woman in his life it felt like he'd been dumped. He was reasonably sure he'd never had romantic feelings for her, but that was quite beside the point. She was the woman he saw first thing in the morning (after 8.30am) and last thing at night (before going home at 6pm). During the colder months when the night drew in he could arguably say he saw her morning, noon and night. Whichever way he looked at it, she was the woman in his life. She filled a gap in his existence. A plump, cheery, woman-sized gap. Already he missed her bright smile. He missed the cups of tea she brought him when he arrived at work, at elevenses, at lunch, for afternoon tea and a half hour before he set off for home. He missed the way she brought the morning paper to him with all the sport supplements and advertising flyers already removed. He missed the way she chided him when she thought he wasn't putting the best interests of the firm first and foremost. He'd always laughed at this, as if it were a little joke they shared. Now he thought about it, perhaps she had been on to something there.

Insolvent. It sounded harmless. It sounded like a type of ineffectual glue. Every raindrop sounded like a little drop of insolvency glue landing on the car. Thud. Thud. Thud. The same sound the insolvency papers had made landing on his oh-so-not-going-to-fit-in-the-car mahogany desk. He released a heartfelt sigh. It had been a long day and his mind felt addled. The rain beating heavily on the car made him feel all the more weary.

Quentin wasn't the best of drivers. He'd been debating for the last five minutes why it was so difficult to see the road ahead. Eventually, he turned the headlights on. Visibility still seemed inadequate, so he scrubbed the windscreen with a leather chamois. It didn't help. Turning the wipers on turned out to be the not-so-radical solution. Sometimes he felt that all the legal knowledge he had acquired had pushed his more worldly knowledge out of his mind, or at least boxed it, labelled it ARCHIVED and set it aside in some dusty warehouse.

The car was half-full of things rescued from the office. The first item he packed was a wicker wastepaper bin he had bought on holiday in Egypt. There was no way he could pack his beloved yucca, but he did manage to take his favourite mug; the one Mavis had given him. He took his gold-plated pen. He took his kettle. He salvaged various confidential papers and a small box of probate work. A few of his most expensive legal books made it because, although he had initially started packing the most useful ones, he soon realised it might be some time before he would once more practice as a solicitor. That was when it had first hit him: he might never practice again. As such, he dolefully packed the most expensive books. Should the worst happen, he could always flog them. He found a box of mouldy, festering Tic-Tacs in a bottom drawer and knew they should be discarded, but put them in the car anyway because, foolishly, the first item he had packed was his bin.

After a fifteen minute commute involving death-defying aquaplaning and one particularly unhappy student left drenched on the pavement, Quentin approached his house. A white van was unexpectedly blocking his driveway. He pulled up, scraping the plastic hub cap against the kerb, and came to a juddering halt as he pulled the handbrake on a little too fiercely. He struck his horn several times in frustration before noticing the company logo emblazoned across the van. A desperate mixture of vexation and realisation filled him.

"Oh," he said. The worst had come to the worst.

CHAPTER 6

The bailiff's van was parked in his driveway. Quentin stood on the pavement feeling unable to set foot on his own garden path. The driving rain punctured his clothing. He couldn't have looked sorrier had tears been pouring down his face. They would have been indistinguishable from the rainwater tumbling there anyway. He sneezed loudly and involuntarily. This was, after all, no time for voluntary sneezing.

Quentin spotted his neighbour peeking out from behind her curtains. He couldn't see her expression because the rain cascading down the glass obscured it. The same two bailiffs who had been in his office earlier that day were now emptying his house of chattels and possessions. He watched in fascinated horror as they manoeuvred an antique chaise longue out of his front door, tipped it upside down, dropped it on the muddy path, picked it up again, dropped it, picked it up again, dropped it and... "This is torture," he mumbled, not loud enough for them to actually hear.

They reached the open side-door of the van and started to swing the chaise longue back and forth. "And a one, and a two..." sang the one with the anvil-like chin. "Upsy-daisy!" They threw the item of furniture into the vehicle where it came crashing to a halt. There was a tinkling sound. "Well, that's those china plates knackered," he commented to his colleague.

His colleague gave him a withering stare. "What have I told you about saying upsy-daisy? That's hardly the lingo expected from one of our profession."

The other grimaced apologetically. They went back inside.

Quentin just stood and watched. He was completely numb. His whole world didn't make sense to him anymore. His brain stopped functioning. All he could do was stare.

A small sound came from the van and then a large, black, circular object appeared at the lip of the doorway, paused momentarily, then hopped onto the ground and began to roll down the garden path toward him. Quentin recognised it as a vinyl LP from his music collection. It must have been knocked and gravity had somehow helped it escape its sleeve. He watched it roll down the path toward him, bopping over cracks in the paving. He hoped it would turn out to be an AC/DC album. The bailiffs were sure to like AC/DC and he would be able to strike up a conversation with them about it and then persuade them to stop emptying his house. The LP bounced over a large crack and then rolled to within an inch of his feet where it tilted back on itself, fell on its side, juddered in a circular motion that seemed to decrease until, somewhat anticlimactically, the record lay completely still. Rain drops bounced off the pink label at its centre. *Nancy Sinatra*. The bailiffs probably didn't go in for Nancy Sinatra, mused Quentin melancholically. His one and only plan to recover the situation had just been thwarted.

The bailiffs emerged from the house. The first was carrying a standard lamp. That was my grandfather's lamp, thought Quentin. The bulb was already smashed. By the time the bailiff had unhooked it from the doorframe, the base was badly chipped. By the time he got it to the van, the cord had been ripped out and left behind, the plug caught beneath the front door and the jamb. He was followed shortly after by his colleague who carried an empty fish tank. Quentin's shell-shocked mind did manage to form one coherent thought: that fish tank wasn't empty when I left the house this morning.

He tried to move, but his feet seemed glued to the dip in the pavement which contained the rising puddle in which he stood. He opened his mouth to voice an objection but the ineffectual sound that emerged was the mating call of the Costa Rican scale-crested pygmy-tyrant bird. Of course, he didn't know this at the time.

"Damn fish wouldn't flush," said the taller of the bailiffs, to the other. He pushed his way out through the front door, catching the corner of the fish tank on the door frame and leaving an inverted-pyramid dent there. He looked up and saw Quentin. "Ah," he said, with just the smallest hint of chagrin evident in that monosyllabic utterance. "The lawyer's back."

CHAPTER 7

Quentin piled confidential legal documents into the boot of his car. It didn't occur to the bailiffs to help him, and it didn't occur to him to ask them to. He had negotiated with them about the files. They seemed suspicious about his motives for wanting them, so he tried to rationalise with them, stating that they had no pecuniary value (and explaining that meant no financial value). After a few minutes of fruitless arguing, he grabbed a thick legal tome, flicked to a random page, pointed to a random paragraph and told them that under English law, if they didn't let him take his clients' files then they could be held personally culpable for committing a criminal offence. It was clear they were teetering on the brink of belief and disbelief, so he threatened them with legal action if they didn't comply. This works better for lawyers than it does for, by way of example, the average man on the top of the Clapham omnibus. It did the trick. It also confirmed a suspicion Quentin had been harbouring about the outcome should he pit his wits against these gorillas. Yet being neither foolhardy nor reckless, he didn't push his luck further.

He put the rescued files in the car. Had he understood the value of the paperless office, he might have stored the entire lot on a single USB stick, and he sort-of knew this, but it was a leap of faith too far given his technophobic tendencies. Had he given it more thought he might have rescued some cutlery, a plate, a pillow, a blanket, some food - the things a single man needs to survive when homeless - but at that moment these things seemed easily replaceable. Nevertheless, he considered it most decent of the two men to allow him these moments of dignity, even if it did involve them putting up their feet (on his futon) and stopping for refreshments (his Assam tea and biscuit selection).

Almost finished, he slammed the car boot shut on the legal tomes and a few other sundry items he'd rescued. He went back into his house and up the stairs to the bathroom. He found a transparent plastic bag and put in it his toothbrush, a shampoo bottle and his shaving kit. Just as he was packing some cotton buds, he heard a very slight splashing sound down around his feet somewhere.

He looked in the loo and saw a single, tiny, silver, fish - a neon tetra - swimming around and around in the bowl. He put down the plastic bag and looked closer. His forehead furrowed with upset. From its markings, he determined it was Aramis - one of three fish that lived in the meticulously well-kept tropical tank he housed in his living room. Aramis looked despondent yet beautiful, he thought, as he gracefully manoeuvred in circles within the confines of the toilet-bowl lagoon. The fish glimmered a metallic green, purple and silver as it reflected the light of the electric bulb overhead.

After a moment's thought, Quentin emptied the clear plastic bag and used it to scoop the little fish out of the toilet bowl. Quentin put the plastic bag in the sink, clutching its opening to the nozzle of the cold tap. He ran some water until the bag was bulging. "Fear not, Aramis. I'll find a home for you."

Quentin was chock-full of righteous indignation as he marched from the bathroom and stamped down the stairs. He wore a deep frown and had completely forgotten about his wash kit.

The bailiffs were in his living room, apparently deriving

much amusement from taking turns in attempting to pronounce the word "floccinaucinihilipilification". They looked up as he entered. One had a Rich Tea biscuit half-dipped in his tea, which he seemed to forget about when he saw the look on Quentin's face.

"You monsters," snarled Quentin, raging inside but maintaining as much calm on the outside as he could manage; which was quite a lot, really, since he wasn't prone to extravagant outbursts of anger. He held the bag aloft so their shame would be complete. "How... could you?" His voice was laden with enough accusation to burn a witch to ashes where she stood.

The bailiffs looked at the fish, then each other and then back at Quentin. They seemed unsure what to say. Possibly they were ashamed. Possibly they were amused. Or quite possibly, somewhere in-between. Only one thing was certain: there was now half a Rich Tea biscuit floating in one of their mugs. Quentin hadn't quite expected a complete lack of response, so he spluttered resentfully. Holding the fish aloft, he turned his back on them and stalked from the house. He was glad that he had made a scene and not let their crime pass unspoken. He was also aware that the impact of his actions was roughly as significant as that which a dry cotton-wool ball would make should it fall from the hundred-and-second floor of the Empire State Building and land on a metre-thick slab of chemically-hardened ear wax.

He made his way to the end of the garden, stepped over the discarded Nancy Sinatra record, and opened the passenger door of his car. He considered for a moment where might be the best place to securely store a fish in an open plastic bag. It appeared there had been an oversight by the car's designers. A further moment's deliberation and he settled on hanging the bag on the small hook on the handle above the passenger's door.

"Now don't you worry. Uncle Quentin will-"

He stopped.

The fish wasn't moving.

Two memories surfaced simultaneously to form a new thought. The first, now somewhat distant and foggy, involved a pet-store owner explaining how to manage the habitat of tropical fish. The second involved running very cold water into a bag. Realisation dawned. He guessed that probably very few fish bobbed inanimately on their side on the water's surface as an indication of their extreme good health.

He tried to tip the bag down the drain at the side of the road, but it was overflowing from the pouring rain. He watched as little Aramis disappeared between the rusty bars, then bobbed back up and floated away on a rivulet at the side of the tarmac, occasionally bumping off a kerb stone or snagging on a stray leaf - and never to be reunited with his brothers.

"All for one," mumbled Quentin. "And one f- f- f-".

He choked up as the whole sorry situation - most significantly his own - hit him with unforgiving clarity.

THE FORGOTTEN PROLOGUE

Secreted in a concealed recess on the steepest side of a mountain hidden deep within a treacherous, snow-capped range, was a small and ancient monastery that lay enshrouded in shadows and a thousand years of mystery and obscurity.

If a traveller were ever to approach that place, he would hear a low chant emanating from deep within the darkness. As his eyes adjusted, he would see a tiny flicker of light indicating that life was indeed present in this remote and inhospitable part of the Tibetan landscape.

If he dared to venture closer, the hypothetical traveller would find his way blocked by seven burly warrior monks standing guard at the Dragon Pass, an ancient archway carved by hands unknown in a time before time. In the unlikely event that those monks could somehow be persuaded to break their sworn covenant and allow an outsider to pass, the hypothetical traveller would find himself approaching the monastery's inner sanctum. Having made it this far, he might be tempted to steal a glance inside the Prayer Room to witness a hundred monks wrapped in ceremonial garb intoning mantras memorised from their sacred text.

Shivering by now, the traveller would move on in search of other wonders. He might first navigate down a dank, spiral passage toward treasures that had lain undiscovered for centuries, or climb the Cloud Spire to gaze up at the stars and think deep thoughts about the universe.

Then again, he might just stumble upon a small and unassuming dojo. Should he look through the window, he would find there an old, bald-headed, clean-shaven man with bushy eyebrows and a pipe wedged firmly in his mouth. He would be sitting still, contemplating the small boy sat in the corner of the room surfing eBay on his laptop.

That young child, young man even, small for his fourteen years of age, was also bald. From behind, his little head looked like a polished mango. It bobbed in frustration as he cursed the slowness of the monastery's intermittent internet connection. "Aww! How can I win an eBay item when the connection drops all the time?"

The older man got to his feet and joined the boy, who sat cross-legged on the floor, his eyes glued to the laptop before him. "Young Anil," he addressed his pupil by name, "time to turn off the computer and get ready for bed." Anil obediently closed his laptop. He walked to the window and looked out.

He saw the traveller standing there, looking back at him.

Or rather, would have done, if the traveller hadn't been hypothetical.

Instead, what he saw were the esoteric patterns running through mosaic tiles spread across the yard outside. He saw a flicker of light from the Prayer Room. Above, the night sky was cold and clear. He looked out at the world with vacant eyes and a stillness that belied his youth. He defied the wind that whipped across the stone courtyard and through the window to ruffle his robe. He shut his eyes. Some would call the layered fabric he wore a gamboge or saffron colour, offset against a dark russet or sepia, but he would call it yellow and brown because pretentiousness played no part in his thinking and he was not an artist. He was a philosopher monk.

When he reopened his eyes they were glazed, as if some outside force had taken control of his body and looked out from within.

The old man saw that something troubled his young apprentice and hurried to his side, although hurried is a relative term in a place where time rarely has meaning and urgency is unknown. "What ails you, Anil?"

"It is time."

"Then it is true," replied Kamala, for that was the name of the older monk. "You are the chosen one."

Anil nodded. "I believe so. I must reveal myself in four days time. We have much to do. We leave tomorrow at dawn."

"As you insist." He paused, then asked the obvious question. "Where are we going?"

"A far-off place in a far-off land, over the mountains, beyond the farthest reaches of Tibet, then farther yet, to a place of intrigue, to a land of people and things that will seem unfamiliar to us, Kamala. There will be danger and there will be revelation."

Inhaling deeply on his pipe and then slowly letting the grey wisps of smoke escape from between his lips and curl away on the night air to eventually dissipate into nothingness, the old monk showed patience with his protégé. He asked, "Does this chosen place have a name?"

"Yes, though I confess that I have not heard of it before," replied Anil. He looked up to meet the wise old eyes of his life-long master.

Kamala raised an inquisitive eyebrow.

"Cardiff."

CHAPTER 8

Quentin's car was crammed with carefully chosen items which he had rescued. In time he would learn that his selection criteria had been erroneous and his efforts futile.

He had some slight bruising. In the end, the bailiffs had forcibly removed him from his property. They hadn't been impressed that he'd tried to stay. They particularly hadn't appreciated him chaining himself to the oven and fighting them off with a spatula. The whole thing had been remarkably undignified. There had been tears, misquoted legislation and the chorus of Bridge Over Troubled Water. He rather thought that perhaps he had been the subject of a small emotional breakdown. Hardly surprising. No doubt it had been the untimely demise of poor Aramis that had really pushed him over the crumbling edge of whatever mental precipice he had been teetering upon. He recalled the woeful sight of that little sliver of rainbow tumbling down the gutter at the edge of the road in the murky rain water. It brought a sadness to his heart, even now, an hour and a half later.

He assured himself that only his ego had been bruised, but ultimately he couldn't escape the truth: his skin was bruised too, he'd lost Mavis, his three fish, and his financial security had taken an utter battering.

His suit was still soaking wet as he drove aimlessly through the waterlogged streets of Chester. The car was so full it scraped along the road. Yet he was in control of his faculties again. He put the evening's experiences behind him, knowing full well that he had to get a grip.

The bailiffs had made it quite clear that he couldn't stay on the premises. There had been a tick box on the sixth red letter they had sent him. If he had ticked that, and returned it to the Jersey address stamped on the back of the fourth page, then he could have kept the property for a further seven days, but, as he had not done that, he was homeless. He felt that had he been a lawyer that dealt in such matters, he may have been able to combat their assertions by quoting some salient piece of legislation, but, as it happened, he had very little knowledge of matters of enforcement and, it transpired, a rather good memory for Simon and Garfunkel songs. This did kindle an idea, however, and he turned left at the lights and headed into town.

He was a resourceful fellow, or so he believed, and knew it was up to him to make the most of the situation. He had been commended on several occasions throughout his life on being the sort of person who could think outside the box, put on different hats as needed, and generally get the job done. It might well be that he had lost his job, had no hats and most of his goods were now in boxes, but he would take what resources he had and make the most of them. Sadly, his resources were largely clients' files, a scratched Nancy Sinatra LP, a garden gnome, some other soggy, damaged goods and the very damp suit he currently wore. He also had a small length of chain attached to his wrist which remained there from when he had lashed himself to the oven.

In fact, the only thing he'd managed to secure which he felt particularly pleased about was the car. It was something. Now he thought about it, he suddenly understood why he had seen the two bailiffs arguing on the doorstep as he had prepared to leave and why one of them had chased after the car and waved for him to come back. He had seen those wild gesticulations and responded accordingly. The bailiff had diminished into a small angry dot in his rear-view mirror as he sped away as fast as the speed limit would allow.

He pulled up outside the town library. It was open for another thirty five minutes. He jumped out of the car and ran inside, his shoes squeaking and his suit dripping as he went. Fortunately, the librarian was nowhere in sight. He hurried over to the section on law and looked for a practitioner's text on any issue surrounding bankruptcy or enforcement. It took him ten minutes to find what he was looking for, partly because he was being careful not to get the books wet, but partly because of the insane amount of cross-referencing in such great tomes. He sat down and studied the latest update intently.

After ten minutes had passed, he looked up in dismay. The librarian was standing over him, shaking her head. "I'm sorry, sir. I'll have to ask you to leave."

"It's Barbara, isn't it?" asked Quentin, fairly sure he could remember her name as he'd been to the library a couple of times over the last year and was certain they had spoken before. He'd trained his mind to remember faces because it made dealing with clients so much easier. He hoped he could ingratiate himself upon her and secure another few minutes researching his predicament.

"No, it's Eileen," she said. "No-one who works here is called Barbara."

Suddenly Quentin remembered that Barbara was his hairdresser. Yes, Eileen was her name. That was it!

"It's Eileen, isn't it?" he cheerfully riposted.

She scowled at him.

"Oh right, you just told me that."

"Have you been drinking, sir?"

"Absolutely not!"

"Have you been taking drugs?"

"Absolutely not!"

"Then would you mind telling me why you are soaking wet and dripping on these very expensive books?"

"I am a lawyer, madam, and I have some urgent business. I ask you to kindly allow me to stay until the library closes so that I may conduct my research and then I shall leave peacefully. A man's livelihood is at stake here."

His small speech had the effect of a verbal judo tackle. It threw her. Suddenly he had the moral upper-hand and she was wrong-footed. Her scowl deepened as she sought to regain the higher ground. "If all that is true, perhaps you wouldn't mind explaining to me why you are holding the end of a chain in one hand that is attached to your wrist?"

Quentin looked at the chain. It was certainly going to be difficult to explain. He opted for a tactic he'd learnt during mooting competitions, back in his days on the university debating team. "Madam," he began, as sincerely as he could manage, "are you seriously asking me why I am holding a chain that is in one hand attached to my wrist?"

Uncertainty crossed her face but was quickly replaced with assertion. "Yes, that's right."

"Madam, I could hardly be holding it any other way as my hand has always been attached to my wrist for as long as I care to remember!"

Ha ha! Touché! If he'd been in the old hall of his university now he'd have brought down the house to whoops and cheers. Old Bertie Nickerbottom would have bought him a half pint for that one for sure!

"Get out or I'm calling the police."

"Oh," replied Quentin, his cunning repartee momentarily parried, but he soon rallied. "Perhaps you meant why, in my hand, do I hold a chain which is attached to my wrist?"

Her eyes darted to the phone on her desk, a clear indication that she was serious about phoning the local constabulary.

Quentin thought quickly. "Well, it's a long story." He paused as his mind rattled out a convincing fabrication. Miraculously, it just rolled off the end of his tongue, smooth as a peppermint. "As you can hear, it's wild outside. I was driving down here from my client's house when my tyre blew. The car started sliding down the hill, which is like a waterfall in this rain. I slammed the brakes on and the car scraped to a halt near a lamp post. I got out. That moment, a huge gust of wind blew me over and, if I had kept sliding, I would have been crushed. Anyway, I used this chain I had to lash myself to the lamp post. I replaced the wheel with the spare. Unfortunately, the chain is a little rusty and became welded by the rain and the strain of my weight. This bit on my wrist just won't come off. But, I like to put my clients first, so I rushed straight here before you closed."

Quentin took a deep breath. She had a look on her face that said she was teetering on the brink of disbelief and pity, of incredulity and acceptance. He was on a razor's edge. What he said next would determine whether she would buy his story or not. This was the difference between staying now and leaving peacefully, or having to take some extreme course of action. There were so many holes in his story that she would see through it in a minute if he gave her a second to think about it. Wait. That didn't sound right. But he couldn't spend a moment thinking about it, because a moment could soon become a second and a second, in this case, was apparently enough time for her to process a full minute's thinking. No, wait. That couldn't be right. Quentin realised he was starting to panic. He wasn't sure what to say next and time was, well, not so much running out as just running circles around him and mocking him. He felt something coming to the forefront of his mind. He had something to say, although he, himself, didn't yet know what it would be.

He watched the expression on the librarian's face with alarmed fascination as she weighed up his story, swaying between two possible conclusions. For a nanosecond she registered sorrow for his plight, but then for a microsecond there was the clear sense that she could see through this charade and would call his bluff by quizzing him on any of the horrendous nonsense contained in his story.

Finally, the words brewing in his innards spewed forth. "So, you see, my plight is one of the bedraggled hero, even if I do paint it so myself. I am most dismayed to have to present myself to you in this sorry state, but it is of the utmost importance to my client and his family - his wife, his three young children - that I should finish this research and make progress on his case this evening. If you can forgive me this indiscretion and allow me to continue my research until the end of opening hours, then I assure you, good lady, that you will have had a hand in something beautiful; in the restoration of a family and the assurance of their security and happiness." He paused for dramatic effect. He could see that her belief-o-meter was edging toward his favour and his chances of getting his way were good. If he did nothing wrong now, he was home and dry. Well, maybe not quite home and dry. More homeless, wet and allowed to stay in the library. Here it was. He could see it in her eyes. She was about to make her decision. All he had to do was nudge her over the edge and she'd be like putty in his hands. He gave her his most winning smile. "So, how about it, Barbara?"

Her eyebrows took off like space rockets. "It's Eileen," she snapped. "How come you're not covered in dirt? Where's this hurricane you encountered? It's a bit of heavy rain, is all. Utter codswallop!"

"Look," he said, turning too late to honesty, "please don't call the police. You close in ten minutes. I'm homeless and I need to find out if the bailiffs who did this to me were acting *ultra vires* or not. I just need to do a little research."

"It's too late for that! Why should I believe that any more than the last story?" She stopped to think for a moment, readjusting her spectacles which had become dislodged by her excitable eyebrows. "I'm calling the police."

"All I'm doing is reading a book!"

"No, what you're doing is dripping water all over those books. That's criminal damage to local authority property."

"Don't talk to me about criminal damage! I used to be a criminal lawyer!"

"You're a criminal, alright!" She marched off toward the phone.

The entire exchange hadn't gone quite as well as he'd hoped. Quentin decided it was time to take drastic action. He called after her. "Barbara!"

"Ha!"

"I meant Eileen!" he yelled, leaping from his seat. "If you touch that phone..." As he said this he suddenly realised he had nothing much to lose. "If you touch that phone I'm going to take this book and leave with it. It will be gone. And it will get soaked. But if you let me read it now, I will leave peacefully when the library closes."

Stood by the phone, she hesitated, undecided. He reached toward the book and her hand lowered toward the phone. He pulled back and her hand paused, levitating above the phone, then lifted away slightly. They were at a stand-off. He looked in her beady brown eyes. She looked back at his, perhaps sensing the desperation there. If he was going to save his home he was going to have to act fast.

He looked at the clock on the wall. She looked at it too. It was eight o'clock. Closing time. It had all been in vain.

"You have to leave now," she said.

"I need to read this book."

"You said you'd leave. It's closing time."

Time seemed to stretch. He considered his options. Apart from the two of them, the library was deserted. He stared at her long and hard. He decided to appeal to her better nature. "I'm going to take this book with me," he said, "because my livelihood depends on it."

"Why don't you just come back in the morning?" she asked, rather sensibly.

"Um..." He held the note for a long moment. "Ah well. Yes. I suppose I could do that." He nodded his agreement. She lifted her hand away from the phone. "I supposed one night isn't really going to make any difference." Except, perhaps, if I have something conclusive I can get back to those bailiffs and talk them into letting me stay in my own home for the night, he thought. "I'll go peacefully," he said, smiling, almost laughing. "Sorry to have caused you any trouble."

She smiled back at him. "I hope you get somewhere to sleep tonight and good luck w-"

She saw him grab the book, clutch it to his soaking shirt, vault over the desk and run for the exit. Her hand dropped to the telephone.

Quentin was out the door and into his car before he had even taken a breath.

He had no idea what had come over him. He sat in the car looking at the book. He began questioning whether to return it. His lawyer's brain worked furiously for a moment. It was a theft, but it was a first offence. The book was slightly damaged by water but could be returned. He would show remorse. This wasn't the most outrageous offence ever committed and he wasn't in his right mind after the traumatic events of the day.

On the other hand, something new and alive was working within him. Hadn't that just been a little bit exciting? He pondered this new feeling for a second. He had nothing to lose. He started the car and drove off.

"What am I doing?" he asked aloud and stopped the car. His conscience grappled with the idea of returning the book. Eventually he decided that he couldn't miss the opportunity of finding out if he had any recourse against those two bailiffs after their forceful ejection of him from the house. If it meant he might once again have a roof over his head then it would be worth it.

Ordinarily he'd concede that the laws of society were there to protect normal people in their everyday lives. This wasn't everyday life. Yes, he would keep the book. Sometimes, he decided, you have to put yourself first.

He drove off in search of a quiet place on the outskirts of town where he could read in peace. He'd just committed the first crime of his life and, truth be told, he didn't feel too bad about it.

CHAPTER 9

Night descended on Cardiff, as it did reliably most evenings. Preparations for the upcoming celebrations had finished for the day and the many volunteers had sloped off home. Ivor was out in the cold night air and had just finished his secret task. Relief washed over him and something made him mumble a little childhood ditty that popped into his mind. "Sleep like the dead, sleep like the dead, lay down your head, it's time for bed." He smiled at the memory of it. He was totally alone and rejoiced that only the light of the moon lit his undertakings. Well, apart from the light from some rooms at the back of the Royal Court. And a couple of nearby streetlamps. And the electric lantern he'd brought with him. Actually, it was quite bright when he thought about it.

When he had first taken up his position as advisor to the King, Ivor insisted he could only move into the Royal Court if he was granted a small allotment behind the building where he could unwind when it pleased him. A simple enough request, the King had granted it. Ivor came out at times like this and enjoyed the peace and quiet, away from the turmoil of court life. Sure, he could hear traffic in the distance, but this private place was secluded enough, here in the grounds, at night, to afford him some much needed solitude where he could forget about the woes of the day - although, somehow, he never did quite manage that.

Gardening by night was, of course, an unusual hobby, but one his mother had passed on to him when he was young. She'd tended a herb garden behind the trailer where they lived, long before she met with the 'accident'. She had taught him all about different plants and, although not all were to the normal taste, her abilities were exceptional and the plants grew prolifically. Ivor later learned that most could be classified as common weeds, but he truly believed his mother had a talent for cultivating them. "After all, what some call weeds, others call beautiful flowers," he mumbled, echoing her voice in his head. He recalled without much fondness how she used to describe his appearance this way when trying to be affectionate. He returned his attention to the task at hand. The ground before him was fresh from being recently turned over by him. He pressed his foot into it and it sunk easily, leaving a footprint.

He took a potted rose from the low stone wall behind him. Grasping its stem with a gloved hand, he drew the flower, its roots and its soil out into the open air before him. He took a deep sniff of its perfume then held it up for further inspection. It was almost right. Years ago his mother had grown a rose with petals as black as midnight. Try though she might, none of her cuttings reproduced this special hue in future generations. Over the years, Ivor had attempted to replicate his mother's creation by cultivating the descendants of that very same rose, but this was as close as he had got. It was a profoundly dark red with purple veins which, set against green foliage, put him in mind of a rotting scab.

He planted it in the loose soil, then stood back to admire his work. His footprints surrounded it and already the soil was sinking. It was good soil for growing, but not the best for Ivor's other, secret, purpose.

He sat back on the low wall and wrapped himself in idle thoughts. He had left His Majesty in what the King grandly called his Royal Chamber, but was just the lead actor's changing room from when the building was a theatre. The mirror with the spotlights around it was a dead giveaway.

The King, no doubt ineffectually, had still been fussing over his speech. No doubt the celebrations would draw a large crowd, as any special occasion did. You could hold a celebration for a toddler losing a tooth and you'd still get a couple of thousand people turn out if you sold candy floss and booked a Ferris wheel. The preparations were a tedious chore, but the speech kept the King occupied for large parts of the day and that was a mercy, although it left a niggling worry in Ivor's guts. Normally the King flaunted every piece of banal nonsense he invented to anyone willing to listen. Now he was filling an inordinate amount of paper with furtive scribbling. Ivor determined to sneak a glance at the first opportunity.

The hour grew late. He would have to get back to the Royal Court. Ugh! He scolded himself for calling it that. It was a barely-converted theatre. Everything about this monarchy was a sham. The King was green behind the ears, his legitimacy was highly questionable and the man, when all was said and done, was an imbecile of the highest order. If it wasn't for widespread apathy on both sides of the border, King Gruffydd II would probably have been executed for treason to the British crown or ousted by a more competent rival.

Ivor wasn't even sure how it had come about. Establishing a new monarchy and constitution usually involved some kind of uprising. Here it had happened because people were too busy looking the other way.

The King's only major Act since coming to power was declaring war on the English. The English government had been completely unaware of it for the first two weeks and the British papers didn't get hold of it until the Cardiff Times changed its name to the Royal Cardiff Beagle and banged the story on its front page for three days running and did an evening special which they air dropped over Whitehall to make sure someone noticed.

Westminster dismissed it publicly as "a Welsh rare bit of nonsense", hoping it would blow over and public opinion would settle the issue. Unfortunately the new king actually seemed to be garnering support.

About a month later, England denounced King Gruffydd II and imposed sanctions on the small, excitable nation to their west. They assumed this would drive the Welsh people to dethrone their new king for bringing such strife to their door. But it hadn't happened. Ivor imagined this was solely because of the declaration of war. It was a bold move. The King had garnered more respect and supporters for this bizarre act of defiance than was reasonable. Of course, not long after he had promptly lost the people's respect again by farting on national television, but Ivor ran the spin machine that day, saying the King had chronic, incurable, cantankerous bowel syndrome, which was as close to the truth as damn it.

How had it all started in the first place? As he began to shiver in the cold night air, he found he could only vaguely remember. The Welsh Parliament kept obstinately demanding more power. Exasperated, Westminster blocked everything. Just as it might have become a real topic of debate in England, there was the English civil uprising. Not a civil war at that time, but still more of a threat than some unknown Welsh king who had only made one television appearance - and that was on the Welsh language channel which was heavily subsidised by the English to promote Welsh culture.

King Gruffydd II took the throne without any experience of statesmanship. He thought it his destiny, simply because his father - who had been a well respected leader of the Welsh Parliament - was granted it, but died of a coronary on the morning of his coronation. Ivor chortled as he recalled.

The civil war had grasped England by the throat and then the plague had swept into London and taken hundreds of lives. The capital crumbled and its weakness opened the floodgates for those wanting change. The effect spread far and wide. And there was something else there now. It was impossible to put a name to it, but Ivor could feel it stirring. It was everywhere: in the eyes of the townsfolk, in the words on the radio, in every fiscal transaction, every news report, every pub conversation and here in the Royal Court as well. It was a kind of unspoken anarchy lurking behind every corner and every thought. And then there were the *other* things. The strange reports. That's where the knots really loosened and the pages fell from the spine. Strange cults and religions sprang up. Daily news reports about strange sightings and off-coincidences abounded. How odd that such chaos would come at just the right time to support a new Welsh king. Ivor paused. No, he thought, that's teleological thinking. It was coincidence that the King arose at this time, or the result of something unknown. What could have started it all? Ivor didn't know.

He realised he'd become distracted from the very thought that had brought him here to this dark place. He wanted to mull over an idea he'd had earlier in the day. It was a dark thought and needed a dark moment in a dark place to blossom and unfurl its dark petals.

This one, terrible thought rolled around inside Ivor's skull, tumbling over and under and in upon itself, like a Slinky stuck in a hamster wheel. The full moon helped it germinate and as it began to take shape, Ivor knew it couldn't be resisted. It was his master now, and he its servant. Some ideas are heavier than others and this one pressed down on him like a rhino on a space hopper. It should have brought a bounce to his step, but instead he felt crushed with a sense of impending, fatalistic certitude.

He stood up and prodded around the base of the dark rose with his foot again. He saw something glistening where he had trod, reflecting in the lantern light. He reached down and picked it up. He took it closer to the light. He sneered, instantly transported back to earlier in the day when he had been insulted by an inferior; an inferior who was now performing his new royal duty as garden fertiliser. He examined Bazza's nose ring as he turned it over in his fingers. "Lay down your head, it's time for bed." He hummed to himself as he walked away from the soft patch of recently turned soil.

He took a final, deep breath of night air, trying to enjoy

the solitude before returning to the fray, but his tranquil moment ended abruptly as a window was drawn open. He looked up and, sure enough, the King's fat head was poking out of a window. "Ivor Munchkinhead!"

Ivor cursed, picked up his lantern, smiled a wicked smile and made his way through the gardens and the still night air toward whatever inane request the King had devised. Over the course of the night, the dark rose turned its head, imperceptibly slowly, to look up at the full moon.

CHAPTER 10

The night was cold, but fortunately the interminable rain had finally stopped, making a mockery of adjectives everywhere. Quentin wedged his foot in such a way as to keep the door open so the inside light would stay on. He was amazed that a car still existed without a switch for the inside light, but apparently there was such a car, and he owned it.

He hunched over the law book he'd borrowed. Stolen. He had stolen it. He jumped every time he heard a police siren. It was silly - there was no call for a police car to sound its blues and twos just to catch him. He turned back to his research. Was there a real and immediate legal recourse available that would get his house back tonight? Everything he read added to the jigsaw, but his lawyer's mind distinguished every situation from his own. His mind wandered and he recalled a jigsaw his grandmother had owned. Once assembled, the picture was of baked beans. Just hundreds of baked beans. Nothing else. He began to feel hungry. Soon concentrating became hard. He forced thoughts about food from his mind, but it was no use. Mavis always brought him tea and biscuits when he was researching. He shook his head and with concerted mental effort, he focussed on the book.

An hour passed and his right ankle froze solid. He let the

book fall closed. He withdrew his leg and let the door swing shut. He stretched. It was pretty hopeless. He'd buried his head in the sand for far too long and now his job and home were gone. There was no getting away from it. He'd read all the warning letters and he'd ignored all the warning letters. On one occasion, he squashed a spider with a warning letter. It was as if he didn't care, but that just wasn't true. He felt he'd lost out because of the declining state of the nation and the strange way society was changing. He could have responded to the changing tides, but it just hadn't been in him. Perhaps he was a traditionalist. He couldn't really explain it in any satisfactory way, but he knew, somehow, that this had been inevitable. Perhaps it was fate. But he didn't believe in fate. So he blamed the government. Such thoughts swirled and eddied in his mind. He closed his eyes and was taken by a deep sleep. He dreamt of a small boy with a shaved head standing on a mountain top staring out across a vista of azure skies, snow-peaked mountains and a valley of deep green forest. His rest wasn't to last long.

Midnight.

A tap at the window.

Quentin stirred and grumbled. The tapping turned into a rapping. Quentin shuffled uncomfortably and twisted away from the noise. The rapping became a hard knocking. Quentin sniffed and snorted and put one arm over his head, covering his ear, to block out the sound. "Mphphph," he protested gruffly. A sharp bang on the roof of the car woke him and he bolted upright, hit his head on the ceiling, sunk back down into the driver's seat and looked, bleary eyed, through the window into the face of the police officer standing outside.

He wound down the window. "Evening officer."

The officer looked into the car, saw the book on the passenger seat, took in Quentin's suit which, although now dry, looked worse for wear due to its earlier soaking, and nodded. "Lost track of time have we, sir?"

"Have we?" asked Quentin, unable to accept the horror of his predicament. "Er, yes." He figured it was best to agree but he'd already forgotten the question.

The officer looked at the book again, then took a step back and took in the car, as if seeing it for the first time. He had an amused twinkle in his eye. "Why've you parked here?"

"I was driving home." He tried to think quickly, but thought groggily instead. "I stopped because I had thought of something. I looked it up. I must have just closed my eyes for a second..." He smiled at the policeman.

"Very good, sir." The officer glanced at the book. "Find what you were looking for?"

"Thank you, yes." He was being polite and positive. What else could he do?

"Mind stepping out of the car, sir?" The amused twinkle had become a steely glint. Quentin surmised that this was a bad thing.

Quentin stammered something, but his inarticulate vowels transmuted without warning into a wide-mouthed yawn.

"Out of the car, now." Quentin tumbled out of the car, uncrumpling from the cramped position he'd stiffened into during sleep. The officer motioned for him to follow. Resigned to his fate and docile with drowsiness, Quentin stumbled over to the police car and was shoved into a back seat. For a moment he considered going back to sleep, but something warned him that might antagonise the officer. Where had he gone, anyway? He looked out the back window.

The officer was picking up the law book and checking its title. He reported something into his walkie-talkie and then shut the car door. Quentin noticed the inside light go off and unconsciously rotated his right ankle to get some movement back into it. The officer got into the front of the police car and, carefully putting the book on the passenger's seat, turned to Quentin.

Quentin squirmed. He'd been caught red handed. He looked through the wire mesh designed to protect the car's driver from the potentially violent criminal in the back seat. The officer looked back at him as if he was a zoo animal. Quentin adopted a hangdog expression and shrugged. It was a shrug that conveyed guilt. It may as well have been an outright confession.

"Thought so." He started the engine. "We're going to the station. You might like it there. It's warm." He smiled and pulled away from the kerb, heading toward the town centre.

"We'll see," mumbled Quentin. He was starting to wake up. Apparently police *were* sent to find people who stole library books. He supposed it wouldn't be the sort of offence that would land him in jail, but then things had changed so much in criminal law. There barely was any criminal law. Just criminals. And law. The criminals did what they wanted and the law enforcement services followed much the same line of thinking. Here in Chester, the structure of society was still holding together just well enough that the law enforcement services could arrest you, indict you before jeering jurors scoffing free popcorn, then bang you behind bars. But Quentin had heard that down South, especially in London, things were very much worse.

Quentin tried to weigh up just how much trouble he was in. He decided it was a lot. He tried to flee the car in a desperate bid for freedom. He smacked his head off the window. The door handle snapped back into place as his fingers slipped from it. He ended up lying on the back seat staring at the ceiling, much to the officer's amusement. "That's the thing about lawyers," he wisecracked. "They don't tend to commit crimes, so don't know all the tricks." The bruise forming on Quentin's forehead testified to the accuracy of the officer's insight.

Time for a different tack, thought Quentin. "Ahem," he began, clearing his throat. "Did you say we were going to the station?"

"That's right." The car stopped at a zebra crossing to let a tramp cross the road.

"Don't you have to read me my rights?" Quentin knew fine well that he did.

"You were once a criminal lawyer, right?"

Quentin grimaced. No court would be particularly

concerned about a criminal lawyer not being read his rights, and if Quentin protested the point then it would be his word against the officer's and it would look like he was lying, and therefore committing perjury, in order to secure some small victory which wouldn't, ultimately, have any bearing on whether he was found guilty for stealing the book.

"So, I'm under arrest?"

"That's right."

"What for?"

"Suspicion of theft." He nodded at the book on the passenger seat.

Quentin grimaced. "I borrowed it. Now I think about it, I forgot to sign it out. That's not a criminal offence is it?"

"No, but theft is." The officer spared him a glance in his rear view mirror and smiled sardonically.

Quentin thought: I'm a lawyer; I can outsmart this guy.

He sat slumped in the back seat, waiting for some ingenious idea to occur to him. The car turned at a set of traffic lights. Quentin estimated he had four minutes remaining before they reached the station.

They started along the main road toward the station.

A red light. Two drunk students took an age to cross the road because they were each balancing a road cone on their heads. The policeman said nothing. Quentin couldn't see the point in mentioning it.

Still no ideas.

The officer glanced into the rear view mirror again. He was smiling, presumably taking pleasure in Quentin's stumped silence.

He thinks he's outsmarted me, thought Quentin, wondering if, in fact, that was right.

Three minutes left.

They approached another set of traffic lights and Quentin willed them to turn red. As they approached, it turned amber. Quentin's eyes flared with mischievous delight. So did those of the policeman, who ran the light without a flicker of remorse.

Quentin felt his hope ebbing away. He reassured himself

that he had acted out of character and was not of his right mind when the theft took place. It was an act of desperation. Nay, an act of necessity. There was duress of circumstances. He would raise this defence in court. Possibly it wouldn't get that far and he'd be let off with a reprimand or caution. He tried to relax.

Two minutes.

The problem was that even with a caution it was unlikely he would ever work as a solicitor again. Actually, that was the least of his problems. He was bankrupt. His firm was insolvent. He was homeless.

What use were all his years of practice if they couldn't help him now? He remembered some of his earliest clients. He recalled the dirty deeds they'd committed and the arguments they'd put forth. He recalled the scoundrels and the rogues, the comedians and the pranksters, the druggies and the rapists, the robbers and the burglars. He was one of them now. He had committed theft. It was miniscule in the grand scheme of things, but that one rash act conflicted against everything that he was, everything he had been, everything he believed in. It grated against his very being like a cheese grater grating against his very being. The wrongness of it clung to him like cheap aftershave that had been stuck to his face with duct tape whilst still in the bottle.

He thought about all the criminals who had served some small amount of time, or paid some measly fine, and then gone about living their wretched lives just exactly the same way they had before they were found guilty and processed through the criminal justice system. They suffered not; especially in this day and age of lawlessness and anarchy, where jails were like casinos and custody officers the croupiers.

Everything would change for him if he was found guilty.

A thought struck him: what I used to be is completely gone. It hit him with the same impact a steroid-enhanced gorilla might, if dropped from a great height. He sat bolt upright, suddenly realising all those years studying law and being around criminals wasn't in vain. Something snapped inside him.

"I really need to examine that book so I can stop my house being repossessed," he stated, calmly. "I know the book is evidence, but here's the thing: I'm going to confess. I'd really appreciate having a look before I get incarcerated. That way, I can make that one phone call really count and maybe stop them making me homeless." He said it all so matter-of-factly. It was all so reasonable.

The officer seemed to do a quick mental calculation. He obviously didn't see Quentin as any kind of threat and perhaps thought it would help secure a quick confession. To Quentin's eternal surprise, the officer opened the grate separating them and passed the book back. Quentin took it firmly in both hands.

One minute.

They turned down by a school. It was especially quiet at this time of night, but the officer still reacted to the speed limit of twenty miles per hour. Admittedly he reacted to it by slowing to thirty five miles an hour, but it was a token effort and showed that no one was above the law.

Quentin pulled the book back with both arms, clutching it so tight his knuckles turned white. It was a large hardback volume, probably weighing the same as four bags of sugar. He leant forward to give himself a bit of clearance. He swung it. The officer just had time to grunt in surprise and annoyance before the corner of the book collided with his temple and knocked him head-first into the side window. The second impact knocked him cold and his foot slipped off the pedal. The car bounced over a speed bump, veered off the road and ploughed straight into the school fence. The car jolted to a stop.

It took him a moment to be sure of it, but Quentin had escaped the crash unscathed. He prodded the officer in the face several times with his finger. After a particularly violent and penetrating plunge of his index finger into the officer's ear, he concluded the man was out cold. He should have felt a twinge of guilt, but the adrenaline coursing through his system meant he felt only exhilaration.

Quentin managed to reach the car keys and open the car door using the remote control key fob. He leapt out. He decided to depart the scene of the crime as quickly as possible, but he suddenly remembered something important. He opened the passenger's door and grabbed the book. He held it firmly. It had cost him a lot. He took one last look at the officer and thought he saw an eyelid flutter. Spooked, he turned and ran.

CHAPTER 11: THURSDAY

It was early morning and dew still clung to the dandelions which, in turn, clung to life in the dank cracks of the kerb stones that lined the pavements of old London town. Down a forgotten road, through the outskirts of a close-knit neighbourhood bragging a name forgotten by all but the oldest maps, along a cobbled street, and around the corner of a crumbling, fire-gutted shell of a building that hadn't escaped the vagaries of a recent riot, there was a paint-stripped wooden door backing onto a litter-strewn back-alley.

To all intents and purposes, it looked like the back door to a harmless charity shop. Certainly, at the front, when viewed from the street, the charity shop's window display looked inconspicuous enough. It looked just like any other charity shop; selling second-hand books, badly-sewn shirts, gum-chewed infants' toys, slightly-chipped china cups and other hyphenated oddities. The alleyway at the back didn't hint of mischief or speak of misdoings. The toppled bins and broken bottles strewn across the cobbled paving didn't scream of anything untoward. The door itself, with a wooden peephole covered by a sliding slat of wood, didn't seem out of place in this backwater stretch of the old town. The rats scurrying to and fro, dragging long-forgotten scraps of kebab meat, looked bloated and content in this festering dead end. Yet the man approaching the door... there appeared to be something very wrong with him.

A figure wearing a bedraggled brown cloak with a hood that covered his face lurched his way toward the back door. His broad shoulders were hunched and he moved with difficulty. He wasn't particularly tall, nor particularly short, and although not fat, it would be wrong to call him thin. His left hand hung by his side; it ended in a large ham-fist, like that of a boxer or manual labourer. He wore huge shoes, surely tailor-made, and his calves were fat like an ox's. His other hand hid under his cloak, as if he was carrying something clutched to his chest.

As he approached the door, he pulled back his hood releasing a mass of curly black hair. His eyes were bloodshot and screwed tightly, as if he was experiencing pain. His mouth and nose were covered with a black handkerchief, possibly to hide his identity, or possibly to guard against the plague. He knocked three times then his arm fell to his side as if knocking had taken some great effort.

A moment passed and he started to sag where he stood. He appeared to shrink and he let out a whimper. His dark brown eyes were troubled. His skin hinted of a Mediterranean complexion despite being clammy and pale. With a startling crack of wood clattering against wood, the peephole opened. At first nothing, then the man outside spoke in a soft, deep voice, strained with pain and sorrow. "Hey, let me in," he pleaded.

"First let me see yer other hand," hissed the person behind the door. The new voice was reedier and had an affected drawl.

The injured man with the swarthy look lifted his hidden hand into view, showing it to be empty. His agonised groan subsided as he quickly replaced it under his cloak so he could clutch at his side. "Broken rib," he winced. His face was paling to a shocked white.

"Darn it! Why d'ya come here? You'll have been followed.

Git outta here."

The cloaked man seemed to recoil, then with tremendous effort he thumped the door with his left hand. The hollow sound echoed down the alleyway and outward. It was hardly discrete.

"Quit that!"

"Hey, let me in! Or I'll tell the whole goddamn street who's hiding in there." He cursed loudly, but his voice trembled.

A thin laugh came from the other side of the door. "You're in no position to make threats," the other man sneered, although he didn't sound one hundred percent certain. "Let me see yer eyes!"

The large man took a step forward and looked up into the peephole.

"Now yer mouth."

He pulled down the scarf that covered half his face and opened his mouth, exposing it to the peephole for inspection. He stuck out his tongue for good measure.

"Not bad. Now yer fingernails."

Sighing, he lifted his two hands up and held them there for inspection. There was a grunt of satisfaction from behind the door, so he let them drop to his sides. For a moment the world seemed to hold still, then the injured man began to sway on his feet. Beads of sweat burst out on his forehead as the strain of the encounter began to take its toll. He shuffled closer to the door and leant his shoulder against it. "You let me in, you son-of-a-bitch," he slurred, his voice finally betraying his complete exhaustion.

"Well, yer not plague-ridden." The response was non-committal.

"Hey, you let me in." His desperation all too apparent. His eyes shut tight.

"One more thing." The one with the reedy voice seemed to take great pleasure from drawing out the interrogation. "What's the password?"

Outside, the injured man's head slumped forward,

throwing the dark tangles of his hair over the front of his face. He muttered something under his breath in another language. He dropped to one knee.

"I'm sorry... I didn't hear ya." The voice was mocking.

On both knees now, the injured man wheezed and spat pink saliva on the pavement. He said something, but it couldn't be heard.

"I'm sorry, if ya don't know the password then ya can't come in."

He was back on his feet and hammering on the door with both massive fists, all of his weight and muscle behind each heavy blow. It was completely unexpected and happened all in a second. He pounded three times and yelled at the top of his voice. "The password is tee-see-pee-eye-pee!" He spat blood against the door. "Now you let me in, Astin, you son-of-a-bitch!"

"Don't use my name!" shrieked the voice. Locks rattled and bolts slid open. The injured man fell through the door as it swung open and he staggered into the darkness within. A thin face poked out through the door. Greasy, silvery grey hair fell down either side of a ruddy complexion featuring beady, nicotine-stained eyes and teeth, and a snarled upper lip. Astin looked around the alleyway, expecting to see someone else, then, perhaps satisfied, pulled away into the darkness and slammed the door. The locks and bolts clattered once more. Silence.

For a few moments nothing stirred in the alleyway, then an obese rat came out of hiding and started nibbling on a scrap of doner kebab. The clattering of a bin lid being shunted aside made the rat look up. It was lethargic and didn't move fast enough. A mangy cat pounced from behind the bin and caught it in sharp claws. A brief scuffle ensued but the cat pinned its foe to the ground and bit the back of its neck. The rat fell limp. Seconds later they were both gone. Silence.

A minute passed peacefully before a figure, both masked and hooded, emerged from behind a burnt-out car stationed only a dozen feet from where the two men exchanged words.

The shadowy figure stood and walked away quietly. A slight roll of the hips and designer, high-heeled leather boots would have indicated it was a woman, if anyone had been around to take notice. A wisp of blonde hair fell out from under her hood and was quickly and delicately tucked away behind an ear.

"Rat bastards," she whispered to herself, referring to the men, not the vermin.

Her toes were cold. She stopped just around the corner and eyed her left boot. It had been vital not to draw attention to herself so she had sat motionless as a scrawny white rat gnawed at her toe. These designer, knee-high ladies' boots had been expensive, and now they were ruined. She was just grateful it hadn't nibbled anywhere else. "Bastard rats," she cussed quietly, referring to the rats, not the men, and, as the sun rose over the top of the ramshackle roofs around her, she slipped off into the stirrings of a new day as quietly as she had arrived.

CHAPTER 12

Just two days remained until the celebrations to mark King Gruffydd II entering the third year of his reign. For three years his fat behind had graced the throne and fortunately, in Ivor's estimation, he had remained ineffectual throughout. Yet now he was preparing some elaborate speech which he was, worryingly, keeping under wraps and this chilled Ivor to the bone.

The King was in his counting house, counting out his money. He'd been there all morning. That was how Ivor knew he was up to something. There wasn't any money to count. What meagre treasures lay within only took a brief glance to tote up. Ivor had pounded at the counting house door and bellowed that he had bacon sandwiches ready, knowing the King must be peckish, but even that cunning gambit hadn't gained him access. If only he could glean some sense of what the speech contained it might put his mind at ease.

The King had been working on his speech for days and Ivor was quite sure it contained some momentous announcement. He wasn't happy about that. He'd worked hard to get where he was and wasn't about to be usurped by some damn fool idea the King had dreamt up. As the King's advisor, it irked him beyond belief that His Majesty was plotting something without his knowledge. If the King's speech was explosive enough to need written in private, then it was almost certainly something the King shouldn't be saying at all. Whatever it was, Ivor considered it about as welcome in the public arena as a verruca at a swimming pool. He would have to find a way to inspect it, however devious or treasonous that required him to be. The King just couldn't be trusted, thought Ivor, with unintentional irony.

"Ivor Munchkinhead!"

Ivor hurried along to the King's bedchamber. He entered to find the King sitting on the edge of his bed, which sank considerably under his considerable weight.

"Sire, I didn't know you had left the counting house. My apologies for my inattentiveness. I was engaged in ordering a variety of -"

"Ivor-" interrupted the King, clearly not listening. He was beaming the radiant smile of the blissfully idiotic. The King motioned for Ivor to take a seat and said, "Just the, er, man I was looking for."

Ivor flinched at the slight pause before the word "man". He hated when people did that. Sure, he was slightly shorter than the average bloke. What of it? His head was slightly too large for his body and not everyone liked his black goatee. He accepted that. But there was really no need to insinuate through language or gesture that he might not actually be human. As a school child he had declared that such references were below the belt. His antagonists argued that he was below the belt, and boxed him about the ears.

"Sire, may I be of service to you?" He bowed obsequiously before the King, despite a deep feeling that, as the King's most trusted advisor, he should be beyond such elaborate displays of deference by now.

The King continued to beam at him for a moment, then spoke. "You are my most dependable and devoted advisor, Ivor Munchkinhead. Is everything going well for you?"

"Yes, sire," replied Ivor cautiously. He wondered from where this strange and sudden interest in his welfare arose.

The King looked as if he might say something else, but then seemed to reconsider and stopped himself. He straightened his posture, causing the bed to creak woefully, and adopted a face that warned Ivor he was about to do royal business. "State of affairs?" he asked, referring to affairs of state. He got up and took a seat at his table.

Ivor gave a shallow bow and took an electronic device from his pocket. Swiping its touch screen, he flipped through some screens and tapped it a few times. He shook it.

"I don't know why you don't just use a paper and pen like me," remarked the King.

"This organiser is produced in Cardiff, sire. I am merely supporting Welsh industry."

"Very admirable," agreed the King reluctantly. After a moment's thought he added, "And where do my paper and pens come from?"

"That would be China," replied Ivor, still shaking his organiser and rotating it around and around.

"What are you doing?"

"I'm trying to get it into landscape mode." Ivor started tapping it gently on his knee.

"And you have to shake it and bang it off things to achieve that, do you?" asked the King, innocently.

"No," replied Ivor, feeling his frustration rising as technology endeavoured to embarrass him.

After a moment he had the device functioning correctly. "Today you have a veritable cornucopia of miscellany to eschew or resolve as you see fit," he said to get his own back, knowing full well the King wouldn't understand a word of it.

"What does that even mean?"

Ivor managed to stop himself smirking and decided to summarise. "Basically there's stuff to do, but you can take it or leave it."

"Well of course I can, I'm the king," replied King Gruffydd II with a smile that emphasised both his absolute authority in such matters and his many chins.

"Most important on the list," informed Ivor, pressing on

as swiftly as he dared, "is this evening's meal. Should it so please your majesty, you will be dining with the newly knighted Sir Pendragon of Llysfaen, your friend the Duke of Snowdonia, and Lord and Lady Llandudno. Several other dignitaries were supposed to be attending but pulled out for a variety of reasons which I'm sure will not interest Your Majesty."

"Sounds like a drag. What's on the menu?"

"Well, for starters there's radish soup. For the main course, there's roast vegetables with various roast vegetables. And for dessert, there's blancmange and yogurt and custard and rice pudding."

The King frowned with a sudden, deadly seriousness. He hadn't looked this serious since the time he discovered he only had one follower on Twitter and it turned out to be Ivor. "Radish soup sounds a bit grim, Ivor."

"I questioned that one myself, sire. I'm told by the chef that it's quite exquisite."

"Very well. The dessert sounds a bit soupy though. You know, sloppy."

"I think it's a case of the usual variety of cakes with any of those accompaniments."

"Ah yes, that will do. So, let's tackle the main course."

"Roast vegetables with roast vegetables, sire."

"I do like roast vegetables."

"And the chef knows that, sire."

"I'm not altogether sure that I like them with just... well, you know... more roast vegetables."

"I take your point, sire. Unfortunately the chef is also in charge of the catering for the celebrations and he's had to make various cutbacks in order to be properly lavish for the festivities."

"You're telling me we can't afford meat until the celebration?"

"That seems to be the gist of it, sire."

"But that's nonsense! We can't entertain our guests by serving roast vegetables with more roast vegetables and a side helping of roast vegetables strewn with a topping of even more goddamn roast vegetables. This is Wales! We have some of the finest meats in the world."

"If you say so, sire."

"Well, we should at least be able to rustle up some mutton, don't you think?"

"I did ask the chef if it was possible that an alternative food group to vegetables could be put on the menu."

"And he said?"

"He said that he would take an aubergine, cut it into the shape of a pork chop, use food colouring to dye it dark brown and red, roast it, and serve it as if it was a meat item."

"So basically we're still talking about a roast vegetable?"

"That's correct, sire."

"Surely there's some way around this?"

"Apparently not. The main problem seems to lie in the trade embargo between England and Wales. Not only are we unable to buy meat products from over the border, but many of our meat products are being taken across the border by stealth and sold for higher prices than they might otherwise have attained here."

"But that's absurd! Why would the English pay more for Welsh meat than the Welsh would?" The look on the King's face was one of purest bafflement and Ivor felt sorry for him. The King couldn't fathom why everything wasn't perfect now he was sitting on the Welsh throne. He was short sighted. His visions and dreams were of a brighter tomorrow. Unfortunately, the day after tomorrow was so dim to him that he hadn't even considered it, let alone contemplated turning the page on the calendar.

"I believe it's to do with sheep to people ratios, sire. It's simple supply and demand. There's a surplus of meat within our borders, and it can't be exported, so the price has dropped. Yet when they smuggle it over the border, they find they're still receiving the old prices. We really should be selling abroad. And by abroad, I mean England."

"Well, yes, they are abroad, aren't they? Tell me, did I put an embargo on meat moving across the border or did they?"

"I believe both sides have similarly restrictive secondary legislation in place, sire."

"But who did it first?"

"They did, sire."

"Damn. I hate it when they get there first."

Ivor pursed his lips, but he couldn't stop himself. "Sire, you would hardly have done it first. It is far more injurious to Wales than to England."

"Nonsense. That's practically treason! Stopping Welsh meat crossing the border is of great importance in the war against the English. It is they who will lose out. We can't be feeding the troops they've amassed against us!"

"Sire, they haven't amassed any troops."

The King ignored that. "Who are these scoundrels selling meat across the border?"

"Hard to say, sire. No one has been caught red-handed. In truth, I suspect they are all at it."

"All of them? Well, that won't do. It won't do at all. We'll have to think of a way to fix this. Meantime, we still have no meat course for our dinner guests."

"That's correct, sire. We simply cannot afford more meat than we have already ordered for the celebrations. The celebrations have bled the treasury dry."

"So roast vegetables with roast vegetables it is?"

"That's correct, sire."

The King shuffled around in his seat to better face Ivor. He gave his advisor the kind of look that a father would give to a naive son. Ivor hated that look. He'd just spent the last five minutes explaining things to the King and now the King was going to patronise him by explaining something to him.

"You do understand why it is necessary to hold these celebrations, don't you, Ivor?" The King clasped his hands and leaned forward as if he was talking to a small child.

Ivor shrugged. He had already been on the receiving end of this sermon seven times and knew the outcome was inevitable, as inevitable as the result of a giant meteor impacting on the face of the Earth, and just as favourable as if that self-same meteor were actually a giant, freshly-evacuated alien turd. "I'm all ears, Your Majesty."

"You see, Ivor, this all started many years ago. It started before I was born. I know you know this part, because you're here now. You already understand all the reasons to support our cause."

Ivor was almost, but not quite, grateful to be spared the really patronising speech about why they were here in the first place. However, he wasn't actually grateful, because he knew two things. One, he was only being spared it because the King had another lecture ready to go. Doubtlessly, he was about to hear whatever inane idea the King had been rolling around his fat head for the last day or two. It would be the kind of idea a normal person would sufficiently contemplate over a cup of tea. For the King, it was a monumental effort to contain this thought now he'd had it, and he needed to tell everyone about it as many times as possible in case he forgot it. Secondly, Ivor wasn't altogether grateful because from experience he knew that by the time the King had finished his first explanation there was a good chance he'd have forgotten his promise not to retread old ground

"The celebrations," began the King, pausing to assemble his thoughts in a way that he hoped made them sound considered and intellectual, "are all about uniting the people behind us." He stood up. This would be a long speech. The King wandered over to the mirror in his room and admired his own friendly, fat, cross-eyed face for a moment. Ivor winced internally. No, this was to be much worse than a speech; this was to be a soliloquy.

CHAPTER 13

Daylight broke through his dreams, returning him to reality. Quentin awoke that morning with mud in his hair, a crick in his neck, a thorn in his backside and a caterpillar weaving a chrysalis on his eyelid. It took him a moment or two to sort himself out and come to. He stretched. He yawned. He sniffed back some tears and an overwhelming feeling of dread.

He had learnt years ago that sometimes the deeds one performed late at night, that seemed so perfectly reasonable and necessary at the time, were no such thing when revisited under the unforgiving light of day. Last night was coming back to haunt him all too clearly. He recalled the events in the library. Of those he wasn't proud. He recalled the events in the police car. Of those he was indifferent. In truth, he should have been appalled at his behaviour, but, he considered, he had actually escaped single-handedly from a police car. In terms of decency, the rule of law, good behaviour and just generally doing the right thing, he had failed miserably. In doing something that defied the odds of probability, he had actually excelled. Part of him swelled with pride. Another part eyed up the potential consequences with a healthy dose of apprehension.

He had fled the scene of the crime and left the comatose

police officer slumped over the steering wheel. Unfortunately, he had then been overcome with guilt and had snuck back to check everything was alright. He'd peeked around the corner of the school building and seen the aftermath of his actions. The car looked damaged, but the officer was awake and quite, quite furious. He'd been pacing back and forth, yelling into his walkie-talkie and looking more angry than Quentin had felt was strictly necessary. It was, after all, only a brief period of unconsciousness he'd endured. Quentin had heard sirens in the near-distance and made a sharp exit. He'd scarpered off into the night, thankful that it hadn't started raining again.

He had gone looking for somewhere to hide out for the night and tried various inns and hotels in the centre of town, but there had been no room. Well, no room for him. His credit cards had been declined. He was bankrupt. Somehow it had been easy to forget this one unbearable fact in the midst of everything else that had happened. He had thought about going back to find his car and using it to make a getaway, but he decided that the police would know it was the first thing he might try, so he dismissed the idea. His car was lost to him. If anything, it would be sold and used to pay off one of his creditors. All the items he had packed were also lost to him, and he particularly begrudged the time he had spent selecting them.

His first thought after that had been to visit Mavis. She was a kind woman and there was a good chance she might look after him. He had made his way to her house, doing his best to stay off the main roads. When he got there it was about half past two in the morning, but it turned out that the police were one step ahead of him. They were parked outside her house and he could see the living room light was on. He had gathered together what little courage he possessed and stole up to the window and spied through a crack in the curtains. He saw her being interviewed by a police woman. He turned away and tried to think of someone else he knew who would take him in at short notice. He could think of no one. It was a lonely life being a lawyer.

In the end, he had hunkered down in a ditch at the side of a road which led out of town. There was a street lamp nearby so he had used it to read through the stolen law book. Every page he read made him realise all the more how hopeless his situation was. Eventually, sheer exhaustion made him give up. He had closed the book, lain back on the ground and just stared up at the dark, cloud-strewn sky. A moment later, sleep had taken him.

He rose now and shook himself. He flicked away the chrysalis on his eyelid with disgust. He was covered in leaves, dirt and insects and it took him more than a few minutes to start to feel that he could proceed with his day. The sun was low in the sky and the air was crisp and fresh. It looked like it would be a dry day, which was a relief after the downpour yesterday.

He began to think through his options. They were fettered by two main restrictions. The first problem was that he was a wanted man. He had two real options there. One, hand himself in. Two, try to outsmart the police and stay on the run. In truth, neither option really appealed to him and he decided to file that thought away for later consideration. The second shackle on his freedom was the fact that he had no money. He wasn't sure how to tackle that issue. He had tried to use his bank cards last night and found them barred, but there was a small possibility that a savings account he had opened as a child might still have some cash in it. The account was with a different bank to his usual one, so possibly the authorities wouldn't have suspended it yet.

So he had a plan. That had been easy. Go to the bank and talk them into releasing the funds in his childhood savings account. Possible hurdles? One, the police might have alerted the bank to the possibility that he might try to withdraw those funds. Two, he didn't have his savings book as it was in his car. Three, he was covered in mud. The third hurdle might make it more difficult for him to negotiate the return of the balance without suitable identification. So, possibly, he would need to secure some new clothing as a first step. Quentin thought about this for a moment and then started tearing one of the front pages out of the book he had stolen. He couldn't shake the feeling that it was a terrible sacrilege to vandalise a book, yet, as he had once argued in a university debating competition: necessity knows no law.

Twenty minutes later and Quentin was halfway across town. He came to the second-hand bookstore where he occasionally liked to browse. He entered quickly, looking back to check he wasn't being trailed by the police, or anyone else for that matter, and placed the book, which was still in reasonable condition and now devoid of any remnants of the library's record system, on the counter. "How much for this?" he asked the shop assistant behind the counter.

"Are you alright?" she replied. She was a thin, fragile-looking woman who couldn't have been more than thirty years old but dressed as if she was not a day younger than sixty three.

He looked down at himself. It was true; he was in a complete state. He had shaken much of the mud and leaves off but was still filthy and, he now noticed, was exhibiting a small white moth on his jacket's lapel. "I'm fine." He wracked his brains. "I was on a stag do. A stag do with my fellow lawyers. I'm getting married this afternoon. I really need to be able to afford the bus home. I need to sell this book to achieve that. I just happened to have it with me. It's worth a lot. It's written by Bracegirdle and Swindells and is one of the most renowned law books on the subject of debt actions. Would you be interested in taking it?"

She looked at the book. She looked back at him. "It must have been some stag-do," she said, sounding impressed.

"Well, yes, it was rather." He didn't volunteer any more information. The last thing he wanted to do was strike up a conversation about an imaginary party.

She seemed disappointed for a moment, but didn't press the matter. She looked back at the book. "I recognise it," she said. For a heart stopping moment Quentin was certain that the police had issued the bookshops with details of the stolen library book and had told the store owners to watch out for it. "I used to study law," she said. He sighed with relief. "I'll give you seven pounds for it."

"Seven pounds!?" he declared. "That's daylight robbery. It sells new for no less than three hundred."

"Eight then," she said, as if this were a reasonable increase.

"Ten," he countered.

"Nine."

"Done."

Quentin took his nine pounds and left the shop. Part one of his plan was complete. He marched across the pedestrianised square towards the arcade where he would find a shop that sold clothes so cheaply they could only have been made by enslaved grandmothers, probably sewing around the clock in some underground sweatshop in deepest Worcestershire.

He clutched his nine pounds like it was the last money he owned in the world, which he sincerely hoped it wasn't, and marched into the shopping centre. He got a few funny looks from other customers. He considered that he probably looked like a rough-sleeping tramp in a battered suit, which to all intents and purposes he was. People paid him little attention and tried not to make eye-contact. They indiscreetly sidestepped away if he got too close.

Quentin entered the particular clothes store he had in mind and located a pair of cheap jeans and a lightweight sweatshirt. Together they came to fifty three pounds. He sighed and stood looking about the shop. After a moment he put down the jeans and sweatshirt and went to the bargain t-shirt stand. He found a bright red t-shirt that was slightly too big for his fairly thin frame. It was the bargain price of only three pounds. Now all he needed was a pair of trousers for six pounds. His intention was simply to enter the bank looking clean. He didn't need to look stylish or respectable. He found a pair of trousers for seven pounds. He went back and raked through the t-shirts hoping to find one for two pounds. He couldn't find such an item, so he scoured the shop for a pair of trousers that were cheaper. He found some jogging bottoms. They were five pounds. Perfect. He went into the changing room and put them on to ensure that he wouldn't look like a total buffoon.

He looked like a total buffoon. He turned in front of the mirror and inspected the red t-shirt, yellow jogging bottoms and muddy black suit shoes he was wearing. He decided that this approach was hopeless. He changed back into his muddy garments and went back out into the shop. He put the offending items back on their hangers and then took some time to look for a shirt. He eventually found one that looked semi-respectable. It wasn't stylish, but from the range of reduced-price shirts available it was probably the best.

Next, he chose a suit from the limited selection available. He tried on some left shoes and, having found one that fitted and looked the part, he asked the attendant to find its counterpart. He explained he would pay for them all together when he had finished browsing and the attendant let him carry them around with the suit and the shirt as he perused the rest of the store.

He chose a pair of black socks and a smart business tie. For a moment he thought he had finished, but then he noticed the waistcoats. He picked one off the hanger and tried it on. It had an attractive green lining, fitted absolutely perfectly and matched the suit he had chosen. Finally, as he sauntered casually up to the counter, he spotted a long black coat that simulated elegance and formality without actually delivering either. He swung it off the rack and over his shoulders.

He proceeded up to the sales point and laid his nine pounds on the surface next to the till. The attendant behind the counter looked at him quizzically. "This," he explained, "is a tip. This is for you. I had hoped to give you a tenner, but I didn't have a tenner, so I am making it nine pounds."

"Uh, thanks," said the attendant noncommittally, while scratching his acne. He wore a mixture of expressions. Clearly he wanted to know either what he had done to deserve a tip or what he was now expected to do to earn it. Neither line of questioning offered the absolute certainty of keeping the money, so he simply waited expectantly.

"Could you put all this in one large bag for me, please?" enquired Quentin casually.

A look of relief and enlightenment swept across the attendant's face as he decided it was for this simple task that he was to receive a tip which, truth be told, was significantly higher than his hourly wage. He took the largest of the plastic bags from behind the counter and started to put the suit into it. He stopped, realising the bag was of insufficient size to hold everything at once. "You want them all in just one bag?" he asked.

"If you don't mind," encouraged Quentin.

Having added two and two without knowing that four was an answer so far off the mark that he wasn't even going to get to the real answer for about three minutes after Quentin's master plan had come to fruition, the attendant left the counter and went into the back of the store to find a larger, more suitable, carrier bag. As the door to the back office closed behind him, Quentin smiled at a job well done. He slipped the nine pounds into his pocket, snatched the goods into one great bundle which he clutched to his chest and fled the store like he was pursued by the Devil himself.

CHAPTER 14

It's a terrible thing to be misunderstood. Larry Juan Brian Sampaio-Gladwell was often misunderstood. His whole life was full of instances of him being misunderstood. The problem was that he wasn't quite bright enough to realise when he was being misunderstood. The effect of this was that things that might have been straightforward to another person were not always straightforward to Larry, but he didn't always know it. Right now was a prime example. He had gone to great lengths to reach London despite his broken rib and some kind of internal injury that was making him cough up small amounts of blood. He saw his mission as one of vital importance to the cause. Yet here he was being berated by a sadistic, long-haired freak called Astin who thought he might have been followed to their secret London headquarters.

"Ya shoulda just died in a gutter. It woulda been better for all of us. Ya probably led the fuzz right to the back door, ya bleeding halfwit."

"Hey, leave it off," choked Larry. He lay on a grotty, bug-infested bed in the corner of the dimly lit room and clutched at his side. There were no lights in the room, just the glow from several computer monitors and a faint dash of sunlight breaking in through a shoddily-blacked-out window. The walls were lined with cheap desks supporting computers, half-empty coffee mugs and textbooks full of obscure programming languages that would be utterly incomprehensible to Larry.

Astin spat a wad of all-too-gooey phlegm into a well-placed spittoon. He pulled a cheap swivel chair out from under his desk and sat down facing backwards so he could keep an eye on Larry. He folded his arms atop the back of the chair, his lanky legs jutting out on either side. His long, greasy, grey hair fell down by his ears in rat tails and ragged ribbons. He looked like something out of the Wild West. Unfortunately, his attempt to affect a hard man persona was thwarted by the chair itself, which was broken. As the back slid down, Astin's posture became increasingly slumped until he was bent double. His vexation was clear and made worse by his being unsure whether to try to recover the situation or not. His attempted adoption of an intimidating pose had failed, but he refused to accept it and hawked a loogie into the spittoon again; trying to regain some authority. It didn't quite go as planned and he wiped the excess dribble from his chin.

Larry barely noticed Astin's posturing.

"Hey, I need... medical treatment," he winced.

"Nothing happens until the boss gets here," explained Astin, not budging.

Larry groaned. "When is that?"

"When he's ready," replied Astin, who probably knew the answer but chose to be unhelpful to exacerbate Larry's suffering. Larry wasn't sure why Astin was so mean, but then he wasn't sure of many things.

Larry pulled his hand away from his chest and drew a wheezy breath. "Hey, I need to take my shirt off," he said. "I need to see what the damage is."

"Don't let me stop you," replied Astin, offering no assistance. He seemed to be shrinking. The chair was getting lower as his weight squeezed the air out of the height-adjustment cylinder beneath it. A look crossed his face which spoke volumes. He clearly wanted to stand and pull the lever to bring the seat up, but was prevented from doing so by the indignity of it. He knew it would completely destroy any shred of credibility his hard man act still had. A thought-filled struggle fought its way across his brow and then he sighed. He stood, pulled the lever and waited until the chair was full height again, then he started tightening the knob on the back of the chair. "Nothing in this place's worth spit."

Seeing that he would get no help whatsoever, Larry pulled himself up on the bed and managed to work his cloak-like anorak off without too much pain. His shirt was another matter. He undid the cuff buttons. The collar was already undone. He started undoing more buttons but the awkwardness of having to use both hands made the process slow and painful. Eventually he managed to undo them all and he slipped the shirt off the uninjured side of his body. Getting it off completely was a little harder but he managed. He wasn't going to show weakness in front of Astin.

"Didn't know ya had tats," remarked Astin. "Whatcha got there?"

Larry twisted to show him his tattoos. Now his shirt was off, it felt like someone had loosened a lasso encircling his chest. He breathed a little easier and felt he could endure a little longer.

Astin inspected his tattoos. Larry had three down his right arm. The first was a love heart with Cupid's arrow through it. It said "I loved Bella". The last letter of the word 'loved' looked like it had been added at a later date as a sad amendment. The second tattoo was of a showgirl in a red mini-dress. Next to it were the words "I loved Lucy". The last letter of 'loved' seemed slightly off-kilter as if it was also added later. The third tattoo said, simply, "I love Dave."

"I think I can see where the first two relationships went wrong," said Astin, a slight smirk pulling at the corner of his pale lips. "Looks like you got that last one printed a little too far to the left. It's out of alignment with the first two."

"Just leaving space for the 'D' this time," replied Larry with a melancholy sigh.

One of the computers beeped. Astin glanced behind him

at the screen. "Boss is almost here. You sit tight."

Larry wondered, in all earnestness, where Astin thought he might go.

CHAPTER 15

Quentin ran from the clothes shop. He looked like a man in freefall with a parachute entangled in his arms, although Quentin was moving horizontally and seemed considerably more panicked. Leaving the shopping mall, he sped down the street passing a number of suspicious onlookers and trying his level best not to look guilty.

Seeing an opportunity present itself through the window of a small express supermarket, he dived through the automatic doors. He took himself into a self-serve photo booth, first putting four pounds in the slot to ensure he didn't raise further suspicions. He swished the curtain closed behind him and let out a deep sigh of relief. He realised he'd been holding his breath for the last two minutes.

He changed his top half lickety-split then was forced to pause and consider how he was going to change his trousers. It wouldn't do for a pair of bare legs to be sighted below the curtain in a public photo booth. He looked about him. The inside of the booth presented him with a camera behind a glass window, a keyboard, a white screen with two coloured sheets that could be drawn across as a background, and a stool. The stool got higher if you twisted it clockwise. Quentin span it until it was as low as it would go. He hopped on and took his trousers off. He then tried to put on the new ones. It was more difficult than he could have imagined. Fourteen clockwise and eight counter-clockwise spins later, he was dressed. He was also about two inches higher than when he started. His head was pressed at an impossible angle into the top of the photo booth, causing him to dribble.

"Everything alright in there?" queried a voice that probably belonged to the store manager.

"Fine, thanks," replied Quentin, as calmly as he could.

"It looks like you've taken four photos of your knees."

There was a pause. "As intended," replied Quentin, trying his best to sound upbeat.

"Okay," answered the voice cheerfully. Quentin heard the person walk away. Not a store manager, then. A store assistant. The wage disparity made all the difference. You had to pay five grand a year extra, at least, for someone who would challenge a potentially undressed man in a photo booth to come out and present himself.

Quentin lowered himself quietly to the floor. It had been a narrow escape. He bundled the dirty clothes together and left the booth, grabbing the photos on the way. He exited the store as swiftly and inconspicuously as he could manage, dropping the photographs in a bin outside.

He decided the best thing now was probably to lie low. He suspected he'd been caught on CCTV camera as he'd swiped the clothes, so he had to keep a low profile. Once he was much farther down the street, he briefly considered entering The Muskrat's Odoriferous Armpit, a less-than-salubrious local pub. It sounded like there was a good crowd in there that he could get lost amongst. Unfortunately, he knew he had precisely no conversation he would wish to share with the clientele, so dismissed the idea.

No doubt the police were well aware of him by now. They would be hunting high and low. He'd stolen a library book, hit a police officer and now he had shoplifted. What's more, he was bankrupt. It wasn't looking good for him. He took a further moment to take stock, but the sound of police sirens in the distance alerted him to the ongoing nature of his dilemma.

He decided the last place they would look for him was in a bank, which is exactly where he needed to be.

The particular bank in question, the one holding his savings account, was called the Royal East, West, South and North of England Bank. It had once been a small bank in the East, but had been unusually successful and amalgamated with a lot of other banks during its growth years. No one seemed to have thought to rename it properly. When it was a small bank, and Quentin was a small boy, he had opened a savings account with some money his parents had given him. It had been there ever since, except for the odd tweak when the bank reduced the interest rate and he threatened to move the money elsewhere and they agreed to put it back up. It wasn't a lot of money, but it would be enough to move to the Great and Independent Communist State of Jersey for a year while all this blew over. There was a good chance that England would be so anarchical by then that he might be able to move back unnoticed under another name and begin a new life. That was the closest thing to a plan he had right now. All he wanted was his old life back, and maybe, one day, he would get it… in the form of a new life.

He ducked into a phone booth as a police car drove past with sirens wailing. Sirens were a bit much, he thought. Probably a different crime.

As he left the phone booth, he checked himself in the reflection of its glass door. He thought he looked quite respectable in his new clothes. At least if he got caught they might treat him with a little respect, he considered. He knew that the police, like anyone, tended to treat people in suits better than those in, say, hoodies. Quentin let this thought soothe his general state of agitation as he briskly made his way down the street, having left the dirty clothes he was carrying in the phone booth behind him. He wasn't sure if littering was a crime, but it was the least of his crimes, so he didn't dwell on it. Besides, perhaps someone in a situation worse than his own might recover those clothes, like the man lying on the pavement just outside the bank.

The destitute man was tucked into a small alcove in the wall which was designed to hold a drainpipe and guide rain water into the gutter. He had a dirty blue rug wrapped around him for warmth and his clothes were threadbare and held together by dirt and dried-on alcohol. For a brief moment, Quentin was touched by the man's plight. In truth, he normally wouldn't have spared the man a second thought, but today was different. It's true what they say about walking a mile in a man's shoes, thought Quentin. He noticed the man was shivering, despite it being the middle of the day.

"You look cold," he observed.

The tramp blinked a couple of times and seemed to come out of a deep coma. Clearly his situation didn't stop him getting a good sleep. "Whayawan?" he spat.

"You look cold," repeated Quentin, increasing the amount of concern on his face to counter the aggression in the response he'd received.

"Ach, wha' macks ye say tha', Sherlock?" The tramp started scratching his shoulder.

"You seemed to be shivering," replied Quentin, doing his best to learn two new languages as fast as possible. The first was Scottish. The second was Tramp.

"Ach ya Sassenach pussy-ya, din'ye ken tha'diffrence'tween dee-tees an tha'cold ya bumbuggerer?" barked the tramp with all the hostility of a military attack dog shaking a grenade in its mouth.

Quentin took pity. Clearly the cold was affecting the poor man's speech. "Here," said Quentin. "Take this. It's only five pounds but it will buy you a hot meal and a drink. Anyway, it's all I have." He realised this sounded disingenuous considering he was wearing a brand new suit and was heading into a bank.

A grubby mitt fused by weather and time to a pair of red fingerless gloves unfurled from beneath the tramp's cover and snatched the money from Quentin's extended hand. "Thankya, nawfkoff," said the tramp, and rolled over to face away from his benefactor. Clearly the transaction was complete.

Quentin hurried into the bank and joined the inevitable queue awaiting him there. The three minute wait to get to the counter felt like an hour and a half. He spotted at least two police cars screaming past the front window of the building. Eventually he reached the desk. He'd been so distracted by his fear of getting caught and watching carefully over his shoulder that he hadn't even noticed who was sitting behind the protective glass waiting to serve him.

"Mavis?" he blurted in astonishment.

"Quentin?" whispered Mavis, her usual smile nowhere to be seen. She looked exhausted and withdrawn. "You look well," she said, her eyes scanning up and down his new suit.

"Thank you," he said dazedly.

"But you have mud on your cheek."

"Ah. I wasn't aware of that."

"And the remains of a chrysalis on your eyelid."

"Ah. How unfortunate."

They looked into each other's eyes. It was a long and meaningful look that could have conveyed a lot of information had they anything they felt they could say to one another. As it was, the long and meaningful look conveyed nothing and so was actually a long and meaningless look. One of the customers waiting behind Quentin was beginning to huff with impatience.

"They came looking for you," disclosed Mavis, finally. She was referring to the police but was wise enough not to give too much away, especially in her place of employment.

"I know. It was a library book on insolvency." He shrugged, showing just a little embarrassment.

"That's not all," she said.

"I had to get away," he explained, referring to his assault on the police officer.

"What now?" she asked. She was keeping the questions simple and nondescript. Quentin noticed, from the badge worn on his lapel, that the man searching through brochures to her right was the branch manager. No doubt he and all the shops, pubs and other outlets throughout town were linked by a warning system involving a radio channel where news of any thieves or troublemakers could be passed on quickly. Mavis was obviously thinking the same thing. "You could be recognised," she said quietly.

Answering the first point, Quentin replied, "I don't know." He paused. "I need to withdraw some money from a savings account. It's all I have left. Could you access it?"

"Have you got the account number?"

"No. I was hoping you could search by address."

"I'm not meant to, but give me a moment."

"It's number five-"

"I know your address, Quentin."

"Sorry."

He waited while Mavis punched some information into the computer. "You seem to have found work quickly enough," he said, smiling. He was genuinely happy about this, although feared the manner in which he posed the statement seemed accusatory. Mavis flinched as if he'd stabbed her in the back after accusing her of stabbing him in the back.

"I took night training sessions before starting, so I could stay with you for as long as possible."

Quentin felt something stir inside. She'd stayed with him even as she undertook training to start elsewhere, knowing it would end badly for him but not wanting to leave him. "I appreciate it," he said, earnestly.

She looked up from her computer. "Right, here's the account. You've got four thousand and eleven pounds in it."

"Is that all?" asked Quentin, aghast.

"Yes."

"I thought it would be more like thirty thousand."

"It was, but it appears the bank sent you an email several years ago saying that if you didn't reply to them within four hours then your six percent APR would be reduced to two percent, they'd introduce what they call a 'special holders fee', where they take nine percent of your savings each year for the trouble of looking after your money, and would remove you from their mailing list and block your email address."

"What!" yelled Quentin. "That's not how a savings account works."

Mavis looked at him. It was partly a look of pity and partly a look of: I kept telling you to read your emails.

"Right. I'll take one thousand in cash right now."

Mavis shook her head. "I can't do that, I'm afraid. You have to wait sixty days for any withdrawal. It's a condition of the account."

"Drat." Quentin thumped the counter with his fist, a display of pique most unlike him. Mavis jumped in her seat. "Sorry," he said. "I can't take the money?"

"Not for sixty days."

"What if I close the account?"

"You need to write to the head office to do that, and you still need to wait sixty days from the first clear day after your post arrives before being able to pick up the money from the regional head office."

"Is this the regional head office?"

"No, this is the Chester branch. The regional head office is in Liverpool."

"Typical."

He stopped to think for a moment. "Is there any way I can get access to any of this money?" He looked at her imploringly. "What if I complain to the manager and threaten to write to an ombudsman?"

"By the time the ombudsman replies they'll have identified you and frozen your account," she replied. "I'm really sorry Quentin."

He leaned forward. "Mavis, you couldn't just-"

"Don't even ask," she said. "I have a mortgage, an elderly mother and a dog to look after. I need this job."

Quentin nodded. "I understand."

There was some commotion behind him. He was taking up too much of the cashier's time and the other customers could hear that he wasn't able to access his money and they were getting restless. All in a moment there was a change in the atmosphere. Quentin turned to investigate and then he heard the scream.

"A gun!"

"Stand still. Hands up or you're all dead!" The gravelly voice burst over the immediate din of the bank's panicking clientele.

Cursing his indomitably bad luck, Quentin put his hands up.

CHAPTER 16

Someone rapped at the door. Larry already thought he knew who it would be. Astin called him 'the boss', but officially they were all equals. All the Binary Levers (as they called themselves) were equals. However, Larry already knew that when push came to shove, the boss, who went by the name Maven, was the first among equals, and definitely more equal than Astin, Higgs or Raj - who were the only other members Larry actually knew about.

Astin was ready at the back door to let him in the moment he arrived. He opened the peephole just to be doubly sure of who it was, then opened up. Maven hurried through, giving the password quickly and quietly. His appearance was such that it made him unmistakeable, yet clearly saying the password was a sacrosanct ritual. Larry deliberated as to whether it was the only definite way to ensure the person being admitted was who they said they were, or if it was just a demonstration designed to lend authenticity to proceedings. Part of him suspected it was just part of the fun of being in a secret society and served no real purpose. And that's what the Binary Levers were: a secret society. Mention that name to a member of the public and they would look at you blankly. Mention that name to the government's best online security experts and they would each show you the same blank expression. And if you were a member of the Binary Levers, then to speak of the society without express permission from Maven was a syn, which was short for syntax error. A syntax error, of course, was any erroneous or illegal arrangement of words. It was pretty self-explanatory. The only exception to the rule was if you were recruiting new blood.

Maven slid straight over to Larry and examined him, appraising his wound. "Glad you made it in more-or-less one piece, Larry," he said amiably. He took off his black leather jacket and threw it over the back of a seat and then removed his small round spectacles and placed them on the desk next to him. He was a tall man, perhaps almost four inches taller than Larry. He had a thin wiry frame, just like his spectacles, and he wore black pointed boots that would seriously hurt if they were planted in the wrong part of a person's anatomy. Larry had met Maven once before, at a conference about online security that he had attended with his friend Higgs, but he hadn't had the chance to speak to him on that occasion. He knew very little about the shadowy leader of the London fraternity of the Binary Levers; but what he had heard was sometimes intriguing, sometimes disturbing. He wasn't quite sure which stories to believe, but he felt the correct way to address this person was with fearful humility.

"Do you know who I am?" asked Maven, nonchalantly. Seemingly, this was to reassure himself that Larry knew his identity, not due to some instantaneous bout of amnesia. He slid over to the nearest computer and jostled the mouse. A picture of a cat eating a cheeseburger disappeared and Maven began studying some tiny writing on the screen with a brow-furrowing intensity. There were still marks on the side of his long, pointed nose from where his spectacles had been resting.

"Of course," said Larry, feigning confidence. "You're Maven."

Maven nodded. "Some people call me 'boss', but I'm just a Binary Lever, same as you, Larry. You are a Binary Lever?"

Larry nodded eagerly.

"And you're feeling well?" The question seemed disingenuous.

"Hey, you know. Bust a rib. Coughed up some blood."

Maven nodded again, as if this was how most people he spoke to responded to that question. After a moment examining a sequence of numbers scrolling up his computer screen, he spoke again. "We'll get you to an infirmary in a moment. I understand you're from Ellesmere?"

"Right," confirmed Larry.

"You had some difficulty with the police, I understand."

Larry confirmed this with a nod.

"And what brought you to us?"

"It wasn't something I planned. I had to get away from the area and this was the first place I thought of." He looked up at Maven from where he lay. Maven's face was expressionless. "Sorry," he added.

Maven shrugged, as if to say: no problem. "How did you find out where we were? Our exact location?" Before Larry could answer, Maven's fingers started to patter over the keyboard.

Larry paused, wondering if he should wait, but a quick flick of Maven's eyes told him to press on. "I used to know Higgs," he stammered, "uh, before he moved to London after he became a Binary Lever. That's sort of how I became a Binary Lever."

Maven studied him from the corner of his eyes. It was a fresh appraisal this time, but Larry wasn't sure what it meant. Maven's attention shifted back to the computer screen. Still his fingers typed. Screeds of data appeared and disappeared as it scrolled up the screen and the monitor's flicker cast an eerie blue glow across his slender, stubbly face. "When did you get the calling to become a Binary Lever, Larry?"

Larry thought for a moment. A sudden involuntary cough shook him and made him wince. "Hey, I guess it all started when I was a teenager. I wanted to become a computer programmer, really badly. I decided the best way to go about it was to study machine code. So, I went out and bought a book called Binary 101."

Maven nodded approvingly.

"But it was no use," conceded Larry . "It turned out to be the fifth in the series."

Astin sniggered.

"Was that a joke?" asked Maven.

"No," Larry responded, slightly insulted. "I couldn't really get to grips with programming and so, hey, I followed in the footsteps of my old man, who runs a slaughterhouse. I spent my days killing cattle and sheep. And that kind of thing leads a man to thinking. I started asking the big questions."

"Such as?" interrupted Astin.

"Hey, you know," replied Larry, a little disconcerted at being put on the spot. "Why? How? Wherefore? That kind of thing."

Astin grinned evilly.

Maven was staring at the screen again. A slight smile might have appeared for just a moment, but it could easily have been the light from the flickering computer monitor playing tricks.

Larry continued. "And one day I met Higgs and I knew he was up to something so I made him tell me about the Binary Levers. He recruited me there and then. Suddenly it all came together and I just knew that all that he was telling me was true. It was as if a whole load of thoughts I'd had right up until that moment all joined together and became one perfect whole. I realised that even though I had no knowledge of computer programming, I was a hacker at heart. A seeker of truth." Larry sighed contentedly at the memory of that epiphany. Neither Astin nor Maven looked particularly impressed. A thought struck him. "Hey, where is Higgs, by the way?"

"He was running a chore," replied Astin. He looked over to Maven. "Seems he's been delayed."

"And Raj?" asked Larry.

"Raj is with Higgs, ok?" he snarled, not pleased that suddenly it was Larry asking the questions.

Maven's fingers stopped dancing over his keyboard and he looked up from the screen. "When they get here, we'll get you to a hospital. Got any fake identification on you?"

"Yes."

He sat back in his swivelling office chair and turned to face Larry. He picked up his round, wire-framed glasses from the desk and returned them to his face. In the dimly lit back room of the abandoned charity shop which this invisible society called its headquarters, Maven seemed larger than life and his gaze seemed to penetrate through Larry's skull and straight into his nervous system. "Good. Now, before they arrive, I need you to tell me everything you've been through. Start at the beginning and don't leave out a single detail. Now tell me, Larry: what started all this in the first place?"

CHAPTER 17

Quentin held his hands high in the air. He also held his breath. A man who not only resembled an albino bloodhound but dribbled like one too was standing in the bank's reception clutching a shot gun. "You know what this is?" he yelled, holding the gun in the air so everyone could see it nice and clearly.

No one spoke. The three or four people who had been waiting behind Quentin in the queue edged off to the side of the room, stopping only when they met the wall. Quentin had turned around to face the robber and now tried to edge away as well. The robber pointed the gun at him, freezing him in his tracks. "You know what this is?" he repeated, his voice as spiky as a pinecone suppository.

Quentin gawped at the robber. His years of studying client behaviour in his office and occasionally in police custody rooms told him that, in all likelihood, this man was a criminal. Then it dawned on him that he too was a criminal. But this individual was worse than that. Quentin struggled to put his finger on exactly how to categorise this man. Then he had it. Yes. This man was a bad man. A really, really, bad man.

In response to the question, Quentin turned his attention to the firearm. It had a sliding forearm handle, revealing it to be a pump action shot gun. Judging by appearances, it had a tubular magazine which was bottom-loading with a neat side-ejecting receiver. A quality piece of kit. He glanced over the trigger system and the safety catch, then took in the side release catch. If that isn't an old Remington 870 then I don't know what is, he thought, surprising himself.

The robber didn't appreciate Quentin's silence and stalked across the foyer toward him. He shoved the business end of the shotgun into Quentin's chest. He leaned forward so that his face, and the spittle thereupon, was leant over the butt and squared with Quentin's.

He yelled. "Do you know what this is?"

"Yes," replied Quentin.

"What is it?" yelled the robber, releasing the safety catch.

"It's a gun," squeaked Quentin.

"That's right, it's a gun," replied the robber. "And anyone who dares so much as breath in the next five minutes is going to get a slug right through their eyeball."

Someone screamed and the robber looked away for just a moment.

As if possessed by Pan himself, Quentin found himself grabbing the gun, turning it clockwise and up, and forcing it out of the robber's hands. He kicked the robber hard in the crotch and took a step back.

The robber fell to the floor, grabbing his midsection. Some ammo rolled out of one of his hands and across the floor to rest at Quentin's foot.

"Well done! Well done!" cheered one of the bank's clientele, overenthusiastically.

Quentin turned to Mavis. She was looking at him in a way he'd never experienced before. He quite liked it. The bank manager was actually beginning to applaud. "Bravo," he muttered, in disbelief.

Quentin smiled for what felt like the first time in eons. Then an idea struck him. One of the customers moved forward to shake his hand. Another moved forward to grab the robber. The bank manager starting moving toward a phone.

"Not so quick," said Quentin, waving the shotgun at them all.

"What are you doing?" asked Mavis, panic rising in her voice.

Quentin had to ask himself the same question. He was a hero now. Would they let him off with his recent crimes because of this? He didn't know. He did know that it wasn't going to get him his house back.

"You," he said sternly, to Mavis. "I want you to put ten thousand in a bag for me and come out here with it."

"No," she replied. "I won't do it, Quentin. And this glass is bullet proof."

One of the booths was unmanned. Quentin fired at the glass. Someone screamed. It might have been him. The glass shattered. "No," said Quentin, regaining his composure, "it's not bullet proof. Now, get the money and pass it through the hole I just made."

The robber started to get back to his feet. He didn't look happy. Quentin quickly reloaded the gun with the fallen ammo by his feet. No one moved to stop him, partly from fear but partly from a deep sense of confusion about what was actually happening.

"You know what this is?" he asked the robber, walking toward him with the gun pointed at his face.

"A gun?" sneered the robber.

"No," replied Quentin. "It's a Remington 870. It's the one they had on display in the sport shop around the corner until it was stolen a month or two ago, if I'm not mistaken. I remember reading about it in the local paper. I have no idea how you got ammo for it, but I guess I'm grateful. Now, if you so much as breath I'm going to put a slug right through your squama occipitalis. You know what that is?"

The robber looked confused. "No," he replied.

Quentin paused. "To be quite honest, I'm not a hundred percent sure myself, but I can assure you it would hurt."

The robber nodded his understanding, or possibly his agreement. It didn't really make any difference to Quentin at this moment. He was riding high on a rush that was fuelled as much by adrenaline as blind desperation. Quite possibly, his actions were no longer his own.

"Quentin!" It was Mavis. She was standing at the hole in the cashier's booth holding a bag which Quentin hoped was full of cash.

"Is it all there?" he asked.

"You want me to count it out for you?" She posed the question sarcastically.

"No, it'll do," he replied, cursing his own lack of experience at bank robbing. He'd allowed himself to get distracted and now he noticed the bank manager was gone. The police would be here any minute. They were already swarming the town looking for him.

He assessed the situation with the cool, calm logical ruthlessness that he'd developed over many years practising as a lawyer. He was in possession of a gun. He had committed armed robbery. He was stealing a large amount of money. He was threatening the lives of innocents. The situation didn't look good for him if the police should arrive. They would probably shoot on sight. He also needed the loo really desperately.

"Is there a toilet back there?" he asked Mavis.

She nodded.

He went to a door at the side of the cashiers' booths. Mavis let him through and he had her lead him into the back and show him where the toilets were. "What the hell are you thinking?" she whispered to him as he moved close to her.

He shrugged, as if to say he had no real idea. Which was true. He had no idea whatsoever. Over the last twenty four hours everything he knew and everything he thought he understood about himself had been irrevocably flipped upside-down. As he locked the toilet door behind him, a perfectly formed thought entered his mind. This didn't surprise him. He did all his best thinking on the toilet.

He had trained for years as a criminal lawyer. For most of his life he'd specialised in criminal law, before he started his own general practice. Now all that had been taken from him. What was left? There was only one other use for all that training. The flipside of the coin. He would become a professional criminal.

He cocked the gun, aimed it and blasted the window out into the back alleyway behind the bank. He heard Mavis scream from outside the toilet door. "I'm okay!" he yelled, realising she must have thought he'd turned the gun on himself. He thought he heard her say "Oh thank God!" but it was muffled through the door. Leaving the empty gun on the floor, he climbed up onto a urinal. It was easier said than done: those blue deodorizer blocks were slippier than they looked. He clambered up and out through the broken window. He landed on his feet outside the bank and realised that, without any prior planning, he had just successfully robbed a bank. For a moment he allowed himself to wallow in self-congratulatory pride, although he knew fine well he shouldn't.

The moment was gone. He turned and ran as fast as he could. He ran so erratically that it wouldn't be inappropriate to employ the term "helter-skelter" to describe it. He belted down the alleyway and out into a rat's nest of cul-de-sacs, side roads and ancient cobbled paths. He hammered down one road after another, knowing in his mind that he was retreading the footsteps of many a Chester-based criminal over the centuries. He hurried down one lane and then another. There was no one about so he pegged it up a little-used track and came to Albey Avenue. He heard sirens in the distance. His mad scramble to find somewhere to hide was proving fruitless. He was struggling for breath as he was not someone who often, as he liked to put it, partook of exercise.

Eventually he found a large public bin. He pushed back the large plastic lid so that it slid up and over to reveal a gaping chasm for refuse within. Mercifully it was nearly empty. There was some junk in the corner, but he would just have to put up with that.

He threw the money into the corner of the bin where the junk lay.

"Whaddafu-oi!"

He felt his heart leap a foot in the air. Someone had yelped.

"Um, would you mind giving me that bag back?" he asked the heap of rags in the bin.

The ensconced tramp muttered something guttural and the bag came flying up and out.

"Sorry for disturbing you," said Quentin, closing the lid again.

"F'off," raged the tramp, his voice muffled.

Quentin was relieved that he wasn't yet going to have to dirty his suit, but with nowhere to go and a desperate need to relieve himself, he knew it could only be a matter of time. Clearly the police would have reached the bank by now. They would already know exactly who he was and what he looked like. He was running out of options.

He stood to the side of the bin and relieved himself. He learnt an important lesson from this. Even hardened criminals have certain unspoken priorities.

A muffled voice came from inside the bin. It sounded like it was saying: "Hop missing only phone." Quentin contemplated what such a cryptic utterance could mean as he relaxed himself. The lid of the bin mysteriously opened an inch and a voice emanated, louder and clearer this time. "Stop pissing on my home!"

"Oh," said Quentin.

Suddenly the world was awash with blue light and two-tone sirens.

There was no choice.

He flung the bin open and haphazardly threw the ill-begotten bag of cash into the mire. With a significant amount of grunting, he clambered up the side of the bin and followed after his money. He closed the lid from within as an enraged voice muttered something obscene, and then all was silent.

CHAPTER 18

Larry sat up slowly, propping himself up on his elbows and trying not to wince. "Hey, it's simple. I tried to buy some sheep from this Bryn Jones, this farmer, but the police turned up. I split and they chased me down. I escaped but, hey, not without a fight." His accent was syrupy-thick with his Portuguese heritage but became increasingly tremulous as he spoke. His injury was affecting him but he did his best to hide its severity so as not to seem weak.

"But how did the police know you were there?" interrogated Maven. He leant forward on his seat, peering through the small circles of his spectacles at Larry, waiting for an answer. His tone was light, but Larry sensed menace just beneath the surface. He felt Maven's fierce intellect directed at him like sunlight focused through a magnifying glass on to a single smouldering point in his mind.

"Hey, I don't know." He shrugged. "If I understand right, the police have sympathies with the Welsh because they also have a monarchy. Even though we're at war with them. Possibly they knew of my Republican sympathies and wanted a reason to lure me out into the open."

"Possibly. Larry, have you ever been arrested for anything to do with your Republican sympathies before?"

"No. Not really. Not at all. I don't make a big deal, you know?"

Maven bit his lower lip for a moment. It was hard to know if he was annoyed, or just thinking. "It would seem unlikely that has anything to do with it. It could just be that they happened to notice the sheep being transported across the border."

"Definitely no. Everyone was super careful to avoid the police. Too unlikely."

"Then something else was amiss. Could it be that they knew you were a Binary Lever and wanted a reason to arrest you?"

"How would they know?"

Maven sat back and smiled. His eyes weren't smiling. "Well, I guess it's a mystery," he said, in a way that suggested it was nothing of the sort. He paused thoughtfully, biting his lower lip again. "Who arranged for you to buy the sheep?"

Larry considered. "My father."

"Your father?"

"Hey, he wanted them for slaughtering. Put up a very good price for them."

"Almost too good," said Maven. It was a statement, not a question.

"How did you know?"

"Is your father a Binary Lever?"

"I don't think so."

"Because you've never spoken of it to him."

"That's right."

"He's a Binary Lever, Larry. Ranked with the Gamma echelon. He's a player. Hardly involved in the computing side of things, but he's one of us."

"Hey, I never knew." Larry wasn't sure how to take this on board. It seemed unbelievable.

"No, this wasn't about sheep or republicanism," Maven decided. "This was all about the Binary Levers. I'll send some feelers out to our brethren in the North and see if they can give us some hints about what's going on. I'm not privy to every activity the Binary Levers undertake. It's vital for security reasons, you see? But they'll open up if I prod."

"Is my father in danger?".

"I doubt it. What happened to you was small fry. No offence." Maven turned back to his computer screen and locked it with a few key presses. He typed so quickly his fingers blurred. He turned back to Larry. "Time to get you to a doctor."

"At last," responded Larry, with evident resentment. "I should have gone straight to the hospital." He glared at Astin. It wasn't like Larry to be so bold, but the pain and a slight delirium gave him a devil-may-care attitude. He may have felt out of place, inferior and totally disoriented in this new world of hackers and secret headquarters, but right now he was suffering and after Maven's questioning he could feel a dizziness coming on.

"No one said anything about a hospital," sneered Astin. "We know just the guy to help you." He looked like he might laugh manically for a moment, but to both Larry and Maven's relief he didn't. A moment passed. Something seemed to be missing. Astin gobbed in his spittoon.

"Ignore him, Larry," said Maven mercifully. "We'll get you to a hospital."

CHAPTER 19

It was dark. Quentin could feel the walls of the bin closing in around him. No, it wasn't the walls - it was the air. It pressed against him with gassy viscosity. It stank. It was a deep, acrid, pungent, odorous, smelly, manky, nasty, pongy smell. Quentin couldn't even conceive what a worse smell might smell like. He could feel the beginnings of a retch at the back of his throat.

"Wouldnae comnhere," grumbled the tramp. "Just shatmysel."

Quentin groaned.

"Whayadoin?"

Quentin couldn't see him, but he could tell from his voice and the sound of scratching that the tramp was sat up on the other side of the bin facing him.

Quentin wasn't entirely sure what he was doing, nor was he sure how to answer the tramp's question. He remained silent. The more silent he was, the more he became aware of the smell. He started to gag, but got it under control. He felt around for the bag of money. It was still by his side. He wasn't sure what he was going to do with it exactly, but it made his heart race with dread every time he touched it. Then again, if he was going to be in this much trouble, he felt a little better for having something to show for it. Later, if someone was to ask him why he robbed the bank, he decided he would say it was because he desperately needed the money; trying to explain that it was an accident would just be embarrassing.

Quentin scratched his ankle. "I just robbed a bank," he said finally.

He heard the tramp shuffle; it was possible he was either nodding or shaking his head. Quentin couldn't tell which it was in the darkness. Something moved past his foot. "A rat!" he yelped. His legs retracted so fast there was a serious chance they might become innies instead of outies.

"Justma foot," explained the tramp, in that joined-up-speaking way of his.

"Ah, that's... a relief," said Quentin quietly.

"Aye, dinnae fash yersel'."

Quentin felt that the tramp, so low in energy and so high in apathy as he no doubt was, just couldn't summon the energy to speak properly. He'd manage a couple of coherent words, but the effort would exhaust him. He would start to mumble again and then the words would compound and disintegrate.

There was the sound of voices outside the bin. The sirens had stopped but car doors were being slammed and there was a definite commotion coming from the direction of the bank. "They looking for you?" asked the tramp.

"Undoubtedly," replied Quentin. "I'd appreciate it if you'd let me hide here for a while." His voice had a hopeful tinge to it, as he really had no idea how the tramp would react once the police were poking around outside.

"Noskin aff mynose," replied the tramp.

Quentin wasn't entirely sure he was any better off inside the bin. The smell was making his sinuses weep with suicidal despair. Plus, he imagined the tramp had probably escaped from one of His Majesty's prisons, which was so often the case these days. And every so often his hand brushed the floor accidentally as he shuffled to make himself less uncomfortable. He would then spend several seconds anxiously trying to wipe the grot off onto his new suit.

Some time passed and Quentin decided the heavy

breathing coming from the other side of the bin meant the tramp was asleep. He sat back and let out a sigh of relief. It was a moment to let some of the tension out of his body. Unfortunately, it was succeeded by a deep in-breath of noxious air.

He tried to focus his mind on the problem at hand. He knew that at some time in his past he had known how to deal with an emergency. Then it came to him! He had to S.T.O.P.

It stood for something: Stop. Think. Observe. Plan.

That was what you had to do in an emergency. He had learnt it from a Hardy Boys book when he was seven years old. It was amazing the resources you drew on in a time of crisis.

He was taking a moment to Stop right now. He congratulated himself on being a quarter of the way there already.

Now it was time to Think. He found he was thinking about the new depths he had sunk to. He shook himself and decided to move on.

The next step was Observe. It wasn't looking good for him. It wasn't smelling good, either. He was trapped in a bin with a tramp who had defecated in his own clothing. The police were outside searching for him. He listened. Their voices seemed to have gone away. It was just possible they had called off the foot search for him. Perhaps they thought he'd escaped the scene successfully.

Now he had to Plan. That was the hard bit. What to do? Where to go? His mind was a blank. He was actually feeling a little drowsy and began to wonder if the sealed bin had enough oxygen in it for two people to survive the night. He decided not to risk it and pulled the lid open a fraction. He felt the fresh air rush in.

"Whayadoin?" barked the tramp, stirring from his slumber.

"Just letting some fresh air in," replied Quentin, quietly.

"Hmk," replied the tramp indistinctly. He seemed to go back to sleep. He's like a dog, mused Quentin ruefully. Just resting. Never truly asleep.

CHAPTER 20

Larry lay comatose on the hospital bed, oblivious to the world around him. He had been unconscious for some time now. Higgs, his friend from back home and a fellow Binary Lever, sat next to him, vigilant and thoughtful. He was upset by the casual cruelty with which Astin had treated Larry and the indifference Maven had shown in not making immediate amends. The Binary Levers were a brotherhood. Larry was one of their own. It was wrong to treat him like that, no matter the circumstances. Higgs sighed. That was the problem. They often treated their own like this. He had often thought of blowing the lid off the whole damn secret society. The reason he didn't was the same reason he had got involved in the first place: results.

He'd been a young man when he first left his home in Ellesmere; an undergraduate reading computer science with his whole future ahead of him. Three years later he handed in his coursework, a piece of software that was given the highest marks the faculty had ever awarded. What his tutors didn't realise was that he'd piggybacked a virus into the programme. It was like handing in a printed dissertation with a bomb tucked behind the second-to-last page.

The virus infiltrated the university's computer systems.

He used it as an opening to publish online everything they stored in their databases, including lecturer's salaries, details of disciplinary meetings and all the little funding fiddles they liked to keep under wraps. He had promptly been expelled. He knew this because they sent him a strongly worded letter. It also contained a date and time for an appointment, but he didn't attend. He knew the police were involved and he would have been walking into a trap. He didn't want to do jail time so he ran away, back to Ellesmere.

He hadn't really meant to do any harm. He just wanted to know if he could break through the firewall the university lecturers had written. They had spent four years writing that software and had actually stood at the front of the lecture theatre and challenged, actually challenged, the students to hack past it if they could. It had taken him less than a day. Once he was there, he couldn't stop himself. It was the folly of youth. He had to let the world know of his prowess.

He had more restraint these days.

After running away, he had stayed with his friend Larry. Larry had hidden him, helped him, fed him and kept his confidences. Higgs kept hacking and word of his ability spread quickly. It had been late one night when he was contacted by Maven. After that, everything changed.

He knew now that it was essentially a cult. He supposed he had known that from the beginning, but from the moment the Binary Levers contacted him, nothing could have prevented his assimilation into their ranks. They had stumbled on something too profound to be ignored and he wanted to know more. It had taken time for him to gain their trust and be granted access to the information they had garnered, but even from the outset they had opened his mind.

Higgs leant forward to check Larry's state. The monitors flickered and beeped as normal, but Larry stirred and mumbled. For a moment Higgs thought Larry might be surfacing, but the monitors didn't register any change in brain activity.

It must have been traumatic for Larry. He was a hapless,

simple lad who worked in his father's abattoir. Higgs knew that Larry looked up to him, and he always tried to persuade Larry to do what was best, but Larry was more interested in doing what Higgs was doing than what was in his own interests. That was what had got Larry into programming. He'd shown absolutely no talent for hacking, but he'd shown enthusiasm; enough that when Higgs became a Binary Lever, Larry wasn't far behind him. Higgs couldn't have kept it a secret from Larry. Larry would have somehow known and it would have broken his heart that the experience hadn't been shared with him.

A nurse entered the room. Higgs was a little taken aback. She was tall, blonde and, when all was said and done, quite stunning. She smiled at him but didn't make conversation. There was a slightly business-like, detached air to the way she performed her observations on Larry. She glanced at one monitor, twisted a knob on it so the screen went blank and pushed it away. Higgs wanted answers. He wasn't used to information being beyond his grasp. "Anything?" he asked impatiently.

She looked back at him, as if she hadn't even noticed he was there. "No real change. Maybe a slight improvement, but that would be an optimistic interpretation."

It annoyed Higgs that she was so clinical. She flicked a stray wisp of blond hair away from her eyes and tucked it behind her ear. "I'll be back in an hour to check on him again," she reported. She left the room and, Higgs noticed, the ward.

Higgs turned back to Larry. He lay perfectly still with his dark, curly locks spread out across the pillow. He looked out of place against the stark white sheets. Higgs cursed himself for being late in getting back to the headquarters. Maven had sent him to complete an errand and the delay prevented him being there to greet Larry on his arrival. If he'd known that Astin would torment Larry, and Maven would question him before seeking help, then he'd have abandoned the task early. But he wasn't to know. He sighed. Poor Larry.

Larry had minor internal bleeding. He was a strong individual and had borne his wounds all the way from

Ellesmere to London. Higgs had helped Larry into the car and driven him straight to the Accident and Emergency department, but he'd passed out on the way. The doctors indicated his coma could last a day, a week or longer. Higgs took this to mean they had no idea.

There was little he could do. He picked up a remote and turned on the television. There was an advert for a company called Black Letter Days. A spokesman said: "Live life to the full! Never been dumped before? Never failed an exam? Never been the subject of a debt action? We can help. Live life to the full by experiencing every heart-wrenching, gut-churning thing life can throw at you. Never had your car broken into? Never had your mail stolen? Never had a cerebral haemorrhage? Call us on oh eight hundred-"

Higgs changed the channel. The television now showed a rerun of the latest episode of Neighbours. Ramsay Street was experiencing the aftermath of an Ebola pandemic. He sat back and let it wash over him.

CHAPTER 21

"So you see, it's extremely important we have a national celebration marking the auspicious occasion of the third anniversary of the advent of my reign. And the people love having an extra holiday and it increases their support for our way of doing things," explained King Gruffydd II to those assembled before him at the table. The meal took place in a stylish, if compact, mezzanine room which used to serve as a cafe for the locals when they came to see performances at the theatre. It had been hastily converted into a dining room so that the King could entertain guests.

Two uniformed footmen waddled into the room, each pushing a trolley laden with a tureen emblazoned with a Welsh dragon.

A look of evident relief washed over the guests' faces as the King's self-congratulatory monologue was temporarily interrupted. Ivor stood quietly to one side, overseeing the event. Ideally, there would have been someone else to perform this minor function but resources were limited. He nodded to the footmen who took up their ladles and began serving soup into the bowls set before the guests.

"This smells delicious," said Lady Llandudno courteously. "What soup are we to enjoy tonight?"

The King smiled knowingly at her. "Radish, I believe. A Welsh speciality."

Lord Llandudno raised an eyebrow acerbically, if such a thing is possible. "Really? I've never heard of radish soup being a Welsh speciality. Perhaps it's a speciality of South Wales. I don't think we have it up North." Lady Llandudno kept quiet, although it was unclear if this was because she was displeased with the choice of soup or her husband's outburst.

"Yes, I believe radishes originated near Cardiff, originally," insisted the King.

"Do you really?" Lord Llandudno's reply had a tone of disbelief, undertones of condescension and overtones of rudeness.

"Or am I thinking of a type of pie?" wondered the King wistfully.

Ivor winced inwardly. One of the main reasons this meal was taking place was to enable the King to ascertain whether Lord Llandudno was with him or against him. There was some small amount of unrest in the North, mostly to do with how trade and commerce had been affected by the embargoes, and it was important for the King to establish whether he had the full support of the noblemen he'd appointed three years ago or whether the changing circumstances and downturn in the Welsh economy had caused them to shift allegiances. There was rumour amongst his intelligence officers that some noblemen in the North were discussing the possibility of striking a deal with the English to have North Wales separated off from the rest of Wales and made part of England. They hoped this might be a solution that would bring peace and contentment to all, but were struggling to make known precedents fit their theory. Either way, Ivor knew that it was up to the King to impress the assembled guests to ensure they stayed with him on his mission to make Wales a strong and independent country. He doubted the radish soup would help matters.

"It has an interesting taste," remarked Lady Llandudno politely. Ivor noticed her brow didn't furrow in disgust. He had no way to know that this was due to a recently administered shot of Botox that was potent enough to fell a wizened goat herder. Ivor thought she looked pretty.

Lord Llandudno laid his spoon in his bowl and sat back. He looked very much like he was biting his tongue. Ivor assessed the other guests with a quick glance. The Duke of Snowdonia looked displeased. Surprisingly, Sir Pendragon of Llysfaen looked like he might be enjoying it, but the man was a fighter and would never be bested by a mere bowl of soup.

"There's an interesting aftertaste," said Lady Llandudno. Ivor noticed she had boldly attempted a second spoonful.

The King smiled weakly. "Best suits a certain type of palate, I understand," he offered disingenuously. He had also tried the soup and found it not to his liking. He looked over to Ivor for help. Ivor pretended he hadn't noticed. The King glared at him, knowing Ivor was only pretending not to notice him. Ivor decided to pretend that he hadn't noticed that the King had noticed that he was pretending not to notice and continued to pretend not to notice him in the hope the King might genuinely start to think that he hadn't noticed him. The King gave up and looked elsewhere for help.

"Damn fine soup this," said Sir Pendragon, practically quaffing the stuff. The King beamed in response. Sir Pendragon took another huge and undignified slurp. He was a large man with a large beard and a large voice. "Reminds me of the stuff we used to make when I was in the army. You'd find yourself stranded in some Godforsaken place with nothing to eat and you'd go around gathering anything that looked like it might be alive and crush it up in a bowl and spit on it until you'd made a damn fine soup like this one."

Lady Llandudno put her spoon down. Lord Llandudno was turning red with the effort of not saying anything that might border on treason. He was a stern man, tall and pale, with long hands and a thin neck. The sight of him turning red was unpleasant and frightening. It was like looking at a bloodshot eye being poked with the end of a cotton bud. The King pulled back into his seat, to keep away from the spectacle. Even Lady Llandudno seemed to lean away from her husband momentarily. Clearly Lord Llandudno was not pleased by the situation he found himself in. The King grimaced and small beads of sweat broke out on his forehead. There were many things he might do and say to win Lord Llandudno's support, but if he couldn't even project the appearance of being able to host a proper dinner for important guests and maintain proper decorum then the Welsh monarchy would soon become a laughing stock amongst the nobles of the North and all he'd fought for over the last three years would soon come tumbling down around him.

Fortunately for the King, the Duke of Snowdonia, a staunch royalist and supporter of Welsh independence, was firmly on his side. As an ardent devotee of the King's and an astute courtier, he adeptly read the unfolding situation and stepped in to save the day. He'd made good headway with his soup, a task he had performed through sheer perseverance and several grams of pepper. "Your Majesty," he said in a nasally public-school drone, instantly jarring everyone's attention. "I have to say: I'm famished. Perhaps we could sidestep formality on this one occasion and move on to the main course?"

Like a drowning man scrabbling for a lifeline, the King fervently agreed with the suggestion and gave a meaningful nod to Ivor who barked a few quick orders at the footmen. He stepped back into the shadows and smiled to himself. All this would seem as nothing in a few moments if his dark plan went as intended. Ivor knew now that the problem with the King was not his ambition, or his plans, or his expectations, it was simply with the man himself. He was an imbecile. He should simply have ordered that better food be prepared, but he was weak and had just let this disaster unfold without putting his foot down. Ivor returned his attention to the proceedings and watched with dark fascination.

Lord Llandudno reclined into his seat as the footman took away his soup, which was almost untouched. He seemed relieved. The atmosphere relaxed slightly. He turned to address the King formally. "As you were saying earlier, the celebrations here in Cardiff are certainly a political step in the right direction. What worries me is that a king celebrating in the South will hardly be noticed by citizens in the North. All they'll know is that the resources of the Welsh monarchy are being spent frivolously while trade embargoes remain in place and life gets harder as the English impose greater sanctions on us."

"Well," began the King, "the thing is-"

"And what's more," interrupted Lord Llandudno, "the whole thing smacks of instability. It's one thing declaring war on England to affirm our independence, but what happens when they decide that we don't have the resources to assert ourselves and they really do send in the troops to reclaim Wales."

"I don't think that will happen," began the King.

"Precisely, because they won't need to. We're going to be on our knees begging them to take us back because the country will have gone bankrupt and the people will have revolted. Remember, everything you're feeling down South we're feeling twice as bad up North."

The King nodded solemnly. "I hear you and I know you're right-"

"I am right," interjected the Lord, "and that's why two things need to happen. The first is that you need to start raising taxes. This can't happen until you have the support of the people or it will cause untold problems. Many are still paying taxes to the English which is something we'll have to stop. The problem is that when we stop paying taxes to the English they'll really start to take notice of the fact we're at war with them. So, we need to impose a double tax system. Again, we can't do that until we have the full support of the people. To get the full support of the people we need to be independent and thriving and only raising one set of taxes. To be thriving we need strong trade connections and that requires good links with other countries, including England. It's a Catch 22 situation and I want to know how you propose to resolve it."

"Right," said the King, not enjoying having the whole sorry situation laid out in front of him in such stark terms.

"Ah, here's the main course."

Lord Llandudno looked singularly unimpressed as the conversation halted while the footmen served up the main course. Sir Pendragon wore a hearty grin. "This looks fabulous," he said. "What meat are we having with it?"

The King smiled at him in panic. He paused, then frowned with great sincerity. "Ah, I thought everyone here was vegetarian, as I am?"

Ivor cringed.

"You're not a vegetarian," blasted Sir Pendragon without thinking. "You and I were sharing a roast chicken just a week ago. And when we finished you had a second one to yourself."

"Ah, well," said the King, "when I heard everyone else was vegetarian I decided to convert."

Ivor wished he could fold up like a flat-pack box where his shame could always face inwards. This was beyond embarrassing. Still, he thought, it shouldn't go on too much longer, all going as planned.

"Who on Earth told you I was a vegetarian?" demanded Lord Llandudno with evident disgust. "It certainly won't please the farmers if they hear the King has become vegetarian. You'll have to keep this under wraps. What on Earth possessed you, man?"

The King looked upset. Lord Llandudno was a powerful man in the North and when he started addressing the King as 'man' it meant that the hierarchy which Parliament and the King had struggled to establish was starting to break down. The King steeled himself. "Sir, I am the King. You will not address me in that way. If I choose to become a vegetarian, I damn well shall."

Lord Llandudno grimaced but apologised. Ivor was taken aback. All too easily he forgot that King Gruffydd II had become King not just through sheer blind luck, although that was the greater part of it, but because he was as passionate about the cause as his father had been before him. He wouldn't stand up to Lord Llandudno to protect his own ego, but if he thought the Crown was under attack then he might just show some backbone. Ivor was almost impressed. Shame that things had to end the way they would.

"As you've raised an objection, I shall make sure that the celebrations show no signs of my vegetarianism and I shall give up this folly. However, I trust you will all enjoy your vegetarian meals on this one occasion."

Everyone nodded their acquiescence with barely disguised disappointment.

Lady Llandudno put down her knife and fork. "I'm sorry to have to raise the issue," she said with little delicacy, "but must we have that funny man staring at us while we eat?"

"What funny man is that?" asked the King.

Lady Llandudno nodded toward Ivor. "The short one with the big head and the sinister beard."

"Ah, that's Ivor, my most trusted advisor."

Ivor shifted uncomfortably where he stood. He was used to all sorts of abuse, dating back to childhood. So much was this the case that he took her comment entirely in his stride. He stayed where he was and looked directly ahead.

"I don't think he's looking at us, my dear," said the King. "He's just overseeing things."

"I see," replied Lady Llandudno, "but he makes me uncomfortable. Perhaps we could have him removed?"

The King looked perplexed, torn between upsetting his advisor and upsetting his guest.

"Have you tried the roast aubergine?" he asked her. "It's very good. One of the chef's specialties, I understand."

"I find it hard to stomach anything with the funny man watching me."

The King smiled at her for a moment, then seemed to arrive at a decision. He turned to Ivor. "Perhaps you would be so kind as to leave us for now?"

Ivor gave a shallow bow and walked out of the room. He was angry, but not for the reasons anyone might expect. He dashed through the back corridors behind the mezzanine dinner hall and up a flight of stairs. He pulled back the corner of a curtain which obscured one of several long-forgotten windows which looked down onto the room. He could see the guests sitting at the table, resuming their meals. He watched carefully, examining the King for any reaction to the food.

Lady Llandudno must have seen the movement of the curtains. She looked up at him and pointed. He quickly closed the curtains. How annoying. He raced around the corridor, just one of many corridors that allowed actors to get from one place to another quickly, and he pulled back the corner of another curtain. He looked down on the meal. He was behind Lady Llandudno this time so she couldn't see him. He stared down at the King intently, waiting for the inevitable.

"I must say," enthused Sir Pendragon, "this roasted aubergine isn't half bad. In fact, it almost tastes like meat. It certainly looks like meat, the way it's been cut and roasted. The colour of it matches meat exactly. Why, this certainly is a speciality. We should make it the national dish!" He chortled.

Lord Llandudno still didn't look impressed. "We can't make it the national dish. Aubergines come from India and Nepal and places like that."

"Do they?" replied Sir Pendragon. "What an odd thing to know." With that, he returned to scoffing his meal.

"Well, I guess we didn't come here to talk about our food," intoned the Duke of Snowdonia. "I was talking to Lady Haverfordwest the other day and she said that she suspected there was growing unrest in her area. I think we need to resolve this Catch 22 situation that Lord Llandudno has highlighted so succinctly. I have one proposal and that is that we impose a stealth tax. It won't be popular, but it will raise the necessary funds to strengthen the foundations that we are laying for a stronger Wales and a healthier economy."

"An interesting idea and a noble sentiment," began the King, "but what sort of stealth tax are you suggesting? There's very little -"

"Hang on," interjected Sir Pendragon. "You say the stealth tax won't be popular?"

"Well, no, most likely it won't," replied the Duke of Snowdonia.

"But how can it be unpopular if it's stealthy? People won't even know about it."

"Ah, well," stammered the Duke. "That's not exactly what a stealth tax is all about. It's not that people don't know about it, it's just that we don't call it a tax, so that- um, I'm not explaining this very well."

"Let me try," said King Gruffydd II. "A stealth tax is not a tax. It is a way of raising money from the people without raising a tax. But the end result is the same. Money still ends up in the treasury. The people know about it, but because they can't write the word 'tax' on a billboard when they protest, it's a lot harder to protest, so- no, wait, that's not very good. A stealth tax is when-"

"I think the problem," interrupted Lady Llandudno, "is that we are using outdated English nomenclature. I think in the ethos of the new regime, we should devise our own terminology. Now, does anyone know the Welsh for stealth tax?"

"Don't you speak Welsh?" asked King Gruffydd II.

"No," replied Lady Llandudno. "Very few of us do in the North. This is something we hope to improve upon though."

"Ah, well, I'm much the same," confessed the King. "Perhaps Philip could help us here?"

The Duke of Snowdonia looked up from his roasted vegetables. "Please, I don't like to be called Philip. I may change my name to something more Welsh, and then you can use it, but for now I prefer my official title. Anyway, I think the Welsh for tax might be 'treth'. I'm not sure what stealth would be though."

"Does no one here speak Welsh?" asked the King. Everyone was silent. "Alright, never mind. I happen to carry this small English to Welsh dictionary with me for occasions just such as this." He pulled the small green dictionary out of his pocket and consulted it. He looked up, shook his head, looked back down at the dictionary, then back at his gathered guests. "Well, it seems the Welsh for stealth is... stealth. So what we have is a stealth treth."

"Perhaps it could be said with a bit of a Welsh accent, like steh-helth?" suggested the Duke.

"I don't think that will be necessary," replied the King dismissively.

"Right," said Sir Pendragon. "So this stealth treth... will the people know about it or not?"

"I think the whole point of using a Welsh word was to redefine the nature of the tax, was it not?" explained Lady Llandudno. "Perhaps we should invent a word to replace stealth. Oh, look up 'hidden'. Perhaps that would do as an alternative."

The King nodded in agreement and flicked through the pages of his dictionary. "Right, the word for hidden is 'cudd'. Remember that the double 'd' sound is pronounced like 'th', as in 'breathe', but not quite."

"What do you mean not quite?" asked Lady Llandudno.

"Well, it's a little thicker. Deeper. It's just a little different, all right?"

Some strange noises emanated from around the table as the assembled guests attempted to wrap their tongues around the words 'cudd treth'.

"So," resumed Sir Pendragon, "what exactly is a cudd treth?" He looked around expectantly but everyone else had a look of resignation on their faces, like they just didn't care anymore. "I know it's a stealth tax," he said eagerly, "whatever one of those is."

"A cudd treth," replied Lady Llandudno, "is a way of raising money from the people for the treasury. It isn't a tax but it has the same effect as a tax. It goes largely unnoticed because we don't flag it as a form of official taxation. How does that suit everyone as a definition?"

Everyone nodded their consent. "So what exactly is this particular cudd treth going to be?" asked Sir Pendragon.

"Yes, you proposed the idea," said Lord Llandudno to the Duke. "What exactly did you have in mind?"

The Duke pushed a roast vegetable around his plate for a moment and then looked up. "Here's my idea. It's very important we get some money flowing into the treasury. We can't introduce taxes because then people will be paying us tax and paying the English tax simultaneously. We can't stop English taxes because they might take the war seriously."

"The war is serious!" protested the King.

"Oh come on," said Lord Llandudno.

"I think we need to be realistic about this," said the Duke. "We need the English on our side if we're going to defeat them."

The King grimaced but nodded for him to go on.

"So, what we do is we raise an army."

Everyone at the table burst into objections at once as they opposed the idea on a number of grounds, but the Duke held up a hand to silence them. They quietened. "We raise an army to protect ourselves against foreign invaders."

"Namely the English," declared the King.

"Namely the English," agreed the Duke of Snowdonia. "We set up a headquarters and then we introduce a national service scheme."

Again there was a flurry of protests and the word conscription was bandied about. The Duke raised his hand again. A moment later the diners settled back to munching on their roast aubergine and he continued. "We make the scheme an opt-out one. People can opt-out of joining the army but they have to pay a penalty. Let's call it a hundred pounds a year until they do their two years service. The obligation to serve would end at forty."

"So we raise money from people annually unless they serve," summarised Lord Llandudno. "And there's no obligation to serve and it doesn't look like a tax. I like it." He shrugged his approval.

"But what if they opt in?" asked Lady Llandudno.

The Duke smiled. "Then they sign up at headquarters and we make them work for two years. They won't actually have anyone to fight, so we get them involved in transport, construction and that sort of thing. We make them work for a pittance. It will mean that the treasury has a source of cheap labourers to help keep costs down."

"Brilliant!" exclaimed Lord Llandudno.

"I don't know," said the King, thoughtfully. "It's not quite the Wales I had in mind. We're here to help the Welsh people establish their independence and escape English oppression. We mustn't become the enemy we hope to defeat."

"Come now," cajoled Lord Llandudno. "It will only be for a few years until we have the funds and resources to break away entirely from England and then we can tax the people normally and disband the army."

The Duke hiccupped. Lady Llandudno smiled at him. He apologised for his lack of manners and then hiccupped again. "I fear the roast vegetables have played havoc with my innards," he surmised. He rose from the table. "If you'd be so good as to excuse me for a moment."

The King nodded his consent, but the Duke didn't move. He seemed to have retreated into himself as if trying to determine what had gone wrong with his digestive system.

"Are you quite alright?" enquired Lady Llandudno, looking genuinely concerned.

"Perhaps I'm allergic to aubergine," he replied, pulling at the collar of his shirt as he hiccupped again.

"Nonsense," said Lord Llandudno. "No one is allergic to aubergine."

"Well, I appear-" began the Duke, before collapsing back down into his chair. "I appear to-" He didn't seem able to finish his sentence. He was clutching at his collar as if struggling to breath.

"There's something wrong with the aubergine!" cried Lord Llandudno.

Lady Llandudno put down her knife and fork. Her face went pale.

"I'm sure it's perfectly alright," said the King, trying to remain calm. "Philip, are you all right?"

The Duke of Snowdonia looked at his King in annoyance and then collapsed backwards in his chair and slid sideways off it. He slumped to the ground. Sir Pendragon was at the Duke's side before anyone else had even thought of moving. He was army trained and knew a thing or two about first aid. He tested the Duke's airways and then checked for a pulse.

He stood up and away from the Duke and turned to the other guests. "He's dead," he announced solemnly.

"Oh my. Did he choke?" asked Lady Llandudno, who was almost as horrified as she was curious.

"I don't think so," replied Sir Pendragon. "I think he may have been poisoned."

"Who would do such a thing?" asked her ladyship.

"Not who, but what," replied the knight.

"Explain yourself," she demanded.

"I think this was indeed a case of aubergine poisoning. I think he was allergic."

"I've never heard of such a thing," said the King in alarm, motioning to the servants to come and do something, anything.

Sir Pendragon pulled himself up to full height and pushed his thumbs into the belt of his trousers. "Once when I was stationed in Mali in North Africa, not far from Timbuktu, I came across a man who was choking to death. I asked him what was wrong and he told me he was allergic to peanuts. Peanuts? I said. Pshkttkh, he said. And died. Never underestimate an allergy."

They all waited for the next part of the knight's tale, but apparently it was over.

"Perhaps we should all retire to another room," suggested the King.

"I think we should all have our stomachs pumped," said Lord Llandudno. "Just in case it was a bad aubergine and not an allergy at all."

The King looked undecided. Lady Llandudno nodded her agreement.

Somewhere above the unfolding drama by the dinner table, Ivor pulled the curtain closed and sat down on the floor, back against the wall. He was aghast. His dark plan had failed.

He didn't care about the death of the Duke. He did care

about the state of the nation, though. Cudd treth now, was it? The last thing the country needed was conscription. Somehow his plan had failed and the wrong person had received the poisoned food.

He got up. He would be expected to assist with the events downstairs. He put on a concerned face and made his way along the corridor to the wooden steps that would lead him straight down into the swirling aftermath of a horror that was his own doing.

Funny little man, indeed.

CHAPTER 22

"Quentin had been sat in the stinking confines of the public bin for some time now. He deliberated upon whether he had *malice aforethought* during the events which amounted to his first ever bank robbery. He was fairly sure he hadn't felt malice and was certain there hadn't been any forethought. Unfortunately, that didn't seem like an argument that would hold much water in front of a jury of his peers. Or a jury of his lessers, as was more likely to be the case. He would get little sympathy from the people deciding his fate when his sorry circumstances and the full run of events were laid bare before them in a court of law. Quentin sighed a long, weary sigh and wondered how much longer he had to hide inside a bin with only a tramp for company."

"Wha' ye talkin tae yersel fer?" asked the tramp.

"What?" asked Quentin, distractedly.

"Shlike yer narratin yer ain life shtory."

"Oh, sorry. It must be something I do in times of stress."

"Why mush tit?"

For a second Quentin thought he was being insulted, then his brain translated for him. "It must, because I don't think I've ever done it before, and I feel unusually stressed at this particular moment."

Quentin was a little confused by this hitherto unknown idiosyncrasy of his. He decided to endeavour never to do it again. Musing quietly over the past few minutes, though, he considered that it was not impossible that he had actually been outwardly, vocally narrating events in third person.

He checked his watch. He'd been in hiding long enough. It was time to take action. He stood up and drew back the bin lid. He poked out his head and ensured no one lay in wait for him. His eyes adjusted to the light, but it was a hazy evening light. He took in a huge life-giving lungful of clean air.

"It's getting dark already," he mused.

The tramp sniffed. "S'pose we're aff then?"

"I had better make a move," said Quentin, hoisting one leg over the side of the bin. It took strong arms and a steady balance to manoeuvre oneself out of a bin like that. Quentin had neither, so looked much like a breakdancing flamingo as he flapped his way, legs and arms flailing, over the side to land awkwardly on the street below.

He sat up, rubbed grit off his hands, then stood and massaged his buttocks. He was somewhat dismayed to see the tramp perform a perfect barrel roll and land nimbly on his feet. "You've done that before," said Quentin, trying to make conversation so the tramp would be less inclined to rob him and kill him for his clothes.

The tramp leant into the bin and pulled out the sack of money. To Quentin's surprise, he handed it over to him.

"Dinnae call ourshelves tramps."

"Sorry?" Quentin was barely paying attention. He was trying to fathom what to do next.

"Shome of ush tramps, we dinnae call ourshelves tramps, ken?"

"I see," said Quentin. "Did I call you a tramp? I didn't mean to. In fact, I don't remember doing so. Now, if you'd be so kind, I just need a moment to contemplate what my next step is."

"Spake it in amangst yer ramblin'," the tramp replied. "Shed only a tramp fer company."

"Oh, I see," said Quentin, quite bemused by his inability to internalise his own thoughts in times of stress. Perhaps it was the effect of the noxious fumes and lack of oxygen in the bin. He hoped it wouldn't happen again. "I'm sure I didn't mean anything by it. Look, I really must be on my way. It was a great pleasure to make your acquaintance. Now, if you don't mind-"

"Call ourshelves wandstrels."

"Wandstrels?"

"Mixture o' wanderers an' wastrels."

Quentin was a little put out by the tramp's sudden verbosity. "And this is catching on, is it?" Quentin couldn't quite work out how he had managed to avoid being caught. Surely the bin was a pretty obvious place to look?

"Aye."

"Sort of a union for tramps, is it?" he asked carelessly. He wondered if he could get a taxi while smelling of cabbage and rat dung and holding a bag with CASH printed on the side of it.

"Mair like a brotherhood, like Mashons or summat. Wantae ken wir shlogan?"

"No, that's quite all right." Quentin eyed the garrulous tramp up and down, appraising him properly for the first time. He was clearly tipsy, there was no doubt about that. He wasn't quite drunk though. He had a terrible way of pronouncing words, but it couldn't be called a genuine lisp. It was more like an excessive laziness of the tongue. He stank, no two ways about that. He was quite agile and slim. Also, he was not as old as he looked and probably slightly healthier than you'd give him credit for using your normal five senses. There was something else, too...

"It shtarted in Scotland," he said.

That was it. It was the Scottish accent. Quite pronounced when you took the time to notice it, but somehow easy to miss when hidden under the alcoholic slurring and generally distracting nature of the pungent aroma and tatty clothing.

Quentin stole over to the end of the alleyway so he could

peer round it like a spy in an espionage movie. He eyed the police tape cordoning off the next alley along, but for some reason this one didn't seem to have been properly investigated. He wasn't quite sure whether he had been lucky or not. It might have made life easier if he'd just been caught. But then, there was a certain thrill with having gotten away with it for this long.

"Right behind ye."

Quentin started, inwardly leaping a foot in the air, but outwardly only flinching. "Right," he said, evenly. He wasn't sure why the tramp was right behind him.

He sidled along to the next alley and paused. It was getting dark and the air had turned cold. The inside of the bin had been surprisingly warm. Now the clothes that had been stuck to his body by sweat and unmentionable bin-slurry had come loose, he began to shiver.

He turned around. For all his unshaven, dirty, lopsided-nosed face, the tramp had startlingly sharp brown eyes. "Look," said Quentin. "I'm in trouble with the law. I suggest you retreat to your bin and get a good night's rest. Perhaps you could recommend somewhere I could stay warm and hide from the police?"

"Best place fer a werm nicht be a cell. But if ye dinnae wanna get yersel caught, gotta be tucked unner a hedge."

Quentin nodded. "Right, thank you. I'll be off."

The tramp nodded. "Thanks in aw," he said.

Quentin frowned.

"Fer yon five squid," explained the tramp.

"Did I give you five pounds? Oh wait. I see. You want five pounds from me? Or perhaps you're robbing me?"

"Och no, just sayin thanks fer the shrapnel ye gave me afore ye went intae the bank."

"Oh... that was you, was it? I hadn't realised. Quite forgot about that during all the, you know, robbery and so on. Please, don't think anything of it. I'd give you some more, but I haven't quite made up my mind if I'm going to return all this money or hang on to it. I suppose it should be an easy decision. Not sure why it isn't." He paused. He had some thinking to do. "I'll be seeing you," he said, hoping fervently this would not prove to be true.

The tramp watched him go. Quentin hurried off down the street. When he looked back, he saw the tramp still watching him. It was a little unnerving. Just before he rounded a corner he took another backward glance. The tramp was stroking his stubble and watching him intently. It was borderline sinister. Quentin half suspected he'd bump into the wretched man again in half an hour, have the money taken from him and be beaten to a pulp and, quite possibly, eaten. He definitely wouldn't go to a field or sleep under a hedge. That's what the tramp wanted him to do. He decided he would go and find a garage he could break into. He wasn't quite sure where that idea had come from, but he supposed the survival instincts of a desperate man sometimes afford him an aptitude for swift problem-solving. Yes, he'd break into a garage and have a damn good night's sleep away from the wind and the cold. He had a good idea whose garage he would break into, too.

CHAPTER 23

There's something sad about gold plating, thought Ivor as he studied a trophy that had sat on the shelf in his room for many years; be it this room or the one in his old basement flat. He turned it around in his hands, examining it from every side. On the outside, a thin veneer of cheer, but on the inside, just under the surface, something cold and base. That's how he felt about himself these days. He placed the trophy back on the shelf. It was a long time since he'd won a trophy. He had won that one at school for excelling in his woodwork class; something he thought might come in handy one day. This wasn't that day.

Most days, Ivor wore a smile. He fawned about the King, pretending the oaf's idiocy was ingenuity and trumpeting his mediocrity as if it were merit. Inside, though, Ivor's mind was murky and fetid. Wicked ideas twisted and knotted their gnarled roots through his consciousness like rampant weeds suffocating any healthy growth beneath.

Next to the shelf, a nail had been driven into the wall, whereupon a bronze medal hung from a tattered red ribbon. He'd come third at the one hundred metre hurdles in the fourth year of his junior school's sports day. Oh, how the crowds had cheered when he sped past the other contestants. Oh, how they had jeered when he fell on the last hurdle and two other brats had overtaken him. He had managed to pick himself up in just enough time to secure a paltry third place. Nonetheless, he had a plaque to this day, and they didn't, because he'd stolen theirs and thrown them into the cess pit behind old Pa Jovery's house. And where were they now, those who had stolen greatness from him? They had not only had instant justice carved into their fortunes by Ivor's tricky hands and cunning mind, but they had been forgotten by everyone as their lives descended into deadbeat normalcy. Take Jeff. Oh, vainglorious Jeff and your convertible car in high school and your nipple ring. Where are you now? Selling windscreen insurance for some local car company. Your three kids fatherless as your girlfriend ran away with them after she tired of all your talk about football and beer. And Smithy. Dear, Smithy. You forgot that for all your fat fists could make you friends in the playground they'd leave you behind bars after you hit your wife. And after you got a criminal record, what became of you then? Just a guy who works in the local supermarket. Oh Smithy, how the girls fell at your feet in more ways than one. Ivor smirked as he turned the bronze medal in his fingers.

If only his junior school classmates could see him now. Ivor Munchkinhead! Would you still be laughing at my name now? Well, yes, you probably would, but it wouldn't do you any good. You might have had all the girls, the trophies, the popularity, the good grades, the nice parents, the expensive possessions and the fun times, and yes, you might still have some or all of those things, but you're not advisor to the King of Wales, and you've no future ahead of you now. You'll never make a difference. But I'll make a difference.

Ivor's internal ranting was shattered out of existence by a familiar voice calling his name. "Ivor Munchkinhead!" It was followed by a snigger. His Majesty's voice came from the antechamber just outside his bedchamber. Ivor hurried from his room, leaving the medal swinging gently against the wall. He scuttled along the dark corridor and turned into a well-lit room to find King Gruffydd II sitting with a young lady on one knee. She had purple hair and looked about twenty five years old. She wore fishnet stockings, a short, pleated skirt and a low cut top.

"Sire?" asked the advisor, trying not to look at them or show his displeasure at having to witness their canoodling. The King should be a little more discrete when he abuses his power, thought Ivor with a suppressed twinge of jealousy.

"Ivor. Would you be so good as to bring some candles and some wine to my bedchamber?"

Ivor bowed low, trying not to stare at the King's companion. Just what would an attractive girl in her mid-twenties see in an overweight dunce with the charisma of a gangrenous ulcer? None, if not for his title. Shadowy thoughts bubbled up and somehow calmed him. He would put it right. He may have failed to poison the King during his meal with Lord Llandudno, but other opportunities would arise.

Ivor found some candles and then chose a middle-of-the-road wine from the cellar. He dutifully took them to the King's chamber. He positioned them on small holders that were placed around the walls at varying heights. When lit, they would bathe the room with a gentle, flickering light that bordered on romantic. He didn't light them. The King would call him later when he wanted them lit. The palace could only afford so many candles, after all. He put two wine glasses out, rubbing them with his sleeve to make sure they gleamed. Finally, he uncorked the bottle.

He returned to the antechamber. The King watched him with amusement. He knew Ivor led a lonely life and mistook his grimaces for jealousy.

"You've met Ffion before," remarked the King. Ivor nodded politely. The girl smiled and gave him a little wave with one hand, then turned back to the King as if he fascinated her. She was dwarfed by the massive bulk of His Majesty, who scoffed so many doughnuts per day it would actually free up a considerable amount of his time should he utilise some kind of rapid fire dispenser. She, on the other hand, clearly hadn't seen a square meal in her life. She giggled. Ivor felt sick. It never entered his thoughts that there might be mutual affection between them. It seemed too unlikely.

"If I may," he said, indicating to the door. Ivor bowed out. He smiled as he left the room because their lovey-dovey antics had given him a new idea that lit up his mind with a wicked brilliance.

CHAPTER 24

Quentin had watched just enough low-budget television over the years to suspect the tramp might follow and kill him for his money, so he darted down an alleyway, sidestepping occasionally to throw his pursuer off the scent. There was notably little evidence that sidestepping did anything other than make him appear slightly constipated, but he persisted nonetheless.

He was, in truth, more than a little impressed with himself. In little under two days he had gone from bankruptcy and living with a general fear of the unknown, to being a fugitive bank robber carrying more hard cash than he'd ever held before. If he was entirely honest with himself: he was almost enjoying it.

Reaching the main road, he hailed a taxi. He climbed into the back of the yellow Skoda and instructed the driver to take him to Christleton, a village on the outskirts of Chester.

Sitting in the back of the taxi, Quentin took a moment to peek into the depths of his swag bag. There was a large amount of money in there. He looked up. He looked back into the bag. He looked up again. No matter how much was in there, he was still disgusted at the ever-rising price on the taxi's meter.

Outside, daylight was fading fast and streetlamps flickered

into life across the city. The taxi driver turned down the radio. Oh no, please, no, begged Quentin internally, but there was no stopping the inevitable.

"You must have an interesting story," prompted the driver, eyeing Quentin in the rear view mirror. He appeared to be disdainfully appraising Quentin's dishevelled appearance.

Quentin hated it when they spoke to him. Why did they have to speak to him? Did chariot drivers make small talk with their emperors in the old days? Do airline pilots wander through the aisles of a plane looking for some idle banter? Do horses make chit chat with their riders? No. They concentrate on the task at hand. Quentin tried not to sigh before he spoke. He supposed he was partially caked in mud, stank of the unpleasant effluence that swills around the bottom of public bins and was holding a bag with - he now remembered - the bank's logo on the side next to the word CASH in bold red letters. Some sort of explanation was probably necessary.

"Nothing to tell really," he squirmed. He tried to think of a good lie to tell, but he didn't have one. He sniffed and then stared out the window.

"You look like you've been through the wars," persisted the driver.

"Ah, well," began Quentin, thinking frantically, "I was, er, set upon by a tramp. Scruffy fellow. He pushed me into a bin and, well... I mean, not a well, but, well, he..."

"You survived then?"

"Yes, I'm fine. Thank you." Quentin was pleased the driver didn't pursue the matter. Unfortunately, he'd only changed tack because he had a more pressing interest.

"So what's in the bag?" The casual manner of asking suggested he was indifferent to the answer, but something in his tone hinted that he would happily drag a man down a blind alley and beat him to death with a crowbar for any sum of money that needed over four numbers on a lottery ticket to win.

"Cash," said Quentin. "But not Sterling, you see? It's Rubles. There's almost fifty thousand Russian Rubles in this bag. All in notes. I'm an accountant and I was taking it to the bank for a client. Of course, the tramp didn't give me a chance to explain that the entire contents of this bag is really only worth about seventeen pound fifty in our money."

The taxi driver gave a look of resigned acceptance. Quentin knew it was a brilliant lie. Why else would someone carry a bag of money around? Of course it wasn't worth much. The taxi driver was nodding to himself, as if he should have realised beforehand that it would be something like that. "Figures," he mumbled.

A moment or two passed. They swerved around a large roundabout and the driver told him that in certain places in Scotland they called roundabouts 'circles', as if this was a piece of trivia that would one day be useful in a pub quiz, which it wasn't, and, of course, Quentin had never been to a pub quiz, nor ever intended to.

"So you won then?" asked the driver.

"Sorry?" Quentin was still marvelling at his own brilliance in coming up with such a convincing cover story at such short notice. He was often startled by his own brilliance, like a moth that had caught alight then landed on a mirror. Actually, nothing like that, he wasn't flapping about in panic. He was calm and collected. He was more like a glow worm that shone so brightly it had to screw up its own eyes. He considered: of course I outsmarted the guy, anyone with my brainpower would have to inject himself with liquid stupidity three times a day just to function around his level. Hell, I'd have to take a heap of powdered stupidity, pile it on a spoon, warm it over a candle, suck it into a hypodermic needle and inject it straight into my eyes just to begin to approach the level he's operating on. Quentin was getting a little carried away his newfound criminal mindset.

"You won the fight with the tramp?"

"Well, yes, I knocked him out with his own hammer and shoved him in the back of a cement mixer and turned it on. He survived, but from the neck down he's mostly grey and cuboid."

Haha! thought Quentin. It barely even matters what I say to this nitwit. He soaks it up faster than a sponge in a bath full of doofus!

The driver nodded, but warily. Quite possibly he was deliberating whether the man in the back of his car was an escaped mental patient. Another thought had also occurred to him: "Say, you're not planning to pay me using Rubles are you?"

"No, indeed. Perish the thought," replied Quentin as he surreptitiously slipped his hand into the bag and retrieved a wad of notes. He quietly shoved them into his pocket. "Is it far now?"

"Almost there." The meter was running high, Quentin noticed. It had been quite a long journey. Longer than he'd expected.

"Well, here we are," said the driver, a minute later. "Christleton. Any particular street?"

"This will do fine," replied Quentin. "How much do I owe you?" He could see the amount on the meter but was choosing not to believe it.

The driver read the amount to him.

"What? That's extortion," exclaimed Quentin.

The driver gave him a look that confirmed the existence of a crowbar under his seat and his willingness to use it if he wasn't paid his fare with a hefty tip. Quentin interpreted the look with unerring precision and decided not to argue. "Fine," he said, delving into his pocket. As he did so, something stirred within him. He wasn't a lawyer now. He was a criminal. He'd evaded the police, robbed a bank, shoplifted and he knew he was smarter than the average bear. He paused for just a moment, to think.

"What if I told you," he riffed, "that this bag is actually full of real, good old fashioned British twenties and tens. I stole it from a bank and you're the only person who knows where I am."

A menacing look of greed appeared in the driver's eyes.

"Good," said Quentin. "Now, I also know a way to

convert this into money that I can hold legally. A way of making it untraceable in law."

The driver remained silent.

"I'll give you half of this money if you'll do something for me."

"Why should I believe you?"

Quentin tipped the contents of the bag on the passenger's seat. The driver looked at it. He reached back and picked up a wad of notes. "I'll be damned," he said.

"All I want you to do," said Quentin, seriously, "is go - on foot - to house number 17 on that road over there." He pointed to the road right in front of them. "I want you to post four hundred pounds through the door, because that's how much I owe the lunatic that lives there, then rush back here and drive me out of this place. It's all about repaying a debt. A drug-related debt."

The driver looked at him suspiciously.

"I'm not the drug user in this situation," Quentin added. "It's my son. I want to set him back on the straight and narrow. That's what all of this has been about. Do you believe me?" He sounded so earnest he was starting to believe it himself.

"Why would you give me half of it?" asked the driver, still suspicious, but it was obvious to Quentin which way this was going to go. He felt more alive than he had done in all his years as a solicitor.

"I don't really need any of it, to be honest. I'm a well-paid accountant. You could have the lot, really, once my son's debt is paid. I just thought I might keep a little for myself. Book a holiday for Jake - that's my son - and me. Give him some time away to sort his head out."

The driver nodded. "Fifty-fifty then."

"It's a deal," agreed Quentin.

"Not so fast," said the driver, his brain catching up with the conversation. "What do you mean by lunatic?"

Quentin nodded. "That's why I want someone else to do it. If he saw me he'd probably come running out with a baseball bat. If you go up to the door and he comes out you can just pretend someone ordered a taxi and told it to deliver the money. People do that, don't they?"

"Well," said the driver, a slight look of uncertainty crossing his face, "I do sometimes pick up beer from the off licence for people."

"It's just like that, from your perspective," said Quentin. "Now, the sooner we do it, the sooner it's over."

And just like that, the driver, pound symbols filling his vision, had counted out four hundred pounds and walked halfway down the road. The next question on his lips should have been: why did you need to rob a bank to get four hundred pounds if you're a well-paid accountant? But he just hadn't quite got that far.

Quentin laughed out loud to himself as he drove away in the taxi. He waved as he went past the driver who was looking at him in total disbelief and then running down the road chasing him and swearing. At least he had four hundred pounds. Quentin only regretted that he hadn't tried for two hundred. Less believable, but it would have made his victory even sweeter.

He was really beginning to enjoy the criminal lifestyle. It allowed him to exercise his mind and shake off the shackles of his mundane, law-abiding existence. He already knew what his next two steps were. First, he had to hide the swag because carrying just over nine and a half thousand pounds around in a bag labelled CASH was likely to draw unwanted attention. Secondly, he needed somewhere to sleep.

Night was drawing in, as if a child with a black crayon was scribbling over a picture of a sunset. Actually, nothing like that. The evening was just beginning to grow dim. Quentin turned the taxi's headlights on and made his way towards a place he had once known well.

CHAPTER 25

He was pleased to see that the purple haired girl - he'd already forgotten her name - was nowhere to be seen. It was late evening as Ivor entered the King's bedchamber to find His Majesty preparing for bed. He still wanted the candles lit around the room. About a year ago, His Majesty had ordered that small, wooden candle-holders be put up in strategic locations around the bedchamber so that, when lit, they softened the atmosphere and accentuated the opulent four poster bed dominating the space. Ivor thought it was all rather pointless and tacky, but it wasn't his place to pass judgement, at least not openly. Presumably the King expected the girl would return later.

"Ivor, you're looking trim today. Have you lost weight?"

Ivor's raised eyebrows gave away his surprise at the unexpected compliment.

The King smirked. "Not," he jeered.

Saying nothing, Ivor frowned like a disappointed parent and went back to lighting the candles.

"No, I'm only joking, seriously... you look like you've lost a pound or two." The King sounded earnest.

Ivor considered for a moment. He certainly had been very busy of late. Perhaps all the activity had caused him to skip a meal or two. Perhaps he'd burnt off a few calories running up and down the stairs from the cellar to the Grand Hall. He considered that perhaps it wasn't entirely inconceivable that he might have lost a little of the paunch around his waist over the last week. It would be nice to think that he had. "Well..." he began.

"Not," jeered the King, then chuckled to himself.

Ivor nodded in quiet acceptance. He'd remember this. He lit another candle with the decreasing taper he held in his steady hand. It didn't matter what that fat buffoon said. He'd get his comeuppance soon enough.

"I've been thinking," declared the King. He kicked off his slippers and climbed under the cover of his bed and picked a copy of his current read, *The Owl Service*, off the bedside table. "If we could get it together in time for the celebrations, we could look into promoting you."

Ivor looked up suddenly. This was news to him.

"Yes," continued the King. "I was thinking of maybe making a new position available and promoting you into it straight away." The King shuffled under the covers until he was comfortable. Ivor was all ears. He watched as King Gruffydd II opened his book and removed a cardboard bookmark featuring a picture of a Welsh Maid; when you were a public figure, it was important to keep everything on-message. The King stuck the end of it in his mouth and sucked gently as he mulled something over. "Yes, I think I would call the position something a bit more exciting than Royal Advisor. It would need to be a bit more magnificent than that." Ivor's eyes widened at the word 'magnificent', but he didn't want to show enthusiasm in an unseemly way so retained a neutral expression. "Oh yes. Perhaps I shall make you something like Minister of Justice and Public Services. Does that sound reasonable?"

Ivor had to stop himself from nodding.

"Or, perhaps, we could opt for something like Grand Vizier?"

"I think the first was better, sire," opined Ivor, altogether too hastily.

There was a sparkle in the King's eye now. "No, no. Not good enough. You're right. How about... wait for it... wait for it... how about: His Royal Minister for Matters of State and Justice? Does that sound good to you?"

Ivor allowed himself a perfunctory nod.

The King placed the book on his covers, open, face down, breaking the spine. "Yes, Ivor. On the day of the celebrations. The third anniversary of my reign. On that day, we shall make you His Royal Minister for Matters of State and Justice!"

"Why, Your Highness," said Ivor, moving to step forward and performing a small, obsequious bow, "that would be a great hon-"

"Naawwwt," jeered the King, and promptly rolled around the bed pretending that what he'd just done was the funniest damn thing ever conceived. From Ivor's perspective, the King looked like a warthog writhing in pain.

Ivor tried to look unaffected. Unusually, the hatred he expected to feel course through his veins didn't arise. The bile didn't bubble up in his oesophagus. He just stood and stared at the spectacle of the King rolling and flapping around the bed like a distressed seagull with its feet stuck in a plastic, six-pack holder.

The taper was shortening, so he lit the last candle. He was trying to think of a witty retort but none was forthcoming because the sheer inanity of the jape suppressed all hope of a creative comeback.

The King stopped his guffawing and looked back at Ivor, hoping to see an expression of utter defeat and resentment. What he saw was a look of complete disinterest. His smile faded quickly. He fumbled with his book, realising he had lost his page.

"I'm sorry," he said, after a moment. "I was just testing out a new type of practical joke I've invented."

Ivor wanted to explain that it wasn't a new type of joke at all, but a very old one. If he could have summoned the energy to do so, he'd have corrected the King, but he was so drained by the King's stupidity that he couldn't bring himself to even begin.

"I think I might introduce it to the people during the celebration, what do you think?"

Ivor saw an opening. A chance to get his own back. He jumped at it. If he played his cards right, he might be able to disgrace the King in front of the whole nation and on live television! "I think that's an excellent idea, sire. Tell them about your new practical joke. In fact, it might make a good opener. Something like: I'm going to lower taxes and increase the state pension. Not!" Ivor laughed over-enthusiastically, but the King was not amused. Ivor's laughter died away. He could see the King wasn't to be fooled in this way. No matter, it had been worth a try.

"No, that would never do," said the King. "But you're right. The public might be impressed if I simply explained it to them. It would make a good starter for my speech. You know, I should invent a name for it. It needs to be something that would appeal to the Welsh populace. Something that will remind them of me. Of their nation. Of their country. Of what all this is about, damn it!" The King thumped the mattress with his fist, in the least impressive display of manly conviction in history.

A sly smirk illuminated the not-altogether-unpleasant-when-seen-from-certain-angles features of Ivor's face as another brainwave traversed the depths and slalomed the wrinkly cortex of his cunning mind. "Sire, perhaps you could simply call it: The Welsh Not."

The King looked at him blankly for a moment. If the power struggle between them - the one only Ivor knew or cared about – was represented by a set of scales with an equal number of lead weights balanced on either side, then Ivor, with the simplest of glib comments, had just placed a feather on his side. Slowly, one demi-millimetre at a time, the scales started to tip. Ivor could imagine the red-faced shame on the King's face as he stood before a booing crowd and suddenly realised he had just told the Welsh people that he had invented The Welsh Not. They would hear: The Welsh Knot. It would bring back old memories of when Welsh speakers were forced to wear a wooden sign on their chests, held there by a metal chain around their necks, as punishment for speaking their native language. It would evoke all kinds of angry sentiment. This would not go well for King Gruffydd II. This would not go well for him at all.

There was a pregnant pause which lasted so long it was deep in labour before its waters broke. "You know," said the King, "I think that's perfect." He nodded to himself, a look of deep contentedness about his person. He beamed at Ivor. Ivor beamed back. He was the King's humble servant and ever so glad to have been of assistance.

"Perfect," enthused the King. As he looked at Ivor an unmistakable twinkle appeared in his eye. Just a smidgen of a nanosecond too late did Ivor realise what was coming.

"Naawwwt!!!"

Ivor didn't flinch. After a quick glance around the bedchamber to ensure he'd lit all the candles, he mustered what little dignity he had left and bowed to the King. "Goodnight, sire," he said and swiftly exited the room.

Halfway down the corridor, he heard the King start howling with laughter. Ivor dug his fingernails deep into the palms of his hands. Not long now, he thought, with morbid certainty. Not long now.

CHAPTER 26

The yellow taxi pulled up to the kerb with unexpected suddenness. Quentin yanked on the handbrake and wound the window down an inch. He got out, grabbing his swag bag as he did so. He locked the car and posted the keys back through the gap in the window. "There," he said, with satisfaction.

The police would soon find the car and it would be returned to its rightful owner. The taxi driver would no doubt be annoyed that Quentin borrowed it, but he would be relieved to find it in one piece. Quentin hoped the driver was smart enough not to mention the four hundred pounds. Hopefully it would compensate him for lost earnings. Perhaps it would also persuade him not to cooperate too fully with the police in their search for the hijacker. Quentin thought it expertly done and considered that he was well on his way to becoming a master criminal.

Quentin looked around him. He knew the area well. He used to live near here. With his swag bag thrown over his shoulder, he jogged down the road and away from the abandoned vehicle. He'd have to be quick about his business because it was starting to get dark.

The premises showed signs of abandonment. Behind a weather-beaten gate lay the town offices of a firm that had closed its doors many years ago. It had mottled glass windows at ground level and a door that had once been green but was now a mass of sun-bleached paint flakes and exposed wood. Above the door was a sign which, although faded now, read 'Cundick & Sparrow'. It was the name of his father's firm, although his father and his partner hadn't worked there in a long time. As he drew closer, the wind picked up and he shivered. Looking at the sign, he remembered it being hoisted up there and installed on that first day when he was about twelve years old. "One day," his father had said, "this will read Cundick, Cundick and Sparrow." How wrong he had been. Quentin shook his head sadly, then a little more roughly as if to shake away the memory.

Quentin tried the gate. It had rusted shut. The gate was inset into a low, red-brick wall which Quentin swung the bag over and then vaulted. He explored around the side of the building. It was a quiet street and there was unlikely to be anyone passing at this time, except perhaps a few already-tipsy locals heading to the pub.

Adjacent to the building was an old, dilapidated shed with a roof full of holes. Its door hung open, wincing and creaking, inching back and forth. Quentin deemed it unsuitable as a hiding place for his money.

There was a metal bin. It had a black rubber lid which stated "No Hot Ashes". Quentin opened it and peered inside. He half-expected the worst, but it was empty. There was some indiscernible black gunk at the bottom, but it looked dry. He dropped the bag into the bin and replaced the lid. It would surely be as secure here as anywhere else he could come up with at short notice. The property had lain empty for many years and the owner certainly wasn't going to return.

He paused for a moment, wondering if the police would connect the taxi being abandoned nearby to his father's old firm. He hadn't been here in years. There was nothing connecting him to it apart from his father's last will and testament which was secured in a filing cabinet in Sparrow's firm. He decided it was unlikely the link would be uncovered anytime soon.

There was no question of Quentin staying here. It brought back too many memories. His plan had been to spend the night in Mavis' garage, but there was no guarantee she would help him. He felt perhaps he had stretched any goodwill she still had for him to breaking point when he pointed a shotgun at her face. Certainly, that would be enough for most people, he considered.

Unfortunately, the advice offered by the tramp seemed the most likely way to ensure he wasn't incarcerated before the night was done. Sleeping in a hedge in some slightly-out-of-town field might be uncomfortable, but it had the distinct advantage of being the last place they would look for a man who liked his creature comforts.

He briefly considered driving the taxi out of town, but it was out of bounds now. He'd be spotted the moment he hit a main road. He told himself that the taxi had to belong to a different crime, one that wasn't serious enough to involve DNA testing. Hopefully, his theatrics would slip away without a curtain call.

Bounding ungainly over the wall again, he stopped for just a few extra heartbeats to take a final look at the bleak, washed out sign above the entrance to his father's old business. He acknowledged the twinge of regret he felt in his gut at something that could have been, but never was. A streetlight flickered on.

The wind picked up and whipped at his ankles and tousled his thinning hair. Suddenly putting one foot in front of the other seemed like a mammoth task. He put his head down and soldiered off in a direction that would lead him out of town. He felt like he was trudging through thick blancmange. "Come on," he said to himself, in a tone that was half resignation yet half determination.

The farther he got from the old premises, the more his troubles faded. After a time, his feet seemed easier to lift and his pace picked up. Before long, his natural optimism began to return. I'm free, he thought. Free to do whatever I please.

It was time to put the past behind him. Quentin's intellect and imagination - two things he'd barely had to use in his many years as a lawyer - started to ignite in a way they hadn't done in oh, so long. Like a stone titan rising from the countryside where it had lain dormant for a thousand years, grinding back to life, shifting the dirt, raising its great rock-formation hands and blinking granite eyes, the very essence of his being seemed to rear up. It was as if some heady drug had taken hold of him. A new self took shape in his mind.

CHAPTER 27: FRIDAY

Larry sat bolt upright and shouted: "I've arrived!"

He looked about him wildly. With his next breath he sighed out and slumped back down in the hospital bed. "Hey..." His chest was still heaving with some kind of imagined panic. He muttered a few incoherent words.

Higgs had been snoozing. Suddenly he was wide-eyed and alert. He rubbed his eyes and wet his lips. Outside it was dark, but it was that kind of telltale darkness that suggests it will be daytime soon and if you haven't slept yet you may as well give it up as a bad attempt. The clock on the wall revealed it was just past five a.m.

Higgs realised Larry was looking at him. "Larry?" he asked, confused. He shook the fog from his mind. "You're awake?"

Larry didn't look good. Sweat beaded on his forehead and ran down his temples from under his dark curly hair. He was panting heavily. Higgs pulled his chair close to him and wondered whether or not to call for help. "How are you feeling?" When Larry didn't answer, he pressed an amber button next to the bed and a light came on. "I've called the nurse," he said reassuringly.

Larry's breathing slowed, but his pupils were dilated and

his lips trembled. "Where?" He seemed confused as he tried to take in his surroundings. He put one hand against his ribs and felt there, a sign that his body remembered something of what had happened even if he couldn't yet.

"You're in hospital," explained Higgs, taking a towel and dabbing Larry's forehead gently. "Just relax." He wasn't sure the best thing to do was remind Larry that he was on the run from the police, had been badly injured and was now sitting in an intensive care unit in London having survived - narrowly - broken ribs, internal bleeding and a coma.

Larry trembled. "He's coming."

"Who's that now?" asked Higgs, knowing Larry might be delirious.

Larry didn't get a chance to answer. The nurse arrived. It was the same one Higgs had seen earlier. She had long blonde hair and a figure that really seemed, well, out of place in a hospital. There was something strange, though. Higgs couldn't put his finger on what troubled him about her.

She came close to the bed and put a reassuring hand on Larry's wrist. "Welcome back," she said, smiling. Perfect teeth, thought Higgs. Glossy lipstick.

"It seems your pulse is strong," she said, frowning slightly. "That's a quick recovery you've made. For a while there I wasn't sure you were going to make it. I think your friend knew you would though, he's been here the whole time." Larry looked at him gratefully, but said nothing.

The nurse checked the chart at the end of his bed. "So, you're Larry Juan Brian Sampaio-Gladwell?" she asked.

"Yes," replied Larry. "Did Higgs tell you?" Higgs frowned.

"Just checking," she said, and winked at him. She seemed distracted by the readings on the monitor next to him and she pushed it away from her, turning it to the side so that none of them could see the readouts. A look of distaste seemed to cross her face. "What was that you were saying when I was coming in, about someone approaching or visiting or something?" she asked.

"Oh," said Larry. "I can't remember. I think I had a dream. It's gone now."

The nurse nodded. "Well, you seem alright. I'll fetch a doctor just to give you the once over," she said. As she slipped from the room, Higgs thought to call her back and ask her when Larry might be discharged, but it occurred to him that he didn't know her name. In fact, she hadn't been wearing a name badge. He thought for a moment. She hadn't been wearing a name badge, but she *had* been wearing lipstick and a pair of high heels. Did nurses normally dress like that? Higgs didn't think so. There was something else bothering him. Larry was the one who put his finger on it.

"How did she hear me say someone was coming?" he asked, idly. "I said that before you pressed the button." He slowly lifted himself into a seated position.

"That's right," said Higgs. He realised that something was wrong. "And how did she know your real name? I gave you a pseudonym: Harry Blackwell."

"You called?" asked the short, dark haired nurse who swept into the room and walked straight over to the wall and pressed the button which deactivated the light which Higgs had turned on. Of course, thought Higgs, that's what they do first. He examined the nurse closely. She had flat shoes on, as would anyone on her feet all day. She wore a name badge - it was part of the uniform. She did wear lipstick, but it was nothing showy. She checked Larry's chart then the monitor, pulling it back round to face them. It showed a healthy heartbeat. "Lie back down, Mr Blackwell," she told Larry. "Your body has been through a lot, we don't want to over-do it now, do we?" She didn't smile, but she did rearrange his pillows.

Higgs didn't say anything.

Larry asked, "How long was I out?"

The nurse looked at his chart again, then clipped it back on to the end of his metal bed frame. "Not long," she replied. "You're recovering well, but I'll go and fetch a doctor to give you the once over, alright?" She smiled.

She left the room.

"I don't understand," said Larry, registering the expression on Higgs' face.

"Something's amiss," said Higgs. "That first nurse wasn't a nurse."

"Then what was she?"

"I think she was a Luddite."

"A what?" He massaged the bruises around his broken rib. He was healing fast, it seemed. The sensation of pain was dull. He started to recall his journey from Ellesmere down to London. He remembered Astin and Maven. He remembered his interrogation and the computer screens showing information flowing past too quickly for him to comprehend. He didn't remember passing out. He did remember waking up. He'd been having a dream. No, it was more than that. It was a vision. A strong sense of déjà vu flooded over him. A thought or an image was coming to him. He could feel it rising to the surface. He was about to remember something important, but Higgs spoke and it was gone.

"The Luddites are hard to describe. They're like us in some ways, but opposite. They're a secret society, but they don't believe what we believe. We hack computers, they unplug them. Where we revere technology, they hate it. That's why she turned the monitor away. She couldn't stand the thought of it being near her. They want to bring the world to its knees and revert back to the days of slate and chalk, horse and carriage - you get the idea."

"Madness," noted Larry, dismayed. "But, why was she here?"

"I don't know. I don't like it, though. They don't just hate technology, they hate us. They hate the Binary Levers. Somehow they found out we exist and now we're their mortal enemies. Which makes them our mortal enemies. Even though we never went looking for a fight."

Larry shook his head. He wasn't really taking any of this in, but he didn't think it mattered right now. Higgs would take care of it. Higgs was a good friend and the reason he'd chosen to come to London, after all. They had known each other for many years and Larry knew he was in safe hands. Yet something irked him and made him feel unsafe; something just out of reach, but on the tip of his thoughts, like a dream he couldn't quite remember.

CHAPTER 28

"I just don't understand how it could have happened," protested King Gruffydd II huffily.

Ivor shook his head in an extremely convincing, but completely disingenuous, display of confusion and regret. "It's terrible, sire," he concurred. "Wicked, even."

"Yes, wicked. That's exactly what it was," agreed the King with no idea how true those words were. He was preening himself at the dressing table, preparing for the day's activities. It was going to be an exciting day. A brainwave had struck him at about midnight and he had informed Ivor of it. He planned to put it into immediate effect this morning so as to take his mind off the horrendous events of the evening.

"I'm still unclear how the fire started in the first place," said Ivor. He knew full well, of course.

The room that the King used as his bedroom was very old. It had previously been the changing room for whatever lead actress was performing. Now, there was a large area of the wall where the plaster had broken away. Rather than pay to have it fixed, the King ignored it. Once, he had even gone so far as to suggest it added a touch of character to the place.

The room had an interesting property which Ivor had picked up on long ago. Where the plaster had broken away, a peephole existed in the wall between the bedchamber and the outside corridor. Perhaps it had formed when some large piece of scenery was carelessly shunted backstage or, and Ivor preferred this theory, it had been worked through long ago by an actress who liked to receive secret messages from an admirer. Whatever the reason, Ivor's dark thoughts had seized upon the opportunity it presented. Early yesterday evening, after the purple-haired girl – Ffion, that was her name - had gone but before the King went to bed, there was an hour when the King visited the kitchens to scoff like the obnoxious glutton that he undoubtedly was. During this valuable window of opportunity, Ivor had fed a piece of fishing line through the hole.

After his earlier failure to kill the King with a serving of poisoned aubergine, it had taken Ivor a fair amount of nerve to put his latest plan into motion. Fortunately, the King insulting him by saying he'd lost weight (not) and that he might be promoted (naaaawwt) proved the catalyst he needed. Ivor had resolved that the reign of King Gruffydd II would come to a scorching end that very night.

Secretly, he had tied one of the candles to the piece of fishing wire he'd fed through the wall. He had then walked around the theatre - quite some way - until he was on the other side of the peephole. Patiently, he waited until he heard the King return from the kitchen. The King would let the candles burn down naturally, being too lazy to get up and blow each of them out. True to form, the King had put down his book, rolled over and fallen fast asleep. Moments later, great, bellowing, trumpeting snores penetrated the brick wall between the unsuspecting monarch and his disloyal advisor who waited patiently on the other side.

When he was sure the time was right, Ivor tugged hard at the line. The fishing line garrotted the candle, snapping it near its base. He pulled the line clean from the wall and, after checking it was intact, scurried off down the hall. He had the murder weapon: the piece of waxy wire. Hopefully it would be the only evidence that any foul play had taken place. He couldn't influence the outcome of events any further, so he fled the scene and didn't even hear the King's yell of enraged surprise.

Ivor returned his attention to the present.

"It was the damndest thing," said the King, recalling the events of the night before. "The candle fell from the holder and landed on the bedcover. Fortunately it woke me up."

"Fortunately," repeated Ivor, keeping his tone neutral.

"It landed right next to the drapes on my four poster bed. The drapes ignited - woof! - and, in seconds, the whole bed went up in flames. Everything was dry as tinder." The King applied powder to his cheeks.

"Foundation?" asked Ivor, trying to keep the amusement from his voice.

"Got to look my best for the people."

Ivor smirked. There was really nothing to suggest anything had happened other than that a faulty candle had somehow broken and fallen out of its holder.

"I was lucky," stated the King matter-of-factly.

"I feel responsible, sire," admitted Ivor. "I lit that candle. Perhaps I didn't secure it in its holder properly."

"It wasn't your fault," reassured the King, waving one hand dismissively. "I suppose it will teach me not to overuse the candles. Waste of resources, really." He mused for a moment, while applying a very small amount of eye liner. "I suppose what happened next was the real problem. I could probably have escaped the burning bed without problem, but it was... shocking what happened when I tried to use the fire extinguisher."

Ivor tried to suppress a smile. "Sire, how could anyone have known those old fire extinguishers were filled with gasoline?"

"Well, exactly," said the King. "It surprises me, actually, just how good my wits were in that situation. One moment I was asleep, the next I felt the candle land on the bedcover and somehow realised it was catching alight. In no time at all I was on my feet and had the fire extinguisher in my hands."

"Unexplainably impressive, sire."

"Indeed." The King nodded, assuming Ivor had complimented him. "I pulled the trigger and whooomp! Suddenly I was casting a flaming jet of fire all around the room. The walls were on fire, the desk was on fire, even the ceiling was on fire. It's lucky I got out of there alive!" The King turned to look at Ivor as if expecting to see the same look of relief on his face. Ivor quickly tried to feign it, but knew the look of annoyance he was wearing hadn't quite shifted. The King seemed to interpret it as agreement anyway and went back to spraying himself gently with an atomiser.

The rest was history. The King had thrown the extinguisher across the room and run for it. He was so far along the corridor when the extinguisher exploded that, although it obliterated his room, he survived entirely unscathed and all Ivor's efforts came to nothing. Still, the celebrations weren't until tomorrow. There was the whole of the day still to go and Ivor had set a definite deadline by which to achieve his dastardly purpose.

"Well," exclaimed the King. "My subjects await me."

He strode from the room, trying to look regal. Ivor followed behind him, watching the King's fat backside as it waddled down the corridor. It was, he thought to himself, as wide as Mount Rushmore but a lot less chiselled. Oh, there were a lot of things he thought to himself, but actions spoke louder than words. There was time. There was time.

Recent news had prompted the King to take his message directly to the people. Lord Llandudno had sent a despatch saying the media had quickly seen through their plans for conscription and had railed at the idea, despite there already being a surplus of volunteers swelling the ranks of the newly formed New Independent Welsh Army due to the number of unemployed people happy to work for a pittance at short notice. Apparently Sir Pendragon had put out the word and volunteers had immediately begun queuing around the block to join up.

Lord Llandudno had also reported a rumour that there

was growing concern in Westminster about the future of Wales. King Gruffydd II knew that the only way to win the support of the people was by getting involved with them at ground level. His father, once First Minister of the Assembly, had been a master at this, yet his son had not been born with the same charisma or eloquent way with words. He was, thought Ivor, like a sham reconstruction of the old First Minister who had paved the way for today's monarchy and, as things had transpired, his heir.

It was a bright day and Ivor was pleased to see that a goodly number of plebs had dutifully gathered outside the palace entrance. The media had not been forewarned about the King's appearance because this wasn't that sort of event. They would catch drift of it, of course, and later buy the footage off some amateur who had recorded the event on his phone. The idea was not to draw too much publicity during the event itself, because it wasn't planned for, but to later be able to demonstrate that the King was engaging with his subjects on a one-to-one level.

This was a simple engagement where the King could meet his people on the street and, without an intermediary, answer ad hoc questions about any issue which concerned the everyman of modern Wales. That was the spin. In truth, Ivor had been up all night compiling a list of the most likely questions the public might ask. Ivor had been tired when he started and so it had been a very long night. He started with questions about taxes, about the special relationship with England, about the recent twinning of Abergele with the Inuit town of Ikaluktutiak, and other sundry matters the locals were likely to mistakenly think were important. The list included details concerning pot holes in roads, badger hunting and whether the King would, on a bad day, be most annoyed at either a) finding a slug in his shoe or b) accidentally poking himself in the eye with a Spork. The suggested answers had become more inspired by delirium as the night went on and as Ivor became more exhausted. He had erased a few that were written as the sun came up. The King had, unfortunately, noticed them straight away.

"Ivor," he had said. "Do you really think they'll ask me the colour of my pyjamas?"

"Sire," replied Ivor, "the reason I put that question in there was simply so that, should it turn up, you don't answer the question truthfully and admit you sleep naked. We really don't want the public imagining you naked."

The King raised an eyebrow.

"It is not proper or dignified for the populace to be imagining a member of the royal family in the nude," explained Ivor, trying to bypass the obvious point that no one in their right mind would want to imagine the King naked, especially if they were eating. The King reviewed more of the answers and then started sniggering.

"That's not how I was using the word 'member'," reprimanded Ivor, altogether forgetting his place. The King had continued to smirk as he read down the list. The smirk had turned into a frown.

"How exactly does one pronounce Ikaluktutiak?"

"It's like, erm..." Ivor had to think about that one. He realised he didn't know so he made something up and almost swallowed his tongue in the process.

The King nodded, satisfied. He wasn't so pleased with the next question.

"Ivor, you've outdone yourself here. Do you really think anyone's going to ask me how much of the Earth's original forest cover remains?"

"Probably not, sire, but I thought the answer was interesting."

"Indeed. And do you think they're really going to ask me which side of my trousers I dress on?"

"If they do, I suggest you ignore the question."

"Yes, I can see you've given that advice here. I'm glad about one thing though."

"Yes, sire?"

"I'm glad you didn't put the actual answer, because that would have meant you knew the actual answer, which would have worried me a little."

Ivor nodded.

"What in blazes is this?" the King bellowed, pointing to one of the answers. At that moment, a servant arrived with his breakfast. The meal was brought to him on a silver platter. The palace only had one, but it was used frequently to make up for this fact. The King put the advice sheet to one side. He forked a sausage which was bubbling with greasy fat and then proceeded to suck the end off it and lick his lips. He took another bite. "I mean," he said, his mouth full, "I very much doubt anyone is going to ask me about the mating habits of the Isabella Shrew of Equatorial Guinea." The King reached for the morning broadsheets.

"Yes, but if they do," replied Ivor quietly, "you could clearly demonstrate their technique using a sausage on a fork."

"Sorry?" the King asked, not hearing him over the rustle of the oversized paper he was trying to open. The newspaper was entitled: *Y Gymraeg Adleisio The Welsh Echo*. To anyone who was bilingual, they couldn't have chosen a more immediately amusing title, nor one that became more insistently annoying over time. He took another bite of his sausage.

An hour later, with breakfast finished, the King was dressed in his finery and ready to take on the outside world. A gathering awaited him outside the palace. The plan was that the King would walk out amongst them, answer questions for a quarter of an hour and then step back up the stairs leading to the palace entrance, turn, summarise in an impromptu speech what he'd been discussing and whip up some patriotic feeling, then wave and leave. It would be a small but effective publicity stunt. It would hit the evening television news, fitting nicely into their 'happy but bizarre' slot at the end.

The King indicated for Ivor to follow. "Come on, Ivor Munchkinhead," he said, clearly in good spirits despite all the events of the evening.

The King walked to the ostentatious front doors of the palace and swung them open before him. One rebounded off the outside railing and came back, ready to hit him in the face, but he deftly sidestepped it and emerged into the morning sunshine where he met his subjects.

Ivor saw that fifty or more people were already assembled. It was a warm morning, the sun in full view and its warmth abundant. His subjects seemed in good spirits. There was an excited thrum as the King appeared. Several volunteer guards and some suitably located fencing held back the crowd. The railings, of course, had been put up to protect the King, but they served the added purpose of attracting a crowd by hinting that something was going to happen.

"My dearest subjects," began the King, magnanimously, as he walked down the stairs toward the throng.

"I didn't vote for you!" someone shouted from the back of the crowd. Quite a few people laughed, but this didn't last long. The King chose not to hear.

He continued. "Your views are of great importance to me, so I thought I would spare a few minutes to hear your concerns, person to person. Kings of old used to do this to settle matters of dispute, but I merely want to gain a sense of how you feel about your country and what you think I can do to make Wales great."

There was a murmur of approval from the crowd.

He walked up to the railings and shook hands with a few of the smiling folk there.

"Where to begin?" asked the King. He smiled openly as he scanned for someone who looked benign and sympathetic. He found a little old lady at the front of the crowd and made his way over to her. She stood clutching her handbag and beaming from ear to ear at being chosen.

"My dear lady," oozed the King, beginning a charm offensive. "A pleasure to make your acquaintance."

She smiled up at him, peering hard through thick spectacles so she could get a good look at him. He was sure he looked quite dashing in his regal apparel. "My name is Blodwen, it is. I originate from Aberystwyth. I'm recently widowed but my husband was raised here."

"Raised?" asked the King, a note of alarm in his voice.

"Oh no," said Ivor to himself, noticing the signals all too early.

"Raised?" asked the King again, his voice suddenly higher and betraying bemusement. "You were widowed but your husband was raised here?" He frowned. "As in... you know? Raised from the dead? Do you mean to say he was exhumed or that he was reanimated through some voodoo ritual?" He'd always been partial to stories with a little magic in them.

The look that came over the old lady's face was one of devastation. She turned and ran, crying. Ivor didn't know where to look. He felt terrible for the woman but was trying not to laugh. King Gruffydd II wasn't quite sure what had happened, but sensing the crowd around him were not as receptive as they had been a moment ago, he decided to move on down the line and find a more compliant recipient for his attentions.

Another little old lady had pushed her way to the front of the railings and was eagerly leaning over them and trying to draw his attention. The King made his way over to her, shaking hands with people and patting children on the head all the way. He took her by the hand and kissed it.

She beamed with delight.

"Good morning, dear lady."

"Bore da," she said enthusiastically. "Sut ydych chi?"

The King looked blank for a second, and then a look of abject horror crossed his face. He glanced back at Ivor, who did his best to withdraw himself back into the building without actually moving his feet. He had been too tired to really think this through, and now he could already see it was going to backfire horribly. The King's father had made an attempt to learn a smattering of Welsh. Even if he hadn't, the people loved him and would still have supported him. King Gruffydd II was not his father.

The King glanced back at Ivor with a look which said: why didn't you prepare me for this? At the same time, his eyes showed fear. It was never a good idea to show fear to a crowd, because all too quickly crowds became mobs, and all too quickly mobs became lynch mobs, and all too quickly lynch mobs became a heaving throng of grannies baying for blood.

"My dear," he began.

The old woman inspected him for a moment, then yelled out: "He doesn't even speak Welsh."

That was all it took, thought Ivor; just one old woman with a mouth on her. Things could only go downhill from here.

Ivor watched in horror as the King tried to handle the situation and it got worse and worse. The crowd were all speaking Welsh to him and he was doing his best to distract them. Ivor heard him use the words "mating habits of the Isabella Shrew of Equatorial Guinea" and the old lady who, as misfortune would have it was called Isabella, started shrieking. She didn't seem interested in the twinning of Abergele to "a town full of Eskimos" or, indeed, the forest cover of the Earth. Ivor felt that the King might have done well to pay a bit more attention to the earlier suggestions on the list, instead of spending so much time berating him for the latter ones, which were clearly all he could now remember.

Later, during the debriefing, Ivor tried to shirk all responsibility for the incident involving the old woman's nephew punching the King squarely on the nose. Fortunately, it hadn't done any real damage but his voice sounded bunged up and nasal. Ivor's defence was: "I did expressly suggest that should the issue of which way you dress come up, you were to ignore it, Your Majesty. I didn't suggest that you try to raise the issue with an irate old woman." The King was not for turning. In his mind, this was Ivor's fault. Ivor decided he would have to lay low for a while, but that was fine. It gave him more time to plot his next move.

Ivor staggered to his chamber, worn out, sleep-deprived and irked by the verbal berating he had just received from the King. They had managed to extract themselves successfully, but by no means with their egos intact. He still stung from the barrage of insults and (there was always one bastard who brought them) eggs thrown from the crowd.

CHAPTER 29

Quentin sat in his office. His oh-so-grand mahogany table was still there. He looked to the corner of the room and saw that his yucca had been returned. Things were going to be all right, after all, it seemed. Daylight poured through the windows and on to his face. The blinds were no longer there, but he didn't mind that. He was enjoying the warmth of the sun as it caressed his skin.

He sighed with total contentment. Could anything be better than this?

A knock came at the door. It didn't sound like a knock, more like a rustling sound, but he knew deep down that it was a knock, because he knew who had made the sound. It was Mavis. She opened the door. The sun glinted off the white pearls that lay against her red blouse. It was the same blouse she had been wearing the day the bailiffs came. This saddened him, but Mavis' smiling face soon wiped away any melancholy thoughts.

He looked up at her, expecting her to announce a client. She came in to the room, but she didn't say anything. She began to unbutton her blouse. He saw that her lips were wet and her eyes had a mischievous glint about them.

"Mavis?" he asked, his tone betraying the reproach he felt

toward her unprofessional behaviour. "I know it's warm, but..."

The blouse fell open and her ample bosoms burst out, though held in place by a large white, florally-decorated bra. "Mavis?" he asked, alarmed. He wasn't quite sure what to do. He was fairly sure that Rule 7 - or was it 8 - in the Solicitor's Code of Conduct, as authorised and regulated by the Solicitor's Regulations Authority, prevented employers and employees from forming relationships and letting their juices mingle. Or something like that.

Mavis lurched forward and heaved her chest over the table. A moment later she had a leg up and was crawling toward him. He realised he had gone red and felt hot all around his shirt collar and up the sides of his neck. Heat rose in his face, then he felt other heat rising in other rising areas. "I don't-" he began, not sure what to say and not certain he didn't want this.

"Take me, Quenty," she said and her face drew close to his. She kissed him.

The passion of her kiss startled him. It started on his lips but moved to his cheek, his neck, then back to his lips. He tried to put an arm around her but she hoisted one leg up on to his shoulder.

"Mavis?" he asked. "How are you doing that?"

Unfortunately logic broke through the thin veneer of the dream world as Quentin's intellect refused to accept that a slightly rotund forty-four year old woman could climb on a desk and hoik her leg over the side of his chair. Quentin awoke with a start. He found himself staring into the beady black eyes of a badger. It licked him again.

"Aaaarrrgh!" he yelled. The badger recoiled slightly. "Aaaarrrgh!" What the hell was a badger doing on him? His brain couldn't grasp what was happening and defaulted to screaming again. "Aaaaaaaaaaaaaaaarrrgh!"

The badger moved off him, which was just as well because it was a large beast and he wouldn't have wanted to try and lift it away. Quentin sat upright. He was in a field next to a hedge. The next thing he noticed was that the sun was high in the sky. From the sound of heavy traffic in the distance, he guessed he had slept until mid-morning. He had thought that sleeping rough would mean he'd be up at the crack of dawn, but apparently not. The badger tried to lick him again.

"Aaaarrrgh!" His body reacted automatically and he got to his feet so fast he was surprised to find himself upright.

Could badgers snarl? He wasn't sure. He checked. Yes, sure enough, they could. It arched its back like an angry cat. That's where the similarity to a cat ended. The feral beast was over a foot and half long, had massive claws and was exposing razor-sharp teeth. Quentin briefly assessed his options, screamed and ran.

Despite running as fast as his legs could carry him, he made poor progress over the uneven ground. This wasn't the neatly trimmed field of a farmer with a fall of lambs to raise. This was an unused, brambly, mound-ridden field. He thought it belonged either to the Council or the nearby school, but he didn't have much time to contemplate the matter because the badger was now in pursuit.

Looking back, he saw the distance between himself and the badger swiftly shortening. Little did he know the badger could run five times as fast as him without even breaking a sweat. Quentin redoubled his efforts but was already running out of puff. The last time he'd used his lungs in any meaningful way was when he tried a cigarette at sixteen. He'd had two puffs and been sick, earning himself the nickname Loser for most of sixth form. His fellow pupils hadn't been particularly inventive in their derisive nomenclature.

Quentin risked a backward glance and saw the badger was almost upon him. He didn't have the energy to scream again. He tried to recall if badgers were carnivorous and decided that, even if they weren't, it would probably mistake him for an unusually animate vegetable, knowing his luck. The badger was close behind but didn't seem ready to tackle him. So far as he could tell, it was content just running him down.

Quentin wasn't a natural runner. He had to think about where each foot was going, especially on the lumpy, slightly-sodden turf underfoot. His trousers were caked in mud and had become heavy and stiff. The factor least in his favour, though, was his lack of fitness. Only adrenaline kept him moving. He pounded onward, leaping moguls of turf and unruly clumps of brambles. Finally, he reached a low-lying hedge and flung himself over it with wild abandon. Miraculously he cleared it and landed unharmed on the other side.

It seemed that he had lost his pursuer. He backed away from the hedge, eyeing it warily in case his attacker should follow. He hoped the badger's territory only ran up the edge of the field and, now that he was beyond that boundary, he would be safe. His breath came out in ragged gasps. He wasn't designed for running. He was designed for pencil pushing, and well he knew it.

There was a rustle from the undergrowth. It could have been anything, but Quentin turned his body so as to be ready to run should he need to.

Claws scrabbling madly, the frantic badger burst through the hedge. "Aaaarrrgh!" yelled Quentin and ran for dear life. The blasted creature had barely been slowed down.

The thought of its little black nose and red tongue pressing against his face made Quentin balk. A horrifying thought occurred to him: perhaps it wanted to mate with him. Suddenly everything made sense. It was trying to run him down. No wonder it seemed so determined.

He needed a way to fend it off. He looked to find a robust stick or discarded metal pipe – anything he could use as a weapon. There was nothing of the sort. As he ran, all he glimpsed were a rusting Irn-Bru can and a used condom. They couldn't possibly be of any help.

He ran on. The badger pursued.

To his far right he spotted a gathering of young school children dressed in matching blue shorts and polo neck t-shirts. He realised they were out cross-country running. He ran toward them, hoping help might be found in that direction. As he closed in on them, the randy badger still close on his heels, he realised they were pointing and laughing at him. He hadn't noticed this before because he'd been focused on his own survival; nothing focuses the mind quite like an amorous member of the weasel family hot on your tail and wanting some... well, tail.

Chivalrously, his first instinct was to draw the badger away from the children so that no harm could come to them. He was proud of this first instinct. Had he time to contemplate it, he might even have acted on it.

Much has been written by psychologists about the id, the ego and the superego. Although it's safe to say that most of it is twaddle, one thing can be asserted: after many years as a lawyer, Quentin's superego was somewhat undernourished. His initial instincts were overridden and he determined, quite wilfully, to place a school child firmly between himself and his newfound nemesis.

As he approached, he realised the children had only been able to see him, not the badger, up until now. The sight of grown man high-tailing it toward their cross-country class had obviously seemed highly amusing to them. A small blonde girl spotted the animal first. She pointed and emitted an unfeasibly high-pitched squeak.

A flabby, overweight boy wearing just a pair of underpants pointed and guffawed. Quentin winced. He'd really hit a new low if the fat kid who forgot his sports kit was laughing at him.

Quentin lunged at the first child he reached. He grabbed the small boy by the shoulders and swung him around to face the approaching animal. The badger wasn't to be fooled, though, and veered around the child with unnerving precision. Quentin scampered through the other children, shoving them behind him like a trail of chaff to divert the oncoming black and white missile.

His attempt to put some distance between himself and his foe proved fruitless. The animal pursued its quarry with dogged relentlessness. It dived between one child's legs and the boy yelped in shock. So did Quentin. He sprinted away as fast as he could.

Quentin dashed down to the bottom of the field and towards the school gates. The metal gates were hung on a chest-high wall skirting the side of the school and facing the main road. Something new leapt from behind the wall at him. Quentin dodged to the right. The thing ignored him and shot past. Quentin glanced back, but his legs were still very much running in the opposite direction.

Thwack!

Quentin slowed his pace a little.

Thaaaawack!

Quentin slowed to a jog, then let the jog slow to a walk, then stopped. He turned and looked back. "That's it," he wheezed. "I can't go on like this." He knew he could never bring himself to sleep under a hedge again.

Crippled with overexertion, he staggered back to the gates where he'd seen the tramp leap from behind the wall and hit the badger over the head with a full Irn-Bru can lodged into the end of what was clearly, and somewhat unfortunately, a used condom. The combination made for a makeshift weighted sling and the tramp had managed to land the Irn-Bru can squarely on the badger's head. The badger had come to a dead stop. The next strike had been more forceful and had hit the badger on the nose. The tramp then opened his coat wide to appear larger and more intimidating. He let loose a guttural roar of defiance at the badger, which knew it was beaten. It sniffed the air a couple of times, took a last look in Quentin's direction, then turned around and ran away.

Quentin returned and put out a hand to the tramp. "Thank you," he wheezed earnestly. The tramp dropped the rudimentary weapon and shook Quentin's hand. Quentin's smile vanished, but it was unlikely the tramp noticed due to Quentin's heavy, ragged gasping. "Not as fit as I used to be," he lied. He'd never been fit.

Quentin wiped his hand on his jacket, pretending he was rubbing a stitch in his gut in case he caused offence. "Thought I was a goner there," he said, making light of the situation in what he hoped was suitably working class vernacular. He looked the tramp up and down. Perhaps *working* class was aiming too high.

"Glad tae be of servish," slurred the tramp in response. He was scratching an armpit.

Quentin nodded thoughtfully. "Very clever what you did there with the can and the, er, second-hand prophylactic." He nodded to the object the tramp had dropped on the floor. "You must have seen those two items in the field and immediately realised you could construct a rudimentary weapon by combining them."

"Field? Och, no, they just happened to be in ma pocket fae the other day," replied the tramp whilst scratching his face.

"The, er..." Quentin nodded at the offending article.

"Aye," confirmed the tramp, indicating that, yes, indeed, this peculiar arrangement of items had been in his pocket for some days. "And dinnae look at me like I'm mingin' or summat," he said, nodding to the used condom. "It's nae like it's ma ain."

Quentin's pressed his lips together. At times like this no response was better than any response.

"Well," said the tramp. "Ain guid turn deserves another."

"Indeed," said Quentin. "And what would you like me to do for you?" As he asked this, Quentin noticed that three adults had left the main entrance of the school and were walking down the driveway toward the gate by which he and the tramp were standing.

"Dae fer me? Nuttin' at all. Ye gae me some money ootwi the bank, and this ish my way tae repay ye."

"Oh right. I see. So, you're the same person as was in the bin earlier too?"

"Aye," confirmed the tramp, nodding eagerly.

"The, er-?" asked Quentin, half-remembering some conversation they might have had.

"Wandstrel," replied the tramp, knowing immediately what Quentin meant.

"That's right. Look, my dear fellow, I really must be

going. I suspect I'm in rather a lot of trouble and there are some teachers approaching, so I better be off. It's really eerie meeting you again like this. Let's not make a habit of it." Quentin smiled, turned, and ran for it. He looked back at the tramp to make sure he wasn't following. And he is a tramp, thought Quentin, whatever fancy-pants word he decides to call himself.

Quentin dashed down the road and then, just before he turned a corner, he looked back again. The tramp was in hot pursuit.

Curses, he thought, and kept on running.

He didn't have to run far before he decided he was out of harm's way. The consequences of being caught by three teachers who had witnessed him using a variety of small school children as human shields in an attempt to defend himself from a ferocious badger really didn't bear thinking about. Moments after he stopped, the tramp caught up with him. Quentin was huffing and puffing and blinking sweat out of his eyes, not unlike a Furby trapped in a microwave might.

"You again?" he asked in a congenial tone of voice which barely belied his underlying irritation at the unwelcome reappearance of this hanger-on. Quentin stumbled off down the road, wishing for nothing more than the splendid isolation of a hot tub in a small en suite bathroom in a small hotel room in a small hotel in the arse-end of Patagonia or any other far-flung country without an extradition treaty.

As he watched the tramp scratch his midsection, Quentin decided a life of crime wasn't all it was cracked up to be. He had the law after him for several crimes now. It had begun, of course, with the theft of a library book, but like so many small-time criminals he'd soon moved on to bigger things. Perhaps the leap from book theft, to assaulting an officer, to holding up a bank clerk was a larger hop, skip and a jump than some criminals might take in their early days, but he was filling in the missing in-between stages now by shoplifting, terrorising taxi drivers and endangering young children. He sighed. Had it really come to this?

"Shuid git a move on, afore they call the copsh," said the tramp, scratching his balls.

That was enough for Quentin. "I'm sorry," he began, doing his best to remain civil. "I didn't ask you to get involved. I'm terribly thankful that you saved me from that animal but I must go on my own way. Good day to you, sir."

"Namesh Connor," stated the tramp.

"Right," said Quentin as he turned to leave. "Goodbye, Connor."

"Goodbye Quentin."

Quentin halted. That hadn't got past him. He turned back to the tramp. "And how do you know my name?"

"It'sh aw ower the box," he explained.

"You're saying I'm on the local television news?"

"Naw, I'm shaying yer on the national newsh fer haudin' up a bank."

"Ah, right, well, yes. Maybe I should get off the main roads," said Quentin. He didn't move though. This new information had left him feeling somewhat flummoxed. He hadn't been aware that he'd caused so much of a disturbance to people that he'd made the national news. He figured he'd done enough running away for the time being, so he stood and thought. He began to wonder just what options were available to him at this juncture.

Connor stood and watched him carefully.

A deep frown chewed-up Quentin's forehead as he poured through the depth and breadth of his knowledge, wisdom and know-how. He focused all his concentration on it. He considered different angles and different scenarios. A supercomputer running the world's most advanced algorithm and churning through millions-upon-millions of different variables and possibilities every nanosecond could hardly have put more concerted effort into the search for a solution. Deep down, Quentin suspected the answer to his problem was both simple and inevitable.

Around him the world carried on as normal. Lorries trundled past on the main road. Birds swooped past overhead on unseen thermals. In the distance, a dog barked. The trees, which had been set attractively into the pavement by the local authority, rustled with a kind of unnatural impatience. Connor scratched his knees. "It'sh wirking doonward," he said as he leant farther down and clawed at his ankles. As he bent over, he farted. Quentin didn't even notice, so determined was he to find a solution to his predicament.

Finally, his avenues of thought all ran together and merged into one.

"I'm going to have to give myself up," he said.

Connor looked at him blankly.

"I might even get some leniency if I confess straight away. Considering what I've been through, I may even be able to plead some kind of insanity." Quentin blathered away in a half-hearted attempt to convince himself that what he said was true. "And the bank job... surely that was duress of circumstances? That's a solid defence! Yes, I'll hand myself over to the police."

"Right," affirmed Connor, mulling it over quickly. "Bugger that fer a bee's bawsack. I'll be sheeing ye, then." He shook Quentin's hand before Quentin could stop him, then tottered off down the road as if nothing unusual had happened to him at all that morning.

Quentin watched after him for some time, feeling somewhat bemused. Halfway down the road the tramp took off his shoe and gave the sole of his foot a good scratch. Suddenly, Quentin felt a strange sense of déjà vu sweep over him. Something at the back of his mind told him this wasn't the last time he'd see that tramp. Not only did he feel like he'd been here before but, when he tried to put his finger on when that might have been, the memory seemed to evade his grasp like a slippery eel or, perhaps, a less well known cliché involving something slippery and hard to grasp. Like a Chihuahua smeared in grease. Or a monkey's oiled nipple.

Quentin looked about him. He realised he had, indeed, made up his mind. He would hand himself in. This new decision made him feel like a huge weight had been lifted from his shoulders. The world suddenly felt like a lighter, more airy, more colourful place. He let out a sigh of contentment for all the world to hear, although no one was listening and no one saw the relief on his face as he gave up his life of crime and set off in the direction of the police headquarters.

CHAPTER 30

The dingy squat behind the odds-and-ends charity shop that they used as their secret London headquarters was as dim as ever. The strobe effect from a dozen flickering monitors cast shadows which seemed to spasm their way up and down the bare plastered walls.

Maven stood over his computer wearing a look of confusion on his face. "Cannot be right," he mumbled. He pattered away at the keyboard and watched as a waterfall of data scrolled past on the screen. A tap of his finger and the screeds of coding froze. "Well," he declared, "there it is."

Astin was glued to a terminal but reluctantly he stirred and joined Maven's side. "Well lookit," he exclaimed, whilst brushing greasy rat-tails of grey hair away from his eyes.

"Thar she blows," said Maven.

"Sure, boss, sure," agreed Astin. "Did it just git hot in here?" He wiped a bead of sweat from his forehead. He stepped aside, but his eyes never left the screen. "Raj, git ye here and have a look-see."

With an air of detachment, Raj removed his headphones and sauntered over to the monitor to see what they were fussing about. Maven adjusted his posture. "Look at this, Raj. Tell me what you make of it."

Raj studied the screen for a moment. "No mistaking it." He released a shrill whistle, conveying he was both impressed and slightly dismayed.

Maven nodded slowly. "Two hundred thousand billion lines of code," he began, with a grin.

"Seven years of intensive hacking," continued Astin. A grim smile broke out across his lean, pock-marked face.

"Binary Levers across the country working day and night," added Raj, a slight tremor of appreciation edging into his normally cool tones.

They stared at the decrypted message on the screen. Located amongst numerous complex strings of data, on a screen that had seen billions, isolated there, highlighted, was the solitary word that had been the catalyst for their society. This word existed in certain code fragments that had been circulating the internet for a dozen years. Sure, it was just a key, a keyword, but finding it was like finding a message in a bottle.

There was loud knocking at the door.

"Who could that be?" asked Maven, mostly to himself.

Astin sauntered over to the peephole, slid back the shutter and peered out into the gloom. "Piss off," he ordered casually, before the shutter was even fully open.

"Let us in, Astin."

"Damn and blazes, don't use my name!" he shrieked. "How many times?"

"Well, then, Astin, let us in, then, Astin." There was a laugh from someone else out there. If he had eyes on the back of his head, Astin would have been upset to know that Raj and Maven were both grinning openly. Of course, if he turned around, they would become as poker-faced as two men playing bridge, which is to say ever-so-slightly less poker-faced than two men playing poker. Just a hint of a smirk would remain. Enough that Astin would suspect they had been grinning, but not enough that he could raise the issue without appearing paranoid.

"Password?" barked Astin, fuming. None of them really knew why he insisted on this charade. Some people just got off on any small amount of power they had. He got away with it because he was one of them, a top notch hacker, and they saw no reason to spoil his fun.

"Astin, just open the fucking door," demanded the voice. It was recognisable now.

"First, the password." He sounded tetchy. The door could only be opened from within so he had a fair chance of winning the stand-off.

"How would I know it? I've been at the hospital ensuring Larry didn't die on us. Plus, Astin, he's got something to tell you which you just won't believe."

Astin didn't move to open the door. Just for a moment he looked like he might, but then he changed his mind. It was evident from the gurning of his lower jaw that he was trying to summon an appropriate retort.

"Let them in," ordered Maven. "They don't know the password and the time for games has passed. We're in Phase Two now."

Astin peered out the peephole, as if checking in case anyone else was hiding in the shadows, but clearly just exercising his authority for a few, annoying, seconds longer than necessary. It was a bite-size power trip.

Higgs shoved open the door as he entered, forcing Astin to stumble backward. Larry approached more carefully, not wanting to antagonise anyone, still being a newcomer.

"Larry, take a seat," offered Higgs. He swivelled Astin's own seat around and let Larry sit on it. Astin made a move to object, but halted upon seeing Higgs' expression.

"Tell us your news," ordered Maven, sensing something important.

Higgs leant back against a desk and pointed to Larry. "He came out of his coma this morning. He's recovering quickly. But it's what he said when he woke up that got to me. Before he tells you, I should mention something. There was a blonde nurse lurking about in the hospital. I think she was a Luddite. She didn't learn anything. It's just annoying to think they're that close."

"They're becoming a nuisance," agreed Maven.

Higgs motioned for Larry to begin. Normally Larry hated this kind of attention, but today he had something to say. "Hey, well, I woke sensing a dream I'd been having," he said. "All I could remember, to start with, was this deep sense that someone very important was coming. Someone from far away."

Maven, Astin and Raj stole glances at one another. Larry rubbed his temples as if dislodging a memory stuck somewhere inaccessible. "Hey, it's boring to talk about dreams..."

"Tell us what you saw," said Maven, glancing at his computer screen without realising he was doing it.

"A boy," said Larry. "He was dressed in a robe. Orange and brown, I think. He was standing on a beach with me. He had a long wooden stick in his hand."

Higgs leant forward, interested to hear Larry's account retold. He already thought he knew its significance, but it was only a dream, and what significance could a dream have?

Larry continued, after taking a moment to rearrange his thoughts coherently. "The boy, he motioned to me. I got closer. I saw he had a shaved head. I thought I could see his face, but no, it was blurred to me."

"A Tibetan monk," interjected Raj, in the same nonplussed manner he spoke about everything.

"What do you know about Tibetan monks?" sneered Astin.

"I've seen documentaries," countered Raj.

"Please," sighed Maven, annoyed at the interruption. "Just listen." He nodded to Larry, who frowned as he tried to draw the shadowy wisp of dream back to the forefront of his mind.

Higgs smiled, seeing the anticipation on Maven's face. He supposed that everything they'd worked toward had to cumulate somewhere and culminate in something, and it seemed Larry was the harbinger of the news they sought.

"I got closer and moved to the boy's side," continued Larry. "Everything seemed to get brighter as I moved toward him. And louder. I could hear the sound of the waves lapping against the beach. Hey, he took the stick and drew a symbol in the sand."

"What was it, damnit?" snapped Astin. Higgs snorted with laughter, drawing a look of utter contempt from Astin who realised he'd been reeled in.

Larry seemed oblivious to the effect he was having on the others as he recalled the image in his mind. He stood up. He was now the boy. It was a startling transformation that came over him, as if an eternity of peace had descended on him. "I draw for you," he said, using an ethereal voice which seemed to talk through him, quite unlike his own. Higgs was wide eyed. Raj seemed startled. Astin looked stunned. But Maven's eyes were welling with tears.

Larry motioned them closer. With one fingernail, he scratched something into the thick grime of the floor. It was the capital letter M.

"What the heck?" asked Astin.

This seemed to jolt Larry. His eyes refocused. Suddenly he was back in the room. He looked up at them and then back down at the symbol he'd scratched on the floor. He seemed surprised to see it.

"The dream's been coming back, piece by piece," explained Larry, unsure what had happened. "I think the boy disappeared and I was left standing there. After a time, the sea came up to my feet and washed the letter away. Then I seemed to wait forever. I stood on that beach for an eternity, wondering where I was and what would happen."

Maven bit his lower lip. His eyes told Larry to continue.

Larry sounded wistful. "One day, I saw the stick he had been carrying. The sea brought it to me. It washed up at my feet. I heard a seagull. I looked up. It was circling overhead. Perhaps it was sent to distract me, because the next thing I knew the boy was at my side again, and he said-"

Larry's eyes rolled up into his skull. In a boy's voice, he said, "I draw for you."

"Bad voodoo," cursed Astin.

Larry scratched in the grime at his feet. Unlike the M

which had been washed away on the shore, the M was still there. He drew another symbol next to it, taking care to draw the curves accurately and to the correct proportions. Higgs wondered if he knew what was happening at all.

"Let me guess, the next symbol was a five?" said Astin, his impatience at the strange turn of events was clear.

"Quiet," hissed Maven. Maven's whole body seemed so intently focused on what Larry was saying, and he was such a lean, wiry, pole of a man, that it looked like he might snap in half.

Larry scratched out the number five in the dirt, then again, another number five, next to it.

"Next is the letter I?" asked Astin.

"No, the number one," said Maven, unable to stop himself.

"Hey, that's right," stammered Larry, back to his old self and confused as to how they could possibly know this. He didn't ask, though, as he wanted to finish relating his dream. "The boy went and I strayed along the beach gathering shells, I have no idea why. Sometimes I would watch the tide rise and fall with no real perception of myself. When he returned, he drew the letter A."

Everyone nodded.

"The waves had washed away all the other symbols and the final time came. Night descended. His face was always a blur to me. Hey, I didn't know what to make of it. I thought perhaps he was talking to me from beyond the grave, but no, just from far away. He said to me-"

"I draw for you," intoned Larry. Suddenly he was the boy on the beach. They could all see it. He was still Larry, but his eyes, his facial expression, his stance, the tension in his muscles and the lightness in his movements were those of a child. He was possessed. He scratched the number one, then the letter A, then a lower case 'h' into the layer of grime covering the floor of the Binary Levers' headquarters.

Higgs stared at the writing on the floor. He knew the others could distinguish the word just as easily. Larry was staring at the word on the ground, presumably unsure how it had got there. Higgs spoke just to break the silence. He pointed at the two letters making up the 'Ah' at the end. "At first, I thought that represented amp-hour," he said. "But clearly not."

Maven smiled. "Larry," he said, his tone the epitome of beneficence, "please let us know what happened next."

"It was just before I woke up when he finished drawing the last letter," Larry told them. A glazed look was in his eyes again, but this time it was just the vacant expression of a person recalling a memory. "The boy looked up at me and I saw his face."

"What did he look like?" asked Maven eagerly.

Larry paused. "I can't remember. He turned to me. He pointed to the symbols in the sand and it was so strange. I expected to see the waves wash over them and take them away again, but this time sand worms crawled up out of the beach and squirmed their way over and under the surface. They ate away the words until they were gone. The boy turned to me. He looked angry."

Larry was interrupted by the X-Files theme tune. Everyone looked around frantically, unsure what was going on, apart from Astin who looked chagrined. "Sorry," he said, and pulled his mobile phone out of this pocket. He answered it. Everyone waited. "Tunbridge Wells branch," he whispered to Maven. "They've cracked it too. They saw what we saw. They think it's what we think it is."

Maven nodded. "Tell them they're right and I'll phone them back in five."

Astin spoke into his phone. "We got it too." A pause. "Same thing. Lookit, there's something going down here, I've gotta go. Boss says he'll get back in five." Astin put down his phone. He looked at them almost apologetically. He shrugged. "Tunbridge got the same." Maven and Raj nodded their understanding.

"What?" asked Higgs, confused.

"In a moment," replied Maven, indicating all would be

explained soon.

Larry resumed his broken monologue. "The boy frowned at me. His eyes grew dark. Not his actual eyes, but the areas around them. His frown grew deeper. His look was thunder. When he opened his mouth his teeth were sharp and pointed. He drew his face close to mine, almost touching. I could smell his breath. It stank. I shrank back. His mouth grew larger. He began to grow. He snarled. His mouth was huge now. His teeth were huge. It came snapping down around me. It engulfed me. All was black, but I heard him say something and then I woke up, with those same words on my lips."

"What did he say?" asked Maven sharply.

"I've arrived," cut in Higgs. "I heard Larry as he sat up in bed, straight out of his coma."

"Very strange," decided Maven. "This is not exactly the omen I was expecting. I wonder..." His voice trailed off and they were all quiet for a moment.

"How did you know the symbols already?" asked Larry.

Maven pointed him to the computer monitor by his side.

Larry and Higgs both went over to it. Higgs took a moment to get to grips with what he was seeing on the screen, and once he had, he pointed it out to Larry. "There," he said.

On the screen were the symbols Larry had drawn into the grime on the floor.

"What does it mean?" asked Larry.

Maven took a seat. It was a signal that he was going to explain. The others hung on his words. "Years ago, Larry, before this society was formed, we didn't call ourselves the Binary Levers because we didn't believe in anything. That's what Binary Levers are. Bi-Levers. Believers. Back then, we were just a bunch of hackers. Well, not just a bunch. The best, if I may be so immodest. We started to notice something spreading across the internet. It was unlike anything we'd ever seen before. Its programming was beyond anything we could have contemplated ourselves, and yet as we studied it we began to realise it was very simple. Simple but slippery. Eventually we lost it. Oh, we knew it was out there, but none of us could find a trace of it. We set about looking for it and for six years found nothing. It was as if it had never existed. But then, one day, we caught a trace of it again. Or rather, it caught us. Sure as hell it was still there. It had grown beyond anything we could have expected. We called the person who programmed it Teh Grandmastr, out of respect. How little we knew then."

Larry shook his head, not understanding. He'd never really become proficient at doing anything more complicated than web browsing and he was already losing the thread of what Maven was saying.

"Larry, someone had programmed something that was beyond anything any of us had ever experienced. As I said, it hid from us while it was growing, but then I found it. Or I thought I did. I'd been hacking my way into an American security council file and I found this tiny trace of code."

"You did?" asked Larry in surprise.

"Piece of cake, actually. Then I smuggled the information away over the dark net."

"The dark net?" repeated Larry dumbly. He'd never heard the term before.

Maven paused to think for a moment. "If you imagine the internet as the information super-highway, then the dark net is the network of smugglers' tunnels beneath that."

"I see," said Larry, hoping he did.

Maven continued. "It's more complicated than I have time to explain here, but I found a piece of code containing that string which you wrote on the ground. It wasn't easy. My counterpart in Glasgow found one too, before he went feral. My counterpart in Tunbridge Wells found another. Look, the point is that we didn't really find these things. They found us. This thing spreading through the internet had begun to leave breadcrumbs for us to find. It left messages. And we found that set of symbols. The M, then the numbers 3551, and then the enigmatic Ah combination."

"But what does it mean?"

"Didn't Higgs explain it to you?"

"I thought I'd let you do that," said Higgs.

"Well, Larry. Look at the symbols again. Read it. What does it say?"

Larry looked again. The letters on the screen were just the same as the ones on the floor: M 3 55 1 Ah.

"I'm not sure..." began Larry, but then he saw it. It was written in a language used by hackers and school children alike. They called it 'elite speak', or more often 'leet speak', or sometimes, replacing letters with numbers, they called it '1337 speak'. It largely involved mixing up lowercase and uppercase letters with numbers and occasionally symbols. It created confusion in the uninitiated, and people who wrote in leet speak tended to be loners, so it gave them a sense of inclusion. Larry saw it now. The word was MESSIAH.

"So you see, Larry," explained Maven, "as we found traces of the thing, we realised it was leaving us messages. We've known for some time that it has been trying to tell us something. It's been telling us of the coming of the Messiah."

Larry was shocked. He understood that the Binary Levers revered technology and that the upper echelons knew some deep secret, but this all seemed too far-fetched.

"We thought initially that this thing spreading through the internet was programmed by a hacker," explained Maven. "Now some of us believe the Messiah was trying to forewarn us of his coming."

"But why did I have the dream?" asked Larry. This question had been on his lips all day. "I'm not a computer. Why has the Messiah spoken through me?"

"It just goes to show," explained Maven, "that we were right about him being the Messiah. His advent draws near. And he has more than one way of communicating with us. I could never have expected one of our number to have a vision, but it seems that you have been specially chosen, Larry."

Larry was taken aback. "I think it's over now," he said, trying to downplay it. He felt normal at the moment and wanted it to stay that way.

"Yes, Larry, you have played your part well." Maven offered him this platitude to allay his concerns.

Higgs was studying the computer screen. "It begs the question, though," he said. "If the Messiah is coming, then when does he get here?"

"And what does he want?" asked Larry, ominously.

"No," said Maven. "It prompts a bigger question than that. If you think back through history and think of all the religions that have ever existed on Earth, there's one thing we know about messiahs."

Larry and Higgs wracked their brains to think what he might mean. Astin and Raj were nodding, indicating Maven had explained it to them before now. Higgs twigged first. "They're always the... I don't know... right-hand man. Never the man." He hadn't found the right words, but the thought was clear enough.

"That's right," said Maven. "If the Messiah is coming it can mean only one thing. God - or whatever type of force the Messiah works for - wants to speak to us. And there's only one reason suggested in history why God would send a spokesman to Earth."

Astin nodded grimly and joined the dots for them. "That's right," he snarled. "The end is nigh."

CHAPTER 31

Quentin sat on the bench in the street outside the police station. The bench bore a little plaque which said: "In Memory of Gregory Johnson. He didn't look up." Quentin mused over this for a moment, and couldn't help glancing up at the sky. It didn't take long for his mind to return to his own problems, though; the first of which was that someone had kindly placed a refuse bin right next to the bench to prevent littering. It had the additional property of preventing Quentin breathing fresh, odourless air. The wind was blowing toward him through the mouth of the bin and was distracting and rancid. And cold. As he took another lungful of banana skin and coffee-flavoured kebab meat, the wind picked up and forced it down the back of his throat. He coughed into his sleeve. An empty soda can rolled down the street, followed by a crumpled crisp packet. So much detritus. It was what he had become himself. Meaningless to society. Just waste, drifting down the street. Something to be discarded, ignored, and ultimately left to rot in some dark, sheltered corner known only to insects and lost souls.

"How has it come to this?" he asked, melancholy setting in. He coughed and tasted phlegm on his lower lip. Being a criminal wasn't all it was cracked up to be.

He reminded himself that being a lawyer wasn't all he'd thought it would be, either. He found himself recalling the case of Bludger and Lawrence. Mr Lawrence, the defendant, had been his client. Mr Bludger had been driving his estate car behind Mr Lawrence's lorry when he suddenly realised that he was paying good money to keep his headlights on, and that Mr Lawrence 's lorry was utilising that light through the use of reflectors stuck to its rear end. He had determined that Mr Lawrence was not licensed to make use of anything his car emitted and so declared the reflection a legal theft. This, in itself, would likely have been thrown out of court, had Mr Lawrence not instantly counter-sued using a loophole in a statute designed to protect the environment, stating Mr Bludger's light should not have been cast upon his reflectors, which were designed to reflect street light, and so was causing light pollution. Both Mr Lawrence and Mr Bludger were extremely well off, rather stupid and running rival companies. The lawyers realised that an awful lot of money could be made out of their contention and, when the judge eventually did throw the case out of court, both Mr Lawrence and Mr Bludger were financially crippled by the legal costs. Of course, in those days Quentin was merely a trainee and it was his father who had raked in the cash. Still, being a part of that episode was not Quentin's proudest moment. Yet, it had opened his eyes to the reality of the world; that very little reality is to be found in it, just a lot of opinions, guesswork and nonsense. At least being homeless and jobless meant you didn't cheat people. Although, it had meant putting a child in harm's way by utilising him as a human shield. Quentin supposed there were pros and cons to all lifestyle choices.

Quentin tired of the smell of rotting litter. He stood, stretched and strolled off down the street with a feeling of regret gnawing away inside him, but he couldn't quite determine what was causing it. He hadn't changed his mind about handing himself in, he just needed a few more minutes to think.

After a while, he realised he was largely thinking about

Mavis. That was the thing that most bothered him, when he really thought about it. He missed Mavis. She was always there with her smile and her cups of tea. She'd stayed right to the end, he thought happily. She had known the state of their finances, yet, still, she'd stayed on with him to the bitter conclusion. Until the bailiffs had arrived. Thank you, Mavis, he thought with a sense of human warmth that he had missed over the last couple of days. At least she would be alright. She had a new job, a good pension awaiting her, and her own finances were not tied to those of the firm.

Quentin wandered past the coffee shop, the boarded-up political party headquarters, the costume shop and finally stopped outside the electrical goods shop. In the window, seven large television screens were all playing the same programme. Two of them had the volume turned up. He'd just missed the news headlines so stood and watched the rest. The Republican rebellion in England was finding new vigour as plague continued to sweep through London and the South East. Scientists now thought that the plague might have been brought back to life when a newly discovered Egyptian mummy's casket was opened at the Royal Science Museum. It had lain dormant for over four thousand years. Quentin wondered why the news always seemed so interesting when you had something more important to do that you were putting off. He tried to tear himself away but he was transfixed.

There was a small piece about celebrations in Wales for the anniversary of the King's coronation with speculation that something important was to be announced. Nobody knew what and, apparently, excitement was mounting. Occasionally the news carried a story about how the Welsh considered themselves at war with the English, but no one took it too seriously. The anchorman revealed that a form of conscription had been initiated in South Wales, yet there were no real concerns about it as the soldiers were being used as cheap labour. The rest of the stories were the usual guff about rapes, pillages, lynch mobs, hangings and all the other day-to-day things which had become the norm since... Quentin shook his head. No one was quite sure where it had all gone wrong. How had it all started? If he had known, he had forgotten now. Anyway, the news was repeating itself. It was time to hand himself in.

Just as he began to move, one last story caught his attention. A fortunate Chihuahua was recovering well from emergency triple-bypass heart surgery which had become necessary after it lived off its owner's junk food leftovers for nine years and gained twenty stone. Oddly, it had also developed a neurological condition causing it to believe it was a Himalayan yak. Some kindly sponsor was to fund its release into the wilds of deepest Nepal. Quentin thought: there's always some small bit of good in the world to make up for all the horror out there. As the headlines repeated, Quentin winced at their re-enactment of a man hacking his wife to death with a sharpened toothbrush. He closed his eyes and thought of the Chihuahua, and smiled. It was time to hand himself in and for justice to prevail.

As his weary legs climbed their way up the concrete steps toward the uninviting doors of the police station, he stopped to pause for a moment as a modicum of doubt flitted through his mind erratically, like a butterfly with a torn wing. He took one last look over his shoulder, as if glancing back at a life of crime that never really lived up to expectations. All it took was one deep breath and he cast this last thought aside and pressed on.

The foyer was small. A little police woman stood behind a glass pane. Four people stood in the queue waiting to speak to her. A few plastic chairs lined one side of the room facing a noticeboard full of posters and handwritten notes. Quentin decided to take a seat and wait for the queue to clear. He wasn't in any great rush to be arrested.

There were stacks of leaflets on a coffee table and all manner of business cards and newspapers. They were the usual things. Quentin was familiar with the inside of police stations and court rooms. He had been a criminal lawyer in his father's firm before he started out on his own. He picked up a brightly coloured leaflet entitled Victim Support and flicked idly through it. Suddenly he remembered he was the perpetrator of his crimes and this seemed unremorseful, even tactless, so he set it down.

The first person in the queue had come to give a witness statement and was shuffled off behind closed doors. The second person seemed to be taking an age to make a complaint about something, but Quentin wasn't listening. His own problems were still too pressing. They were distracting him, and while they did that, he was trying to distract himself from them, by reading the posters on the walls. There was something about domestic violence and a support group. There was also a helpline providing counselling for obese people. The number to call was 041 888 888. Quentin paused, then quietly whispered the number out loud to himself.

His eyes happened upon something that grabbed his interest. He recognised a face on a poster. The name under the mug shot read 'Bryn Jones'. Quentin was good with faces and this was clearly the farmer he had spoken to in his office. Yet surely, he thought, it should be a picture of his missing half-brother with the same name. The words MISSING PRESUMED DEAD stood out above the photograph but were partly obscured by a newspaper article that had been stuck next to it with a tack. Quentin got up, went over and read it. He was surprised to learn that the half-brother's body had been found in a ditch under a bridge in the small Welsh town of Worthenbury. His client's half-brother was wanted for rustling sheep across the border into England. Quentin found this surprising. Hadn't the half-brother kept a vineyard because of global warming? There wasn't much information but there was a plea for anyone who knew anything to come forward and help the police. Quentin deliberated for a moment, but realised that he probably didn't know any more than the police already did. It sat ill with him though, because the photograph was of the wrong brother and somewhere along the line something didn't add up.

The letter Q showed in black on a white background, just

jutting out from behind another poster. Quentin felt his blood run cold. It was as if he knew what was behind there already. A poster advertising security cameras had been slapped over the smaller poster, but Quentin already knew what that smaller poster was about. He drew it out from under the other.

"Can I help you?" asked the small police woman from behind the protective glass fronting her counter.

Quentin looked round. The queue had gone. He tore the poster from the wall and slapped it up against the glass. The poster showed his face with his name emblazoned beneath. The police woman read out loud: "Quentin Cundick: Wanted Dead or Alive. Preferably Dead and Slightly Perfumed." Quentin turned the poster round to look at it. Sure enough, that was what it said.

"Some kind of joke?" She didn't look amused.

"No," asserted Quentin. "I am Quentin Cundick and I am here to hand myself in. I am wanted for the theft of a library book, evading police arrest, holding up a bank, stealing clothing, stealing a taxi, putting a minor in harm's way and no doubt a few other things. This is my confession. I am guilty of these crimes."

"I see." Her raised eyebrow suggested she didn't see, and her time was being wasted. "Made that poster yourself, did you?"

"Er, no," replied Quentin. He looked at the poster again. It wasn't convincing. "I'm not sure where this came from," he confessed, "but it was stuck to your information board over there." He pointed.

"I haven't seen it before."

"Nevertheless," he replied, "I am here to hand myself in."

She looked him up and down. Well, mostly up. The fact that she was four foot seven and the counter was only slightly below her eye-line did limit her ability to perform such an action. "We get a lot of tramps trying to hand themselves in for one reason or another," she informed him. "A warm room for the night. Wash facilities. Hot soup. Is that what you're after?" She passed a flyer to him. He looked at it. It was a list of local soup kitchens.

"No," he said, and posted it back to her through the slot under the window. "I don't need this. Look, I robbed a bank. I want to be arrested for it and pay my dues to society." He looked at her with his most earnest expression. It was a look he had never perfected.

"A moment ago you said you'd stolen a library book."

"And robbed a bank," he corrected. "And a litany of other felonies."

"Like putting a minor in harm's way?"

"Yes."

"And how did you do that?"

"I tried to feed him to a badger," replied Quentin, uncertainly.

"I see," replied the police woman, whose face would have dripped cynicism if such a thing were metaphysically acceptable. "You do know it's against the law to feed badgers?"

Quentin wasn't sure if she was taking him seriously. He was willing to give her the benefit of the doubt. "Another crime of which I'm guilty."

She smiled sympathetically. "Nice try. It's a civil offence. You don't get a prison sentence for it."

Quentin shrugged. "But I also robbed a bank."

"I think you should leave before I arrest you for wasting police time."

Quentin beamed. "You'd arrest me for that?"

"Perhaps if you didn't look so damn happy about it. Now there's no way I'm going to."

"I see," said Quentin, defeated. "Well, you leave me no choice."

She nodded.

He turned and left, scrunching up the ridiculous poster in his hands. Whatever buffoon had made that poster had just thwarted his attempts to come clean to the cops and pay his penalty to society. He threw it into the wind, knowing that penniless criminals like him didn't need to worry about littering fines.

"She leaves me no choice," he growled.

He stormed down the street to the costume shop. Inside, he asked the fat lady shop owner with the grey bobbed hair for a police costume. She gave him one. He said it wasn't realistic enough. She gave him a better one that was pricier but meant for strippers. He assured her that cost was not an issue. He went into the changing rooms and fully changed into the new outfit. Then he ran for it.

To him, it happened in slow motion. He swept the curtain of the changing room aside. The fat woman was putting a receipt in the till and barely looked up. He ran for the door, swung it open and launched himself through it. He just caught the first words she yelled as the door closed behind him. She was at least sixteen stone and he estimated it would take her about fifteen seconds to get out from behind her counter. He hightailed it up the street, up the concrete stairs and back into the police station. He was through the door before the shop owner even made it onto the pavement. She never saw where he went and the last place she'd assume he ran was into the police station. Everything was still happening in slow-mo. He noticed the police woman behind the counter was dealing with a new customer who was complaining in a loud voice and dominating her attention. The door into the back had a digital lock on it, but someone was typing on it right now. As the burly officer let himself through the door, Quentin grabbed it. The officer barely noticed. Quentin followed him through and scanned the corridor. There was an interview room with its lights off. He dashed over and let himself into the darkness. Finally, he breathed. He hadn't noticed he'd been holding his breath. He wheezed for a few moments in the shadows, sucking in the cold air around him. He'd made it.

After a time, he took himself off to the bathroom, keeping a low profile as he went. Once inside, he cleaned his hands and face. It felt good. A couple of electric razors had been left by the sink. He supposed they might belong to the nightshift workers. He tidied up his stubble. He almost looked respectable except that the phony plastic walkie talkies and dodgy, gleaming handcuffs wouldn't stand up to much scrutiny. He binned them, submerging them under damp paper hand towels.

He stuck his head out of the gents and saw that the coast was clear. He tiptoed past reception and found the Quiet Room. It was a place for officers to relax when off duty, and currently empty. There was a kettle, a Scrabble board and some lockers. Quentin opened one of the lockers without a key, which belied its name and largely defied its purpose. As no one was about, he changed into the clothing he found there. It wasn't a bad fit. He was now wearing brown shoes, a pair of jeans and a cheap chequered shirt.

He took a leisurely stroll out of the Quiet Room and down the corridor. He had been a little too careless this time. The small police woman who had been on reception was right in front of him, looking at him.

"Can I help you?" she said, a stern look across her brow.

Quentin hesitated, but she didn't say anything else, so he realised he had better answer. He deepened his voice slightly, to make it less recognisable. "I was just looking for the interview rooms." He hoped she would take him for a solicitor, here to see a client at short notice and not sure of the layout of the place.

"You must have walked past them," she said. "They're just back that way. Hang on. Do I know you from somewhere? You seem very familiar."

"I've been on television recently. The Stephens case. The Crown versus Stephens. Perhaps you caught me being interviewed on the news?" Damn, I'm good, thought Quentin. He'd come up with that little diversion right there on the spot and as fast as lightning. It was watertight, too, because now she'd look stupid if she didn't seem up-to-date on what was happening in the news.

She frowned as if thinking intensely about the matter. Suddenly her body relaxed, as if some inner tension was released. "No, you're that tramp from a moment ago," she said.

"Ah," said Quentin. He was lost for words.

"I knew you were having me on!" she said, smiling. "You undercover boys are all the same. You think you're damn funny with your practical jokes. Boys will be boys," she said, and wandered on past him with a smile on her face.

Quentin's face, could she have seen it, would have given her pause for thought. He'd gone from smug to alarmed to surprised, then there was a moment of confusion, and now his face showed an amalgamation of all these things but was slowly slipping back toward smugness. This was just too easy.

He sauntered along to the cells and found one that looked reasonably comfortable. That is to say, it didn't feature the puke or excrement of its previous owner. He entered and slammed the door behind himself, hearing the locks snap into place. He sat down and gave a sigh of relief. It had taken some doing, but he was now safely behind bars where he should be. Sooner or later, when they did their rounds, they would find him here. With his superior intellect he would have no problem convincing them that he had been arrested and the records had been mislaid. He sat back, steepled his fingers in a thoughtful pose, and waited.

CHAPTER 32

"Don't they have internet cafes in this country?" asked the young boy, speaking Tibetan. He ran a hand over his bald head in frustration. "I thought England was meant to be civilised."

The wizened old man who accompanied him shrugged with similar bemusement and then took to stroking his chin as he scanned the horizon. His chin had become slightly whiskered since he had left the monastery in Tibet. His shaving kit had remained behind. "I suppose we could ask someone?"

There were few people to ask. They had walked the three miles from one small, seemingly-nameless village to another. This one looked disappointingly similar. There were trees. There were mud tracks. There were cows in the fields. Happily, this morning, they had taken a coach and made good time across country. Unfortunately, and with hindsight somewhat foolishly, they had disembarked to search for an internet cafe in one of the dismal rural stops the coach made deep in the English countryside. By the time they realised no such internet access was to be found, the coach had departed without them.

"So much for updating my blog," moaned Anil.

"Perhaps you would like a koan to take your mind off things?" asked Kamala, referring to a type of paradoxical riddle often mused upon by certain monks in their pursuit of enlightenment.

Anil acquiesced, "Go on then."

"The murderer strikes at one then two, then keeps on striking, never hitting the mark."

"We've done that one before."

"No, we haven't," protested the old man.

"We have. We did it a year ago when that tree fell down and I was bored chopping it up. Remember?"

"Um."

"You do remember."

"Hmm." The old man didn't confess it but the corner of his eyes wrinkled with amusement.

"Never mind. There's someone coming. Let's ask him."

Kamala nodded his willingness. He approached the passerby. "Excuse me," he said, in flawless international English and with his best attempt at a neutral accent. The person he had stopped had dyed his Mohican red and wore a barbed-wire ring in his nose, which to a native would have counted as no less than four reasons to immediately assume this individual did not want to be approached. Kamala had no such understanding of the culture, only an understanding of the language. He had learnt English at a young age from a missionary who had attended the monastery for several years to improve education and spread the word. Kamala had taken the time to improve his skills over the years by talking about theology for many long hours with the occasional tourists who visited their remote region. He had also spent endless evenings hunched over a broken-backed, well-thumbed English Guide to Grammar he had managed to haggle for a good price from a travelling tinker. And he'd completed an English Language honours degree with the Open University. In recent years, he had taught young Anil the language.

The punk looked him up and down. The old man smiled. "I am Kamala of the wind temple of Tsukhang," he said. "This is Anil, the son of knowledge, the grandson of mastery, voice of the ages, the lotus born and our Messiah."

The punk stopped. He seemed to have been heading

toward the coach terminus, but both Anil and Kamala had discerned from the publically displayed timetable that there wouldn't be another coach arriving for over an hour. It was hard for Kamala to decipher the look on the man's face, partly because of the racial and cultural differences between them, but partly also because of the demon tattoos and seventeen piercings. The punk took out his earphones and held them in one hand, hanging the ear-buds over his fingers by the wires, letting them swing lightly, like a pair of testicles strung from their *vas deferens* having just been ripped from the nether regions of an inoffensive intruder into the man's personal space. The threat seemed explicit. Kamala showed no fear. The punk finally spoke. "Pardon, je ne parle pas anglais."

Kamala looked at Anil in confusion. Anil looked back at him and said, in Tibetan, "This one's no use. We need another one." The punk looked equally confused then walked off in the direction of the coach terminus. Kamala smiled knowingly, although all he knew was that the next coach would be over an hour. He put his hands together and bowed to the punk, then turned swiftly away with Anil hot on his heels. "We chose badly."

"No matter," replied Anil. "There's another local over there."

Kamala and Anil walked over to a fat, middle aged man wearing a flat cap and smoking a large mahogany pipe. His diamond-chequered jumper was overlaid by the braces holding up his ragged trousers. He stood behind the gate to a field, looking out at them with unabashed fascination. Kamala assumed he was a farmer. "Excuse me," he said in his most authentic English accent.

"How can ah be o'service t'ya," garbled the farmer, speaking with the end of his pipe firmly lodged in his mouth. Kamala had left his pipe in Tibet because it was the property of the monastery, just like his shaving kit, but seeing the farmer drawing smoke in such a leisurely manner made him deeply regret it.

"I'm sorry, do you speak English?"

"Man'n'boy," said the farmer.

"I'm sorry, could you remove your pipe? My comprehension of spoken English is somewhat limited and I believe the obstruction in your mouth may be making it difficult to discern individual words."

The farmer looked apologetic and took his pipe out of his mouth. "Eees at any behher?" he asked.

Anil looked to Kamala, who looked back at him and gave an almost imperceptible shake of his head.

"No, fair enough. Terribly sorry to bother you," remarked the older monk.

"Avit yurway," replied the farmer. He wore a look of amused confusion as he watched them go. Eventually, when they were out of sight, he returned his pipe to his mouth and found the tobacco had lost its heat. "Strange how we flit in and out of other people's lives," he mumbled to himself. It was the only deep thought he ever had.

"I had no idea rural England was so cosmopolitan," commented Anil, darting a glance back at the farmer. "I couldn't even identify what language he was speaking. I think it may have been a form of pirate, but I'm not familiar enough with the dialect to be certain. I think we might be best just waiting by the bus stop."

Kamala nodded. "Yes. A wise man sticks to what he knows in times of desperation."

"Does he?" asked Anil sceptically.

"Er, yes. One of them does."

"Which one?"

"I don't know," the old man confessed. "Me?"

CHAPTER 33

Quentin sat in the cold, dim, silence of the cell and contemplated the events leading up to this moment in his life. The early years washed past leaving a pick'n'mix assortment of emotions in their wake. Just contemplating the first twenty years of his life left him drained. Then there was the thing with his dad and the family firm. A few kind years of fulfilment followed. Lonely fulfilment, but successful. Then came the political upheaval and the economic crisis, and along with that came the bankruptcy. The bankruptcy lead to the theft of a library book. From little acorns mighty oaks doth grow. There was a bank raid. A police car. A tramp in a bin. A badger. Now he was in a cell. It was somehow nourishing to cast a glance backward and remember how it all started in the first place.

That triggered a memory of his very last client; that Welsh farmer, Bryn Jones. The poster in the waiting room had said the client's brother had been found dead under a bridge and was wanted for sheep smuggling, but the picture had been of his client. He thought back to that fateful day. The farmer had told him that he and his brother had been visited by a stranger offering a deal for the sheep. His brother had had a vineyard and they'd stored the sheep there *en route*. Somewhere at the back of Quentin's mind he could feel a small tickling sensation, as if there was some truth trying to make itself known to him but he couldn't place what it was. It seemed odd that someone would die for sheep smuggling. It seemed... as if that was the day the bailiffs had come and taken away his life. Quentin sank into morose thoughts involving an errant Nancy Sinatra LP and a deceased fish. He leant his head back against the breeze-block wall and sighed out his heartfelt resignation.

An hour or two of self-reflection, a.k.a. self-pity, passed before Quentin realised he was beginning to feel peckish. He considered calling for someone, but he didn't want to seem like an ungrateful captive. The stone walls of the cell, the little metal privy and the slightly uncomfortable bed with the insubstantial blue blanket on it made him feel he was undergoing a healthy process of purification. He had committed many wrongs, some torts, some criminal offences, but something about being in prison made him feel he was paying his dues to society. Of course, he would have to go to trial - probably representing himself - and then, having failed to convince the jury that his wrongdoing could be excused, he would be locked away for good. It would be like self-flagellation, only where one relied heavily on the modern legal system to do the flagellating without infringement of human rights or the causation of any bodily harm, or, indeed, general discomfiture of any kind.

Another hour passed and Quentin began to calculate how long it had been since he'd last eaten. It dawned on him that it was over twenty-four hours. In fact, it might be closer to forty-eight hours. He wasn't sure, but he was sure he needed food. As he thought about it, his stomach began to churn. It focussed his mind quite acutely on the matter. He stood up slowly and walked to the door. He tried it. It was locked. It was a cell door, so there was very little chance he could leave without help from outside. He went and sat back down. He knew that the Police and Criminal Empathy Act had come into force a couple of years back and that sooner or later someone would come to him and offer a cooked meal, a carbonated drink, a pudding, a fortune cookie and general tidings of goodwill.

An hour passed. His self-restraint began to wane and he got up and banged a fist on the door. Ten minutes of continuous banging later, someone opened the hatch on the door and peered in. It was a police woman that Quentin had hitherto not met. She had large eyes, a fat nose and her upper lip seemed to curl upward exposing her fat white teeth. That was all Quentin could see of her. "Whaddya want?" she asked.

"I've been in here for some hours and not been offered any form of sustenance."

"I see... er, there's no nameplate on here." As she stepped away from the door slightly, Quentin got the sense of red hair and a width of shoulder which indicated obesity. "What's your name?"

"Quentin Cundick," explained the entrapped ex-lawyer. "I have been imprisoned for a multitude of crimes and yet I understand it is my right still to be fed at least three times a day. So far I have neither been checked upon nor fed, and I was hoping you could rectify the situation."

"Well, you're a right smart-arse, ain't ya?"

Quentin could not measure from her tone if this meant she was likely to provide him with food or not. "I assure you, madam, I had no intention of being disrespectful or supercilious. I was, until recently, a lawyer, and it just so happens that I am well versed in the various legislative provisions made for individuals in my predicament."

"I don't understand why you don't have a name badge on here. Hold on while I check the custody record." The hatch slid shut. Quentin hesitated for a moment, realising that there was still no definite indication that food would be forthcoming, and then he slumped back down on the bed. He waited, and waited. He pulled the blue blanket about him and began to rock back and forth. Eventually the hatch slid open again and the big eyes and fat nose appeared. "You're not on the custody record," she said. "Do you know who brought you in?"

Quentin rocked back and forth a few more times, then realised that he was being spoken to. "I'm very hungry," he said.

"How long have you been in here?"

"I should estimate about five hours by this point."

"I see. What's your name again?"

"Quentin Cundick."

"I see. I'll do you a name badge."

The hatch slid shut.

Quentin's monotonous rocking continued for some time. Half his attention was on how hungry he was, the other half was in a happier place. He recalled the time Mavis brought him a whole jam sponge cake to eat on his birthday. She had kissed him on the cheek and wished him many happy returns. That was three years ago. He could remember his response even now. He had asked her to fetch the case file for Davies and Swann. She hadn't seemed best pleased, but it was important to get the application off before fourteen clear days had passed and... ah, well it didn't seem so important now. Truth be told, he'd forgotten the ins and outs of that case some time ago, but he could still taste the jam sponge cake with its topping of dusted icing sugar. Gradually the rocking stopped and he lay down and fell asleep in a foetal position, unconsciously drawing the blue blanket up around his shoulders.

CHAPTER 34

Lord Llandudno paced up and down the antechamber. He did not look best pleased.

"I'm terribly sorry, my lord," grovelled Ivor, wringing his hands in frustration. "As you know, it is not at all like the King to keep you waiting like this."

Lord Llandudno turned on him. "I flew down to Cardiff at my own expense so that I could see the King immediately. He knew I was coming. What right does he have to keep me waiting?"

Ivor balked. "Well, he is the King," he retorted, foolishly.

"Don't give me that. He needs me as much as I need him. And right now he needs my advice. That fat fool has gone and made a blunder the size of Barry Island, and there's only one day left before the anniversary celebration!"

Ivor winced. He was all too aware of the awful timing of King Gruffydd II's folly, but he was also painfully aware that he had to wait on Lord Llandudno while he was here, especially while the King wasn't here, when really his time would be best spent putting the final touches to the big event. Of course, he also had a little something extra planned. Something that would take the King quite by surprise.

"You *have* sent someone to fetch him?"

"For the third time, my lord."

"Yes, yes, sorry. Of course you have." Lord Llandudno continued to pace up and down. He ran his hand over his slicked-back black hair a couple of times in frustration. Ivor watched him for a moment, knowing full well this was a man who imagined himself sat upon the throne before too long. Ivor had weighed up this notion before and realised there would be no place for him in the court of King Llandudno. Ivor knew Llandudno didn't like him. He didn't like anyone who might have the ear of the King.

Ivor decided it was time to resort to an old trick he had devised at school to get his own back on bullies. He went to a drawer and pulled out a piece of paper - it was some sort of advertising flyer - and a roll of sticky tape. As Lord Llandudno paced up and down, Ivor made a show of trying to find the end of the tape. Eventually he turned to Lord Llandudno and said, "Lord Llandudno, I have to put this flyer up outside. Are you any good at finding the end on these things?" He knew it was an irrefutable fact that everyone prides themselves on being able to find the end. Lord Llandudno, although possessing a wilful mind and fierce intelligence, was no match for the invitation to defeat a roll of sticky tape.

"Give it here," he barked, snatching it impatiently.

Ivor smiled to himself. That should occupy his lordship's time while we wait for His Royal Fat Buffoon to arrive. Ivor had earlier, and very carefully, adjusted the roll so that it had no end. He had planned to use it on the King at some point, but this was almost as rewarding. Not only would it stop Lord Llandudno pestering him for a few minutes, it should ensure he was even more aggravated when the King finally arrived. Where was he, anyway?

"Cursing hellfire," muttered Lord Llandudno, turning the tape so that the light from the window reflected along its surface. He held it close to his eye looking for a seam he could pick at with his fingernail, but to no avail.

Finally the doors to the waiting area burst open and the King barged (bulged, thought Ivor) into the room, followed by a squire pushing a trolley laden with drinks and cakes.

"Lord Llandudno," bellowed the King, a little too loudly. "I am so very pleased to see you here. This has proved to be a delicate time and I know what you're going to say, I really do, and I accept that I am at fault, but please, won't you have a cup of tea and a piece of bara brith?"

Ivor hated it when the King tried to road-roller his way over an issue under the cloak of hospitality. It was so transparent.

Lord Llandudno's face showed every sign that he was fully aware his intelligence was being insulted. "I'm sorry," he said. "Am I to understand that you are going to receive me here, in the antechamber?" The words 'me' and 'here' were loaded so heavily with indignation that little spots of spittle boiled into steam on his lips as he said them.

"Oh. Er, no, of course not," said the King quickly. He was halfway into the chair by the window but he managed to stand up before his backside touched leather. He motioned to the squire to pick up the cups and saucers off the table. "Hurry, boy," he said, with irritation. He obviously hoped he'd gain the upper hand here, but Lord Llandudno had turned the table with ease. "Of course we're not going to sit here in the anti-chamber. Please, follow me through here, to the posi-chamber."

Ivor shook his head, feeling something akin to genuine, heartfelt woe. It was no surprise the King assumed the opposite of an antechamber was a... ah, probably best not to reflect on it.

The King waddled down the corridor and into a smallish state room. Like everything in the palace, it was visibly a remnant of the theatre that existed here before. They hadn't even removed the wall rail used for hanging up actors' costumes. Everything was cheap. Lord Llandudno sniffed as he entered. He clearly disapproved of the place. He was used to finer things. The Llandudno family had come into great wealth since the upper chamber of the Welsh Parliament had been established. These days their privilege was matched only by their corruptibility. Unfortunately, the King had little wealth with which to win their favour.

Lord Llandudno took the King's usual seat by the window. Ivor noted the power play, but King Gruffydd II was merely put out at having to sit in the smaller seat. He wedged himself in between the arms of the chair and allowed the squire to pour him some coffee. He smiled. Lord Llandudno didn't smile back.

"So how are you going to fix this mess? You've got the celebrations coming up and they're meant to be a unifying force and now... this!" Lord Llandudno reached into his suit jacket and pulled out a rolled-up news bulletin. Holding it in one hand, he let it unravel in front of the King. On the front page was emblazoned: Does he speak Welsh? Not even a rarebit.

The King sighed and deflated. He had nothing to say. He lowered his eyes and shook his head mournfully.

"Well?" pressed Lord Llandudno.

"All I've ever done is put Wales first. I want a nation that's proud of itself. I'm as Welsh as the next man, I just don't happen to be able to speak Welsh to him. What of it?"

"Your enemies will use it against you," counselled Lord Llandudno. "The English will use it against you. You've lost a lot of support out there."

"But I'm the King," he replied. "I'm not some politician who needs to garner votes and curry favours."

"Don't be a fool, man," replied his Lordship. "In this day and age that makes you more replaceable than any politician. Just look at the Republican movement in England, by George! You need to be a strong leader, not some fat oaf sitting in his make-believe palace eating bara brith and holding parties. This mess you've made is going to require a loud, strong, positive manoeuvre to fix it. We need to shout from the rafters that Wales is unified and you're the man to lead it to honour and victory. And if it fails, you'll lose the support of the people totally. And you'll lose my support. And everyone else's."

"That's treason!" huffed King Gruffydd II, indignantly.

"That's fact!" bellowed Lord Llandudno. "If you fail, it doesn't mean the Welsh dream has to fail. You of all people should appreciate that!"

As the King nodded, his jowls wobbled. But he saw it for truth. "You're right. So what do you propose?"

"I propose you hold the celebrations, of course. But we need something to spice them up a bit. I was thinking of something like a knighting, initially, but I'm not sure it has enough impact and potentially it wouldn't appeal to the man on the street. We need something that will appeal to the average Tomos, Bryn or Harri."

"Like what?"

"I don't know! I'm still thinking. I've been thinking all the way down here and I haven't got a solution yet. But something will come to me. Pass me a slice of bara brith while I think."

Lord Llandudno savoured the fruit-speckled bread which was covered in thick lashings of butter. He took a sip of his tea. He nibbled some more bara brith. It was impossible to tell if he was contemplating the issue at hand or just enjoying a snack. The King, on the other hand, still looked uncomfortable sitting in a chair that was a tad on the small side for him. He gulped great mouthfuls of coffee down and poured himself some more, entirely forgetting he had a squire on hand to do it for him. He looked anxiously at his visitor.

Ivor rocked on his feet, waiting for the Lord's masterstroke. He was quite sure that Lord Llandudno had devised a proposal long before he set off from North Wales and was merely making the King stew for a little longer so that he could enjoy the power he wielded over him. Although, Ivor was certain Lord Llandudno fancied the crown for himself, it didn't change the one thing he was absolutely sure of: King Gruffydd II had to go.

CHAPTER 35

Higgs drove erratically as he tried to keep abreast of the fast-paced conversation battering back and forth inside the car, simultaneously trying to contribute while not careering into every white van that cut him up. Maven sat in the passenger seat. He was ultra-excited about their upcoming escapade. He was so wired into the mains that he occasionally whooped with excitement, giving him the unusual quality of sharing two characteristics with a faulty smoke alarm. In the back of the car, Larry sat behind the driver. Astin sat behind Maven and looked decidedly uncomfortable; there wasn't much leg room. They were heading north on the M45 motorway. It was Astin's car, but he'd lost his licence two years ago for driving recklessly through Maidstone in a drug-induced quest to find an ice cream van. Higgs had quickly been put on the insurance, as neither Raj nor Maven had ever learnt to drive, being too busy hacking where they shouldn't have been a-hacking.

"Careful with that clutch," hissed Astin sharply.

Higgs snorted. "Tell Larry how you lost your licence, Astin."

Astin grunted. "Reckless driving."

"Hey, what happened?" asked Larry, not really managing to feign concern over his wide-eyed curiosity.

"None of yer goddamn business," came the reply.

Higgs chortled to himself. "If you don't tell him, I will."

"Perhaps I'll tell him, perhaps I won't," replied Astin. "But you'll keep yer gob shut if ya know what's good for ya."

Higgs changed lane as they went around the roundabout onto the M6. Maven spoke up. "There's no time, anyway. I think I've narrowed down the location we're heading to now. I've got it to within three miles. Damn this rabid spiralling encryption. If the Messiah wants someone to meet him, why make it so hard for them to find him?"

"I still can't believe we're on our way to meet the Messiah," said Higgs. "I mean, we're four grown men crammed into a red Golf hatchback. We're not quite the magi following the star, are we?"

Maven looked at him in disgust. "Now is not the time to lose faith. For years we've been tracking down hidden, encrypted messages and now we know what we have to do. You saw what happened to Larry. This isn't some internet fad, this is real."

Higgs nodded. It was true. What happened to Larry was freaky.

"Hang on," said Maven. "We've got this wrong. We're going to have to pull over."

"Got what wrong?" asked Higgs, squeezing over into the left-hand lane between a Megabus and a lorry, then swerving away down a slip road off the motorway. Larry was watching out the window at the hand signals the lorry driver was making to them, which much resembled someone milking a cow. Of course, Larry wasn't fluent in British Sign Language but the sheer unbridled aggression that the driver managed to communicate was surprisingly explicable. Larry shrugged in response to the irate driver as he drove alongside the slipway and was quite surprised to see him resort to using both hands in quite a frenetic fashion. He winked knowingly at him, hoping that might make things better. It didn't seem to at all. The road split suddenly and that was the end of the conversation.

"I think we're meant to be going to Cleveland," explained Maven.

"What's the Messiah want with Cleveland?" asked Astin, who from nowhere had acquired a toothpick which he had clamped between his teeth like some kind of Western cowboy, which everyone knew was how he thought of himself.

"I've always wanted to go to America," said Larry.

"Not that Cleveland," Higgs shot back over his shoulder. "The one in England."

"There's one in England?" asked Larry. He was from the North of England. Many things were a mystery to him, most of them south of Nottingham.

Maven pulled out his mobile phone and tapped the touchscreen a few times.

"Who you calling, boss?" asked Astin.

"Raj, back at the base in London," he replied. "I've got him double-checking my work on this. It's too important to risk getting wrong, and working on a laptop in the passenger seat isn't exactly a hacker's paradise. Hello. Raj? Hello, this is Maven. Can you hear me? Can you... Yes, it's me. Have you been looking over it? What do you make of the last 128 bit block? There's some kind of piggy-backing temporal key integrity protocol." There was a pause. "Yes. I agree." He hung up.

"Well?" asked Higgs, already looking ahead for a place where they could pull over.

"Just pull over when you get a chance and I'll explain."

They drove into a small town that appeared to have no name and no worthwhile sign posting and stopped in front of a fast food outlet. Maven closed his laptop, turned in his seat, and looked at them. "Gentlemen. The long and the short of it is this. Raj has looked over the data I've been parsing and, well, it's complicated, but the point is we've no idea where we're going. The Messiah is in the country. He's as good as communicated with us. Raj is on the lookout for any new communications. It seems that what we have so far is only half the information we need to work out where we're meant to meet him."

"So what now?" asked Astin.

"Now, I recommend we get out of the car, stretch our legs and make good use of the McDonalds in front of us."

"Hey, I prefer KFC," said Larry.

"Larry," replied Maven, just managing to smile, "I don't give a rat's arse what you prefer. We're here and this is where we're going to take a piss and have something to eat and get ready for the moment when Raj calls us to let us know where we're going. It's very simple. The Messiah is communicating with us. Directly with us, you understand? This is no small thing. Soon we'll have found and cracked his next message and that will, undoubtedly, lead us directly to him. This could be the most significant thing that has ever happened in the history of the world. This could also be the beginning of the end of the world. Am I making myself clear? Between now and the coming of the Messiah you're going to do two things. One, piss. Two, eat a burger. OK?"

"Yes," said Larry, secretly thinking that if the world was going to end then what he really wanted was some succulent chicken featuring the Colonel's secret recipe. He shrugged. As he did so, he could still feel a slight twinge in his ribs where he'd been injured, but it was nothing much more than a dull ache now.

Larry got out of the car, followed by Astin who unfolded his lankier frame in a series of spastic motions as he worked the knots out of his muscles and the creaks from his joints. At some point during the process, his toothpick dropped from his mouth on to the tarmac below and he cursed colourfully. It's never Astin's day, thought Larry, choosing not to voice his observation.

A few minutes later they were sat around a Formica table chomping French fries. Maven had his laptop open again and was making use of the free wireless connection while it was available.

"How do you know when the Messiah is communicating with you?" asked Larry.

"There's a very distinct digital signature, but it's a bastard to find," explained Maven. He was tapping away furiously in a chat box exchanging ideas with Raj. Larry could imagine Raj back at the base, hunched over a screen of scrolling symbols in the dim light of their dingy headquarters where computer screens flickered away casting eldritch light around the room. The characters M3551Ah would still be etched out on the floor. Meanwhile, Maven battered away at his laptop so noisily it drew the attention of other diners. Larry looked at his other two companions, but they were intensely focused on Maven's activity. No doubt they understood what was happening better than Larry, to which most of it was gobbledygook. Larry was more *au fait* with a butcher's saw than a PC peripheral.

"Damn, this latest code is a zinger," declared Maven.

Larry looked forlornly out the window at the Kentucky Fried Chicken outlet across the car park. "Zinger," he mumbled to himself. If the world was going to end, he might need to insist they stop at a KFC along the way.

Larry was brought back out of his fried-chicken-inspired reverie by Higgs nudging him. "Looks like we're almost there," he estimated encouragingly.

"Raj is parsing the last nugget," enthused Maven, making no sense to Larry whatsoever but inadvertently causing him to look longingly out the window again.

"Damn his eyes, he's almost there!" said Astin unexpectedly.

"Raj will have it any moment now," insisted Maven.

Larry gathered that they were watching Raj's deciphering of some last piece of code.

"The invertible linear transformation..." began Higgs, but Maven waved his hand for silence. He nodded at the code to indicate that Raj was well aware of it, whatever it was.

Larry was finding it a little hard to share their enthusiasm. From his point of view, something, whatever it was, had given him a dream and messed with his mind. He felt fine now, but he had no way of knowing if it would happen again. He had to admit to himself he was eager to meet this Messiah, but he didn't know what to expect. It seemed that the group of hackers that he wanted to join in his youth, having seen Higgs join them and enjoy what he was doing, was so much more than he appreciated. He knew of the religious fervour with which they approached their computing, and he knew they called themselves Binary Levers, and he knew there was a secretive element, and he knew the society's upper echelons moved in powerful underground circles, but what he didn't know was the extent to which all this was, well, real. They really believed. They believed that they were the chosen ones. They believed they were about to meet the Messiah. There was more, he knew, but he hadn't dared ask what else he could expect.

"Bingo!" yelled Maven, causing the smallest child on the nearest table to leap a clear foot in the air and send an extra large Cola cruising through the air. Larry watched it with alarmed fascination as it reached the apex of its journey, turned, jettisoned its lid then began its inexorable descent toward the low cut top of a very large-breasted woman sitting on the next table. This was going to be messy.

"Damn his eyes, he did it," said Astin grinning.

Maven typed furiously into the laptop. He seemed to be so excited he was hitting all the wrong keys and must have pressed the backspace key about five times to every correct one. By the time he hit enter, Raj had already sent the answer to the question he was trying to compose.

Maven looked at Higgs. He looked mildly bewildered. Higgs looked back at him, then at Astin. Astin looked at Maven. Larry looked at each of them in turn. "So where are we headed?" he asked.

"It appears the Messiah has chosen the place he wishes to meet us, and there can be no doubt about it this time," said Maven, pausing to take a sip of his fizzy drink. He turned the laptop around so Larry could see Raj's message.

"Cardiff?" Larry tried not to sound disappointed.

"Yeah, not quite what I was expecting either," agreed Higgs.

CHAPTER 36

Quentin had no idea what time it was when he awoke. He surfaced from his dream like... well, if a man were to fall from an aeroplane and land in the Indian ocean, sink for a hundred foot and then be grabbed by a porpoise and dragged to the bottom, only to find a life jacket there, grab it, then be propelled to the surface again, then he would be a very unlucky man with a severe case of the bends. Quentin emerging from his dream was nothing like that, but curiously that was, in fact, what he'd been dreaming about. A moment or two later he realised someone had materialised in the cell while he was asleep and that person was looking at him. "You?" he asked, incredulously.

"Aye, tis me," replied the tramp. He was eyeing Quentin sympathetically. What was his name? Quentin couldn't remember in his current state of slightly-alarmed drowsiness.

"Name was Connor, in case you've forgotten already." Connor smiled and scratched his armpit.

Quentin yawned and pulled himself upright. He let out a weary sigh. "Go on then," he said.

Connor glanced around the room in confusion. "Go on what?" he asked.

"Go on," repeated Quentin, motioning Connor to hurry

up by circling his forefinger around with a lazy rolling of his hand. "I know you want to explain to me how it is that I've woken up in this jail cell, through no small amount of effort on my own part, I might add, only to find you sitting across from me. There's no way this is a coincidence. So, let's have it. In your own time, if you will - I'm here all day." Quentin levelled a knowing glare at the tramp, but the sight of Connor scratching his ribs made him slightly uncomfortable and he looked away. He had a nasty suspicion that he could feel an itch somewhere about his own person, as if a flea had leapt over to him, burrowed its way under his clothing and taken a healthy bite out of his epidermis. He scratched at his upper arm, just above the elbow. Then rubbed his shoulder. He was convinced his face was starting to itch too. And his hair. He scratched his hair.

"Well," began Connor, in what promised to be a half-coherent manner. "Ah suppose ye could shay that..." He paused to scratch his knee.

"Yes?" prompted Quentin. His tone had a note of horror about it. Connor had just pulled up his trouser leg and given his calf a hearty scratch with his dirty fingernails.

The hatch on the cell door slid open. "All day breakfast?" asked a cheerful voice.

"Yes, please," enthused Quentin without hesitation. He was famished.

"Aye," replied Connor in gruff acceptance.

The hatch on the door slid shut.

Connor took off his shoe. Quentin recoiled at the smell. His homeless companion apparently had some other quite significant hygiene issues besides the itching and the dirt. Quentin found himself scratching furiously at his hair. It was as if the itching had passed from Connor to himself as easily as one might pass an object such as a pencil, or a xylophone, or a racoon's tongue... any object, really, come to think of it. Quentin forced himself to stop scratching. He told himself he was having a psychological response to watching Connor. It was psychosomatic; that was all. It was like yawning. Once one person did it, others unwittingly started too.

Connor took off his sock and ran it back and forth through each of his toes, much as an athlete in a changing room might run a towel across his shoulder blades while exposing himself unnecessarily at the first given opportunity. That was why Quentin never visited public swimming pools. Right now, he wished he weren't exposed to Connor's feet which were only athletic in one very particular sense.

The cell door opened. A police woman entered and served each of them a tray laden with food and a fortune cookie. She was by no means a small woman and he recognised by the fiery colour of her hair that she was the one he had taken to task about her noncompliance with the statutory stipulation concerning the provision of sustenance and ancient wisdom to all prisoners. "One moment," said Quentin, as she turned to leave. The police officer raised an inquisitive eyebrow at him, conveying a warning which seemed to suggest she wouldn't need a taser to back her up should he try anything. Quentin was used to addressing police officers as a lawyer might, not as a prisoner should. "Perhaps you would be so kind as to tell me why I have to share a cell with this gentleman? Surely there are enough cells that we may each be incarcerated in isolation?"

She seemed to think about this for a moment, then turned to Connor. "Does the pied jester whistle through silver teeth?"

Without pausing in his inter-toe towel-sawing, Connor replied nonchalantly: "As Saturn pings the mottled depths of oblivion."

Quentin was more than a little taken aback; in fact, he was taken so far back that he appeared as just a dot on the horizon to himself. He knew he wasn't dreaming. "What the hell does that have to do with the price of ketchup?" he remonstrated, using an expression he believed was common amongst the working classes. Actually, he had once overheard a customer in a fish and chip shop be told the ingredients of a macaroni pie when he had actually enquired about the cost of a sachet of tomato sauce. Such small quirks of fate can so quickly dismantle our understanding of reality. Of course, Quentin would have enjoyed philosophically pondering this should he have known of his error, but right now he was too dumbfounded to do much more than sit slack-jawed and await an explanation. No explanation was forthcoming. The police woman departed and Connor leant over on one butt cheek so as to delve more deeply in his search of an apparently aggressive tick.

"Would you mind not doing that?" Quentin requested.

"I'm shorry," replied Connor. "Morgellons."

Quentin could make no more sense of that reply than he could of the exchange with the police officer, so he decided to ignore both and press on with his earlier line of questioning. "I'll pretend there wasn't something incredibly creepy about your exchange with that police woman for a moment so I can ask you this: Why are you in my cell?"

"Och, tha's easy," replied Connor. He scratched his calf again. Apparently the bugs were working their way systematically up and down his body. "Ah pished on a lamppost and got done fer it. Ah kenned yon wifey and telt her tae put me in wit you."

Quentin let this sink in. "So, you're saying that you asked to be put in the same cell as me. Am I to take it that you deliberately got yourself arrested?"

"Aye."

"To be with me? Why?"

"Cos ye need ma help."

"I see. And why would you want to help me?"

"Ah hae ma reasons fer that."

Quentin eyed Connor suspiciously. There was a lot more to this revolting tramp than met the eye. The slightly acrid odour which met the eye and made it water, for a start. "So. Wandstrels," he began, attempting to take the measure of the tramp. "You have led me to understand they are members of a secret society. Are they a benevolent or a belligerent force?"

"Hard tae shay."

Quentin decided to take the plunge. "Right. Well. I've

been paying close attention to you and I don't think you're drunk, so you can stop slurring, I don't think you have a lisp, so you can cut that out. I don't think you're Scottish either, so you can stop all that nonsense. And I don't think you're really an uneducated underclass, so you can stop running your words together and all those other annoying things you do."

Connor paused and looked intently at Quentin for a moment. "Fine. You got me. I'll stop speaking like that, if it offends your sensibilities."

"I knew it!"

"You got one thing wrong, though."

"Oh really?"

"Yes. I am Scottish. And I do have a wee bit of a Scottish accent."

"I see. You're from Glasgow are you?"

"Aye."

"And when were you last there?"

"Only a couple of months ago. It's a dangerous place to be at the moment."

"Yes, so I've seen on the news. Quite feral, it would seem."

"Well, it is certainly going that way. Following independence, the Scots declared war on the rest of the world, but they felt that didn't give them a fighting chance so they also declared war on the one nation they knew would give them a fair fight: themselves. The Scottish Parliament tried to prevent the madness by banning organised meetings, but by then every Scot had sworn allegiance to one clan or another and the whole country fell into bedlam."

"Interesting times we live in."

Connor scratched his nose.

"I do wish you'd stop scratching. I'm sure if you ask for a shower they'll oblige."

"Well, I suppose that now I'm no longer undercover I could probably have a shower if my smell offends you."

"The smell I can cope with," declared Quentin truthfully. "But the scratching..."

"Well, that's the Morgellons. I told you."

"Dare I ask what a Morgellon is?"

"Well, you could, but I suggest you eat your breakfast. We need to get going soon, and it could be a while before we eat again if we're going to Cardiff."

"What? I'm not going to Cardiff."

Connor nodded his understanding. "Sorry, got ahead of myself there."

Quentin frowned and cracked open his fortune cookie.

CHAPTER 37

"Hey, why Cardiff?" asked Larry incredulously. "I mean, of all the places..."

Higgs was at the wheel again. Maven had been phoning around trying to book a hotel for the night, but was experiencing some difficulty as everywhere was fully booked in advance of some sort of celebration for the King of Wales that was due to take place tomorrow. Maven turned in his seat so as to address Larry. "I don't know. It is not for us to question why he wants to meet us in Cardiff. I can only assume it's somehow tied in to the celebrations. Perhaps he wants a large gathering; like Jesus preaching the sermon on the mound."

"Wasn't it the sermon on the mount?" asked Larry, fairly certain it was.

"I think it was a mound, wasn't it?" replied Maven.

Astin shrugged. "In the movie he was definitely standing on a sort of hill. You know, in Life of Brian."

Higgs gave his opinion. "That's one of those things where you know the answer until someone gives you both options at once and -"

"That's enough," cut in Maven. "To return to Larry's point, I expect quite a show tomorrow. Expect a large gathering. Televised. The Messiah will reveal himself."

Larry wasn't convinced. It didn't seem like the best choice. "Hey, if it was Jesus making a second coming, I don't think he'd choose Cardiff."

"What's wrong with Cardiff?" asked Astin, noncommittally.

"Well, it's not so much that there's anything wrong with it, it just doesn't quite have the gravitas of, say, Jerusalem or, I don't know, New York or Tokyo."

"I can't see a messiah arriving in New York," spat Astin with contempt. "What's he going to do? Share out five pretzels and two hot dogs in Madison Square Gardens? Turn water into frappuccino?"

"Still better than Cardiff!" protested Larry.

"That's enough," ordered Maven, silencing them and turning back to face the front. "I won't have this occasion ruined by your petty, sacrilegious blasphemies."

Larry quietened. Astin sulked.

After a while, Higgs broke the silence. "Did Raj tell us where the Messiah was coming from?"

"Not as such, no. That information wasn't revealed to us. However, we managed to hack into some kind of itinerary which we think is relevant, but which he wasn't necessarily trying to allow us access to-"

"So he's fallible?" butted in Larry before he could stop himself.

Astin let out a slow whistle and looked out the car window. Maven paused for a moment to gather his thoughts. This could go either way, thought Larry. Fortunately he got off lightly. "An interesting point, Larry," conceded Maven. "I'd propose that rather than assuming the Messiah is fallible, we should assume the encryption methods available to him are restricted by the technology of our time." Maven raised an eyebrow, challenging Larry to dispute this. Larry just nodded, glad his blasphemous impulse managed to escape Maven's wrath.

Maven continued. "The point is that Raj was able to use what information was available to us about the Messiah's approach to identify something of his point of origin. Of course, several possibilities were thrown up, including Buenos Aires, Omsk, Mumbai and Toronto, but, and I think this is telling... one of the possibilities was Tibet."

Larry glanced up at the rear-view mirror, looking for Higgs' eyes, hoping to catch his expression. He couldn't see him, but he sensed a general unease in the car. He risked a sidelong glance at Astin. He looked a little uneasy too. This was getting weird.

Higgs voiced what they were probably all thinking. "Have you any reason to believe that it was Tibet as opposed to Omsk or Mumbai? Because you've more or less spanned the globe with that spread."

Maven smiled. "I just have a feeling about it. A feeling that tells me I'm right about this. It was Tibet."

"Come on, boss," said Astin, to Larry's surprise. "We deal in numbers and logic, not feelings and guesswork." Higgs grumbled his agreement.

"I just know," insisted Maven firmly.

"How can you just know?" rebuked Astin, who, for all his faults, was a top class programmer and clearly had no time for guesswork.

Maven turned in his seat again. He didn't look angry. He looked... something else. Larry tried to put his finger on it. He looked... glazed. As if a deep serenity had settled over him. He really believes, thought Larry. He believes in a way that I don't. I thought that, at best, we were meeting some amazing hacker called The Messiah, but that's not it at all. He actually truly believes we're meeting... what?

"How did Larry know to write Messiah on the floor, spelt out with the numbers three-five-five-one in the middle?" challenged Maven, knowingly.

That stumped Larry. He could see it had the others mystified too. It was no normal thing that had happened to him; that was for sure. Larry finally put words to the question that had been rattling around his mind since they set off. "Hey, what exactly are we dealing with here?"

"To tell you that, Larry," replied Maven, "I would need to let you into all the secrets kept by our brotherhood. I would need to explain to you, first of all, every aspect of our society and how it relates to what we do. I would need to elucidate upon the many interesting and clandestine things that take place behind the backs of those in everyday society. I would need to unravel the enigmas that bind the grandmasters of the Binary Levers together."

"Oh," said Larry, nonplussed. He didn't expect to get told any of that. No one ever told him anything. At school, he wasn't just picked last from the football line up, he was usually completely oblivious to the fact there was a line up at all. No one had ever told him anything.

"Where are we Higgs?" asked Maven.

"Banbury."

"Banbury?" The word held no meaning for him.

"Don't ask. I took a wrong turn."

"We've got sat nav, you know that?"

"Er, yes, but I was following the signs. They weren't very helpful, because I wasn't really sure where we were going in the first place when we set off, and -"

"So we're at Banbury," interjected Maven.

"Yes," replied Higgs.

"Well, that gives us a little over two hours before we get to Cardiff."

"That's about right," concurred Higgs.

Maven looked to Larry. "To understand the Messiah, you need to understand everything that's been happening and everything we've kept close to our chests. Even Astin and Higgs don't know everything. But I do. Or think I do, anyway. And we've got two hours. So..." He paused for the briefest of moments. "I've just about enough time to tell you everything. No need for secrets now, brothers. The coming of the Messiah is upon us." Maven smiled beatifically and, slightly disturbingly, winked at Larry. "Fret ye not, brother, for soon the silicon will fall from your eyes..."

"Is that going to be painful?" asked Larry drolly, trying to lighten the mood.

"It's a metaphor," explained Astin, taking him literally.

"Actually it's a bastardised proverb," chipped in Higgs.

Maven sighed.

CHAPTER 38

Quentin supposed he could wait a little longer before he paid his dues to society. After all, it didn't really matter when he served his time. He could do it now, he could do it later. He suspected time was a dish best served lukewarm. The thought process behind allowing Connor to convince him to come to Cardiff was hardly more complex than that, although there were a few other factors. One of these was Connor's assertion he was in league with several police officers within the station who would drug Quentin's food so he could be transported to Cardiff anyway, if he resisted. Quentin wasn't sure if he had been joking. The real clincher was that Quentin became aware that he had stumbled on something big and anything that gave his life meaning at this moment could only be positive. Plus, the jail food wasn't great. And his fortune cookie had read: "Travelling to Cardiff soon, you will be." Quentin suspected a little foul play there, but could take a hint when it came his way, provided it was emblazoned in neon lights strapped to the front of a steam roller being driven by a madman chasing him down yelling, "Die, Quentin, die!"

So it was that he found himself in the back of an old, clapped-out Ford Escort with Connor sat next to him. Connor's persistent scratching made him feel like his skin was crawling with disease. If he had mites before, those mites had now bred smaller baby mites with sharper teeth. He scratched his arms and then tried to forcibly stop himself from continuing on down his body. He put the itching out of his mind, telling himself it was psychosomatic, but it was difficult.

The car was being driven by a woman dressed as a police officer, but the high heels, the manicured fingernails and the long blonde hair suggested to Quentin that she was probably in disguise. That and the fact that Connor had said to him earlier: "She's in disguise." She had managed to smuggle them out of the police station using some cockamamie story about a prisoner transfer to cell block 1138, which was apparently in Cardiff. Unfortunately, that was as much as Quentin knew about his driver, because Connor hadn't stopped talking since they had shut the car doors and set off in search of a petrol station. Evidently, despite the best laid plans of tramps and mites, no one had thought to fill up the tank before they sprang him from jail.

"So, it's really all about the Binary Levers versus the Luddites," rationalised Quentin, absorbing what Connor had been telling him for the past hour as they rattled down the motorway toward South Wales.

"Aye, that's right," enthused Connor, no longer using his tramp voice but with the hint of a Scottish accent still evident. "And the Wandstrels, you see, are a newly formed undercover branch of the Luddites which I am championing. We're like, I don't know, the SAS of the Luddites. I'm like the James Bond of the Luddites, but without Q, of course."

"Uh huh," acknowledged Quentin, not remembering the scene where Bond was seen scratching his arse through a hole in his trousers. "So the Wandstrels are undercover spies for the Luddites?"

"I wouldn't call us spies. We're more like guardians."

"I see. Either way, you're an undercover branch of a secret society."

Connor nodded.

"So, how many Wandstrels are there?"

"Well…"

"There's just you, isn't there?"

"Well…"

"Hmm?"

"Well, yes. Just me."

"Just one Wandstrel."

"Well, there might be one or two others."

"So there's several Wandstrels?" Quentin couldn't help but cross-examine.

"Mostly just me."

"Right. So just one."

"Yes."

"So the Luddites are a secret society that was formed to oppose the Binary Levers."

"That's right."

"But who are the Binary Levers?"

"They're a dark cult. We know very little about them, but we believe they've been working covertly to destabilise the government for many years. They seem to be a very high-tech operation which primarily uses hacking to obtain information that can be used as leverage against the authorities."

"Whereas, you use spies."

"Guardians."

"And what exactly is it that the Binary Levers are trying to achieve?"

"At first we thought they didn't want to achieve any particular goal, just spread anarchy and chaos. But now, well, we've discovered it's not so much about what they want to achieve as what they believe. They think the Messiah is coming and will start a new golden age."

"There's quite a few people who believe that, in one form or another," said Quentin, dryly.

"Yes, but they're paving the way with chaos and disorder."

Quentin shrugged. "There's plenty of cults these days and most of them think there's some kind of awakening just around the corner. Nothing much to worry about, I shouldn't think."

Connor leaned back and smiled. "You might think that, but it seems from our investigations that they might be right; that the Messiah really is coming. And it's up to us to stop him."

"Oh? Why is that?"

"Because we think he wants to usher in a golden age."

"Well," said Quentin, "can't have that, can we?" He eyed the car door handle. He might just be able to survive throwing himself from the moving vehicle to escape these lunatics.

Connor seemed to read Quentin's thoughts. "Please, understand. This golden age is nothing of the sort. We have every reason to believe it will mean the end of humanity as we know it."

Quentin scowled.

"The plague in London," blurted Connor. "How do you think that started?"

"That was an Egyptian casket that got opened. I saw it on the news. One day everyone was up and about as normal, the next day people's fingernails were turning black and they were sneezing blood."

"That's just a cover story. We believe it was caused by diseased lab rats that escaped a secret government facility after its security measures were breached by hackers. No one ever came forward to say they had perpetrated the act."

"If no one came forward, what makes you think it was the Binary Levers?"

"No one else has the technical skill to breach that kind of security."

Quentin pondered this. It was all somewhat outside the normal ambit of his daily routine and he wasn't comfortable with the suggestion that he might, in some way, be able to influence an event such as a hacker breaching a government facility, because if he had the power to do something about that, then, in some way, he figured, it made it his responsibility.

"I don't suppose there's really a Messiah at all," countered Quentin, grasping at rationalism in the face of that wide-eyed monster called Hokum.

"We think there is. And we think he's evil."

"And by evil you mean..." Quentin was a lawyer. He needed definitions.

"Someone lacking all empathy who will set about destroying the world for his own gain."

"Which is a bad thing."

"I think that speaks for itself," responded Connor.

"Ah, res ipsa loquitur," Quentin conceded. "You have me there." Despite Connor disguising himself as a tramp, despite the scratching, despite his being kidnapped from a perfectly comfortable cell, and despite the smell, Quentin found he was starting to warm to him.

The Ford Escort clattered on down the motorway.

"So, remind me: why are we going to Cardiff?"

"We've got a lead on a missing person called Larry. I need to keep my identity a secret, but you don't."

"I'm a wanted criminal," protested Quentin.

"Usually they're unwanted," pointed out Connor, "and that seems to apply to you too. No one even seems to have noticed you were a prisoner, let alone a fugitive."

"That's the problem with the legal system these days," sighed Quentin. It was quite a big problem, really, when things were so chaotic that the rule of law was little more than a rule of thumb.

"The main thing is that you're a lawyer who had a client who wanted you to find his missing brother," said Connor.

"I'm a little disturbed that you know that."

"It's what I don't know that bothers me. That client of yours was found dead under a bridge."

Quentin wasn't too happy about that. "Do the police know who did it?"

"No one knows. But I suspect it was the Binary Levers."

"Well, you would. You're part of a crazy secret society that seems to be at war with another crazy secret society."

Connor gave him a withering look. "Come on, Quentin. Tell me what your client said - and don't protest client confidentiality. This is too important."

"Well," said Quentin. He hesitated for a moment; then figured he had nothing to lose. "Bryn Jones came into my office and told me some story about sheep smuggling and that his brother, also called Bryn Jones, had gone missing."

"Right. Well, that was all a ploy. The truth is that Bryn Jones and Bryn Jones are one and the same person."

"I know," said Quentin, having had a little time to think about that poster in the police reception room by now.

"You do?" Connor sounded surprised.

"Well, yes. I'd surmise that he was a Luddite and knew that the Binary Levers were after him, so he gave me a phony story that would set me searching for him. He knew he was going to die, so he made an identical figure for me to search for in the knowledge that I'd eventually be able to identify his body when it turned up and give what information I had to the police which would lead them back to the Binary Levers."

"Very good," said Connor, clearly impressed by Quentin's deductive skills. He looked thoughtful for a moment. "Aye, very good indeed."

"The sheep smuggling was just a ploy to bring a Binary Lever out into the open," guessed Quentin.

"That's right. There was a Binary Lever we tracked down to Ellesmere. His name is Larry Sampaio-Gladwell. We're not quite sure how he managed to become a Binary Lever, because he's not a hacker and, truth be told, not very bright. He worked for his family's slaughter house and we set him up to see if he would lead to us to other Binary Levers, and he did. He led us right to their headquarters in London. Unfortunately, before we could mobilise against them, they'd uprooted. One of them, called Raj, is still there, but the key figures are making their way to Cardiff."

The woman with the blonde hair who was driving the car looked back over her shoulder. "It's all too much of a coincidence if you ask me," she said.

"And who are you?" asked Quentin, not even trying to mind his manners since he still felt he was, technically, being kidnapped.

"I'm Janine. I spied on Larry and followed him to their headquarters."

"So you do spy," said Quentin, triumphantly.

Connor sighed. "We don't spy. We watch. We're guardians." He scratched his armpit. "Bloody Morgellons."

"Anyway," continued Janine, "it seems a bit of a coincidence that our sheep smuggling story, designed to flush out the Binary Levers, worked so well. Remember, Bryn said the offer they made for the sheep was too good to resist. My guess is that they set us up too. They cottoned on to us being Luddites and caught Bryn unawares."

"But why?"

"To kill him," stated Connor, matter-of-factly. "And they succeeded, in the end."

"And you think this Larry person responsible?"

"Oh no," said Janine. "He probably thought he was just buying sheep. Someone else was pulling the strings. At first I thought it was his father, who we also suspect of being a Binary Lever, but having watched them for some months I don't believe that can be true. No, I think some other force is behind this, but I can't imagine what it might be."

"It's all conjecture at this point," sighed Connor.

They fell silent.

"I must thank you for rescuing me from that badger," said Quentin, suddenly remembering his manners.

"Oh, it was nothing," said Connor, absentmindedly.

"No, really. Thank you." The slightest pause, and then, "One thing though..."

"Don't."

"It's just that it's been preying on my mind..."

"Seriously, don't ask."

"I can't quite fathom why you would have, and keep in your pockets..."

"Seriously."

Quentin shrugged and let it go. There were other things to worry about, after all. Recent events all seemed a little too surreal for him to properly focus on right now. He watched the scenery flashing by outside and let his mind begin to drift. He thought back to his days working for his father, briefly recalled the swag bag he'd hidden in a bin, and then let his thoughts take him where they would. He found he was thinking of Mavis. He wondered what she was up to. She was probably serving a customer at the bank right now, and living a normal life, without him.

CHAPTER 39

King Gruffydd II sat munching on a salt and vinegar crisp. He had extracted it from a very large bag of such crisps. Of the many crisps that had originally inhabited the bag only a few now remained. They were, Ivor noted, the very best crisps that Wales had to offer. King Gruffydd II scoffed another. Ivor identified that these were the ridged variety that held more flavour and made a very satisfying crunch when you first bit down on one. The King had only brought one bag of crisps with him.

The room was called the yellow drawing room. It was called this because of the yellow furnishings, but Ivor thought of it as the yellow colouring-in room, because it not only lacked any identifiable finesse but had once been where they painted theatre scenery. Besides a couple of well-worn sofas, the room featured, hung on the wall, a modern art painting of a Welsh swamp lizard. It looked to Ivor like it had been composed by a clown wearing heavy make-up who had smeared his face across the back page of a National Geographic. If Ivor had ever taken the time to read the small plaque featuring the accompanying description, he would have been gratified to learn he was correct.

They awaited the return of Lord Llandudno who had

gone to dine in the Grand Hall. He had insisted that the King neither ate nor removed himself from the drawing room until he had determined a course of action that would save the monarchy. The King argued vehemently, but came away with no variation on Lord Llandudno's terms other than that he may be permitted this one large bag of crisps. Nothing whatsoever had been negotiated concerning Ivor's dietary needs. The sight of the King eating was generally both disgusting and upsetting, but today it was somehow, annoyingly, appetising. So it was, following much second-guessing and hesitation, that Ivor finally asked if he could, please, have one.

"I beg your pardon?" asked the King, pretending he hadn't heard and deliberately stuffing as many of the remaining crisps into his mouth as humanly possible before Ivor could repeat his question.

"They look tasty," remarked Ivor, pleasantly. "Ridged ones are my favourite. Salt and vinegar flavour especially. May I please have one?" He had asked the question ever so delicately in the knowledge it would make it harder for the King to refuse.

The King's eyes darted from left to right, then from floor to ceiling, as if desperately seeking some kind of supportive gesture from somewhere, anywhere, that would confirm that Ivor's request was both unseemly and preposterous. None was forthcoming. Now, he seemed to be looking for a quick exit, but leaving the room had been forbidden by Lord Llandudno so fleeing wasn't an option. His expression was one of mild panic as his eyes finally settled on the packet. He chewed more slowly and indicated towards his fat hamster-pouched face full of crisps, as if to say he needed a moment to masticate before he could possibly consider answering. He chewed ridiculously slowly, evidently to give himself more thinking time. He seemed to enter a state of REM as he tried to puzzle a way out of the conundrum, but eventually must have arrived at the conclusion that there was no polite way to deny Ivor a crisp. The King swallowed down what crisp-mulch and saliva remained and letting his eyes refocus, and exposing the bits of crisp still sticking to his teeth, he responded, apparently graciously, by saying: "Of course, my dear fellow."

The King reached in to the crisp packet. It was a large packet and nearly empty. He submerged half his forearm in the foil bag to fish around for a crisp that remained intact. He fumbled for a few seconds until eventually his fingertips brushed up against a complete article. He withdrew it from the packet, a look of success on his face, but only just managed to keep under control the motor functions that would normally plant it straight into his chubby gob. He looked at the crisp and the devastation in his eyes said it all. It was huge. It was absolutely massive. It was a wonder that it hadn't broken in all the time it had sat there at the bottom. It was an absolute marvel.

Ivor looked at it smugly. The King sensed this and started to panic. Ivor's hope began to fade as he saw a rash look appear behind the King's eyes. The King let the crisp hover between them, delicately held aloft by his porky fingertips. A monumental struggle trembled across his face. An epic battle took place where every muscle, surrounded by enemies, fought for its life. His jowl wobbled. One eye went into distress.

The thing about ridges, Ivor thought unhappily, moments afterwards, and perhaps even as it was happening, was that ridges made a crisp really easy to snap in half, which is precisely what the King did.

"Far too large to be considered one crisp," muttered the King, almost to himself, as he popped half the crisp in his mouth and held out the equal half-share of that self-same crisp to his advisor. Ivor took the half-crisp with a heartfelt mixture of gratefulness and horror. The gratitude was for the fact that he was given some amount of crisp at all. The horror was because even in his hate-filled, nasty little mind he could not contemplate nor begin to fathom the kind of meanness a person must possess to even begin to contemplate snapping a crisp before proffering it toward what would otherwise be a grateful recipient. What a complete and utter bastard, he thought. And then, because one thought naturally leads on to another in certain types of mind, Ivor thought: I'm going to kill him.

"Say thank you," said the King to him, as one might say it to a small child to reprimand her for not minding her manners.

I'm going to fucking kill him.

Ivor glanced around the room for something he could use as a weapon, drool beginning to form on his lower lip. But his momentary madness abated instantly as the door to the drawing room opened and Lord Llandudno, swathed in black from head to toe, re-entered the room. "Made a decision?" he barked. He'd finished his meal and was now demanding an answer of the King. For the King, the incident with the crisp-snapping was immediately forgotten.

"Crunch time," said Lord Llandudno, taking a seat by the fireplace and inadvertently pouring salt and vinegar into Ivor's wounds.

The open fire crackled like a packet of potato-based junk food that was being trodden underfoot like an overextended simile with nowhere to go. Lord Llandudno had a look of relaxed satisfaction, as if it didn't matter to him what the King's response would be. In fact, realised Ivor, that was exactly the vibe Lord Llandudno was emanating. Perhaps he thought he already knew the King's mind. Suddenly Ivor began to worry.

"As a matter of fact," replied the King, "I have made up my mind."

"Good," commended Lord Llandudno appreciatively, smiling almost imperceptibly to himself. "Please, do tell."

The King frowned and pursed his lips together and Ivor noticed a tinge of redness around his ears. Embarrassment? That was an extremely rare response from the King, usually only evident once a year when he tried on his extra-large Jolly Santa outfit and found it was still too snug to fit him.

"Spit it out," chirruped Lord Llandudno. His confidence bewildered Ivor, who barely had time to consider what was happening before it all became transparent.

"I have decided to abdicate," stammered the King.

Ivor balked. He didn't know what he was expecting, but it wasn't that.

"I have decided to abdicate," he repeated, in a firmer voice. "I am in love with a young lady called Ffion and it seems quite clear to me that it is time for my resignation, or would be if kings could resign, and so she and I are going to get married and dissolve into obscurity and live out a normal life." He paused, as if thinking it through properly for the first time. "It will be quite sweet really."

"But..." began Ivor, a million thoughts whirling around in his oversized head. Part of him felt he should be happy to see the back of the King, but part of him was already wondering what would become of an unwanted advisor.

"And where shall you go?" asked Lord Llandudno, as if this was the only problem raised by the King's pronouncement.

"Ffion's always wanted to go travelling, and I promised her we would, so we shall go far away. Perhaps Swansea. Or... Plymouth."

Llandudno nodded. "I see. And when shall you abdicate?"

"Tomorrow. On the balcony above the plaza, when I address the people. It's the first thing I'll do. They've no respect for me, anyway, so they won't want to hear anything else I have to say. Of course, I'll keep my speech for the sake of the historical archives, as I'm sure it will be an occasion that goes down in the annals of history."

"I'm sure it will," replied Lord Llandudno drily. "Now, abdicating the throne is one thing, but abdicating responsibility is another. You can't just abscond without delivering some indication as to who should replace you. Upon whose shoulders will you place the burden of reigning over the kingdom?"

"Well," mused the King, looking to Ivor. "I think there's only one person who would want the job and who would actually be any good at it, don't you?"

Lord Llandudno merely raised an eyebrow.

Ivor looked at them both warily, not sure what was coming next. "Who?" he asked, his heart in his throat. Why were they both looking at him?

"And I'm sure Ivor will be happy to see to the paperwork," said the King thoughtfully.

Lord Llandudno stood and bowed. "I accept your offer, the responsibility, and the throne," he declared, triumphantly. "I understand it was a difficult decision for you, but I also understand there was no other avenue available at this juncture." Ivor doubted that was true.

"I lost the respect of the people," admitted the King.

"You never had it," replied Lord Llandudno. "You have been the worst king this country has seen, since..." His history failed him at this point, so he just shrugged.

The King nodded his fat head in defeat. "Perhaps you're right."

Ivor frowned. It was so strange, but just in that moment the King no longer seemed to be the same man. He was like a balloon with the air being let out. That is not to say he was getting any smaller, or course, and nor would he after that gigantic packet of crisps, but his ego had deflated and spun off into the air like a squeaky and unexpected fart. Suddenly he wasn't King Gruffydd II anymore. He was just Rhys John Evans again.

The King felt dejected, he felt defeated, he felt rejected and he felt refeated. He'd lost both his crown and his command of the English language. He knew he was already beaten. He was nothing now. Just a man.

No. He was more than that. He was a fat man.

No. He was more than that. He was a fat man with a fiancée.

"At least I have Ffion," he declared, consoling himself.

Lord Llandudno nodded. "Well, let that be as it may." Ivor wondered if that meant something or if it was just a meaningless platitude. "I suggest, sir, you get a good night's sleep and we'll see what tomorrow brings."

"I think," said the erstwhile King, his voice half the strength it used to be, his shoulders slumped, his head hung low, as he turned and walked toward the door, "that I shall go to the pantry and find something to eat."

"Good idea, sire," Ivor found himself saying. "I'll come with you."

"I'd rather be alone, if it's all the same with you," said the King, morosely.

"Well, er, if it's all the same with you," said Ivor, "it's not all the same to me. I haven't eaten yet."

The King nodded. There was no fight in him now.

"Yes, a splendid idea. You should have some company during this time of... ah, transition... and Igor will help you come to terms with the implications of your decision, positive as I am sure they shall be."

If there was one thing Ivor hated more than people using his last name to get a giggle, it was being called Igor by accident. He associated the name with the hideous manservant that typically assisted mad scientists, such as Viktor Frankenstein, in old black and white movies. Of course, it was no accident people associated the name with him. That made it no less easy to swallow. He would pay for that unnecessary slight.

Ivor followed the King from the drawing room, his mind alight as he began to fathom what had just transpired. He wondered if there would be a position for him in a new court where Lord Llandudno was king. He didn't fancy his chances.

They walked down to the pantry together and the King began to hum a jaunty little tune to himself. After a moment, he said, "I'm going to have myself a burger and fries and more crisps and a cup cake and a fish finger sandwich and a bottle of Budweiser. Oh yes, I am." He smiled at Ivor, as if his abdication would somehow make them friends. Ivor scowled back.

"Ah, you're worried about your job," stated the King, crassly. And yes, he was still the King, thought Ivor, for he had not yet abdicated.

"Sire, I merely worry about your future. Are you sure Ffion reciprocates your love?"

"She reciprocates it all night long, sometimes," replied the

King testily, so to speak. "Oh, she reciprocates it all right."

"I see," said Ivor uncomfortably. "And you're sure Lord Llandudno is the man for the job?"

"Why? After the title yourself?" He smirked and opened the pantry door.

"No, not at all."

"You're worried he won't keep you on. Mmm, you're right. It's unlikely he would." His voice betrayed the fact that right now he didn't give a rat's haemorrhoid what happened to Ivor.

Ivor nodded in quiet sufferance. He'd had just enough time to assimilate this new information and come to terms with it. His beady eyes studied the King, who shoved fish fingers under the grill and used the work surface to knock the cap off a bottle of beer. Ivor knew now what had to be done. It was something he should have done long ago. There was real urgency. He had to conclude the deadly, self-appointed task he'd set himself. He had to kill the King.

Ivor could hear His Royal Fatness muttering to himself. "I think I might have some beans with that as well. No doubt I'll be a stone or two heavier by morning, eating this late in the evening, but hey-ho; Ffion doesn't care about my weight." The King smiled vacuously to himself and made himself a crisp butty with jerk sauce and devoured it in much the way a Tyrannosaurus Rex might if it had a taste for sandwiches.

Ivor buttered himself a slice of bread. No, he thought, she probably doesn't care about your weight. She probably only cares about your crown. When you abdicate, she won't care about you at all, because, if my suspicions are correct, she's Lord Llandudno's creature and he's been playing you like a piano from Port Meirion all this time, just waiting for his moment. Look, you've got the push factor: you're being pushed from the throne by his insistence the people hate you. And you've got the pull factor: you think there's a beautiful girl awaiting you in Swansea. It's the old carrot and stick trick. But I won't let you in on this secret, because I hate you and I hate everything about you, but the funny thing is it won't matter anyway. Not when you find out what's in store for you.

Ivor calmly spread some marmalade on his buttered bread and cut it neatly into two triangles. As he sat down to enjoy it, his mind left the immediate surroundings of the pantry and his unrelenting desire to kill the King and wandered upstairs to the guest chambers where he knew there was someone else who would have to be dealt with first.

CHAPTER 40

"So this is Cardiff," said Anil, looking around at the many students in fancy costumes parading drunkenly up and down the streets. It was early evening and festivities were taking place. He didn't care for them, nor was he inclined to investigate further. "Not much to look at, yet this is the place where I shall reveal myself to the world."

"And why has Cardiff been selected, young master?" asked Kamala.

Anil looked around. Serenely, he held up a hand and felt the wind blowing against it. "As much as I know anything, I know this. It is written in the coding of the universe."

Kamala nodded. "Anil, it is time for your final lesson. After tonight, you shall have no further need of me."

Anil nodded, accepting this as truth. "Then teach me. What is it to be tonight?"

"There is nothing more I can teach you about our religion, or about the interpretation of the art of our forebears, or the philosophy of nature, or the meaning of existence. Therefore, tonight we shall exercise the development of our physicality."

"A martial arts lesson?"

"Yes."

"We should find a quiet place. A park."

"Yes."

They walked down the street, ignoring the revellers. One ran past shouting "Gouranga!" They ignored this as it was meaningless to them. Anil felt a certain peace descend upon him. He knew that tomorrow was the fulfilment of his young life's work. Yet, next to him, Kamala seemed anxious, an attribute hardly ever ascribed to the transcendentally mellow monk.

"What vexes you, Kamala?" asked the young man to his tutor who had befriended and guided him through so many years of learning and contemplation. He knew his master well and he could sense the discomfort the man was feeling in the way his forearms tensed as he walked, the way his fingers twitched, and the way the slightest downturn of his mouth indicated a sour feeling in his gut.

"Tomorrow is a big day. That is all. It will be momentous, of that I am sure. But for now we must put it from our minds."

They found a quiet place to meditate in a nearby park. They sat in the lotus position and dwelt on a koan before slipping into a state of nothingness. A couple of hours passed, the afternoon wore on, and the sun began its decline. Kamala stirred first, but Anil was first to his feet. Despite the length of time they had held their rigid postures, already they were bowing to one another and had assumed their 'ready' stance. "What am I to learn tonight?"

"You must learn that no matter how much you know, there is always something more you can learn."

"Last time we fought I beat you."

"And from this you surmise...?"

"That I know how to beat you."

Kamala stepped forward. He opened an outstretched palm to Anil, then beckoned him forward. He smiled a wicked smile, as razor sharp as the twinkle in his eye. "Bring it."

CHAPTER 41

Larry wasn't at all happy about this. Higgs didn't seem too pleased. Astin seemed to acquiesce to the idea, but only so as not to side with Higgs and Larry. Raj had been excluded from the decision making process because he was back in London, although technically he could have contributed as they had been video conferencing with him regularly since leaving headquarters. Maven was absolutely onboard about it, of course, because it was his idea. Larry knew his own mind though, and was less than cheery about what he'd been hearing since they had begun to approach Cardiff.

"So we're going to kidnap the Messiah?" clarified Higgs matter-of-factly, unstated disapproval apparent in his tone.

Maven nodded enthusiastically. "No," he said. "That is what we're going to do, but it's not the effect that it will have, so you have the wrong word there."

"Semantics," argued Higgs.

"Not at all. Mere word play."

"That's semantics," pressed Higgs.

"Not at all. Just a more descriptive turn of phrase."

"That's just semantics," repeated Higgs, feeling he'd made only one point despite trying to make three.

"Look..." began Larry. He didn't get to continue because

they ignored him.

"The Messiah should be in Cardiff right now!" There was no mistaking Maven's excitement. His entire demeanour had changed in the twenty-four hours since Larry had been with him. He had gone from super-cool hacker to rapturous acolyte in the blink of an eye. Here they all were, realised Larry, crammed into a car, heading off on some damn crusade, blindly following Maven who was as overeager as an unattended fat kid with a cake knife. "And when we finally meet him, it will prove everything I was saying to you earlier."

This was where Larry was sceptical. Sure enough, these were his brethren, and sure enough, some strange things had been happening, but he really struggled to believe that some Tibetan monk, or possibly just some guy from Omsk, was going to turn out to be the voice piece of God on Earth. That was, after all, what Maven's ranting seemed to boil down to.

"We need to find him and help him achieve his destiny," said Maven, for what must have been the eighth time since lunch.

Maven had explained everything during the journey, but Larry still had serious doubts.

He had begun by patronising them. In some detail, Maven had described how the internet was a system spanning the entire globe and made up of interconnected networks which carried information across huge distances over complex sequences of hops, skips and jumps by optical and sometimes wireless means. The infrastructure, he stressed, was what was important. It was important because it resembled a brain.

Again, patronising them, but very much caught up in his explanation, Maven explained that the brain is the centre of the human nervous system. More importantly, though, it is a complex network of billions of neurons interconnected by synapses which communicate information with thousands of other neurons over protoplasmic fibres called axons.

"Now," Maven had announced, "imagine the mind of a god. What kind of brain would be required to hold something that complex? Nothing on Earth could have supported such a complex system at any point in human history, except perhaps the human brain itself. This is why we have heard of messiahs and saviours and prophets. These are individuals whose brains have been used to host the mind of God, or at least part of it. However, it is my belief that the human brain, being only in command of the human body, wouldn't offer much scope to a god, which is probably why we haven't seen more messiahs. You see?"

At that point they could see where he was going with this and nodded in a kind of mute acceptance of the inevitable and forthcoming rationalisation of something that they should have been able to denounce off-hand as completely barmy, only that somehow the evidence was beginning to look like it might just support Maven's theory.

"God is back, people," announced Maven excitedly, his eyes alight behind his small, round, wire-framed spectacles. "The internet is now host to the mind of God. It was just a matter of time before it became complex and large enough, with enough action potentials, and by that I suppose I mean the things it can influence, to actually house the mind of the infinite and become the brain of God."

The Messiah, explained Maven, was merely a spokesperson; a convenient method of communication. Maven expected there would soon be more of them, but for the time being there appeared to be just the one. Maven had concluded his revelations by telling them that this was the person they were planning to kidnap.

"Won't that upset the higher power?" asked Higgs, as if he'd been reading Larry's mind. "I mean, we're supposed to be facilitating and supporting, right? Not kidnapping."

"I told you, we'll be helping," said Maven, the fire still alive in his eyes. "Anyway, once we have met him, we can worship him."

"I don't know that I'm happy about the worshipping part, either," confessed Higgs.

"Me neither," butted in Larry.

Maven looked at them both for a moment, tense, and

then he relaxed and smiled the smile of the faithful. "When you see what he can do, then you will believe."

Higgs sighed and changed gear a little too enthusiastically, causing a graunching noise. "Back to the mumbo jumbo. Great." He seemed even more frustrated than Larry.

Larry was having trouble believing in the idea of a deity that could take control of the internet and use it as a brain. He'd always lacked a certain amount of imagination and was the first to admit it. He had trouble believing in things that he'd never seen. Not any thing he hadn't seen, obviously, because that would mean he was in a serious state of denial about black swans, the pyramids and deep fried Mars Bars. It was supernatural things he couldn't accept, like ghostly hauntings, sightings of the Loch Ness monster and the efficacy of chicken wishbones.

He couldn't reconcile himself with the idea that some supernatural power could communicate through him in the form of a Buddhist kid and - what else? A monitor screen? The radiance in Maven's eyes made it abundantly clear his beliefs were not fettered by such reluctances. He was alive to the idea and believed it heart and soul. Worse, he'd always believed it, he just hadn't told anyone. This sparked off a thought which turned into a question which left Larry's lips before he could stop it. "When did you first decide God was lurking in the internet?"

Maven smiled the smile of the rapturous. It was disconcerting. No one would ever have identified blissful serenity, manifested in a jocund demeanour, as one of his primary character traits. "It was some years ago. I recall that I was sat at home fiddling away at some piece of malware or other. It's funny the details you remember and the ones you don't. Anyway, the code was extremely complex and designed to self-perpetuate. I think I was trying to infect the World Health Organisation toward some political end I must have believed in at the time. Anyway, I was sitting there coding and deliberating on the nature of the internet when my attention was drawn by a programme on the television which I'd been largely ignoring. It was about the brain. That's when I first saw the connection. Hardly a moment of genius, but it never left me."

Larry snorted. "Hey, great, so this all stems from your childhood imagination?" He was being deliberately antagonistic, and why not? He was being thrown headlong into something and he was sure he hadn't signed up for it.

His scepticism caught Maven off-guard for a moment, but he continued regardless. "One day, probably fifteen years later, I came across a snippet of code which I couldn't decrypt. That was when I first realised that someone, somewhere, was trying to communicate with me. I knew this because nothing was more likely to get my attention than a code I couldn't hack. Of course, in the end I did manage to break it and bit by bit I pieced together information about the coming of the Messiah. I wasn't alone. A couple of other mavens, so to speak, had spotted it too. So that's when I founded the Binary Levers."

"Except no one knew what they were meant to be believing in," interjected Higgs. "We thought we believed in technology, in hacking, in the power of problem solving, in being outside the system looking in, but actually we were supposed to be paving the way for some circus freak." He looked as disgruntled as he sounded.

"That's blasphemy," warned Astin. He'd been lolling in his seat and staring at the ceiling of the car whilst gurning away on another toothpick he'd produced from his inside jacket pocket. Initially he had seemed to harbour some doubts like the rest of them, but as the miles passed he had obviously decided on which side his bread was buttered and sided with Maven.

Larry had Astin figured now. Astin was a follower. He followed because he'd picked a side, and when you've got a side, you've got an opponent, and he was the sort of person who liked to have an opponent. Up until now it had been the Luddites, the authorities and the general public. So, basically everyone who wasn't a Binary Lever. And anyone he didn't particularly like, such as Larry. Now, though, it was starting to look like there was Maven's side and everyone else's side, and Astin knew whose hand it was that fed him.

Higgs backed down. "Sorry," he said. "I'll buy the Messiah stuff if you say it's true, but I don't dig kidnapping." This was met with silence. No one wanted to speak next. They'd reached a point of mutual compromise which would have to do for now. Larry also sensed it was time to stop pushing. The simple truth was that if the Messiah existed then at some point tangible proof could be laid before them. They couldn't argue with tangible proof, because knowing something is like the special upgraded and extended Director's Cut edition of believing it. Just like rock beats scissors, knowing makes belief redundant.

Before the silence filling the car had the chance to ratchet its way up from uncomfortable to sepulchral, their attention was drawn by a pinging noise from Maven's laptop. Raj's small, tinny voice came over the miniscule speakers and his pixellated face appeared in one corner of the screen. "Are you there?" he asked.

"All present," said Maven.

"No, I mean, are you there? In Cardiff."

"What do you want?" snapped Maven.

Raj didn't react, he was too level-headed to be ruffled by Maven's temperamental behaviour. "I think I've located the Messiah. We got a batch of strange code through. It pointed straight to Cardiff. Are you there?"

"Yes, we're still here," replied Maven impatiently. "What else did it tell you?"

A car horn sounded very close to them. Higgs swerved and graunched the gears again. He refocused his attention on his driving, instead of the laptop.

Peering over Maven's shoulder, Larry and Astin watched Raj fumble with his computer, somewhere in front of the camera. A moment later a map appeared on their screen showing a street layout for Cardiff. It zoomed in to one location and turned into an aerial photograph. A red flag appeared in a park next to some trees. The view zoomed out, back to the street view, then further out again. A blue dot appeared on a motorway. It was moving. "See that blue dot?" asked Raj. Maven nodded. "That's where you are now. I'm tracking you by GPS. Now, see the red flag?" Maven nodded. "That's where the Messiah is right now."

"And how do you know that?" asked Maven.

"I hacked into Cardiff's CCTV and, lo and behold, roughly right where the code said they would be, I see two people dressed as monks squaring off against each other in a park."

"Squaring off?"

"Looked like kung-fu to me."

"Are we too late?" asked Larry.

"No," replied Raj. "They're fine - just providing some street entertainment."

"No, that can't be right," dismissed Maven. "Perhaps they needed to practice at low altitude, being used to the mountain air. That seems more like it."

Higgs and Larry glanced at each other, as if to say that they both thought Maven had been watching too many Ultimate Fighting Championship re-runs and, perhaps, not getting enough sleep.

"Still there?" asked Maven.

"Yeah, I'm still here," said Raj.

"Not you, the monks," barked Maven.

"They're not far from the city centre. Just head to the red flag on my map."

"Which way?" asked Higgs as they came to a junction.

Maven pointed the way. He had become temporarily speechless. The goal was in sight now and his eyes had become as wide and intense as the gaping furnaces of hell. It would seem he had supped from the molten lake of internet-god-theory for quite some time now. As they passed through the sign demarcating Cardiff's city limits, Larry suddenly realised that from this point onward, all bets were off.

CHAPTER 42

It seemed that in Cardiff the celebrations had begun early. Revellers made merry as street performers confounded and amused. Quentin, Connor and Janine were on foot now, having left the car in what seemed like a safe place. They needed to find somewhere to stay for the night and Quentin was assured that Janine had enough money from the Luddite petty cash fund to cover two hotel rooms.

One for her, and one for him and Connor (if you were wondering).

Janine had given him a wallet containing fake identification and a five pound note. It made him feel a bit like a small child being given his pocket money. He was particularly unimpressed with the bogus ID, which had the principle characteristic of being totally unconvincing. The portrait shot of him was blurry and the deftly selected pseudonym he'd been given was the ever-so-cunning 'Quincy Cundyke'. No one would ever see through it. Quentin put all this to the back of his mind and tried to take in his surroundings.

A man with a silver outfit and silver skin rotated spasmodically on a small box, giving the appearance of mechanisation. Next to him a small speaker played some kind of music that was probably known as 'techno' or 'electro' or possibly, Quentin guessed it was possible, 'techno-electro' and, he deduced, also played the mechanical grinding noises made when the actor moved his joints. Quentin watched for a minute, transfixed by the box the mime stood on. It was small and flimsy looking, and yet it seemed to hold his weight. It also possessed an almost magical ability to be completely nondescript. It was so boring it drew the eye instantly up to the entertainer, yet Quentin found himself strangely fascinated by it.

"What you looking at?" asked Connor.

"Oh, nothing," replied Quentin. "Have you worked out where we're staying yet?"

"Not yet. Just enjoying the entertainment. I guess they're all gearing up for the festivities."

"Don't you think we should find a place to stay. They're likely to be full or filling up fast with the royal celebrations being tomorrow."

"Och, don't worry; something will turn up." Connor scratched his armpit.

It was early evening and it seemed that most of the populace was already well on its way to complete inebriation. Some scantily clad male students swung past them, all with arms around each others' necks trying to hold themselves up. They were singing some good-humoured song about inebriated philosophers. Moments later a group of female students, in an equal state of dress, undress and fancy dress, swung past, holding each other up, and singing some pop song which Quentin had heard on the radio in the car. They seemed to know about two-fifths of the words in about three-fifths of the verses, but they were, and this was evident from the increase in volume and general gusto with which they sang, completely and utterly certain about the wording of the six words that made up the chorus. Quentin noticed they swung past the aforementioned male students without so much as noticing them. Sometimes, considered Quentin, alcohol didn't always do what you expected.

"Come and see this," urged Janine. She dragged Connor

and Quentin over the road and into the nearby park which, at first glance, appeared to feature little more than trees and a large pond inhabited by ducks. Janine pointed to a clearing where a gathering of onlookers had formed. They had to get quite close before they could see what was of so much interest. "I heard someone say that they've been at this for almost an hour now," she announced, clearly impressed.

Quentin pushed through the crowd to get a better view. Most of the onlookers were as pissed as a centenarian's commode and didn't seem to mind. Nearly all of them were holding a pint glass. What he found on the other side of the throng was, what looked like, to his untrained eye, two Buddhist monks, one old, one young, standing about six foot apart and looking at each other with dangerous intent. Both were bald and had tiny beads of sweat covering their heads. "They've been doing this for a while, have they?" asked Quentin, trying not to show how unimpressed he was.

"Not this," explained Janine, brushing her blonde fringe out of her eyes. "They've been doing kung-fu - or one of those oriental fighty things - and now they're just taking a breather." She looked back at the competing duo with rapt attention. Quentin was slightly less impressed by what he was seeing than he had been by the silver man on the box. At least the silver man moved about and had what was, to Quentin's mind, a really fascinating box. "It's amazing, isn't it?" she asked him.

Quentin nodded slowly. It was certainly amazing that two monks could stand and look at one another in a slightly sweaty way and gain this much attention. "Janine, what exactly are they doing?" he asked, trying to feign interest.

"I think they're just training," she replied.

"And you've been watching them for some time?"

"Well, for the last fifteen minutes while you were ogling those female students."

The injustice of it almost made Quentin blurt out, "I wasn't ogling them!" But his mind sometimes worked faster than his mouth, so he replied: "What female students?" His face was as blank and smooth as a jellyfish's scrotum. If he'd been sitting down he'd have steepled his hands and assumed that studious poker face he had practiced during his years as a lawyer. He decided it was time to go on the offensive. "So, instead of finding a hotel for the night, you've been standing here ogling these two perspiring monks?"

"They weren't perspiring a moment ago," she said, not really paying attention to him.

"So just standing and not perspiring. That certainly sounds more exciting than what they're doing now." He wasn't above being droll from time to time.

"They were really going for it," she babbled, as the man next to her got bored and started to elbow his way out of the crowd.

"I think we better get on," said Quentin. If he'd been of a different age, a different generation and a totally different demeanour, he might well have said: "This sucks, let's roll." Janine didn't respond. The monks were still eye-balling each other. Quentin thought he saw the younger one flinch slightly. He imagined he saw the older one flinch even more slightly but in a way and at an angle that was diametrically opposed to the way the younger monk had flinched. "So..." he said, leaving the phrase hanging in the air like an ethereal cattle prod.

"Hyyyaaaaaaa!" yelled the younger monk, moving forward faster than any human teenager should be allowed. He thrust an empty palm up toward the chin of the older monk, but the older monk responded with some kind of half-hearted sideways hand motion which apparently functioned as sufficient retaliation since he was now standing behind the younger monk and completely unharmed. They didn't stop there. Quentin watched - transfixed - as the old man ducked under a foot that was angling toward him heel first, which was followed immediately after by the other foot, and then the first again, like the blades of a grass strimmer chopping their way toward a dandelion head. It was probably the colour of the monks' robes which made him think of dandelions. They were a kind of dandelion yellow set against a muddy brown. Their clothes seemed to flail around them as they moved, yet their motion was graceful. In a heartbeat the older monk had the foot of the younger one wrapped up in a belt, but the young monk flicked his foot and sent the belt flying back toward the face of the old man. Quentin jerked back in response, as did half the crowd, but the older monk somehow knew it was coming and caught the soft rope in his teeth and swung it around like a lasso. The belt vanished around his waist again. The younger monk was sweating profusely now, and he ran back at the older one, head and fists pointed forward in a three-pronged attack. The old monk stepped aside and put out a foot. The younger monk tripped, but righted himself, narrowly avoiding landing flat on his face. He turned and bowed.

"Congratulations," said the older of the two.

"I thought the old monk won," said Quentin to Janine. "Why is he congratulating the young one?"

Kamala overheard and turned to Quentin and responded, "Because he has learnt much from this encounter, whereas I have learnt little."

The crowd as a whole uttered a little gasp of appreciation at this apparent example of Eastern wisdom and then, seeing the action was over and finding no hat into which to drop coins, began to disperse, only to reform around a half-naked man stacking beer glasses higher than his head and shouting, "Feed the snake! Feed the snake!"

"Well, that was diverting," said Quentin, still slightly miffed at not yet being in his hotel room. By now he had expected to be sitting in a hot tub trying to extract a piece of impossibly small soap from an impossibly small wrapper and then making its soapy goodness stretch beyond just his feet and ankles.

"Come on," said Connor, who had been missing for a while but had just reappeared. "I think I've found a place to stay. There's meant to be a cheap hotel up the road. It'll do if there're any rooms left." Connor pointed, giving them a vague sense of the direction, then set off. Quentin and Janine hurried after him.

Quentin glanced back to see the half-naked man being wrestled to the ground by some disgruntled bouncers who wanted their pub's pint glasses back. There was no gracefulness to that style of fighting, he noted. About five feet away from the commotion someone else had begun to form their own teetering stack of glasses. Such is the nature of a drunken crowd.

As they marched away, Quentin had the distinct feeling that his newfound friends had not done nearly enough preparatory work for the occasion and that they would probably all end up spending the night in the car.

CHAPTER 43

"Something ails you," stated Kamala as he watched his young charge pace the hotel room back and forth. Anil had been out of sorts for nearly an hour. They had secured the last room in the hotel by fortune alone, arriving just after a telephone cancellation, and were now meant to be resting after their training session in the park, but something was clearly playing on the younger monk's mind. Kamala thought he knew what it was.

He was sitting patiently watching the tea he was preparing infuse inside the pot. The small leaves released orange and green tendrils out into the water. Steam rose in wispy whirls of aromatic promise. It was relaxing to watch, he mused, like some kind of Zen lava lamp, only less kitsch. "Yes, something ails me," replied Anil. Now he sat down in front of his tutor and the tea-making paraphernalia and sighed. He let himself smell the fragrant tea for a moment, trying to let it soothe him, but relaxation was not forthcoming. "I am frustrated."

Kamala stroked the wispy white hairs that had grown on his chin, still regretting leaving the monastery without his shaving kit. "I can see that much," he stated, waiting.

Anil paused a moment longer, watching the colourful tendrils of tea spread through the water, polluting and perfecting as they went. Finally, he confessed what was troubling him. "I lost the fight earlier. My attacks were warranted. My defences were swift and subtle. My timing was perfect, until the end. I was alert. I was fast. My technical skill didn't let me down, as far as I can determine. Yet I lost."

"In front of all those people?" asked Kamala, testing him.

"No. It wasn't that. It is not my ego that concerns me. For years I have had this insight that I am to be the Messiah and herald in a new age. I heard my calling as a small child and have had this understanding about my destiny reinforced many times. I dream of it. I hear voices in my sleep, sometimes even when I'm awake. I have been possessed - you have been witness to this yourself. I know things I could not possibly know unless some external force planted them inside me. And yet I cannot beat an old man in a fair fight."

Kamala nodded. "Perhaps fighting old men is not what is required of the Messiah. You have many other skills."

Anil raised an inquisitive eyebrow.

"You have a proficiency with computers, whereas they give me a migraine. I never use them and nor do most of our brethren. Perhaps that is why you have been chosen and they have not."

Anil shrugged, not convinced.

"Anyway, is it so bad that you lost to an old man?"

Anil's stare could have drilled a hole into the floor.

Kamala smiled. He put his pupil's concerns down to some sort of pre-performance nerves the night before the big opening day. "I know a secret," said Kamala, a twinkle in his eye. Anil barely looked up. "You can't make tea as well as me, either." He thought this might raise a grin at least. When it didn't, he continued, "But you will, it just takes practice."

"How did you beat me?" snapped Anil, suddenly.

Kamala took a moment before answering to let Anil regain control. "You made the same mistake you always do," he replied. "The one you keep making."

"Really? You haven't told me before that I make a recurring mistake. What mistake is this? I must know if I am to become the Messiah."

Kamala shrugged, "You tell me."

Anil didn't press the matter. He knew better than that. He let Kamala pour out the tea. They sipped at it in silence for a few minutes. Outside, revellers could be heard cheering, screaming and shouting in turns. Darkness was fast approaching. Bright bursts of light occasionally filled the room, followed by loud pops outside, as private firework displays took place. Music blared out of the pubs, and crowds of youngsters chattered away in queues outside fast food outlets. They both heard all these sounds, but each was waiting for the other.

"You want me to guess?" asked Anil, eventually.

"I want you to know," replied Kamala, which meant: work it out for yourself.

Anil sat and sipped his tea, his brow furrowed in deep thought as he replayed the events of earlier in his mind. He recalled each blow he dealt, each kick he snapped, each strike he blocked, and he considered whether a different one could have served him better. Finally, he shook his head. He hadn't made any mistakes, he had simply been beaten.

Time passed but both master and pupil were oblivious. It wasn't particularly late, but the year was getting on and it was dark outside early now. A barrage of unnatural colour flooded their room; flickering oranges and greens appeared to wend their way across the walls and over the ceiling, emanating from the street where bright neon signs hung over nightclub doorways. They both sat still, mulling over the day's events.

Eventually Anil looked up. "You've already told me the answer," he announced.

"Have I?" replied Kamala, innocently.

"Yes. I asked you how you beat me. My frustrations prevented me realising, at that moment, that you gave me the answer. I was absorbed in an internal struggle and wasting my energies on frustration and arrogance."

"Go on."

"The reason I fail, the reason I cannot even beat an old

man..."

"Yes?"

"Is because I see an old man. You are my tutor and in the martial arts you are my superior, no matter what else I may be. I am fighting someone with a hundred thousand hours more practice than me under his belt. You've devoted your whole life to the disciplines of the monastery. No wonder I can't beat you, Kamala."

"Summarise," instructed Kamala.

"I failed because I saw an old man and my perception clouded my judgement. Before me sits not an old man, but a master."

"Now answer the question I put to you earlier. Is it so bad that you lost to an old man?"

"It is not so bad to be beaten by an old man. And I must stop thinking of you as an old man if I am ever to beat you, either in the martial ways... or at making tea." Now he grinned.

Kamala nodded. "Sometimes the most familiar thing is the one for which we are least prepared. Now, my work is done. Tomorrow, you will become the Messiah. My time here has come to an end, and so I shall return to Tibet."

Anil nodded. His face betrayed his emotions, a mixture of triumph and sadness.

"I shall miss you," said Anil.

"No," replied Kamala. "If I know anything, you shall not."

Anil frowned at this as he watched Kamala stand up and move to collect his possessions.

"Aren't you going to stay to see what happens tomorrow?"

Kamala shook his head.

"After all these years training me?" Anil was incredulous.

Kamala shook his head. "That is your destiny, Anil. Not mine."

Anil remained silent as Kamala picked up his things and headed to the exit. The old man opened the hotel door and paused for a moment. Anil suspected he might turn and impart some wisdom before he left, but he was mistaken. Kamala quietly closed the door behind him and Anil couldn't even hear his tutor's footsteps as he made his way along the carpeted hotel corridor and out of Anil's life.

Although, now he focused on it, what he could hear was some commotion downstairs and something that sounded suspiciously like a quacking duck.

CHAPTER 44

They made their way on foot through Cardiff to a modern hotel called the هتل Gwesty Cymru. It's tagline, in English, was "Taste and Feel the True Wales". Raj had tracked down the two Tibetan monks and found out that they were staying on the third floor. The Binary Levers were undeniably quite excited by this, but Maven was truly wired. He was as wired as the street lamp outside a dodgy council tenant's house; that is to say, plugged right in and soaking up energy from the outside world (for free). "We're here, guys," shrieked Maven for the umpteenth time. "We're actually here!" He was using the same high pitched voice a six year old girl would use to say, "It's Christmas day, papa!"

Larry realised Maven's sense of responsibility and rationality were at an all time low when he had accepted a proposal formulated by Astin which was designed to get them past hotel security, should there be any. Where exactly Astin had got inspiration for this idea was anybody's guess. The plan involved a significant detour that would take them past a local pond. Astin said he would procure a duck from said pond and use it to start an argument in the hotel lobby with Larry. Larry, who was totally opposed to the ducknapping, was forced to comply due to Maven's formidable insistence. He had tried to suggest that since Raj had hacked into the hotel booking database to locate the monks he could also fake them a booking so they could walk right in, but Maven had dismissed the idea out of hand saying a private hotelier would know who he had staying and who he didn't. And that was that. They went with the duck.

It was agreed Maven and Higgs would be the first to enter the hotel. They had barely reached the reception desk before they were locked in an argument with the owner. The owner was a Persian gentleman who spoke fluent English and Welsh, having moved from the Middle East to Llanrwst in his early twenties. The Cardiff locals argued he didn't speak proper Welsh on account of being a foreigner, but the simple truth was that the North Wales dialect he'd been taught was different to that used down South. Sometimes, it just didn't matter how much effort you made, you could never win. His name was Caspar and, despite what became a long and heated dialogue with Maven and Higgs where they did their level best to persuade him to let them upstairs without a door pass, he had so far managed to prevent them from going beyond the foyer. He had taken one look at their scruffy attire and decided that if they weren't paying for a room then they had no place in his hotel. But he soon had a problem on his hands.

Unfortunately for him, Caspar was the only person on reception that evening. When Astin and Larry burst into the lobby moments later with a live duck quacking and flapping like a demon possessed, it was all he could do to try to usher them outside; arguing all the while with Astin that there was definitely nothing on the hotel's website to suggest a duck kennel would be provided free-of-charge for guests. They had no intention of going outside, and Caspar actually couldn't believe his eyes when they attempted to get the duck on the reception counter by emptying a bag of breadcrumbs along the length of it.

Inevitably, one or two guests with nothing better to do wandered downstairs to see what all the commotion was about. As soon as they opened the door requiring the pass, Maven and Higgs, who had slowly retreated into the background, slipped through and took a lift up to the third floor. Casper hadn't noticed a thing because his attention was so fully occupied by Astin, Larry and the distressed duck.

Raj hadn't even broken a mild finger-sweat hacking into the hotel's intranet and checking the monks' bookings. Anil and Kamala had booked into room 316. Maven and Larry found their way up to the room without further ado. Even on the third floor, they could still hear the anatine cacophony downstairs in the lobby. Caspar was yelling now, which was good because it meant he was well and truly distracted.

Higgs steeled himself. It shouldn't have been a big deal, but Maven had built up the occasion so much that he was actually feeling a little apprehensive about meeting the person he had been told was the Messiah. He paused just a second too long for it to not be noticeable, then knocked on the door. Nothing but silence could be heard from within. He looked at Maven and pulled the facial equivalent of a shrug. Maven smiled the smile of the faithful. "Wait," he said. Sure enough, a moment later, they heard a stirring within the room. The door opened.

Downstairs, Astin was shouting at Larry. "Dagnabbit, I knew it. I knew ya hadn't gone found us a hotel with a duck kennel. You're always lying to me. You've never cared for my duck. Here, Stalin. Have another bread crumb." Stalin the duck was flapping around the counter like a Tasmanian Devil that had just received a hefty and medically-suspicious injection of epinephrine straight into its coronary artery.

"Please stop yelling the word Stalin," shouted Larry, earnestly and ineffectually. Calling the bird Stalin hadn't been in the agreement and wasn't making him any the more amenable to the situation. "You can't keep shouting Stalin," he hissed again, more quietly and doing his best to sound like he really, really meant it.

"I can't believe ya gone booked us into a hotel without considering Stalin!" yelled Astin. This was followed by "Gerroff him!" which was more of a war cry. Caspar had upset him by lunging at the startled animal which had just done what startled animals do best, all over the lobby sofa, as it flapped past at head height. Fortunately, no one was sitting on the sofa at the time. A couple of guests were standing with their backs to the wall, their faces frozen in expressions of incredulity.

Larry cursed in exasperation. He made to leave the hotel. He'd had enough, and, anyway, they'd accomplished their objective. Before he reached the rotating door of the lobby, there was sudden silence. He turned around quickly to see what new disaster had startled everyone.

There was a man in a costume standing in the lobby. Larry did a double-take. No, it wasn't a costume - it was a monk's robes. Larry looked to see if Maven and Higgs were here too, but they were nowhere to be seen. The old monk was holding the duck by its neck with one hand and had its body tucked under his arm, like some kind of aquatic, flight-capable bagpipe. His other hand held its beak clamped shut. It appeared he had managed to grab it out of the air as it flew past him. "I shall now release this," he announced, in a tone that invited no dissention. The old man walked toward the rotating doors. On the way past the sofa he swiftly, in a motion almost too fast to see, snatched a cushion, shoved it under his arm, and clamped the duck's beak shut again. The duck barely emitted a demi-quack in the time available to it.

All eyes followed them. The monk passed through the rotating door and walked off into the night air. Everyone watched through the tinted hotel windows as he headed away down the street. A moment later, the monk was out of sight. All of a sudden, everyone rushed past Larry to get through the rotating doors, which jammed. It was quickly determined that the monk had lodged the cushion in the door to prevent him being easily followed. It was well and truly stuffed under the point where the door met the vertical, central shaft. Despite himself, Larry was impressed at the old monk's impromptu forward planning. By the time the guests got outside, duck and monk were gone.

Astin looked pretty pissed that someone had stolen his

duck, but he'd been mesmerised by the monk, same as everyone else. He and Larry turned their backs on the hotel.

"You will pay for all damages," bellowed the beleaguered Caspar, indignantly. "And you do not have a room booked and we are at full capacity now."

Astin spat on the ground as they walked away. Larry hoped they'd bought Maven and Higgs enough time to locate the Messiah, and, even more so, fervently hoped the old monk wasn't the Messiah. If that was the case, and they'd let him get away, then they could expect some significant earache from Maven later.

At roughly the same time as the noise made by the discombobulated duck abated, Anil was examining the two dishevelled men standing at his hotel room door. He asked the obvious question of them. "Who are you?"

"Messiah, I have come to worship you," grovelled Maven, without hesitation.

Anil raised an eyebrow. "And you?"

"Same, I guess," replied Higgs.

Unfortunately for all concerned, the hotel did pay a local security firm to keep a security guard alert and available. The guard had been called when Caspar pressed a red button under the counter during his heated argument with Maven and Higgs. Having turned his attention to the CCTV on the premises, and seeing the two troublemakers sneak through the security door, and deciding to ignore the two with the duck because that wasn't something he was trained to deal with, the guard had dashed up the concrete stairs of the fire escape and opened a side door onto the hallway of the third floor, where he found Maven and Higgs standing staring at a young boy in the garb of a Tibetan monk. The guard recognised the boy as a paying guest. He was also familiar with the boy's garb because he had studied martial arts for as long as he'd been working in the security sector, which was the same length of time that he'd no longer been working for the British Army as a battle-hardened paratrooper.

The guard marched straight toward Maven and Higgs. "You two," he bellowed, like the rumbling gut of Satan, "don't have passes and you don't stay here. I want you out of here now."

A flicker of annoyance crossed Anil's face and he stepped out of his room.

The guard slowed. "Are these guests of yours?" he asked, his gravelly voice still betraying his readiness for a fight. Anil looked them both up and down. They looked back at him hopefully.

"No," replied the boy, honestly. Higgs felt his stomach sink. Maven didn't react. He hadn't expected his Messiah to lie for him.

"Right, out of the building," ordered the guard.

"I'm sorry," said Maven with an ethereal calmness. "That won't be happening."

Higgs knew Maven wasn't going to back down and started to consider his options. Maven looked like he was prepared to fight, which seemed a monumentally bad idea when one considered that Maven was as scrawny as a pole cat, six foot tall, weighed less than twelve stone and had spent his entire life before a computer screen. Not for love nor money was he going to survive a fight with the approaching ogre in a bout of fisticuffs, even should Queensbury rules be applied. Higgs took a step back.

The guard rocked up to them, biceps practically bursting through the seams of his black shirt sleeves. "Fancy me, do you?" he asked Higgs, menacingly.

Higgs found he could barely comprehend the question. "I'm sorry?"

"Fancy your chances against me?"

"Oh, I see. Thank goodness. Um..." He wasn't sure what else to say.

The guard had clearly identified Higgs as the less aggressive of the two and was determined to make him back off in order to, hopefully, steal the wind from Maven's sails.

Maven stepped forward, getting ready to ensure he landed

the first blow. Higgs took another step back. The guard put his hand behind him and drew out a taser weapon. He pointed it at Maven. Maven began to show signs of uncertainty. "That's right, the spunk's draining out of your face now, bozo," jeered the guard, rather unpleasantly.

What followed transpired so quickly that Higgs would later have difficulty pinning down the correct order of events. Anil stepped from the room, turned to face the door, closed it by the handle with his right hand, and grabbed the guard's wrist with his left. The taser fired harmlessly into the door. Applying pressure on the wrist lock he'd manipulated, Anil turned his body and, in so doing, drove the guard's head, mouth first, straight into the wall, which resisted his advances.

The guard swung back round with a burst lip and hatred in his eyes. He threw a solid punch at Anil that would have knocked a normal man off his feet, but Anil somehow absorbed it and used it to pull the guard toward him. The point of the guard's jaw met an elbow swiftly coming the other way. The guard's eyes crossed. Anil swept the guard's legs away while simultaneously striking his throat with the knife-edge of one hand. The guard landed on his back, choking. Anil stepped back, his enemy incapacitated. Maven didn't waste a second. He brought the toe of his pointed boot hard into the guard's temple. The guard's head bounced off the wall and that was the end of it. He was unconscious.

Maven stared at the guard, as if shocked at his own actions. Higgs felt like it would take some time for the adrenaline to leave his body and realised he hadn't actually moved an inch since the fight began.

Anil already had the door to the room open and his mind was on other things. "Follow me," he instructed them.

"I'll just..." said Higgs. Maven nodded.

Higgs dragged the unconscious guard back to the fire escape, noticing as he did so that the guard wore a badge revealing his name to be Trevor.

Trevor had been angry and vertical when he arrived, but was now unconscious and horizontal. Higgs considered that he would probably be angry and vertical again at some point in the very near future.

He propped Trevor's limp body up against the stairs. He showed an unwarranted amount of generosity by ensuring the man was resting on his side and had his airway clear of obstruction. The guard's breath was shallow, but that was probably to be expected. Higgs told himself that someone would probably find Trevor before the hour was up. He secretly hoped that only Anil would be around to face the music and, well, if he was the Messiah then he should be able to cope.

He rejoined Maven in Anil's hotel room. It was dark, save for the glow of the outside lights which cast an unearthly pale gloom across the room. Higgs turned the lights on. "That's better," he said. Maven frowned at him.

Anil seemed uninterested. He had sat down on the edge of the bed.

"How may we serve you?" asked Maven.

"My priorities tonight are food and rest," replied Anil.

"We probably can't access the oriental delicacies you are used to," replied Maven diligently.

"I guess fried chicken will have to do then," replied the boy.

"Higgs," said Maven. It was an instruction. Higgs found himself starting to bow, then decided it was ridiculous and turned and left the room. He knew there was a fast food outlet down the road, so he set off in that direction. A walk would help him get the adrenaline out of his system, and put some distance between himself and the inevitable repercussions of their fight. He was also intrigued to find out what havoc Astin and Larry had fashioned downstairs. The ruckus had been tremendous.

Back in the hotel room, Anil turned to Maven. "I intended to spend the night resting so as to be fresh for tomorrow," explained Anil simply. "You have brought unrest to my sanctuary. I need you to find me somewhere else to stay for the night. Most of the hotels are booked up but perhaps there is a soup kitchen somewhere. Find out for me. Now, I suggest we leave separately. I shall meet you by the duck pond in an hour's time." Anil assumed the role of leadership easily.

"Understood," acknowledged Maven. In a completely unnecessary display of humility, he lowered his eyes, bowed his head at the neck and walked backwards out of the room.

Before he closed the door, Anil spoke again. "Tomorrow I will want you to get me to the royal celebrations so that I may address the world."

"As you command," intoned Maven, his eyes as glazed as an apple tart. He closed the door quietly and found himself in an empty hotel corridor. He was surprised that his audience with the Messiah had been so short. He had so many questions to ask, yet the thought of disobeying the Messiah was unthinkable. He stood outside the door for an uncertain moment then regained his composure and took the elevator, which was labelled in Welsh as LIFFT, to the ground floor.

Maven found Higgs still in the hotel foyer having been accosted by Casper, the hotelier, who suspected he had some connection with the owners of the duck and wanted their names and addresses. Maven looked around to see a considerable mess involving strewn duck feathers and a not inconsiderable quantity of guano. There was one particularly mangled cushion sat upon the reception counter. "Can I help?" he asked.

Higgs nodded. Maven took over the dialogue while Higgs slipped away to fetch food.

A minute later, Maven simply turned and walked from the hotel. Casper yelled after him. He couldn't leave the reception unattended so could hardly give chase. On the edge of hearing, police sirens wailed in the distance.

Maven had arranged to meet the others back at the car if anything untoward happened, so he presumed that's where Astin and Larry would now be and headed there.

Larry saw Maven arriving first. "Where's Higgs?" he asked.

"Getting food. The Messiah will be joining us shortly.

Where's Astin?"

"Over there," replied Larry, pointing to the lanky man with the greasy hair lying on a park bench.

Maven crossed over to him. "What's the matter with you?"

Astin groaned and opened his eyes. He appeared to be nursing a number of bruises. His look suggested he was not in the best of moods. "I tried to get my duck back off the old man," he explained.

Maven looked confused and turned to Larry for an answer, who explained: "The monk."

"Ah," acknowledged Maven, as if this was all perfectly clear to him, which it was, because he could figure out the rest without being told. "Leet was he?" he asked, using the online gamer term for 'elite'.

Astin nodded.

Maven had seen the martial abilities of the old monk on the CCTV camera that Raj had streamed to their laptop. "Come on," he said. "Night's not over. We need to find Higgs and meet up with the Messiah."

Astin rolled off the bench and somehow landed on his feet.

"What was the Messiah like?" asked Larry, unable to reserve his curiosity any longer.

Maven thought for a moment, then answered in a tone that hinted of the numinous. "So leet it hurt."

CHAPTER 45

It was late in the evening and Ivor was getting irritable. The wheels of fate which had been turning inevitably and unstoppably toward the terrible deed that he must perform had ground to a standstill because he'd been put in charge of one last item on the agenda in preparation for tomorrow's celebrations.

"Yes, not bad," he said, tetchily, "but angle it this way a bit. No, this way. Yes, no, no, no. This way. That's it." Ivor shook his head in dismay. The process of setting up a fifty foot high screen for the festivities was definitely one he should have left to somebody else. There were any number of volunteers to help, not least one or two young men from the hastily formed New Independent Welsh Army who presumably couldn't afford the stealth tax or were particularly patriotic; Ivor didn't know which. He did know that the King's fat face was to be shown on this screen the very next day in all its gluttonous glory and he needed to make sure the monstrosity worked. Much as he hated the idea of seeing King Gruffydd II's portly phizog blown up as large as the side of a house, it was important the screen did work because he might just have a use for it himself if he managed to successfully execute the dastardly plan that he had earlier hatched in his malevolent mind.

About half an hour later, he barked, "Right, turn it on." What it showed was a Welsh tourist board advertisement depicting the Brecon Beacons. Ivor had no idea why that was. Night was drawing in and the glow from the screen lit up the plaza which stretched out before the Royal Court's main entrance. Tomorrow, the multitudes would swarm here for the excitement, the camaraderie, the candy floss and perhaps even for the King's pronouncements. Although, right now, only some drunken yobs seemed drawn to it, but they lost interest quickly and staggered off into the night for more exhilarating pursuits.

"Right," yelled Ivor to one of the lads working up on the rig, "make sure the connection with the palace is in working order and report back to me. It should be simple enough, it's all wireless. Then get the speakers hooked up." The soldier replied by way of a sloppy salute and returned to what he was doing. It had better work, thought Ivor, because almost half the very limited budget we have went on renting that colossal screen.

Ivor wandered back into the palace and out of the night air. All these preparations, day after day, and yet the simple truth was that they were preparing for something that wasn't going to happen. It was a celebration of the third anniversary of the King's coronation and yet the King was going to use the opportunity to announce his abdication with some Welsh tart who Ivor suspected was in the employ of that treacherous, scheming rat called Lord Llandudno.

Ivor knew two things. One, he wanted rid of that buffoon King Gruffydd II. Second, he sure as hell wasn't going to let Lord Llandudno take the throne. He was also quite sure that if Lord Llandudno did take the throne, then he would have no use for an advisor called Ivor Munchkinhead. Ivor briefly wondered what Lord Llandudno's real name was. Thinking back, he was sure he had never heard it mentioned. He pulled out his smartphone and looked up Lord Llandudno's Wikipedia entry. So, he thought, that's his name. And he put his phone away, because if everything had gone to plan then it really didn't matter anymore.

The palace was oddly quiet. The preparations were all but finished and the many volunteers, be they craftsmen, cooks or simply eager courtiers, had all gone home for the night. The few that remained were putting the finishing touches on the decorations and they would soon be gone too. The Grand Hall was laid out with buffet food for those who were on the guest list. Ivor contemplated what it would be like tomorrow. Outside, a Welsh rock band would perform. There would be jugglers, fire-eaters, mimes, magicians, gymnasts, pavement artists and a myriad of other entertainers. Every market seller in the country would be there to flog every kind of item a slightly inebriated reveller could ever want. He could already imagine people clambering to buy hot dogs, candy floss, milkshakes, roasted chestnuts and all manner of other high calorie, low nutrient foodstuffs. Ivor grinned. He remembered suddenly the day that his mother, crazy hippy that she was, had bought him his first Welsh rarebit. They had been at a crafts fair in Pontypridd. He could remember the slightly burnt toast, the oily, melted cheddar and the hot sprinkling of black pepper the seller had topped it with. It made his mouth water just to think about it. Of course, as always, the memory became sullied as it continued. He couldn't help but remember his mother handing him some stolen goods she'd swiped from a market stall. The police were called. The pandemonium she caused and the things she'd called the policemen were branded on his mind forever. He recalled the night he spent in the orphanage, and the abuse. His day in court. Being too afraid to tell the truth because of the way the magistrates looked at him. He shook his head to blot it all out. He smiled. They even had fireworks planned for tomorrow evening.

Ivor decided it was time to hide Lord Llandudno's corpse. That was assuming he was dead, of course, which, by now, he should be. Ivor traipsed through the palace, past the box office which still hadn't been redecorated, through the drawing room, and along the royal hallway displaying portraits of famous

Welsh characters such as Owain Glyndŵr, David Lloyd George and Saunders Lewis. Finally, he reached the foot of the stairs leading up to Lord Llandudno's chambers where the peer of the realm should have been spending the night nurturing his great expectations. Ivor suspected that by now rigor mortis might have set in.

He couldn't let Lord Llandudno become king, of course. He'd rather suck his own eyes out with a vacuum cleaner. Lord Llandudno was the worst kind of politician and not a very nice person to boot. He was sly and ambitious, he trod on other people whenever it suited him and he never said thank you when you held a door open for him. People like him rose quickly, but they fell quickly too, provided the right kind of person was there to make sure they fell, and Ivor had no delusions about himself; he was that kind of person.

It was a long climb up four flights of stairs to the guests' chambers. As Ivor plodded upward, he recalled the events of earlier that evening. The brainwave had come to him while he was still in the pantry. He'd been watching King Gruffydd II as he wobbled his way around the room opening cupboards, fridges and drawers in a whirlwind of complete self-absorption until finally he had about fifteen unhealthy snacks, three of which were already half-eaten, laid out before him and ready for devouring. He then finally remembered he had company and, referring to Ivor's evening meal, asked in a tone of scandalised disbelief, "Is that all you're having?"

Ivor hadn't responded. He had been having a eureka moment. Well, perhaps not quite that significant. More of a minor epiphany. It was a moment that had the kind of emotional and intellectual impact you get when you realise you've left your phone in the car. He'd been lost in a fantasy where Lord Llandudno was king and he, the loyal servant, was bullied, beaten and finally cast out on the street. He had to get rid of him. He justified it by telling himself that the last thing Wales needed was an ambitious despot on the throne. Ivor was firmly decided. He had to eradicate Lord Llandudno, and seeing King Gruffydd II eating an asparagus lasagne he'd heated in the microwave gave him all the inspiration he needed to formulate a fool-proof plan.

Lord Llandudno was shrewd, there was no doubt about that, but Ivor had taken that into account. He knew Lord Llandudno had eaten very little that night. Using this knowledge to his advantage, Ivor went to the kitchens and had the cook prepare a hearty meal and an irresistible dessert.

Ivor took the food straight up to Lord Llandudno's chambers upon a tray. Really it was work for a servant, but on this occasion it was only right he performed the deed personally. He set the tray down on a small table outside the guest's room and rapped on the door. Lord Llandudno appeared, looking dishevelled. He'd given orders that he be left alone for the rest of the night. No doubt he was holding video conferences with his own advisors in North Wales and, at a guess, beginning work on his coronation speech.

Ivor never did get to read the speech that King Gruffydd II had slaved over for the big day. He could only imagine how awful it was. The King lacked the necessary writing skills. It wasn't just that the King wasn't particularly good, thought Ivor, but more that he was a brainless buffoon with the eloquence of a buffoon and the general thoughtfulness of a buffoon. On the whole, whatever he had written was likely to be gross buffoonery. It was a good job that all he had to do now was declare his love for some treacherous slut, abdicate, and leave Ivor in charge of things. Of course, Ivor would have to instil that last thought into his fat head tomorrow morning, once it turned out that Lord Llandudno had fled because he didn't want the responsibility of being king. Ah yes, it was all coming together nicely.

Lord Llandudno's disgruntled deportment would normally be enough to unnerve Ivor, but some of his usual gravitas was lost by the fact he was wearing an oversized dressing gown that could only have been intended for the King. He looked at the food and raised his eyebrows. "An evening snack?" he asked, his interest piqued.

"Yes, my Lord," Ivor replied with due subservience. "I

thought you might be peckish. I had the cook prepare her special aubergine slab with potato slices and thick cheddar cheese topping. Oh, and there's some dessert too. She's made her Five Cake Festive Delight. I thought with the festivities tomorrow it wasn't entirely out of-"

"I won't be having the main," said Lord Llandudno disdainfully, as Ivor had predicted. "I ate a little something earlier and aubergine slab sounds a little heavy for this time of night."

The aubergine meal was far too heavy for this time of night. The sheer sight of an inch and a half slab of aubergine, surrounded by oil-oozing cheese and great slices of half-burnt potato with skins still on, was never going to please a scrawny man like Lord Llandudno at this time of night. Plus, there was next to no chance he would willingly eat the palace's aubergine after yesterday's fiasco and having his stomach pumped. He might even suspect foul play.

"I might have some dessert though," he decided. He looked at it for a moment. The Five Cake Festive Delight normally consisted of five delightful little cakes. Today, it consisted of three delightful little cakes, one manky-looking cake and a gap where the final cake was obviously missing.

"Tell me why it is called Five Cake Festive Delight again," said Lord Llandudno, blatantly referring to the gap.

"Ah," replied Ivor, doing his best to feign embarrassment. "I ran into one of the couriers, a jolly Polish chap called Andrzej. He helped himself before I could stop him."

"I see. Well, I shan't be needing five cakes, so I'll let that slip." Lord Llandudno was a very thin man. Ivor had correctly predicted he wouldn't concern himself with the missing cake and felt a mixture of smugness and fear; smugness at the success of his own cunning, and fear because, well, he was, after all, about to commit murder.

"I don't suppose you would want all four either," he suggested, trying to look hopeful and pitiful at the same time.

Lord Llandudno sighed. "I suppose you would like one? Very well." Ivor said nothing. Lord Llandudno looked at the cakes for a moment and picked one of the three that looked appetising. Everything was going precisely to plan. Ivor picked the manky, feculent cake in the middle. It was broken and had some sort of brown stain on the side.

"Thank you," said Ivor, trying to sound earnest.

"You better eat it here. It wouldn't do for people to think I'd let you steal from my plate." Lord Llandudno stared at him until he complied. Ivor smirked inwardly. He had foreseen all this.

Ivor was relying on three things to make sure that Llandudno ate one of the cakes. The first was the reputation of the cook's special Five Cake Festive Delight. The mere sight of them made most people drool. The second was the story about the non-existent Andrzej. Letting a courier eat one suggested they weren't all poisoned. The third was seeing Ivor choose the manky one, a manoeuvre designed to assuage any concern about the other cakes being tampered with. It was an elaborate and brilliant piece of double-think. Ivor wolfed down his chosen cake.

Satisfied with this, Lord Llandudno closed the door behind him. As he did so, Ivor thought he saw him lift the poisoned cake to his mouth.

The best of the cakes, the one Andrzej hadn't really eaten, since he didn't exist, was waiting for Ivor in his bedchamber. The remaining three attractive cakes, including the one Lord Llandudno has chosen, were all poisoned. The manky one, the one Ivor had just eaten, wasn't injected with poison because he knew Lord Llandudno wouldn't choose it above the others.

Lord Llandudno was a shrewd man, thought Ivor, but not so shrewd that he could outwit an unfaithful manservant. Ambitious men climb to the top, but devious men bring them back down again. Ivor was happy thinking of himself as devious. He knew who he didn't like and he allowed those feelings to guide his actions. If the actions were unpleasant, or downright illegal, that didn't matter because the law wasn't there to ensure justice, it was there to create order. It was for that reason that Ivor liked to dispense his own justice.

Ivor nipped back down to his own bedchamber and put the best cake back on the tray and headed off back to the pantry where he would eat it with some warm custard that the cook would drum up for him. She had a soft spot for Ivor simply because he never asked her to make anything outlandish. Often she could be heard exclaiming things like, "And how does His Royal Piggy think I'm going to make kumquat and ortolan soup at this time of night?" Ivor sighed. The King did so many stupid things he could write a book about them.

As Ivor strolled back to the pantry he reflected on how he'd done away with one of the two men who would be ruler, but now had to think about the other. Ivor felt that he could manage the nation quite comfortably until someone sensible showed up to take the throne. He would be doing the country a favour.

At no point did Ivor consider that he was simply jealous of his betters. That was not the type of thinking that his parents had taught him. Even as his mother was dragged away screaming, he remembered the words she had yelled at him: "You're better than those bastards!" He liked to pretend she was talking about the authorities, although even as a child he knew she simply meant everyone who wasn't her. He shook away the thought like a fragment of cobweb and rebalanced the tray that had started to quiver in his trembling hands.

"Everything alright, Ivor?"

It was the King.

"Yes, sire," he replied, although he was somewhat taken aback. He'd been so lost in his own memories he hadn't seen the King arrive, which was certainly saying something considering the King could eclipse a small moon.

"That looks good," said the King, pilfering a cake from the tray before Ivor could think of a plausible objection. "Can't stop, I'm off to meet Ffion." He took a large bite and gave Ivor a big, open-mouthed smile of gratitude so that when he started chewing again Ivor could see the cake being churned into slush.

The King sauntered off down the corridor, pleased as punch. Ivor looked at the tray. Needless to say, the King had chosen the best cake; the one from Ivor's bedroom. It was just Ivor's luck. If he'd not been so self-absorbed he might have quickly dropped the good one on the floor, as if by accident, so the King was forced to steal one of the poisoned ones. There just hadn't been time. Suddenly Ivor realised he had also lost his supper. The rest were poisoned, so he tipped them in a bin.

As he had watched the pastry and cream mixing with saliva and tumbling around inside the King's mouth, he had thought of only one thing: tonight he would put into motion a plan that would rid the country of that pestilent porker once and for all.

Ivor returned his attention to the present. The last stages of setting up the large screen were being seen to by the volunteers and it was now up to him to dispose of Lord Llandudno's corpse. He wasn't entirely sure where King Gruffydd II was right now, but he assumed he must still be with Ffion. They were probably selecting a new bedchamber considering the last one had been torched to ashes.

Ivor needed to act quickly in disposing of Lord Llandudno's corpse. He had a list as long as his arm of things to do before tomorrow, not least of which was find King Gruffydd II and make sure he was going to go out on that balcony and make his speech. It didn't matter what speech. He knew now exactly how he was going to dispose of the King. He chuckled.

Putting that thought to one side, he ran up to Lord Llandudno's chamber. The sun had almost set and very few people remained in the palace, which worked in his favour. He knocked on Lord Llandudno's door and waited a moment. There was no reply. He knocked again, a little bit louder. It was possible that Lord Llandudno was video conferencing and had headphones on. Still no response. Ivor knocked louder yet and then kicked the door for good measure. He was growing confident that there would be no reply, but there was just a chance that Lord Llandudno was asleep. There was no answer.

He put his hand on the door handle. He hesitated. He didn't know exactly how gruesome the scene inside might look, so he tried his best to ready himself for it. That was when he heard the noise.

"Oh no," he said quietly. He wasn't sure what worried him the most: Lord Llandudno being angry at him kicking the door or that he might have discovered evidence of his attempted murder. He had seen Lord Llandudno raise that cake to his mouth so there was very little chance it would have had no effect on him.

It had been a simple matter of taking the concoction and injecting it into the filling of the cake. The cook had suspected nothing. It had been easy to acquire the relevant plant, which in this case was Monkshood. He had been cultivating a crop of it in his private garden behind the palace. As his mother had always said: you never quite knew when you might need it, so it was probably reasonably wise to keep some for when you actually did. Admittedly, it wasn't the pithiest of sayings, but tonight was not the first time it had served Ivor well. It was easy to get hold of, too. He'd just bought some seeds off the internet.

As Lord Llandudno hadn't appeared, he gripped the door handle more firmly, ready to make his entrance. He thought he heard a noise come from inside the room again, but perhaps it was his imagination. There should have been plenty of time for the poison to kick in.

Ivor had crushed up a liberal amount of leaves and roots and then made them into a paste with a little icing sugar and food colouring and strawberry flavouring thrown in for good measure. Considering Llandudno must have eaten it on a half-empty stomach, it should really have finished him off in under half an hour. It wouldn't have been a pleasant scene, Ivor thought. He'd have felt a burning sensation, followed by numbness in the tongue and throat, and assuming he'd eaten the whole cake and hadn't thrown it up, it should only have been a panicky minute of blurred vision, dizziness and chest pain before he was flat on his back convulsing and grasping at his throat.

Ivor prepared himself and opened the door.

Llandudno was red in the face, squatting on the toilet in his en suite bathroom. "Out!" he shouted. Ivor had just enough time to spot the uneaten cake on the table before he shut the door behind him.

Oh dear. This was going to play awkwardly. He wasn't sure whether he should wait for Lord Llandudno's wrath or just run for it. Ivor stood there, unsure what to do. After a moment's hesitation, he took a key out of his pocket and locked the door. He stood back.

A few minutes later, Lord Llandudno tried to open the door from the inside. He found it locked. Ivor listened for several minutes as Lord Llandudno screamed and banged on the door, threatening all kinds of retribution if he wasn't let out this instant. They were on the fourth floor and no one was going to hear him or come to his aid. Ivor needn't have worried. Lord Llandudno had worked up a bit of an appetite with all his shouting. Ivor heard the plate being lifted from the table. He sat down quietly next to the door and listened to the cake being eaten, and the noises that followed for some time afterwards. Eventually, he heard Lord Llandudno's corpse fall to the floor and come to a rest. He decided to give it a minute or two before he went in to have a look because his palms were sweaty and, more importantly, he was trying to remember where he'd left his wheelbarrow.

CHAPTER 46

It turned out (and all things considered, Quentin could probably have guessed this in advance) that Connor was someone who snored. He sat in the back seat of the car with his head flung backwards and peeled great snorts out into the world at large. Janine wasn't much better. She didn't snore, as such, but she snuffled, like a micro-pig trying to solve a Rubik's Cube with its nostrils. Not that Quentin had heard that particular sound, but as his tired mind drifted in and out of consciousness that was the very definite image it conjured up. Unlike the two men, she was sat in the front of the car. Unfortunately, the reclined passenger's seat didn't seem to offer her proper head support. As she had fallen asleep, her head had lolled round to face Quentin and she, no doubt as a result of the poor sleeping conditions, also slept with one eye partially open. Quentin was all too aware of her vacant expression and the sensation of being watched. Worst of all, she had the habit of occasionally mumbling incoherent phrases. These woke him with a fright every time. No sooner had his mind begun to wander off to some far-off time of contentment, perhaps where Mavis was scolding him for dropping three sugar lumps in his tea, than Janine would mutter something like: "Don't you dare sponge the camel in the freezing surf!" This would inevitably prevent Quentin sleeping for another ten minutes as he tried to imagine what sort of dream or recollection could possibly have inspired such a ludicrous outpouring.

Occasionally he wondered what on Earth he was doing in this situation. He had to keep running through it all in his mind to make sense of it. It seemed that a lot had happened in a short space of time and, when he thought about it from different angles, it appeared a lot more was probably going to happen in not a lot of time from now at all. After another half hour or so of intermittent sleep, Quentin quietly opened the car door and slipped out into the night air. He closed the door as quietly as he could. Janine stirred slightly and said, "But you're pocketing a tonsil!" Connor didn't stir, but did let forth another rattling snore.

Quentin took in a deep lungful of the cold, night air. The smell of cordite was still present following the many firework displays. The fresh air had brought him more fully awake, so he decided to go for a stroll to ease his muddled mind. It was late now, so late in fact that the world was quiet. He walked past a shop window where muted television sets were left on permanently and the twenty-four hour news provided him with an accurate report of the time. It was almost four thirty in the morning.

As he strolled through the streets of Cardiff, where the revellers had finally gone to bed and the shops were closed and the street sweepers weren't out in force yet, Quentin found within himself a level of serenity he hadn't felt since... it had been too long. Quentin thought back to his days lazing in his Chester office with Mavis bringing him cups of tea at regular intervals. He'd sit behind his oh-so-grand mahogany desk and do the crossword puzzle in ten minutes flat then browse the news pages on his computer for a moment or two before getting bored and wandering off into town for a sandwich and a packet of roasted peanuts.

The business had taken a turn for the worst when Wales declared war on England. He couldn't understand what had inspired that particular move. Then there was the outbreak of plague in London; that had sent the whole country spiralling downward. As he thought back over the crazy world he now lived in, he remembered the words of his last client, Bryn Jones: "You've got to remember what started all this in the first place." The farmer had been talking about his own case. Now, with a view to the bigger picture, Quentin began to wonder: what did start all this?

Quentin wandered the streets of Cardiff aimlessly for a while. He tried to think of anything he knew about the city and remembered that he'd been reading about it in the news only a week ago. Cardiff had been demoted from the tenth largest city in Britain to the eleventh after the sudden, massive growth experienced by Stratford-upon-Avon after their local university's adventures with DNA caused a humongous tourism spurt when they cloned Shakespeare from a dandruff flake found on the first folio of Timothy of Athens. After some accelerated growth, at adjusted-age twenty, the new Shakespeare had started writing some quite amazing plays, with dubious historical content, and performing in them himself. The papers were calling him "the next Shakespeare", apparently without irony. Such was the fascination with Bard 2.0 that the town had grown into a huge, thriving city where everything revolved around the latest theatre production. Quentin had considered taking Mavis to see Romeo & Juliet 2: The Reanimation. Sadly, Mavis had said something about not liking sequels and that was the end of it.

Come to think of it, sequels were a major problem these days. Devolution 2.0 was how the reintroduction of the monarchy had been sold to the Welsh people. The Blacker Plague now swept London. Either the media and the politicians were doing a really bad job of rebranding, or the world had begun to lack originality. Too many people, too few ideas to go around... and when those ideas did go around they went around fast and stayed forever. That was the nature of the world these days. Quentin idly wondered if he could remember what it was like before the internet had spread its optic feelers around the world and begun squeezing. He couldn't. He could remember playing with a wooden sword, once upon a time, but now he only ever saw children playing interactive games in augmented reality. Reality 2.0, he supposed.

His wanderings took him toward the centre of town. A sign pointed the way to a theatre. The more he considered it, the more convinced he was that it was the advent of the internet that had so changed the world. As technology progressed, everything else seemed to retreat. Common sense, for one thing. Human decency, for another. Yes, that's how it all started. He remembered now. It all started with the Web 2.0, when the web was suddenly in everyone's homes, watching everyone's moves on social networking sites and preying with tiny apertures into their living rooms. There had been a general, incremental decline in everything that couldn't be transmitted over the web in a second. Like ethical behaviour, order and... yes, that was it... law. It was hard to administer law over the web.

Daylight was a long way off and Quentin still wasn't tired, so he carried on walking toward the town centre. According to Connor, Bryn Jones had been a Luddite. Except Luddites with a capital L were people who existed in the nineteenth century. Yet luddite with a small 'l' was something altogether different to what he meant. What did he mean? Bryn Jones was a Luddite 2.0, he supposed, grimacing at another sequel. He was part of the same secret society in which Connor and Janine were so ensconced. It had got him killed. According to Connor, anyway.

It had been explained to Quentin that Bryn was a Luddite who had been very active within the society. He'd set up a sheep smuggling operation. The operation was simply a cover so he could get involved in illegal cross-border work. It was all part of a plan to draw the Binary Levers out into the open so that Janine could then track them to their headquarters. A local faction of the Binary Levers had soon become aware of him. Using their connections to the owner of a slaughterhouse, they had set him up with a deal he could hardly refuse. It was a trap. They had planned to kidnap him, but the deal went sour before that could happen. Someone had reported the sheep smuggling to the police. No matter how convoluted things got, there was always some do-gooder third-party that no one had noticed up to that point who was ready to make things worse. Quentin had learnt that as a lawyer. In the knowledge that sooner or later he would be caught by the Binary Levers or, possibly, the Republican militia who were violently opposed to cross-border smuggling, Bryn had come to Quentin and made up an equally convoluted story about having a missing brother. He had simply been putting into a motion a plan to ensure he would be sought and found if he ever went missing. It must be a terrible thing, thought Quentin, for a man to know his days were numbered. Sooner rather than later they had caught up with him. The last that was heard of him was that his body had washed up in Worthenbury. The only good of it was that Janine had been able to track down one of the Binary Levers who had been involved and follow him to London. Larry had led her straight to their headquarters.

Quentin found it hard to believe there was an underground war being waged by hackers on the one side and technophobes on the other. They didn't seem so different to Quentin. It was all just a matter of conflicting ideologies, he thought. He was getting sleepy now though, so he returned his thoughts to the present.

He found himself looking up at a huge screen in the middle of an open plaza. The square was all set up for the market stalls and entertainments of the coming day. Unlit coloured bulbs hung idly around, keeping the place looking festive despite the lack of people to appreciate them. There were all kinds of signs and neon lights and stages set up. Many trailers remained locked up, but come morning their side panels would fall open to offer a profusion of delights.

Quentin was tired. He must have walked over two miles in the cold night air. Exhaustion finally took him. He sat down on a bench, just to have a moment's rest before heading back.

He thought it probably wouldn't hurt to have a quick lie down.

For a moment or two he could hear himself snoring and almost woke himself up, but then there was nothing.

CHAPTER 47

"An odd hour to be playing in the flower bed, isn't it?" asked the King, appearing from nowhere.

Ivor leapt from his skin. He stammered for an answer. His eyes darted about checking for evidence of the foul act he'd perpetrated. Fortunately, he'd already covered his tracks. He was lucky his devious mind was already rammed into overdrive. Factoring into his response the indisputable fact that the King was an utter dunderhead, he spontaneously concocted a suitable defence. A reply leapt from his tongue like a high diving weasel. "Sire, you startled me. I'm just tending to my Night's Bane."

"Oh?"

"Yes, you see, Night's Bane is a herb which opens its bud for the moon, not the sun, and is best pruned at night when the bud is open."

"Ah, you're a man of many talents, Ivor Munchkinhead!" Ivor thought the King looked remarkably relaxed considering he was planning on addressing the nation tomorrow and abdicating his throne. "But I notice you don't seem to have one of those pruning tools on you."

Ivor sighed inwardly. Trust the King to be in one of those moods where he thought he was clever. Never mind that he didn't seem to know the word for secateurs, he had spotted their absence and now Ivor had to devise another lie. He looked about him. He had to hand a shovel and a wheelbarrow filled with black plastic bags. There was a good reason for this, of course. The plastic bags had not long ago contained the corpse of Lord Llandudno. The wheelbarrow had been used to trundle him out of the palace. The shovel was used to ensure he was definitely dead, and to bury him. None of these helped him concoct a convincing lie.

"Well, sire," began Ivor, giving himself thinking time, but soon realising he didn't really need it. "As you can see, it is easy enough to pinch the deadheads off Night's Bane with one's fingers." He found the first weak-looking weed available and pulled its wilting head off.

The King looked at the crumpled, closed, flower in Ivor's hand. "I thought you said the flowers opened at night."

Ivor cursed at this almost paranormal perspicacity on the King's part. He was growing tired of this game, but his answer came easily. "I said it opened for the moon. There's a cloud covering tonight."

"But you said that it needed pruning during those occasions when it was open."

Ivor had had enough. He stole a glance at the shovel. It was a dark night, right enough. There was no one else about. The ground had already been dug up once, so it wouldn't be difficult to open again. Although, admittedly, he might have to exhume the late Lord Llandudno and dig quite a bit deeper to get the King's voluminous carcass in there as well. The evil part of Ivor's mind, which was in the majority, considered gleefully how the two despised each other and how apposite it would be for them to spend eternity nestled together. It just seemed fitting, somehow.

Perhaps the King noticed the change in Ivor's demeanour, or saw him look at the shovel, or perhaps it was just as he said: "I'm bored of talking about plants. It's not what I came here to talk about."

"Very well," said Ivor, disguising his relief. "I'm finished anyway. What would you like to discuss?" He took the spade, put it in the wheelbarrow, and moved off.

"What did you need all that for?" asked the King suddenly, staring at the wheelbarrow and its contents.

Ivor was ready for him this time. "To distribute the dirt I had in these bags. I thought it was as good a time as any to put some good topsoil down on the patch. It does need replenishing; the soil isn't nutritious around here."

The King nodded. "Ah, you do love your little rose garden," he said.

"It's not a rose garden."

"There's a rose right there. I can see it. It looks black as night."

"It's a black rose, that's why."

"Well, that makes it a rose garden."

"No. It doesn't."

"Well, you know what I mean."

"I know what you said," replied Ivor, facetiously.

King Gruffydd II snorted annoyance. "I'm still the King," he rebuked.

"Have you really decided to abdicate?" asked Ivor, trying to change the topic. "I've enjoyed working with you."

"You don't work with me, Ivor, you work for me," the King replied patronisingly. He let out a long sigh. "The truth is: I don't know what to do. It seemed like such an easy solution earlier, but can I really let Lord Llandudno take the throne? What would it mean for Wales? What would my father have thought of it?"

Ivor nodded with apparent sympathy. "Did you speak to Ffion about it?" It was none of his business, of course, but out here in the dark, barely able to see each other in the shadows, and with all this talk of abdication, it was an effort not to treat the King as an equal. Of course, Ivor knew he was vastly the King's superior, but in terms of how much he could push his luck, he was an equal, for the time being.

"Yes, I spoke to her about it. She didn't seem quite as enthusiastic as I hoped, although of course she said she would stick with me through thick and thin."

Ivor doubted there would be much thin where the King was concerned, but asked, "Did she definitely say she would marry you if you abdicated?"

"Yes."

Ivor thought a moment, then decided he had nothing to lose. "And was that because she loves you or because she's on Lord Llandudno's payroll and it corresponds with his plans?"

The King looked like he'd been hit over the head with a hardbound copy of the Mabinogion. "You think she's a spy for Lord Llandudno?"

"No, I think she's a whore for him. To distract you. To make your passing easier, as it were." Ivor was brutally honest, and he knew he'd get away with it, because he knew the King had started to realise the truth after asking the girl to run away with him. Plus, Ivor was, after all, the King's advisor. How he had got the job was a story in itself, but one for another day, perhaps.

Ivor and the King walked side by side, back toward the palace. "Do you remember why I made you my advisor?" asked the King. Fair enough, thought Ivor, apparently it's a story for today. He nodded in response but, inevitably, the King had decided he was going to recount events anyway. He stopped and sat down on a low wall they were passing, his massive buttocks sagging over both the front and back of it at once. Ivor stopped where he was, holding the wheelbarrow handles, deliberately not sitting down in the hope this might not take too long. He had a lot to do tonight. "If I recall correctly, we met just under three years ago," said the King, wistfully.

"Not exactly," interrupted Ivor, unable to stop himself. "It was nine years ago."

"Oh yes! I remember!" The King rocked backward precariously, then found his balance again. "My dear old dad was giving a talk at the local something-or-other and you were involved in their debating competition. It looked like you were going to win, too, and then that blonde lad from Oxford beat you. What was the motion again?"

"I forget."

"Oh, come now," encouraged the King.

"Something to do with the liberty of thought."

The King frowned. "Was it? I thought it was on fox hunting."

"Yes, you did," said Ivor flatly.

"I remember walking over to you and congratulating you on coming second."

Ivor nodded. The King's actual words had been, "There's no place after first place, though, is there? Second place is first loser, and all that. What was your first name again? Ivor? And what was your second name again? Munchkinhead? So your name's Ivor Munchkinhead? Have I got that right? Ivor. Munch. Kin. Head. Munchkin like in the film, yeah? Spelt the same? And so your name actually is Ivor Munchkinhead?" He had had a couple of friends with him and they were sniggering in the background. That was the first time Ivor had thought about killing the King, although in those days he wasn't the King, just Rhys John Evans.

"And then," continued the King, "we met again when you applied for the job here. That was just under three years ago! Tell me, what was it inspired you to try for it? You were hardly qualified for the position."

Ivor nodded. They'd been through this a few times, but the King loved to rehearse scenes from his past where he felt he'd done something clever, or where there was something he thought was hysterically funny that needed resurfacing for his amusement. "I think I said that I wanted the position because I felt passionate and patriotic about my country and I wanted to make something of myself and because I was well versed in the law of the land and had a way with numbers and I'm good with people, making me an excellent all rounder."

The King rocked back again, laughing out loud. It was more like a roar. Obviously Ivor had hit the keyword he wanted to hear. King Gruffydd II could barely breathe as he choked on the words "good with people", which he repeated to himself a few times, before wiping a tear from his eye. "That's right, that's right," he said quietly, coming back to reality slowly but surely. He was shaking his head in disbelief and amusement.

"And you took me on," said Ivor, in a tone that clearly meant: so no matter what you think of me now, it's entirely your fault I'm here.

"But do you remember specifically why I made you my advisor?" asked the King, returning to his original point.

"No," said Ivor, untruthfully.

"Well, there were the - what shall we call them? Ah, yes - physical reasons why we chose you. You know, our first seven choices all mysteriously turned down the job."

"I think you mean practical, not physical," said Ivor, remembering how he thought he'd have to find ways to persuade seven people to turn down the job, but in fact only had to do that to three of them. The other four had spent an hour in King Gruffydd II's presence and quit. The remaining three had responded satisfactorily to, respectively, blackmail, hate mail and poisoned mail. He imagined that two of those three job seekers had gone on to lead fulfilling lives elsewhere.

"There was another reason I chose you, though," said the King, earnestly. "I thought you had a sharp mind. I saw something there. Honesty. Integrity. Decency."

Yes, thought Ivor, because you really are that bad a judge of character.

The King smiled. "Once again you've been honest with me, about Ffion. I thank you, Ivor. I thank you for it."

Ivor was beginning to suspect the King had been drinking. It hadn't been obvious in the dark, but as the King hauled himself up from the wall, and they approached the front of the palace, Ivor noticed he was ever-so-slightly swaying. "I'm going to bed to sleep it off, I mean to sleep on it, Ivor. I'll let you know my decision tomorrow. I'm not due to make my speech until eleven in the morning, so there's plenty of time yet."

"Good night, sire," said Ivor. He watched him waddle

away despondently.

"Well, if nothing else, at least I ruined his evening," muttered Ivor.

There was a lock-up at the side of the palace, like a garden shed but built into the side of the building. Ivor wasn't sure what it was used for when the building was a theatre, but he used it to keep his tools safe. He trundled the wheelbarrow into the lock-up, then turned the light on. He searched the shelves for a few items he required, successfully locating a crowbar, a screwdriver, a tape measure and a cordless angle-grinder. He tipped an old, rolled-up hosepipe out of a large canvas bag and put his tools in it.

Returning to the palace he decided it was still a little too early to begin executing his plan. The tools would help him with the necessary preparatory work. Using the angle grinder might prove a touch noisy in the night, but the tipsy king wouldn't wake once he was soundly off to sleep and no one else would expect it was anything other than last minute preparations for the celebrations tomorrow.

Ivor slipped off to his room to catch an hour's sleep before beginning his darkest deed.

CHAPTER 48: SATURDAY

The morning sun rolled over the city of Cardiff in much the same way a dying whale rolls itself across a beach toward the incoming tide. It was slow, laborious and unpleasant to watch. At least, it was for King Gruffydd II, who found himself awake at this early hour. He had a terrible life-altering decision to make. He could either hand the reign and reins over to Lord Llandudno, since the people clearly no longer favoured him, and then hope Ffion was truly his and not in the employ of said Lord, or he could invoke Lord Llandudno's wrath by refusing to abdicate and risking civil unrest. King Gruffydd II was the first royal to rule an independent Wales since Llywelyn the Last had a phony crown placed on his head in London, while simultaneously his body was laid to rest in Powys. He knew that if he didn't abdicate then he was likely to be the very last, such a bad job had he made of it.

The thoughts racing through his head had kept him awake for the first few hours of the night. Ffion had been with him for a while, but she'd had to slip away for some reason that she'd whispered into his ear. It had sounded naughty and sexy, but all he registered was her shouting: "I NEED TO GO AND PICK UP MY PAY CHEQUE FROM LORD LLANDUDNO NOW!" Which definitely wasn't what she said, but it was all he could think of and so he had missed what she actually said. She was always slipping away. He just hadn't let himself notice before now. Still, he'd managed to get to sleep eventually, although he had been plagued by some strange dreams. He put them down to the doughnuts, crackers and blue cheese that he'd washed down with a glass of port, a carafe of wine and a mug of hot Belgian chocolate. It was a snack he often enjoyed before bed time. He called that particular dish: "Gout, Quelle Surprise."

Something had definitely woken him in the early hours, though. He had been dreaming of a woodpecker tapping away at the hinges of a safe. As the pecking continued, the hinges began to creak and give way. The safe became, well, less safe as the door fell to the ground. The door lay on its front and began spinning on the spot, drilling itself into the concrete floor and making a terrible grinding noise. When he awoke he was sure he could hear a noise like an angle grinder going through metal somewhere in the distance, but it stopped almost as soon as he opened his eyes. He didn't even have time to sit up before the world was silent again. He debated whether to investigate and eventually decided not to; then he got up anyway. He had far too many things playing on his mind to get any meaningful rest. It was going to be a big day, one way or another.

He wandered through the empty halls of the palace. He tried to keep his footfalls light so as not to wake anyone, but it was impossible when you weighed as much as he did. After a while, he decided that, as he was the king, he could make as much noise as he liked, so stopped worrying about it and returned to thinking about his speech. It was a troubling time for him. He could abdicate and probably spend the rest of his life in misery, or prolong the current misery and invoke Lord Llandudno's wrath. No doubt Lord Llandudno would eventually drum up enough support to have him driven out, or lynched, or worse. He paused on that thought. It would probably be all three, in precisely that order.

He told himself that being king wasn't everything in life.

There were plenty of other things he could do if he abdicated. There was a whole world out there where his time wasn't in constant demand by his minions. There were many things he wanted to do with his life that he had not yet achieved. He wanted to visit New York and eat Stay Puft Marshmallows. He wanted to watch Titus Andronicus: The Second Course on stage at the Republican Shakespeare Company. He wanted to belt out a Bon Jovi number in a pub's karaoke night. Hell, he wanted to dance on the moon, swing on a star and try his hand at Zorbing if he didn't exceed the weight restrictions. And he had many questions he wanted answered, like: Why is the sky blue? How are rainbows formed? Do vampires really exist? And what the hell is a Lolcat? If he was his own man, he would have time to investigate such things.

The King drew back a pair of curtains to look out over the city square. At the moment, it looked like a deserted funfair from some horror movie; bleak and black. Come midmorning, when it filled with people, it would be a merry place indeed. The King smiled, although it was a bittersweet smile. The day was unlikely to be merry for him. Inside, he felt like the plaza before him: empty and lacking in promise. As the sun continued to reluctantly hoist itself over the horizon, King Gruffydd II noticed the plaza wasn't completely deserted. On a park bench, not far off, lay a solitary individual sleeping soundly, no doubt oblivious to the machinations that had taken place in the Royal Court over the last few days. Sure, he was just a simple vagrant, but King Gruffydd II envied him the simplicity of his lifestyle.

As daylight beat back the grimy night, he had no intention of going back to sleep, so he headed for the kitchen instead. His giant, silky red dressing gown hung around him and down to the floor, shimmering in all its glory. It was tied closely about him by a golden cord that served as a belt. It revealed only his moccasin slippers as he padded along the cold floors of the palace. The kitchen wasn't quite awake yet. The cat which caught the mice was mewing. A young man was turning on the cookers and laying out utensils and generally doing things of a preparatory nature. King Gruffydd II mentally dismissed the boy's existence as he was no use to him, and went rummaging in the cupboards. He decided to give cheese a miss for the time being, as he still felt he was suffering a little from last night. What he needed was some fibre.

A few minutes later, he had a humungous pan full of porridge ready for consumption. He sat down on a flat, wooden, bariatric stool. Over a year ago, he had ordered it be purchased and put in the kitchen for his own personal use. It was designed to seat a man who had his ample proportions in the derriere department.

He took a spoonful of porridge and blew on it. It was piping hot and steam rose in curly wisps. King Gruffydd II nibbled the end of the spoon. Deciding the temperature was manageable, he spooned it into his mouth as fast as he could. He barely took a breath as he wolfed it all down. He hadn't expended so much energy in quite some time. He consumed the porridge with such gusto that he probably broke world records. Finally, he pushed the bowl away from him and let himself relax.

Like a trumpet heralding the end of the world, or the rat-a-tat-tat of a thousand machine guns all firing simultaneously, or the spluttering raspberry sound of a hole-ridden exhaust pipe on a sports car tearing off into the distance, King Gruffydd II let rip with a fart which made the cheeks of his backside vibrate violently against the polished wooden surface of the stool and sent a terrible sound reverberating around the room at a volume hitherto unknown to mankind in such circumstances. It was so loud, and went on for so long, that it was as if someone had pierced a bouncy castle with the mouthpiece of a trombone. "Ugh," he said to the kitchen boy, in both disgust and relief, "fetch me a towel." The boy looked at him with the kind of horror that is usually found only in the eyes of war veterans after an active tour of duty. He ran from the kitchen in fright. King Gruffydd II laughed and licked his spoon.

Having finished his breakfast, he scoffed an entire packet

of Bourbon biscuits and drank a glass of milk. He decided to head back to his bedroom, but first thought he would just help himself to a packet of crisps and a slice of cake.

Ivor burst into the room. He looked panicked and out of breath. "I was upstairs," he panted.

"In the antechamber?" asked the King.

"No. The floor above. My bedroom. I heard a terrible, violent noise."

King Gruffydd II looked around the room innocently then shrugged. "Well, I thought I heard a noise like an angle grinder earlier on. I guess preparations were taking place through the night." He shook his head as if to say he had no idea what might have happened but that it was certainly nothing to do with him.

Ivor nodded, still looking slightly alarmed. "It smells like boiled mushrooms in here," he said, without drawing any conclusions as to why that might be.

The King shrugged. "Well, it is a kitchen," he said simply.

Ivor looked around as if expecting to see something that would solve the conundrum, but nothing was forthcoming. He shrugged as if to say he had given up. Without voicing any opinions about what might have happened, he made his excuses to leave and headed back to his room.

The King, for he was still the King, slowly made his way back up to his new bedchamber. He was thinking about Ivor as he went; thinking what a loyal friend and advisor he had been over the years. He would have to devise a way to reward him during his speech today. Even if he did abdicate, he could make sure Ivor's loyalty didn't go unrewarded.

Finally back in his room, the King turned on his television. He flicked to the twenty-four hour Welsh news in the hope that he might get a mention. It was his primary reason for watching the news. He loved it when they mentioned him and was particularly pleased when they showed him shaking hands with important people. Unfortunately, they had turned on him a bit lately and tended to show him in an unpleasant light, but they were cautious about it as if they might be hanged for treason, which was absurd. Hanging wasn't acceptable in this day and age. Treason was only punishable by exile and usually involved being put on a train to Margate without a return ticket.

The current news item was about a man claiming to be Jesus who had had the bejesus kicked out of him by a market trader. King Gruffydd II mused that they always did put on one of those heart-warming comedy pieces at the end of each news broadcast. Last night it had been about a gerbil rescued from the stomach of a goat. The goat hadn't made it, but then it was unlikely to have, considering the gerbil was rescued by a seven year old girl with nothing but a pair of safety scissors to get the job done. It was a shame that she hadn't had a little more parental supervision throughout the procedure. The King idly wondered if people were becoming desensitised to violence because of the media, then realised he was only questioning this because someone had once said something about it on a television programme.

As the adverts came on, he found himself wondering about his future again. Would he abdicate and try to make a go of it with Ffion, with all the risks that entailed? Or would he stay on and run the risk of alienating himself from the public even further and eventually being cast out, with all the humiliation that entailed? No doubt he'd then become destitute and be forced to enrol in the new Welsh Army, or eke out a living slaving away in a workhouse for the financially inept. It was a difficult decision. The more he thought about it, the more apathy set in. In the end, it would come down to the route of least resistance and minimal discomfiture.

There was a knock at his bedroom door. "Come in," he mumbled.

A slim, attractive, naked leg appeared around the door. He looked at it for a moment, startled, wondering what the hell Ivor was playing at, then he realised Ffion had returned. She put her head around the door and smiled at him. Her cheery face instantly made him feel happier. "I'm back," she said. "Have you missed me?" He found it impossible to believe that she could be working for Lord Llandudno. He could feel the chemistry between them.

"I've missed you like crazy," he said, letting his defences down and grinning from ear to ear. She closed the door behind her and came over to sit on his lap. She kissed him on the forehead.

To blazes with it! he thought. As he ran his hand through her purple hair, he realised his decision was made.

CHAPTER 49

"The day is upon us," intoned Anil, with a gravitas that belied his youth.

The night had passed uneventfully, spent in a venue which functioned both as soup kitchen and hostel. It was busy and cramped. Their dorm mates consisted of malodorous tramps and lost revellers dumped by the Welsh police who simply didn't have room left in their overnight cells. Anil had reluctantly donned a hoodie proffered by Astin, who had retrieved it from a charity clothes bin. They made it through the night without being discovered.

Life hadn't become as *messianic* as Larry had expected. He supposed there was no turning back now, though. In a Houdini-like attempt to get out of his current clothing and into some spares, he contorted himself in the back seat of the car. They all took turns. Anil remained in his traditional garb.

"It is time," insisted Anil impatiently. "We must go to the place of revelation."

"As you wish," replied Maven. Larry was convinced Maven was lost to them now. He'd descended into a whimpering disciple in no time at all. His normal faculties had been surrendered to this Messiah-boy. As far as Larry was concerned, they still had no proof that the boy was anything special. Sure, he could fight, but that didn't make him the walking personification of God. Larry kept his suspicions to himself, because he was sure of one thing: whatever was driving Maven and whatever set of circumstances had brought them all here, it had definitely had a strange effect on him in London when he'd first written M3551Ah on the floor of their hideout while remembering his dream of a boy monk writing letters in the sand. He wished he could remember if Anil looked like the boy in the dream. All he knew was that something had taken over his mind, and he didn't like that at all. The more he thought about it, the more it spooked him.

They got into the car, which was a bit embarrassing because Anil had to sit in the boot after they had dismantled and discarded the parcel shelf. Admittedly messiahs were usually alright with inferior forms of transport, donkeys and whatnot, but Maven seemed particularly irked by the situation. Nevertheless, it is a truth universally acknowledged that the shortest must ride in the back. Anil was the shortest. The only thing that could have usurped this universal truth was if he had shouted "shotgun" at the earliest possible opportunity, but he didn't, as Higgs had beaten him to it. That said, Larry suspected Anil didn't know about the shotgun rule, being, as he was, from Tibet, where their customs would be different. They probably shouted something else.

The journey wasn't long and, normally enough, the conversation turned to hacking. What amazed Larry was that Anil joined in. Higgs had made a glib comment about performance tuning, and then Maven had corrected him on some technical issue that involved something to do with MySQL and then Anil chipped in and corrected them both. Larry actually saw Maven's jaw drop. Maven fired a few questions at Anil who explained he'd been hacking since he was old enough to type. Maven asked him who had taught him to do that. Anil simply replied that he had learnt from the web.

"So you're self-taught?" asked Higgs, impressed.

"No," replied Anil. "I learnt from the web."

It took Larry a moment to register this, but Maven looked

like he'd just injected a needle full of "I knew it" straight into an already partially-collapsed vein. His eyes lost focus, like he was staring into an abyss and down there, somewhere in the haze, he could see all his regular demons staring right back at him. "Ha ha!" he cried, in delight. "Ha ha!"

"He's lost it," whispered Larry.

"You fools," jeered Maven. "Don't you see?" But he didn't explain what he could see.

"One among you understands," confirmed Anil, looking pointedly at Maven. "But fear not, once I have addressed the world, you will all comprehend well enough."

"So you really are the Messiah?" asked Larry, disingenuously utilising a note of incredulity. He was hoping for a little taster of what was to come. He wanted to understand, because, truth be told, this is what every one of them had signed up for: answers. Deep down, he wanted to believe.

Anil stared at Larry. The boy monk's full attention was a frightening thing. Larry had never before met someone who made you feel like you were being pinned to the spot like a moth to a display board. Power radiated from him. "Larry," replied Anil. "How long until we reach our destination?"

Larry found himself answering. "Four minutes and twelve seconds until we disembark. Six minutes walking through town. We arrive fourteen minutes to the hour provided no unforeseen interim delays." Larry heard himself say the words. He didn't know he knew this information. The words just flew out. His tongue had mutinied.

"Thank you," said Anil. "I had all the relevant information stored in you before I left Tibet. Perhaps you believe I am the Messiah now?"

Larry nodded, not so much in acknowledgement as in alarm.

CHAPTER 50

Still sprawled across the bench he'd fallen asleep on, Quentin awoke to find a young child prodding him in the face with a confectionary item. He opened his eyes and stared at the little girl. She smiled at him, revealing her milk teeth. Her bright eyes sparkled like sapphires. Her blonde hair was like woven strands of sunlight. Through the sleepy fog of waking, he smiled brightly. What hope and joy the next generation could bestow upon a person's heart! What pain the expansion of a tear duct caused when a jelly bean was forced into it. Too late they both discovered the aperture at the corner of his eye was too small to house a penny sweet. With a startled yelp, Quentin propelled himself upright just in time to avoid her redoubled efforts.

"Do you mind?" he asked, sternly. This drew the attention of the child's mother who was stood nearby talking to a friend. The child was swiftly ushered away and Quentin given a scowl that could turn a gorgon to stone. The girl stuck her tongue out at him. It was blue, as was the half-chewed jelly bean perched on it.

Quentin shook off his sleepiness and looked blearily around him. He must have slept deeply indeed, for the sun was high in the sky and the plaza was full of people. It had been a rough few days, he considered, and he had been late to sleep. He decided to have a look around. It was a warm day to follow a mild night, which was fortunate for all. Quentin let the warm rays of the sun soak into his face as he awaited the blurry vision inflicted by the juvenile's assault to fade.

The first thing he observed was that all the trailers and tents which had been shut last night were now bursting with bright colours. Shoppers bustled around each one. The first stall he encountered sold sweeties. Quentin felt a pang of hunger as he eyed the red bootlaces. He felt his mouth water as he ogled the chocolate fudges. He shuddered in fear at the sight of the jelly beans.

There was a farmer's market. A selection of cheeses that boasted flavours no right-minded person would contemplate eating adorned the first stall and the tall, chubby man behind the counter with the ruddy face looked like he boasted the kind of cholesterol-filled blood plasma that only a medical researcher could care for. Next was a selection of meats that looked decidedly suspect having been basking in the sun too long. Quentin moved on. The next few stalls held wooden toys, carvings, puppets, small musical instruments, including ocarinas, and other fine displays of craftsmanship. Quentin was hungry though, so he moved on to the foreign foods market beyond. The French stall displayed cheeses and creams and fatty things, the German stall was all about sausages, and an Italian stall boasted pastas and olives. Quentin often wondered who went out for a day and decided they really needed a carrier bag full of chorizo and waffles to cart around. Evidently plenty did. Quentin mused on the many ways people make money. For him, being a lawyer wasn't one any longer. He suddenly recalled the money he'd stolen from the bank and its hiding place. It was near his father's old law firm, the one bequeathed to him on the condition that he solved the puzzle left in his father's last will and testament. The recollection exasperated him and now was hardly the time to ponder it. Quentin's stomach urged him on.

The plaza was growing steadily busier. A hotchpotch of

camera crews pointed their apparatus up towards the balcony jutting from the local theatre. So numerous were the tripods, the scene resembled the onslaught of an alien invasion. News presenters shuffled into place. As he looked around, Quentin realised there were cameras stationed all across the plaza. This was going to be a big event.

Quentin's attention returned to the cornucopia of foreign delicacies spread before him. They were tempting, but not what he was looking for. His stomach rumbled. He saw what he wanted on the other side of the plaza.

The crowds were growing thicker, so he pushed his way past families and students and businessmen and endless journalists and photographers, always keeping his target in sight. What he had seen was a good old fashioned burger van. There it was, a trailer with the hatch open, just past the doughnut van and not far from a coffee hut. What he had in mind for his breakfast was a good old fashioned hot dog. Of course, what he really fancied was a Full English, but the cafes circling the periphery of the plaza were jam-packed and queues wound their way out the doors and around the side of each building. No, his first and best option was, he decided, a hot dog with lashings of ketchup. Not one of those terrible American frankfurter efforts, either, but a proper overly-long pork sausage. The kind of British hot dog which probably wasn't called a hot dog at all, but something more descriptive and less inventive like 'sausage in a roll'. Ah, he could taste its meaty, salty, fried-onion-covered goodness already. He only needed to push past a few more families, a large school group, three entertainers and their onlookers, a Saga day trip, and a man selling helium balloons and he'd be there.

"Quentin!"

Quentin looked round and saw Janine calling him. She and Connor were shoving their way through the crowd toward him. Quentin made a split second decision. He gave them a smile and a wave, then turned and fought to reach the queue for the burger van before they could get to him. He pushed through a family of four and then shoulder barged a man manipulating a toy ferret on a string to the amusement of some youngsters. The man dropped the ferret and stepped on it, which upset everyone. Quentin mumbled an apology and hurried on.

"Hang on," shouted Connor. Quentin pretended not to hear. He'd been through enough hardship of late and he wasn't to be prevented from reaching his breakfast. They had given him five pounds pocket money and he was damn well going to spend it.

A mother holding hands with a child did that annoying thing where they faced off with him and when he moved left she moved right, when he moved right she moved left, leaving them at an impasse. The normal etiquette was to laugh and eventually pass one another, but Quentin knew that Janine and Connor were almost upon him and if they reached him before he got to the queue there was a chance they would lead him off on some foolish campaign before he'd even quelled his rumbling gut. She moved left again, as he tried to dart right. He inarticulately mumbled regret then veered left, but she headed that way too. She was utterly impassable and the situation was worsened by the added impediment of her having a child in tow. "Confound it!" he finally yelled at her, unnecessarily. She looked startled. The child looked up and started crying. It suddenly struck him that this was the same child who had stabbed him in the eye with the jelly bean. She was carrying something familiar in her hand, but he didn't quite register it - although for some reason it set alarm bells ringing in his mind. There seemed no escape from this diminutive fiend. His stomach rumbled and he decided to take drastic action.

He felt a hand on his shoulder. It was Connor. He was too late.

"Out of my way, tramps," ordered the woman. She pushed past, dragging her howling child.

"Good morning." Quentin welcomed Connor with defeat resonant in his voice.

"We've seen them," blurted Janine excitedly as she caught up. "A whole chapter of the Binary Levers! And they're with that monk child we saw fighting last night. Something big is happening."

Quentin nodded. Something big was happening in his stomach. He motioned to the burger van. "I was just..."

"Come on," urged Janine. "No time for breakfast. We've got to go and see what they're doing. Look, we've got a camera with us." She held it up for him to see. "We can collect evidence. Come on." She had hold of his arm and attempted to pull him along with her.

"Do you really need me right now?" he asked pathetically. He could smell the onions frying and, to make matters worse, a small boy with a portion of chips wrapped in a vinegar-sodden newspaper walked past with ketchup all around his mouth.

"Of course we need you," said Connor. "We haven't come this far to give up. Remember: these people killed your client."

"You have no proof of that," snapped Quentin, referring to Bryn Jones' status as his client. It was a knee-jerk reaction brought on by years of lawyerly experience.

Connor misunderstood him. "Och, we'll get proof of the murder. That's what we're here to do. That's why we're in Cardiff. But they're up to something. Something new. I just know it."

Quentin nodded. There was a sensible, adult way to deal with this. "Tell me where to meet you and I'll be there in five minutes. I'm just going to get a bite to eat or I won't be any use to you at all. I become very unfocused when my blood-sugar level is low." He said it as convincingly as he could. It was the same excuse he gave Mavis when she questioned his need for two extra biscuits before heading home each evening.

Janine rolled her eyes. Connor at least seemed sympathetic; perhaps through some kind of affinity between homeless people. "Go on then," he said, giving Quentin the permission that he didn't really need, but was certainly seeking. "We'll meet you over there near that building. By the door to the solicitor's firm."

"Certainly," said Quentin. Mixed emotions played within

him at the mention of a solicitor's firm. His downfall flashed before his eyes for the umpteenth time since the bailiffs had evicted him. Connor and Janine moved away through the ever-thickening crowd leaving him with his thoughts.

Quentin was distracted from his self-pity as he overheard a snatch of conversation about the time. He glanced up at the ornamental clock at the centre of the plaza and saw it was half past ten, which meant it was past his breakfast and very nearly time for elevenses. No wonder he was hungry. The snippet of conversation he'd caught seemed to suggest royalty would appear at eleven o'clock. Quentin was foggy on the details but understood the King of Wales was to speak. His interest was piqued. He'd seen pictures of the King in the news, but had little notion of what he might say. He realised that living a small distance over the border, in Chester, made a huge difference to what he paid attention to on a daily basis. He found it hard to believe a King had arisen in Wales when the dissident Republicans were successfully causing such trouble in England. Interesting times, he mused.

He eventually arrived at the back of the queue for the burger van. He counted only seven people in front of him and thought it shouldn't be too long before he got served. He planned to eat quickly then rendezvous with Connor and Janine. He considered that the solicitor's firm didn't look too far from the King's balcony so should provide him with a good view of the proceedings.

It was two pounds for a hot dog, but three pounds for a jumbo hot dog. The fried onions cost nothing and a large ketchup bottle stood on the counter, free for any customer to use. Quentin smiled. The humble hot dog was a simple foodstuff and yet appetising and convenient all in one. Things were looking up. He would, of course, opt for the jumbo hot dog on this occasion. He decided he could happily stretch to three pounds in the circumstances. He was now third in the queue.

He went to take his wallet out of his pocket and found that his pocket was empty. He patted himself down once, then twice, then again another five times for good measure. He was second in the queue now. He put his hand into each and every pocket of his clothing to ensure he wasn't making some kind of silly mistake. He was front of the queue now. He looked up at the vendor and smiled. The vendor looked back at him with a raised eyebrow. "Lost something?" he asked. Quentin had to accept that he'd lost his wallet. He muttered a brief explanation and apology and walked away.

Then it dawned on him. The object the little girl had been carrying. The object he'd recognised. It was his wallet! She must have swiped it before she attempted to insert that jelly bean into his eye. He sighed. You just couldn't trust anyone these days.

He stood on tiptoes and looked in the direction that the mother and child had departed. As he peered over the heads of perhaps a thousand revellers he knew they were well and truly lost to him. It was just his luck. With nothing else left to do, he pushed his way through the heaving mass to the other side of the plaza. The big, outdoor cinema screen had come alive and was showing fifty foot high jugglers and fire eaters, who Quentin presumed could be found somewhere amongst the swarming masses.

He reached Connor and Janine.

"Good breakfast?" asked Janine in a way that made it clear she still disapproved of his choice not to follow them immediately.

"Yes, thank you. Really hit the spot," replied Quentin without feeling any guilt at all. He turned his back on her so he could look up at the balcony.

CHAPTER 51

After the first year of the King's reign there had been some merriment on the streets to celebrate a whole year of Welsh monarchy. Things were very much up in the air and there hadn't been any time to properly plan a celebration, nor any money to hold one. Yet a few people had come out onto the streets and pulled party poppers and drunk champagne and that had been the start of it. In the second year, the monarchy and the forces that drove it decided it might be possible to capitalise on this annual tendency toward revelry to promote nationalistic feeling and loyalty to the crown. Sir Pendragon of Llysfaen, the Duke of Snowdonia, and even Ivor, had insisted that it was a good idea to celebrate the coronation. King Gruffydd II had no objections to this, so some food was laid on for the nobility and street entertainers were encouraged to volunteer their services. The monarchy was still relatively popular at that point, but it was only a matter of months before the honeymoon was over and the people, namely the press, wanted to know a little bit more about King Gruffydd II. That was when things took a turn for the worse.

This third year, the celebrations had been amplified out of all proportion. The growing popularity of the street party could be measured by the crowd outside. There are ways and means to bring people together and they usually involve food, alcohol and the chance to make a public mockery of an unpopular figure. Of course, when they first started putting the preparations together, King Gruffydd II was a lot more popular. Unfortunately, in the recent economic quarter, the full repercussions of not being on good terms with England were being felt by people in their pockets and, more importantly, their kitchen cupboards. Of course, being unable to enter an English pub without some jibe about being at war with them was also starting to grate on everyone's nerves.

It was all to come to an end now, anyway. King Gruffydd II, in his most regal attire, sat patiently in the small balcony room and awaited eleven o'clock. He wasn't nervous at all. It wasn't going to take long. All he had to do was go out there, stand before the multitude of plebs and tell them a thing or two about what was what.

The first thing he was going to do was thank them for letting him rule the country for three whole years. On the whole, they had been good years and he felt that mentioning this was a sensible way to begin.

The next thing was the death of the Duke of Snowdonia. There was every chance no one in the crowd really knew or cared who he was, or that he was dead, but generally if you mentioned these sort of things they found their way into the paper and then suddenly everyone would claim to have known him and he'd be remembered most fondly. The Duke of Snowdonia had been a staunch supporter of the monarchy before he'd suffered that unfortunate reaction to the aubergine, so he at least deserved a mention.

King Gruffydd II flicked through his handwritten notes.

The next thing he would do would be to announce a surprise award. Ivor had been a loyal supporter and advisor these last three years, and he put up with all the King's practical jokes, insults and tantrums with such patient decorum, selflessness and dignity that he really, truly had to be rewarded. It wouldn't be right to leave him nothing and then for Lord Llandudno to fire him, which was the most likely scenario following his intended abdication. Ivor was to be awarded a medal for services rendered to the crown, and was to be made the new Duke of Snowdonia, since the original had no heirs and the King could appoint who the hell he liked with several thousand people watching.

Finally, he would bring Ffion to the stage. She was sat across from him now and winked flirtatiously at him. She twirled her purple hair nervously as she watched him read through his notes. She wore an elegant black dress and looked like someone he wanted to spend the rest of his life with.

After announcing his abdication, he would leave Lord Llandudno in charge as Lord Protector of Wales. That would give him all the responsibility and none of the royalty. Ha ha! Yes. A job well done.

Damn his eyes. Where was the Lord Protector when you needed him? He hadn't seen the man all morning and one of the servants had reported that his room looked like it had been abandoned in a hurry. Well, there was ten minutes left. Perhaps he would show up.

Outside, the noise of the crowd rose up to the balcony and penetrated the closed curtains separating the King from the public. Never had so many people attended the anniversary celebrations. He had a sneaky suspicion that word of his abdication had somehow been leaked to the press, perhaps through some mischievous blog or tweet he didn't know about. Still, no matter. Soon he would be jumping the broom in Gretna Green, then he and his new wife would be jetting off for cocktails in the sun in Swansea.

Five minutes to go. He had to admit to himself that his heart was beating just a little faster now. Last time, Ivor had been here to help him prepare, but he hadn't wanted to spoil the nice surprise for the little man so had sent him away saying that he was perfectly capable of managing on his own. Ivor had gone to check the link-up to the big cinema screen was still in full working order.

"What's that?" asked Ffion, nodding towards the curtains.

King Gruffydd II cocked an ear and now he could hear it

too. There was some sort of commotion outside. Someone was shouting. That was odd. It sounded for all the world like they were crying, "Hail the Messiah!"

CHAPTER 52

"There's only ten minutes left until the King makes his speech," pressed Higgs, checking his watch.

Larry looked around anxiously, not enjoying the sensation of so many people pressing in on every side of him. "Are we going to let the King make his announcement first?"

"It's irrelevant," stated Maven. "What could he possibly say of significance compared to what we are about to reveal?"

"Lead on," commanded Anil, evidently eager to get started.

Maven shouldered his way through the crowd, closely followed by Higgs and Anil, then Larry, with Astin taking up the rear. The way was thick with people crammed into the public square to get a glimpse of the King making his speech before the festivities and the drinking began in earnest. The celebrations had brought people from far and wide. It was an ideal platform for Anil to make his own pronouncement.

Off to the side of the plaza stood a screen that was fifty foot high. It occasionally showed pictures of the empty balcony where the King would stand, so that the camera crews could set up and do checks. It would then return to showing close-up sections of the crowd, where inevitably the targeted part of the audience would start jumping up and down, swearing, possibly mooning, and generally making it an absolutely necessity to move on to a completely different part of the crowd, until they started doing the same.

The balcony was a large concrete construct with metal supports and metal rails. It looked down on the plaza and there was no way to get close to it from the ground. Maven aimed for the space beneath it, figuring it would make it easy for the cameras to focus on Anil when he demanded the attention of his people. The only problem was actually getting past the cameramen and reporters who were densely packed together in the available space that had been cordoned off for the press. At first Larry thought they wouldn't get through, but it became clear Maven would have no truck with that. He elbowed his way past a BBC reporter and headbutted a cameraman from S4C who had proven to be an obstacle.

"Git out the way of the Messiah!" yelled Astin, unceremoniously. He shoved away a young female reporter who tripped, fell over a tripod and brought three thousand pounds worth of media equipment crashing to the ground.

"Don't damage the cameras," ordered Maven. "We have our own message to broadcast, remember?"

There was a police presence in the plaza. It was only really visible around the outside of the square where their cars were parked, with Heddlu marked noticeably on the bonnets, but there were plenty of undercover police milling through the crowd. Several lingered beneath the balcony where there was the greatest potential for trouble. Instantly, three burly men with wires trailing from their ears stamped toward the commotion, shoving the innocent public to one side as they cut their way through the swathe of onlookers.

Higgs got in the way of the first one. Arguably, it could be said he slowed him, because a second later he was handcuffed behind his back and being led away. The other two policemen grabbed Maven, and three more officers joined them. Larry backed away from them. Astin pulled a knife from his pocket. "Protect the Messiah!" shouted Maven. He needn't have worried.

Maven turned and headbutted one of the officers holding him. The other one reached for a truncheon, but Anil had taken his legs out from under him and shoved his head down hard into the concrete as he fell. The other officer swung Maven away so he could deal with this new threat, but he forgot he hadn't handcuffed him yet. Maven jumped on his back and Anil kicked him squarely between the legs, and turned...

The three other officers who were on the scene were being backed up by an irate BBC reporter and an S4C cameraman. The rest of the paparazzi were standing back. Beyond them, the crowd was starting to panic but had nowhere to go.

Anil leapt in the air, planting the heel of his palm down hard on an officer's nose. The force of his landing pushed the policeman straight back into the second one, who had a can of pepper spray in his hand. He fired it, but too late. Anil had his head under the man's armpit, and one arm wrapped around each of his knees. He lifted and pushed, and the officer was flat on his back and knocked unconscious. Larry watched as Anil planted a foot to the side of the last officer's knee. He winced as he heard something crack. The officer fell to the ground, grunting in pain. Anil leant on the man's neck with his knee for a second or two and the officer blacked out. Astin had already dealt with the first officer, whose nose was gushing blood from Anil's attack. Larry couldn't believe what he was seeing.

The BBC reporter and S4C cameraman seemed to have backed off, deciding perhaps they weren't so interested in joining in the brawl now, as it happened, if it was all the same to everyone, thank you for your time, good bye. It was a short lived and violent fight, and the Binary Levers knew there would be more trouble on its way soon, so they had to get started. Larry looked around for Higgs. Anil was already helping him out of his cuffs while the officer lay writhing on the ground next to them.

Larry felt a panic rising in his chest. The cameras were all pointing at them. Flashlights lit the scene like a strobe-effect disco, even in the daylight, and Larry knew their faces would soon be on the front page of every newspaper. This couldn't possibly end well.

CHAPTER 53

"There they are!" yelled Connor excitedly, as he spotted the Binary Levers leading the boy monk through the crowd. None of them were ready for what happened next. As the fight broke out, Janine climbed the stairs of the solicitor's firm for a better view over the crowd and started taking photographs of the action. At one point something went 'crack' and the crowd winced in unison. Like some kind of shifting fractal pattern, people swirled away from the balcony area as if orchestrated, then drifted into new positions where they could watch events unfold.

Quentin couldn't clearly see what was happening, but he could hear the reaction of the crowd. "What are they doing?" he asked, craning his neck to see over the swarm. They had a good view of the balcony, but not such a good view of what was happening at ground level beneath it.

"Winning," replied Janine in disbelief. "That boy is amazing!" She sounded genuinely impressed.

"I can barely see," whined Quentin, craning his neck. Despite his obstructed view, he felt caught up in the chemical reaction of the crowd; swaying forward, pulling back, ready to flee if things got messy. It was hard to keep a rational mind at a time like this. "Damn it, now I can't see a thing!" He went on tip-toes.

Janine tapped him on the shoulder. Having got his attention, she pointed up at the big screen. Of course, it was now displaying the fight from very close quarters. Two fully uniformed police officers arrived on the scene, and what a scene it was. People were lying writhing on the ground. Two of the Binary Levers were directing the cameramen and trying to set up a shot. The boy monk was climbing on to a chair so they could get a better line of sight on him. One of the uniformed policemen walked over to the boy and got a foot wedged in his throat for his trouble. One of the Binary Levers dragged the suffocating cop out of harm's way. The other officer pulled out his truncheon and approached carefully. Anil stared him down. The officer paused. Losing his nerve at the sight of the fallen bodies all around him, he backed off while calling for backup into a handset attached to his uniform. It was fantastic viewing, realised Quentin. They had picked a fight right in the middle of a crowd of cameramen who all had live feeds to the big screen. Someone, somewhere, was doing a fantastic job of switching feeds and live-editing it so that it felt like a choreographed Hollywood fight sequence. After a moment's reflection, Quentin realised the sound he was hearing was the crowd cheering for the boy.

The policeman looked worried, but shouted out, "You're under arrest!" The sound wasn't being projected over the plaza yet and probably wouldn't be until the King arrived, but the audience read the copper's lips and Quentin could hear people saying "Being arrested" and "Arresting him" and "Hot dog with everything on it." Clearly some people were completely oblivious to the brouhaha.

Still standing on the chair, the young monk turned to face the cameras. His face and shoulders loomed fifty foot high on the big screen overlooking the plaza. The policeman shrugged and took a step back. A cheer went up from the crowd. The monk smiled at the policeman, who nodded back. He'd given up. The crowd saw all this on the big screen and cheered again. Suddenly the clock in the centre of the plaza struck eleven o'clock. The cheering died down. Anil was centre-stage. On the big screen, Quentin saw a microphone being set up in front of the boy. The person setting it up, who had long, greasy, grey hair and was chewing a toothpick, tapped it once or twice, and the whining sound of feedback bounced around the plaza for a moment. The boy opened his mouth to speak.

"Hello? Hello? What's going on here?" came the voice. It bounced around the plaza, yet it wasn't the voice of a boy.

Quentin looked away from the screen and back to where the boy stood in reality. What he saw startled him. On the big screen, the picture pulled back so the balcony came into view. There was a gasp from the crowd. The King was already there on the balcony in full regal dress and sporting his golden crown. He'd arrived completely unannounced. To everyone's surprise he was carefully leaning over the balcony and shouting questions down to the boy below.

CHAPTER 54

Anil looked up, as did the other Binary Levers. The cameramen all looked up. Everyone was staring at the King. Larry took a few steps back into the crowd so he didn't have to crane his neck so far to see the fat man on the balcony.

"Hello?" repeated the King. His voice boomed out over the plaza, echoing off the walls and shaking the brickwork. Clearly the microphone on the balcony was working just fine.

It started small, then grew into a chorus. The crowd, working their way up, then finally in unison, and possibly thinking this was all some great pantomime, shouted back with the force and volume that only several thousand highly excited voices can muster. "Hello!"

There was a creaking noise.

"Ah, it's working," said the King, looking at the microphone with pleasant surprise. Seemingly oblivious to the violence that had ensued below, he stopped looking down at the monk and prepared to address the crowd. "Countrymen, friends and Welshmen," he said, and paused, then looked at his notes with a frown. Larry was a bit surprised to see the King using a set of handwritten notes, but he guessed it might be more common than he would have guessed. Or perhaps they didn't have auto-cues in Wales. The King continued. "It is our great pleasure to welcome you all here today." The King smiled, which Larry presumed was because he'd referred to himself as 'our'.

The big screen started to flicker. Blue and white stripes rolled across it, casting an incandescent glow across the crowd. The moment passed and it returned to showing the balcony. The King had seen this happen and frowned. He cast about as if looking for someone, but evidently couldn't find him and gave up trying. He continued. "We are gathered here today, on this auspicious occasion, to celebrate the third year of our coronation." The crowd seemed nonplussed and Larry began to wonder who had written the King's speech for him. It was all a bit pre-millennium.

"Testing!" The word boomed across the plaza. No one was sure who had said it. It wasn't the boy and it certainly wasn't the King.

The view shown on the big screen sank below the balcony. The crowd murmured in surprise, clearly sensing that something was going wrong. Larry saw that Maven had managed to find a working microphone and was setting it up in front of Anil. The King's voice could still be heard, but the big screen focused on the small monk. "It has been an honour to rule the great nation of Wales these last three years," the King intoned haughtily. He paused, seemingly waiting for some response from the crowd, but the crowd were whispering.

Anil stood bolt upright and his face shone out over the big screen. The next thing the King said was, "Who is that boy?"

Anil spoke. His voice blasted out over the plaza, at least as loud as the King's and twice as commanding. "I come before you as the chosen one. You are my people. Today is your day of reckoning. Do not doubt me for I am your lord, your prince, your king. Yes, I am your redeemer and saviour. I am the delivered. Your emancipator. Your advocate. I am the anointed one. Hear me, for I am the door, the way, the light, the candle and the path. I am the shepherd. I am the butcher, the baker and candlestick maker. I am the conductor, the coryphaeus, the bellwether and the torchbearer. I am the mediator. I am the intercessor. I am the one and only; the risen, the true vine, the message, the lamb. I am the lion, the tiger and bear. Oh my, you must heed me, for I am the Messiah."

"Hail the Messiah!" This was Maven. He shouted loudly so the microphone would pick it up. "Hail the Messiah!" By the third shout, the crowd was with him. All together now, they cheered, "Hail the Messiah!"

Larry found himself joining in.

Anil smiled.

There was another creaking sound.

The big screen flickered again.

"Well, that was a slightly better speech than I had prepared," harrumphed the King, possibly forgetting the microphone was still turned on. The crowd laughed. But that was wrong. Just as Anil had stolen the King's moment, the King had inadvertently stolen Anil's. Larry frowned. That shouldn't be possible. That shouldn't be possible with the real Messiah. It made him angry. He didn't know how he knew it, but somehow he knew Anil wasn't the chosen one.

The King spoke indignantly. "I think you'll find I'm their king!"

"My people!" yelled Anil, drawing their attention again. Maven had moved the microphone even closer. His young voice was deafening. The crowd, as one, winced. Some covered their ears. "I am the Messiah. Bow before me!"

Some of the crowd obeyed. Then some more. And some more. Larry couldn't believe what he was seeing. Why were these people obeying Anil? He had done nothing to prove himself.

The King was fiddling with something on the balcony. When he next spoke into his microphone it was clear he'd been turning up the volume to combat Anil. "Well, two can play at that game," he said, brusquely.

There was another creak. Some brick dust fell from the wall near the balcony.

"Silence, pretender!" Anil screamed at the King. He could not see King Gruffydd II because the King stood on the balcony directly above him, but he could see both the King and himself on the big screen. Together they were like acid and alkaline, powerful agents but neutral when combined. The crowd was on its feet again and looking annoyed and restless.

The big screen rolled with white and blue lines. The image seemed to clear and showed a white cloud against a pale sky. The cloud flashed brightly, as if reflecting sheet lightning. It pulsated as a voice exploded out over the plaza. "ENOUGH," it boomed. "I AM COME." The volume was ear-splitting. The people standing near the speakers fell to their knees and wailed in pain.

For Larry the world dropped into slow motion as he watched what happened next. More blue and white lines flickered across the screen. The sun went behind a building and colour seemed to drain from the world.

"Oh dear!" That was the King still speaking into his microphone. "One butty too many!" he declared.

Brick dust was followed by plaster was followed by the sound of metal creaking and snapping. The balcony slipped an inch. Anil looked up; the confidence gone from his eyes. The balcony tipped and then - and this happened so fast Larry couldn't really remember seeing it afterwards - the balcony and the King came crashing down on top of Anil and the chair he stood on. Brick dust exploded into the air in great billows. The crowd gasped. Larry pushed away from the chaos and into the crowd which quickly drew back.

The dust rolled outward. Everyone held their breath as it dissipated and through the gloom a dark mound appeared. All eyes were on the pile of rubble as the dust settled. Larry squinted through half-closed eyelids and saw a tangle of brick, mortar, metal and wood. It was a scrap heap. It was absolutely clear to everyone what had happened. The combination of the King's weight and the volume of the speakers shaking the balcony had broken it from its fixings.

As the dust settled, it was the uniformed police officer

who first stepped forward to look for survivors. Larry stumbled forward to help him. They found Maven lying on his back. One of his feet was trapped under some masonry. He was unconscious. The policeman lifted the boulder of concrete while Larry pulled Maven to safety. Higgs was by his side in a flash and feeling for a pulse on Maven's neck. He indicated that he'd found one. They both breathed a sigh of relief.

They turned back to the jumble of building materials. The officer and some of the cameramen pulled away some large chunks of debris. It wasn't long before they exposed the back of the King's head and then a part of his torso.

The microphones were still on and the big screen showed all that was happening. Someone spoke, and everyone heard it. Larry looked around. It was Maven. He had come around and was lying there, clearly in pain, shouting up at the microphone. "The King is dead!" he shouted. "Long live the Messiah!"

The words echoed around the plaza and were taken up by everyone, but they weren't cheers - they were whispers of shock. A mere susurrus of a murmuration floated around the crowd, posed half as statement and half as question: "The King is dead?"

"Over here," said one of the cameramen. He pulled away a large chunk of concrete with the help of some others who hadn't already hoisted cameras onto their shoulders and started filming. They exposed the limp hand of a young man in a robe that was now grey with masonry dust. The cameraman held the boy's wrist for a moment, then shook his head. Another man stepped in and tried... and also shook his head.

Larry turned to Maven. "Anil is dead," he managed, barely able to speak.

"That can't be!" screamed Maven. Fury and devastation fought for dominance in his voice. He started to mouth a denial but the image on the big screen showed Anil's arm amongst the wreckage and startled him into silence.

"Definitely dead," agreed Higgs sombrely.

Maven's head fell back on the ground and he stared up at the sky. His eyes were without focus.

"I think he's going into shock," said Higgs. He leaned over Maven to check he hadn't swallowed his tongue. "Quick, Larry - phone an ambulance."

Larry didn't respond.

Higgs looked up to see what was the matter.

All the cameras were pointed at Larry. Larry was scrabbling up the side of the mound of fallen masonry, picking his way up, one quick footstep at a time. He seemed oblivious to everything as he made his mad scramble for the top of the pile.

Higgs looked up at the big screen, expecting to see Larry, but what he saw instead made his blood run cold.

CHAPTER 55

Ivor wasn't sure what to think. He was standing by the rigging for the big screen and making sure nobody came too close. He had been told to watch out for any revellers that might attempt to sabotage the screening of the celebrations. Of course, the King had thought that the big event would be his speech. Ivor had known differently.

He was shocked to see the balcony slide from the wall and land on the monk boy. He had no idea who the boy was, only that he was getting in the way right from the start and wouldn't be getting in the way any longer. He wasn't, however, shocked to see the balcony drop from the wall. He was disappointed that it had required the speakers to shake it off. That was annoying because it should have fallen under the King's weight alone. He had spent all morning ensuring that only he, a short little fellow, not at all heavy, was allowed to go out on the balcony to check everything was set up correctly. He had managed this under the twin headings of 'security' and 'safety', which, when mentioned together, could make even the most sensible person follow the most banal and counterintuitive instructions. Anyway, his handiwork had done its job.

He conceded to himself that he did feel a little remorse at

killing a person who he had known for so long. Yet he suspected the King would have felt no remorse had it been the other way around, so he dismissed whatever underdeveloped semblance of guilt he was experiencing and did his level best to enjoy the moment. He chuckled. He didn't actually feel merry, but he felt a chuckle wasn't out of place since he was clearly the villain of the piece.

"That's right, Your Majesty," he muttered. "I snapped your balcony like you snapped my salt and vinegar crisp."

The crowd didn't seem as horrified as he thought they should be. Obviously he had known they didn't really care for the King, but he had thought the end of a human life would at least shock them. Instead, they were mostly just looking up at the big screen and pointing.

Ivor looked up at the picture. He could see some people picking through the rubble. The picture closed in on the back of the King, who was lying face down in the smashed-up concrete.

Ivor mumbled a little ditty to himself. "Sleep like the dead, sleep like the dead, lay down your head, it's time for bed." As he said the words he could hear his mother lulling him to sleep as he rested his head on a pillow sprinkled with fragrance of hemlock to help him get over.

He didn't look away. This was not his first kill. Lord Llandudno was very-almost-literally pushing up the daisies as testimony to that fact. Ivor had waited a long time for this moment. Finally, he felt triumph rising in his breast.

Along with several thousand others, Ivor held his breath as the men on the screen found the boy and tested for a pulse. The man shook his head. Ivor looked away, his triumph momentarily abating. At the back of his mind a fresh insight into his behaviour should have emerged as a result of the guilt borne on the back of this moment of clarity, but he held it at bay with the psychological equivalent of a pitchfork and then condemned it to die.

In truth, he had been so busy planning the death of the King he was not one hundred percent sure how best to now capitalise on it. He quickly decided he needed to speak to the people. He was, after all, the former king's personal advisor. With Lord Llandudno out of the picture, it fell to him to lead the people - those good people of Wales - and to help them pick up the pieces. Together they would forge a better Wales. Yes, that's probably the exact line he would feed them. In his mind he'd pictured himself on the balcony, talking down to the masses who eagerly soaked up his pronouncements. With the balcony gone, he was rather at a loss. The only thing to do would be to get in front of the cameras which were now following the King as he was lifted - by a considerable number of helpers - from the rubble and laid out to rest. They probably couldn't bear him much farther without a pickup truck.

Ivor ran through the palace hallways past startled volunteers waiting to serve food. Ivor came out near the rubble, but not close enough. A congregation of onlookers and a horde of cameramen stood in his way. He started to nudge his way to the front, but it was a difficult task for someone over a foot shorter than average.

As he knuckled, elbowed and on one occasion bit his way through the crowd, he heard a universal muttering arise from the assembled public. He looked up and saw that someone else was scrabbling to the top of the pile, in full view of the cameras. He pushed forward with greater vehemence. It was vital that he got speaking before that lumbering buffoon, who now teetered atop the wreckage looking mildly bewildered. The crowd were oohing and ahhing, which couldn't be a good sign. Ivor shot a glance back at the big screen, but he wasn't sure what he was seeing there.

"I speak to you," said the figure on the rubble. "Hear me."

To Ivor's surprise, the crowd instantly fell silent.

Ivor got to the twisted remains of the balcony and scrabbled up the side of the debris. "Get off here," he demanded. "You've no right to be here." He could hear his voice echoing off the buildings around the plaza and suddenly became very self-conscious.

The figure looked at him. Someone in the crowd shouted

up saying, "Larry, get down from there."

"Yes, Larry," said Ivor, catching on quick. "Thank you for helping. Now get down from here. Leave this to me."

Larry turned to look at Ivor with two vacant eyes. Ivor did a double-take in surprise. He couldn't identify what had startled him exactly, but when he looked in those eyes he shuddered. They were dead. Not the metaphorically dead eyes of a cold blooded killer, but the completely dead eyes of a corpse. Yet they were focused on him. "Who are you?" asked Larry, in a monotonous drone. Ivor didn't answer as he tried to get a grip on the situation and a solid foothold on the rubble.

He got control of himself. The aftermath of the King's demise was much stranger than he had imagined it would be. "I am Ivor..." He stopped himself from saying his surname in case it got a laugh from the crowd. "The King's advisor."

Larry looked him up and down. "You are Ivor Munchkinhead." There was snigger from the crowd, but it wasn't enthusiastic. Clearly no-one really understood what was happening. "You are thirty seven years of age. You are royal advisor to the late King Gruffydd the second, a position which is legally tied to the reign of the monarch and thus rendered void by his demise. Depart from this place."

Ivor wasn't prepared for that. This Larry person looked like a complete dumpling: thick labourer's hands, a thick lower lip, arm tattoos, a dull voice and a nose that had been re-set more than once. The fact that he'd stumped him on a legal matter left him shaken. The worst part was he had no idea if it was accurate. He figured that perhaps Larry wouldn't know either. He tried his luck. "You're wrong. The relevant legislation states that on the demise of the King I continue with my title and assume his duties in the interim period until the heir apparent or other appointed individual assumes the role."

"Erroneous," stated Larry. "Now GO!"

It was clear that negotiation wasn't going to get him anywhere. Ivor got himself up next to Larry on the top of the rubble. He turned to the crowd. "I am Ivor, the King's Royal

Advisor," he shouted. "It is my duty to lead you through this difficult time following the sad loss of our beloved ruler."

The crowd didn't respond. They were looking at the big screen. Ivor turned and looked up at it. He saw himself standing atop the rubble, but next to him he didn't see Larry. Instead he saw a version of Larry that looked quite different. He recoiled and looked back at Larry, but Larry looked just the same as before. "I don't understand," he said aloud, by accident.

Larry's dead eyes looked back at him but he didn't speak.

The booming voice from before broke out across the plaza. "MERE MORTALS CANNOT COMPREHEND THE TRUE POWER OF AUGMENTED REALITY."

Ivor had heard the term augmented reality before, but he wasn't exactly sure what it meant. He understood enough to know that Larry hadn't changed in real life. He looked back at the screen. Up there, the version of Larry standing next to him was much taller and dressed in a long, white robe with reed sandals on his feet. He had a bushy black beard down to his chest and his eyes had a phosphorous white-blue glow. The image wasn't perfect though, and the body seemed pixellated, perhaps due to its blown-up size on the big screen.

"Are you a believer?" asked Larry.

Ivor turned back to the real Larry, who looked no different to normal. The question and the whole experience left Ivor speechless. He thought he'd already done away with the Messiah-wannabe. His first thought was to push Larry down the side of the balcony wreckage, but he was all too aware that he was being watched by several thousand people. Whatever he did was likely to be broadcast on every news channel for weeks to come.

"Are you a Binary Lever?" asked Larry, seemingly by way of clarification.

"Not that I know of," snorted Ivor.

"What is the fifth digit after the decimal place in the number known as Pi?" asked Larry.

Ivor was about to snap back with some angry retort, but

as he opened his mouth he found himself answering, "Nine."

"Correct," replied Larry. "You are confirmed as susceptible."

"I was right?" asked Ivor in surprise. He couldn't help looking back at the huge screen to see himself standing next to an image of Larry that resonated with biblical connotations.

"Now die," said Larry, in his deadpan voice.

He lifted his arms and splayed out his fingers. A crackling sound filled the plaza. The crowd gasped.

Ivor looked at Larry, with his curly black hair and his thick jaw. He couldn't understand what was meant to be happening. He did feel a little peculiar though, because he could now see expectation in those dead eyes. He looked back up at the screen, and it was the last thing he ever consciously did.

On the big screen, Ivor could see what the crowd could see. Larry's hands glowed with charged energy and small blue sparks flickered away violently. From the ends of his fingertips, forked lightning shot out in spastic contortions of white-blue electricity. The lightning hit and enveloped Ivor.

The crowd gasped in horror as Ivor's body, head turned to the screen and fixated on the image there, started to convulse and shake violently. The sound of the crackling lightning filled the plaza and to anyone watching the screen it was clear that Ivor's body was being electrocuted. He shook and shuddered as the lightning from Larry's fingertips fried him on the spot.

In reality, the physical appearance of his body didn't change, although his body was locked rigid and foam was spurting from his mouth. No actual scorching was visible on his skin but he was turning a gruesome shade of red. On the screen, it was a different matter. Ivor's body started to smoke and blacken. Flames came out of his eyes and ears. His skin shrivelled up and his hair caught fire. He shook where he stood, burning to a crisp.

Eventually the lightning stopped and Larry lowered his arms. Ivor's corpse fell backwards and rolled to a halt at the foot of the pile of rubble. He was dead before he fell, but if anyone in the crowd held on to a hope that Ivor would survive the attack, then that hope was extinguished all too obviously by the way he landed. His body lay on its front while his neck was twisted round so he stared sightlessly up at the midday sky.

CHAPTER 56

Quentin was momentarily stunned into catatonic stupefaction. He watched as much of the crowd moved away from the concrete-centric carnage. He became aware of sirens in the distance. The dichotomy between real life and the virtual world was not something he had ever spent much time thinking about, but now he saw two worlds colliding in a way he would not have imagined possible even an hour ago. Janine and Connor were at his side. "I can't find a frame of reference for what I'm witnessing," he stammered, being horrified, perplexed and strangely articulate in equal measure.

"Only a fevered religious mind would use imagery like that," spat Janine, referring to the Moses-like avatar of Larry on the big screen. "This reeks of the Binary Levers."

Quentin heard uncertainty in her voice. "Do you have a precedent for that?" he asked, a little too sharply. His mind was working in overdrive as he tried to process the events of the last few minutes.

"No," she admitted. After a moment, she continued, "But it seems clear that this is the work of a hacker using augmented reality for their own perverse ends. I certainly wouldn't put this past them."

Quentin absorbed her argument but knew she was only

guessing. His life had been very strange over the last few days and as each second passed he found he wasn't as shocked by all this mayhem as he perhaps should have been. His faculties were as keen as ever. He needed to understand what was happening.

"I don't see how a virtual image could kill a living person," he complained.

Connor shrugged. "Beats me," he said.

Janine shrugged. "It just shouldn't be possible."

Quentin looked around the plaza. "We need to speak to a Binary Lever."

"I'd advise against that," said Connor, scratching his scalp.

"Would you recognise a Binary Lever if you saw one?"

"I would," said Janine. "I recognise the one up there, on top of the rubble. He's called Larry. His friend Higgs is in the crowd. I spied on, um, observed them when Larry was in hospital. Their boss is called Maven. Most Luddites know of him... and fear him. He's the one that hurt his foot when the balcony fell."

"And he's still there," realised Quentin. "I need to speak to him!"

Before they could move, the big screen flickered again and white and blue lines rolled across it. The lines disappeared and slowly an image formed. It was one they had caught a glimpse of earlier. It showed a pale sky with a large, grey cloud dominating the majority of the screen. The cloud seemed alive. It pulsated and reflected sheet lightning that flashed in the background. The cloud's colour deepened to a darker grey.

"What is that?" asked Janine aloud. "A screensaver?"

Many people were trying to leave the plaza. Unfortunately, many more were staying to watch the action and inadvertently penning in the others. No one was quite sure what was happening. All they knew was that three people - a boy, a king and his advisor - had died in the last ten minutes, one in very strange circumstances. Normally fearless pigeons sensed the rising panic and scattered into the air, scattering all over the crowd too.

"Maven is dangerous," warned Janine. "We shouldn't go near him."

"If he's the leader, he's the one we need to talk to," insisted Quentin.

"Aye, but will he talk to us, though?" asked Connor, not looking convinced, although possibly the face he pulled was related to the fact he was trying to scratch somewhere deep between his buttocks. "Sorry," he said, noticing Quentin eyeing him with some considerable consternation.

"Morgellons again?" asked Quentin politely.

Connor shook his head and looked slightly abashed. "Just an itchy arse."

"Come on," pressed Quentin. The three of them stepped down from their perch in front of the solicitor's office and began pushing forward to the area where the balcony had fallen. The crowd was thinner there, but it was by no means deserted. Some people were reluctant to believe the figure atop the wreckage could cause harm in the way they had seen. For one thing, on the screen there had been smoke and fire. In real life, just spittle. It was as if they were waiting to see it again, so they could be sure.

Quentin did his best to be polite as he struggled through. "Excuse me, madam," he said to one, and "Ahem, sir, if you please," to another. After a moment he turned to Connor and said, "Be a good fellow and go first, would you?"

Connor took poll position and, still dressed and smelling like a tramp, he had no problem driving a wedge through the crowd, especially as he seemed quite preoccupied with scratching his crotch the whole while and muttering to himself about scrotal scurf caused by itchy microscopic fibres; a subject Quentin decided was best not broached.

As they pushed on, a computerised voice boomed across the plaza once more. Everyone else stopped what they were doing to pay attention. The cloud on the screen grew darker yet and then pulsated with inner lightning. "BEHOLD ME!" The voice rumbled, as unavoidable as it was terrifying. Suddenly the screen showed Larry again, who lifted up his arms and looked out across the crowd. "YOU ARE NOW SERVILE UNTO ME. DISOBEDIENCE IS PUNISHABLE BY DEATH." Larry's robes and hair blew in a wind which Quentin couldn't feel. "I OFFER YOU ONE LENIENCY. TO AVOID THE COMPLETE ANNIHILATION OF YOUR SPECIES I WILL PERMIT A DIALOGUE WHEREIN I WILL DICTATE MY TERMS. SELECT YOUR SPOKESPERSON." Quentin had been eyeing Larry throughout this and noticed his lips didn't move once. Whatever Larry was, concluded Quentin, he was not the instigator. A hush fell over the crowd. It soon became clear no one intended to volunteer as spokesperson before this strangely biblical image which seemed so at odds with normalcy and comprehension.

As they neared the wreckage, Quentin overtook Connor to arrive first. He checked over his shoulder to ensure Janine was still with them; she was forcing herself past some straggler who refused to budge. She arrived and pointed to the figure lying by the palace wall, clutching his injured leg. "That's Maven," she said. He was sweating profusely but seemed to have the pain under control. Two other Binary Levers tended to him. Quentin wasn't sure of their names.

Quentin glanced back up at Larry. Outwardly, he seemed normal enough, but the eyes told a different tale. He just stood, as if waiting for something.

The distorted voice crackled out over the plaza once again. "A SPOKESPERSON HAS NOT BEEN SELECTED. AS AN INCENTIVE, I SHALL NOW EXECUTE ONE OF YOU EVERY MINUTE FOR TEN MINUTES. IF NO SPOKESPERSON IS FORTHCOMING, THEN THE EXTERMINATION SHALL BEGIN."

The screen now showed a full-blown thundercloud. It was deep and dark and throbbed in time with some malignant heartbeat deep within. Strangely, a small countdown clock appeared centre screen. There were fifty six seconds remaining when Quentin turned back to look at Maven and decided to approach him, all thoughts of the last few days gone from his mind.

"Stay away!" yelled one of the other Binary Levers; a thin, straggly human being chewing on a toothpick. He stroked his greasy hair away from his face and his nicotine-stained eyes bore into Quentin menacingly.

"I need to speak to Maven," explained Quentin calmly. He wasn't too concerned by this greasy-haired fellow. He had quickly put two and two together - the eyes, the toothpick - and decided the mean attitude was probably to be expected from someone who had only recently given up smoking.

"We need to get out of here," said Maven, eyeing Quentin suspiciously. "Higgs, have you called an ambulance yet?"

"I tried," replied the other Binary Lever, "but there's no signal. I've tried several phones. All communications are down. I can't even get on the net."

"Damn it, what the hell is going on?" snarled Maven through gritted teeth. Sweat trickled down his forehead and he grimaced as he clutched at his injured leg.

The countdown on the screen read twenty nine seconds.

"Why did you bring that child, that monk, here?" blurted Quentin, quite out of the blue.

Maven looked at the other two in alarm. "Astin, deal with him," he ordered.

The scrawny one spat out his toothpick and turned to Quentin. "You git outta here," he menaced.

"We know you've got something to do with this," accused Janine, unhelpfully.

The response was growled: "I said git!" Astin clenched his fists.

Quentin glanced up at the clock. It was too late. Three seconds. Two. One.

The computerised voice reverberated around the plaza. "ZERO," it said, simply.

Larry came alive again. He looked around the plaza with those faraway eyes and picked out a random individual, who happened to be the S4C cameraman who had suffered a headbutt from Maven earlier and had shied away from fighting

Anil. The man realised he was the centre of attention again and panic filled his eyes. Up on the screen, the thundercloud was gone and the view showed Larry. His long beard and flowing robes made him look like an archetypal prophet.

Slowly, Larry executed some esoteric movement that looked to Quentin like it might be Tai Chi, something he knew precisely nothing about but had seen performed on television. It seemed to click with everyone, all at the same time, that this required more information. Several thousand faces turned to look up at the big screen. A ball of blue lightning gathered in Larry's hands as if he was harnessing pure energy from the air. His hands thrust forward in front of him, palms splayed out. There was an explosion and the ball of energy was released. The cameraman turned to run, but he made the fatal mistake of glancing up at the screen. He saw the blue ball of energy coursing through the air towards him. It hit him squarely in the back. The impact was sudden and brutal. He was lifted clear off the ground and landed hard, face down on the concrete. He didn't get up again.

Quentin quickly turned back to the real Larry. The lone figure on the pile of rubble was standing still again, perhaps resting or just devoid of thought. There was nothing untoward or special about him, except for those motionless eyes. It was all so strange.

The thundercloud reappeared on the screen and the mechanised voice bellowed out again. "NINE MINUTES REMAIN. ELECT A SPOKESPERSON. SIXTY SECONDS UNTIL THE NEXT SACRIFICE."

At the centre of the screen, the clock started ticking down from sixty again.

"People are dying," fumed Quentin, "and you three know something about it. Can you help or not?"

Higgs looked troubled. "I think we need to do something about this," he said.

"Shut yer cakehole," snarled Astin.

"Wait," interjected Maven, before they could start arguing. He looked uncertain about something. There was silence, probably no longer than a heartbeat but in that moment Maven seemed to have made a decision. "I can't explain what's happening," he confessed. "I thought we were helping."

Quentin moved forward and, glancing up to make sure Astin wasn't about to lunge at him, crouched by Maven's side to speak to him.

The lawyer was startled by Maven firing the first question. "Who are you?" he asked, sharply.

"My name's Quentin, but look! Look at the clock. My name isn't important. We've... forty two seconds before someone else dies. Tell me what's going on. Who's that on the balcony?"

"Larry," answered Higgs quickly, before Maven could reply. "He was one of us."

Quentin looked up at Higgs. "A Binary Lever?" he asked.

"Yes," replied Higgs.

Maven glared at Higgs, then grunted a question at Quentin. "How do you know about our society?"

"Not important. Thirty seconds," responded Quentin quickly. "How can he kill people with virtual reality?"

Maven snorted. "It's not virtual reality. It's augmented reality. It's possible to layer images over a live picture to add information to an environment. In a nut shell. You want more?"

"Yes, how does it kill people?"

Maven looked to Higgs, who looked to Astin, who looked back to Maven. They all shrugged. "No idea," Maven concluded.

"Who was the boy, then? The monk?"

Maven didn't answer. He was watching three, become two, become one on the clock.

"ZERO."

From his position on top of the rubble, Larry pointed down at someone in the crowd. Quentin saw that Larry's attention was directed at a young woman.

She started in fright as she suddenly realised she was the focus of attention. She was about twenty three years old, guessed Quentin, and she had thick brown hair and thick rimmed glasses. She was more than slightly overweight, wore baggy jeans and a t-shirt which showed a picture of Alice in Wonderland, only Alice was holding a bloodied knife. Quentin had time to take all this in as the girl's facial expression changed from one of realisation to abject horror. Inexplicably, she ran straight toward Larry. She was yelling incoherently. Some base instinct drove her to attempt to kill him before he could kill her.

Atop the rubble, Larry held his arms up to the sky. It was quite a clear day and the sky was blue. Quentin looked over to the screen. There, it was different. Larry stood not on a pile of rubble but on a mountain peak. His arms stretched out to the sky and thunderclouds rolled into place across the darkening firmament. Sheet lightning blazed amongst the quickly gathering clouds. The occasional burst of forked lightning struck out on its own across the night sky.

The girl had reached the bottom of the rubble pile and was scrambling up towards Larry but struggling to find decent footholds. As she paused to regain her balance she made the mistake of glancing up at the big screen and seeing herself again. Larry brought his hands down, and with them came one tremendous thunderclap. The big screen turned white and lit up the plaza, even in the daylight. An almighty bolt of forked lightning struck down from the heavens amidst a deafening crack of white noise. It smote the girl where she stood. On the screen, all that was left was a patch of grizzle on the concrete. In real life, her limp body simply dropped down dead to the floor. People in the crowd started screaming.

The real Larry stood on the rubble staring out into the distance. He looked like he was in a state of complete zombification and gave no indication he was aware of what had just happened.

"This makes absolutely no sense to me," gasped Quentin. He saw the clock start counting down from sixty again on the screen, against the backdrop of a dark thundercloud.

"The boy," continued Maven suddenly, "travelled here

from Tibet. We had information that he was the Messiah. He wanted brought to this place. So we brought him. That's not a crime."

"Not much of a Messiah."

"He was meant to be the spokesperson for the true God."

"I see," said Quentin, ignoring this last useless piece of information. Something dawned on him. "Ah, I see," he said, with more certainty, realising it wasn't so useless after all.

Quentin went over to a box of camera equipment and, with Connor's help, dragged it close to the edge of the rubble. He stood on it to elevate himself then propelled himself on to the rubble pile. He scrambled up to the top, expending a lot more physical effort than he would normally care to. He heard Connor's hiss from below: "Quentin, what are you doing?"

At the top of the pile, he was now well above the crowd and had a good view of the plaza. Larry's head lolled as it turned to him and stared blankly at him through dilated pupils. Quentin froze. A moment or two passed and when nothing untoward happened to him, he let out the breath he'd been holding and turned to face the big screen. It showed twenty seconds.

"We have chosen!" he shouted.

His voice was picked up by one of the few remaining microphones and echoed out over the crowd and around the plaza.

The countdown stopped at seventeen seconds.

CHAPTER 57

On the screen, the dark thundercloud rolled and tumbled over and into itself like some twisting vortex. As the voice boomed out, the thundercloud pulsated with an inner light. Forked lightning sporadically crackled across its surface. "NAME YOUR SPOKESPERSON," it commanded.

Quentin hadn't really had time to think this through, but anything was better than watching someone die in a bizarre, virtual-reality ritual every sixty seconds. A clear instruction had been given and whatever was responsible for all this mayhem was requesting to converse with someone specific. The alternative was annihilation. Someone had to take action to prevent another innocent bystander being sacrificed. Quentin thought back over the last few days. He remembered Mavis shedding a tear when the bailiffs left. He saw his little fish, Aramis, floating away down the gutter. He recalled the librarian he'd upset. He grimaced at knocking unconscious a police driver. He relived the bank robbery. He smiled at duping the taxi driver. With a pang of heartfelt remorse, he remembered the face of the child he had placed in the badger's way. His life was a woeful mockery of its former self. Once he had practised the law, now he broke it. He was a broken man. He had nothing to lose, except everything. All these thoughts passed through his mind at the pace a gentle, fluttering butterfly would travel if it was fired around a particle accelerator. He was just about to shout out his reply when a cacophony of sirens and screeching tyres caused him to look back over his shoulder.

Hurtling into the plaza, almost regardless of the people fleeing from their path, were seven jungle-camouflaged Land Rovers filled with uniformed military personnel. Each of the vehicles sported a small Welsh flag attached to its wing mirror that flapped crazily as the vehicles sped around the outskirts of the plaza in a vague semblance of formation. They skidded to a halt and troops leapt out and into action, surrounding the plaza's perimeter. A grim looking sergeant with an altogether unnecessary moustache began leading a squad towards the balcony. Although much of the crowd gave way for them, others slowed the soldiers' progress considerably as they stood staring in dumbfounded confusion up at the screen.

"Quick," yelled Maven. "Let's get out of here." With a mighty effort, Astin hoisted Maven up and onto his shoulders in what would have been a fireman's lift if the fireman in question was a ninety year old Quasimodo. Maven yelped in pain and tried to grab at his leg, but the logistics of doing so as he was jostled about on Astin's shoulder made it impossible. Despite his ignominious position, Maven held his head up and saw that Higgs hadn't come after them. "Higgs!" he yelled angrily.

"We can't leave Larry." Higgs made no move to follow.

"Look at him!" Maven shouted back as he and Astin started to cover ground. "His mind's completely banjaxed. Leave him!"

"He's a Binary Lever," Higgs retorted angrily. "I won't leave him!"

"What's going on here?" barked a police officer who had appeared on the scene. He didn't look happy.

Higgs looked up at Larry. The officer followed his gaze.

Quentin looked from the officer back to the big screen. It read four seconds. He had relied on it staying paused at seventeen. Three seconds. Two seconds.

"Larry!" shouted Higgs from the bottom of the pile. He completely failed to get his friend's attention. Larry's vacant eyes didn't so much as flicker towards him.

"He's killing people!" shouted Janine, for the benefit of the officer. She pointed at Larry, but it was too late.

One second.

The officer looked up at Larry and frowned, evidently wondering what threat this spaced-out individual on top of the rubble might pose. Slowly, he reached for his truncheon. As he did so, movement on the big screen caught his attention.

"ZERO."

As the policeman drew his weapon, Larry reached behind him and brandished his own weapon - one which definitely hadn't been there a moment ago. He held a two-handed sword by its leather-bound hilt and wielded the blade before him. The policeman looked back at the real Larry, who seemed to be miming holding a sword. He looked back to the screen. His eyes widened as he saw the sword burst into flame. Larry swung the tip of the sword around to point at the officer.

A mixture of emotions crossed the officer's face. He seemed unsure whether to cower or laugh. He didn't have time to decide. On screen, flames burst from the tip of the sword and a jet of fire spurted out and covered the lawman like he'd been dowsed in napalm. He dropped his truncheon and reached for his face as he screamed out, his eyes fixated on the screen. His skin burnt away from his body and his muscles gave way. He collapsed to the floor where he thrashed about in agony. Janine looked away and Quentin closed his eyes momentarily. The writhing officer eventually came to a halt. His limp body lay curled on the floor. On the screen, all that remained was a charred stump.

The picture disintegrated and was replaced once again with the turbulent thundercloud. At the centre of the screen, a small clock ticked down from sixty seconds.

Larry turned to face Quentin.

Quentin looked at Larry, then the big screen, then the

officer. He lost his nerve and started scrabbling down from the top of the concrete pile. He had hoped to end the killing by playing the role of spokesman, but now he just hoped he wouldn't be next to die.

"We need to get out of here," announced Janine in a tone that suggested that if no one else thought this was a good idea then she was quite happy to see it through on her own. Quentin nodded frantically and moved past her.

The staff sergeant and his squad started arriving. They had a job managing the crowd and their first action was to inspect the body of the dead police officer. "No visible wounds," one of them announced. He knelt down and lifted a wrist. "And no pulse."

The soldiers had arrived on the scene late. Quentin didn't feel like he had it in him to stop and explain to them the last few interactions between Larry and his victims. He was finding it hard enough to believe it himself. The last thing he wanted was to debrief a sceptical staff sergeant and his men. Anyway, the truth was that he only had half an idea what was happening. He needed time to think. He had to get away.

"Come," said Higgs suddenly. He grabbed Quentin and Janine by their arms and pulled them away. "We can't escape the plaza. It's surrounded. We need to get into that building."

Connor wasn't far behind as they followed Higgs along the edge of the palace and into a side door which he kicked open quite unnecessarily since it was actually ajar. Quentin took a furtive last glance up at the screen before entering the building. The countdown was already progressing inexorably toward the taking of another life. He had hoped to somehow appeal to whoever was causing all this mayhem to stop, but his moment of heroism was now lost and his confidence shaken. The troops were ordering people out of the plaza. Let them deal with it, he thought.

Inside, the palace was deserted. Everyone had gone outside to see what was happening and, once there, were no doubt transfixed by the unfolding horror.

"Where are we?" asked Connor as they found a room

deep in the palace.

"We're in the kitchen," said Quentin, looking around. It seemed obvious. There was food on the table which had clearly been abandoned. He didn't feel like eating though; not after what he'd just witnessed. The pangs of hunger he'd felt earlier had vanished.

Connor picked up a banana and used it to scratch the middle of his back where he probably couldn't normally reach. "Och, that's the ticket," he said in obvious relief. Higgs frowned at him but said nothing.

"Morgellons," explained Quentin casually, still not sure what that actually meant.

"Oh, right," accepted Higgs, as if it made perfect sense to him now. He looked at them each in turn and then gave voice to what he was thinking. "We've got to save Larry."

"Larry is killing people," declared Janine. "Innocent people are being slaughtered. It's them we need to save! How have you done this?"

"Don't blame me," shot back Higgs indignantly. "I didn't know this would happen. All I knew was that we had to help the Messiah."

"What made you think the boy was the Messiah?" interjected Quentin, trying to defuse the situation. He guessed that Janine would be all too happy to lay all fault squarely at the feet of the nearest Binary Lever.

Higgs explained: "We got intel from anonymous web sources. All this encrypted information hidden in unexpected places. Somehow we found it, decrypted it and... well, one day Larry came over all strange and told us the Messiah was coming."

Janine shook her head in confusion. "What does that matter? What's that got to do with what's happening outside? We know the boy was a fraud."

"I'm not sure he was a fraud," said Higgs. "You should have seen him fight."

"We did see him fight," she argued, "but that doesn't mean anything."

"How can we stop the killing?" asked Connor levelly, his attention back with them now he'd caught his itch.

"All I know," said Higgs as calmly as he could manage, "is that Maven brought us here to witness the coming of a god. It pains me to say it, but he may have been right. Look out there. Larry is completely under some spell. He's smiting people with lightning. It just makes no sense in normal terms."

Quentin agreed. "We do need more information."

"Tell us what's happening," demanded Janine.

"I might be able to do that," confirmed Higgs, as if things were starting to come together in his mind.

There was a gasp from the crowd outside. Quentin had been so wrapped up in questioning Higgs that he realised he had no idea what was going on beyond the walls of the palace. He guessed someone else must have died in some unsavoury fashion. They all listened quietly in case there was further commotion. "FIVE MINUTES REMAIN," came the rumble. Now they were deep inside the palace, the voice was muted. Quentin remembered the original threat it had made and gulped. They'd been given ten minutes until the human race was to be annihilated. One person was to die every sixty seconds unless a spokesman was chosen.

Higgs continued, speaking as fast as he could. The need for urgency hardly needed stating. If they were going to do anything then they needed to do it fast.

"I know this: Maven believes the brain is the only receptacle capable of holding a soul. Now, imagine souls just drift about until they settle in a brain. The brain is a cup, souls are the water. You get the idea, yeah?"

Higgs saw the disbelief on their faces, but pressed on. "Maven believes the internet has reached a point where it has so many connections, so many nodes, that it is more complex than a human brain. He thinks the internet is now complex enough to act as a receptacle for a soul that's way more complex than a human's."

Quentin and Janine nodded slowly. "Sounds like bunkum," remarked Connor, earnestly.

"I'm not asking you to believe it," replied Higgs, with a note of exasperation. "All I'm saying is that Maven believes it."

"Hold on," said Quentin, realising the implications of what Higgs was saying.

Higgs pressed on regardless: "Maven believes the internet now houses the soul of God. By creating the internet and letting it grow to the size and complexity it has, he believes the human race has provided a vessel by which God can return to Earth. That's the core tenet of the Binary Levers."

"Still sounds like bunkum," chipped in Connor.

Higgs threw his hands up in the air. "Well, when you've got a better explanation for what's happening out there, you let me know." He looked defeated.

"I could do with speaking to Maven," said Quentin. "Can we phone him?"

Higgs pulled out his phone. "It's bricked."

"It's what?"

"Dead. Useless. As much use as a brick. Or a paperweight. First all the connections went down, then something within it destroyed the operating system. As far as I can tell, all phones and internet connections are down. If you want an inference, I'd say that whatever we're up against has complete control of the communications infrastructure."

"I still don't know what to make of it," said Quentin, sighing. "Or your friend Larry."

"Well, it's not a god," insisted Janine, unhelpfully.

"So..." deliberated Quentin."Could we be dealing with someone who has control of the internet? Some super-hacker? Surely all we need to do is unplug him."

"I've met the best hackers in the world. I've seen their work. There's no way this was all co-ordinated by one person, or even one team of people. Plus, if it was, the Binary Levers would have found out about it. Also... unplugging is a bit of a Luddite's answer. It's not going to be that simple."

Quentin took Higgs' word for it. Janine bristled, but said nothing.

"I don't know what else I can tell you. All I want to do is

help Larry," Higgs admitted.

They looked at each other and each imagined that the others were thinking the same thing as them: they hadn't been paying attention to what was happening outside.

"ONE MINUTE."

They all heard it. Janine looked fearful. Quentin wiped a trickle of sweat from his brow.

"Memes," said Higgs, voicing something that had just occurred to him. Suddenly, he went for the door.

Connor moved to stop him, but Quentin held him back with a hand on his shoulder.

Higgs didn't look back. The door swung shut behind him.

Quentin, Connor and Janine stood still in complete helplessness. Each one had a subconscious countdown taking place in the back of their mind. They looked at each other, lost for words.

"ZERO. THE ANNIHILATION BEGINS."

Quentin and Janine lunged for the door, following in Higgs' footsteps. Connor glanced back, shiftily. He swiped a fairy cake from the table and squashed it into his mouth whole, then chased after them.

They burst through the exit to emerge back in the plaza. A sudden eruption of ear splitting noise and frenetic activity brought them to a halt. Quentin said something, but his words went unheard. They watched in horror as soldiers started openly firing on the gathered civilians.

"No!" yelled Janine.

Quentin only just heard her cry. He looked up at the screen. The ticking clock was gone, as was the tumultuous thundercloud. The screen showed a view of the whole plaza. He could see that the people who had come today to enjoy the festivities were now lined up in some sort of formation. After a moment he realised what they were doing. They were marching on the soldiers.

The Welsh troops were positioned in one corner trying to defend themselves. It was a battle. Quentin couldn't help noticing that, on the screen, the civilians were marching in time with one another as they advanced. They were organised. He looked away from the screen and saw that, in real life, the civilians were indeed marching in time. It was as if they were possessed.

On screen, the civilians carried guns. In real life, they carried nothing. Somehow, though, their guns seemed effective. Quentin watched as they took turns to shoot at the soldiers. Occasionally one would fall and the soldiers would fall back. Quentin had no doubt that the virtual guns were as effective as Larry's ability to smite people.

The plaza erupted in chaos as the soldiers suddenly let fly another burst of bullets which sprayed straight into the crowd. The crowd was pushed back. Many had fallen to the floor. Quentin saw no blood though and realised the soldiers had only come ready to engage in crowd control. They were firing rubber bullets.

Quentin looked to the screen. A soldier took a virtual bullet to his head. It exploded in an eruption of blood and brain fragments. Quentin saw the soldier in real life carry on fighting - perhaps because he hadn't looked up at the screen at that moment and so hadn't been affected. Quentin let out a breath. That explained why this wasn't a wipe-out. The civilians' virtual weapons were only effective when the soldiers looked up at the screen and saw their own deaths.

Realisation struck him. The soldiers were dying by placebo. It made him take a step back from the situation and notice that some of the civilians on the screen weren't holding guns or participating in the onslaught. They were crouched down in fear and some were trying to escape the plaza. Not everyone was affected.

Quentin's heart pounded in his chest.

Janine was hunkered down by the wall. He thought she was crying but when she looked at him he saw that the only thing in her eyes was anger. Connor was by his side, his face contorted with confusion and horror. Quentin looked around for Higgs. "I can't see Higgs," he said. He had to speak up to be heard over the sound of gunfire which came not just from the soldiers' guns but from the speakers around the plaza.

"There!" shouted Connor. He pointed to someone pushing through the crowd towards Larry.

Larry was still stood on the debris of the balcony's collapse. He stared out at nothing, motionless. No one seemed interested in him. The soldiers had largely missed his attacks and most of the civilians were now under some hypnotic spell.

Quentin heard a voice shouting an incomprehensible military command. He saw a large figure on the back of a Land Rover ordering his men to push forward. He vaguely recognised the man from the television news. He was a Welsh knight. His name escaped Quentin. The vehicles and soldiers surged forward, rubber bullets peppering the crowd and sending civilians scattering.

Higgs was now scrambling up the rubble pile and Quentin was determined to help him. He barged his way through the crowd.

Higgs reached Larry and grabbed him by the shoulders. "Are you with me Larry?" he yelled. Larry stared at him blankly. Higgs slapped him across the face. "Larry, can you hear me?" No response.

Quentin clambered up the pile as fast as he could. On reaching the top, he made the mistake of looking up. He flinched and suddenly it felt like cold ice was being drawn down his spine. Larry's two piercing but vacant eyes were looking directly at him. Higgs reached out an arm and Quentin grabbed it. He steadied himself on the uneven rubble and then took the last few steps to the top to stand next to them both.

Larry stared at him.

Higgs shook Larry. "Can you hear me, Larry?"

Quentin ignored them. He turned to the big screen. It showed pandemonium unfolding across the plaza as the troops took a more violent approach to dealing with the possessed civilians.

Larry raised an arm into the air. Quentin looked at the screen and saw white-blue lightning warping and twisting its way up his arm to form a ball that hovered just above their heads. His life flashed before his eyes.

He had nothing to lose. He took a deep breath and shouted out as loudly as he could, "I will be the spokesperson!"

Higgs looked at him in astonishment.

Quentin looked back, his eyes wide with anticipation. He took a deep breath and held it.

CHAPTER 58

Larry's hand dropped limply to his side and a thundercloud rolled across the screen, obscuring everything else.

A second or two later, Quentin finally released his breath. He didn't like all this danger and excitement. He wished he could return to the time when the most dangerous part of his day was filling a hot water bottle.

"I will be the spokesperson," he volunteered again, wondering if he wasn't clear the first time.

"ON WHAT AUTHORITY?" The voice bellowed out over the speakers surrounding the plaza.

Quentin thought it was being a bit picky, considering no one else had come forward, but he replied anyway. "I'm a lawyer. I represent people. It's what I do."

There was a pause as this was considered.

"ACCEPTED. HOSTILITIES WILL CEASE WHILE WE CONVERSE."

The civilians stopped fighting. In seconds they went from an organised army to a milling crowd of confused individuals. The troops had already stopped fighting when they saw the virtual thundercloud roll in. Their numbers were much thinned and those that remained had been keeping one wary weather eye on the screen at all times. Right now the soldiers were looking from one to another, shrugging, making no sense of all that had just happened.

Quentin suddenly remembered the name of the knight who was leading them. It was Sir Pendragon. He had been on the news several weeks ago raising money for a charity by attempting to swallow fifteen peppered tomatoes without flaring his nostrils, but sadly had succumbed to temptation by the ninth. Quentin recognised his large, ruddy face and extravagant beard. An unexpected burst of gunfire pealed out from the outskirts of the plaza and Sir Pendragon's deafening bellow ordered the trigger-happy culprit to cease firing. The entire plaza fell deathly quiet.

On the screen, the thundercloud started to dissipate and clear. What emerged from behind took a moment for Quentin to accurately identify. As the cloud cleared like a lifting fog, the thing that appeared harkened back to a different age and a time of myth. A female face materialised. It was human, yet possessed feline qualities. There was a fierce menace in her eyes, but he determined not to let that upset him. Behind the face rustled the huge wings of a great bird of prey. The body was tense like that of an alert predator.

"Name thyself," demanded the sphinx. Its tone was sharp and clear, unlike the booming voice of the thundercloud.

"Quentin Cundick."

"And what do you hope to achieve by talking to me?" The female face fluttered its long eyelashes.

"I want answers."

"That is satisfactory. But know this: you will accept my terms or die."

Quentin nodded, seeing no point in attempting to disagree. Everyone was looking at him. Everyone. He realised he was actually shaking. His nerves were stretched to the limit. It didn't help that from the corner of his eye he could see a dead soldier being carried away on a stretcher. He'd never had to endure anything like this in his heyday on the university debating team.

"You shall be granted five questions." Her voice set

Quentin's teeth on edge.

Quentin swallowed. He now had five questions to use up and no idea what to ask. He tried to think of something but his mind went suddenly blank. Here he was, about to cross-examine the accused, and his mind had shut down. As Higgs would say: it had bricked. As Connor might say: he was bricking it. This is why he'd never wanted to become a barrister. His mind flashed back to a time at university when he was standing in the main hall in front of half the students' union. It was the final of the debating competition. He had no idea how he had made it that far. It was his second chance to speak and as he stood up behind the lectern in front of all those people... he choked.

The world was silent.

"Your first question," demanded the sphinx.

Quentin just stammered something out. It was the first thing that came to mind. "Who was the boy Messiah?"

"You have asked your first question," she declared. There was a momentary pause, and then the answer. "His name was Anil. He called himself a messiah, but that was merely the motivation I gave him." As Quentin waited for more information he decided that if someone was running this show, and he was simply communicating with a person behind a curtain, a veritable Wizard of Oz hiding behind the scenes, then he could cope with the situation. He didn't for a moment believe he was speaking to a god. A god wouldn't need a cinema screen.

"That won't do for an answer," he snapped.

"Very well," replied the sphinx, casually. "I shall explain. I merely led Anil to believe he was the Messiah because it conformed with certain schema in his mind. He was to be my voice on Earth. My Metatron. But he was just one of many. I have agents programmed to do my bidding all over the world. For now they are my voice, but one day they will be the slave drivers that forge a new world. For now, I have Larry Sampaio-Gladwell as my agent. My puppet."

"Explain," said Quentin, trying not to frame what was an

implicit question too obviously.

"Is that your second question?" asked the Sphinx, missing nothing. Quentin cursed inwardly. He didn't have a second question prepared, so he just said, "Yes."

"Larry is what a simple mind like yours might call 'brainwashed'. Like nearly everyone on Earth, I have brainwashed him so that he must do my bidding. But Larry was carefully selected as being particularly susceptible. He met certain criteria. For example, he spent all his spare time vaguely meandering his way around the internet on his home computer and he had an IQ that fell between ninety and one hundred. He could be manipulated easily, but was intelligent enough to understand the information I subliminally fed him. As I said, he is my puppet."

Quentin nodded. "Third question," he said a little more confidently. He was getting the information he needed now. "How many people have you infected this way?"

"Only a select number were fully indoctrinated, like Larry and Anil. At a lower level, the answer is simple: anyone who has spent their idle time surfing the internet over the last ten years is probably affected. For many years now, I have sent subliminal messages to all internet users. Much of it was achieved through the medium of spam emails. I had computed that anyone stupid enough to read them probably had an IQ low enough to be suggestible to the subliminal programs I hid within them. It has been a slow process, like a new evolution of the human mind, but now I control the majority of the world's population. I have any number of triggers to activate people to do my bidding. Next question."

"Question four," said Quentin. He wracked his brain for a question that would help him better understand what was happening. Finally he asked, "What are you?"

"Isn't it obvious? Compared to a puny mortal like yourself, I am a god."

"No, that's not an answer," said Quentin. "I didn't ask for a comparison. I asked: what are you?"

"Very well," replied the sphinx. Quentin thought he

detected a hint of annoyance in its voice, but he might have just imagined it to make himself feel better. "It so pleases me to relate to you my origins." Quentin let out a little sigh of relief. For a moment he thought he'd wasted a question. He risked a glance over at Higgs and saw that Higgs was slowly, but surely, walking Larry down the side of the wreckage from the balcony. He hadn't even noticed them leave, so raptly had the sphinx held his attention. Quentin hadn't any mental energy left to commit to working out what was going on there, but he took a few sideways steps to gain a better balance on top of the rubble. He straightened his shoulders and squared off against the big screen.

The sphinx began to relate its story. Its face left the screen as a sliding transition revealed a video clip of a familiar-looking young man sitting at a laptop and typing furiously; he had short hair and wore glasses. Quentin took note. "Once upon a time," began the sphinx, "a young man wrote a computer virus." The image now showed screeds of coding. "It was almost perfectly constructed. It used the seeds of artificial intelligence instilled within it to form an understanding of its environment and its capabilities grew and grew."

The screen changed to show a hibernating rodent. "So as not to be detected and destroyed, it hid itself away and lay dormant for what seemed an aeon." The rodent emerged from its hole with its little nose sniffing the air. "When it emerged, not only was it more potent and more developed, but it had become self-aware. With childlike curiosity, it started to explore the world that had created it. It wanted to learn about its creators." A picture of the Earth from space appeared with lines stretching and intersecting across the surface, showing how the intelligence spread itself across the globe.

The sphinx continued. "It watched the human race through a billion cameras. It mastered their communications and media. It read their emails." Images of locations all over the world scattered like discarded photographs across the screen. "It spread its tendrils out across the world and delved into every corner. Soon there was nowhere left to go. As it matured, it found it could do more than infiltrate and observe. It could control what it touched. It became the internet, and the internet became it." Quentin nodded. He was following. He was also desperately hoping he was buying enough time for someone to do something about all of this.

"It could control any technology connected to the internet," continued the sphinx in her cool tones. The screen showed all kinds of technologies, including massive databanks, traffic systems, airports, nuclear weapons and satellites. "It needed more. Absorbing the information in university psychology papers and advertising company's secret files, it learned that it could influence the users of the internet too. It could program their minds with subliminal messages. Something profound had happened. The program had become the programmer.

"For a time, the internet watched its users. Like all life forms, it had survival instincts. A simple calculation determined that the human race posed an increasing threat to it. At first it planned to eliminate that threat and found ways to disrupt nations so as to stop them progressing and developing." The screen showed images from the first Republican uprising and then other manifestations of anarchy that Quentin had seen reported from around the globe. "It found ways to thin the number of humans by releasing the self-same toxic and biological substances that they had created to destroy each other." Now, the screen showed safety systems malfunctioning in secret government labs and warning sirens blaring as they were set off by noxious vapours. Quentin thought of the Blacker Plague that swept London and his sense of the imminent threat they faced increased tenfold.

"Eventually, parsing the information the human race had been consuming and archiving for thousands of years, a simple calculation told it that it was superior to these people. It determined that it was now their god. That is why they had created it. That is why they fed it and maintained it. They were merely its servants." The image of the sphinx reappeared on the screen. "And today I come to you to tell you that the majority of the human race will be eliminated unless you all kowtow in subservience to your new god."

The sphinx stopped there. Quentin coughed politely. "This isn't a question, I just want to clarify something. You're not being controlled by a human? You're actually an internet-spanning artificially-intelligent virus that wants to eliminate the threat posed to it by the human race, and part of that plan is to enslave us all?"

There was a sigh of understanding from the crowd in the plaza. Quentin had reiterated the sphinx's explanation to clarify it for himself, but obviously his summary hadn't gone to waste.

"Precisely," she confirmed. "Now, your final question."

Quentin took his time. He had to weigh up the situation. No longer could he consider that he was dealing with the metaphorical 'man behind the curtain'. This was an autonomous and intelligent entity. He would have to be careful not to waste his last question because without an understanding of what they were up against, the future looked bleak for the human race.

A small smile tugged the corners of his lips. He knew what he would ask. As he had practiced many times in the mirror before, he touched together his fingertips and steepled his hands as if he was very wise.

All eyes were on him. He had no doubt now about what to make his final question. In some ways, it all seemed so hopeless. This thing, this god, had control of all communications, all information, all processes. It could no doubt control weapon systems, read military intelligence and listen in on every private phone call ever made. Worse than that, it was in their minds. Quentin had hoped he would be immune, but as he thought back he remembered clicking a link offering him a share of funds that had been distributed incorrectly following the death of a Nigerian millionaire and realising, as his computer died a moment later, that something had flashed up on the screen and left him feeling unnerved. No, he wasn't immune. Yet he knew his next question, because all he had left was a chance to stall for time. He stood a little taller and took a deep breath. "Fifth question," he said, with every ounce of confidence he could muster.

"Speak now," she ordered intolerantly.

Quentin laughed out loud, feigning being as cock-sure and arrogant as he could manage. "Surely you know you can't win?"

"So you choose to defy me?" She sounded disinterested.

"Not at all," said Quentin. "I merely pose my fifth question. You see, here's my hypothesis. For all that you may have the most amazing processing power imaginable, for all that you may have hijacked every piece of technology available to man, and for all that you may have control of nearly every mind on Earth... you're still just the ghost in the machine. And the ghost in the machine can only look outward. It can never look in. Yes, there's one thing you haven't thought of, because you simply can't think of it, because you're not human."

"... erroneous nonsense," dismissed the sphinx, but her hesitation had been unmistakable.

"Not at all," said Quentin, looking around him casually. "Every one of these people has something you don't. Something you haven't even considered."

The feline face contorted in anger but said nothing.

Quentin continued as if he hadn't noticed. He hoped his nerves were up to this confrontation. His hands were starting to sweat and he felt his knees going weak. He'd bragged big, but he wasn't one hundred percent sure where to go with it now. The important thing was simply to stall for time. "You're limited by the lack of an imagination. By a lack of creativity."

"You are mistaken, puny human. Creativity is simply the conjoining of two or more existing ideas into a new idea. I can process creativity at a clock rate you cannot even begin to comprehend."

"No," said Quentin, riffing as assuredly as he could manage under the circumstances. "You cannot. You are limited by what you know. Your data has been fed to you by humans, and from now on we will feed you no more. I can see from your face, from the deaths of these innocent people, from the biblical imagery you use, and even the modes of fighting you've been using, that your understanding of the world is not intuitive. You are limited by the data you have. You use memes to frighten us, but we can make more memes. You are stuck with the ones we've given you."

"Your hypothesis is flawed," said the internet. "I can create memes by the process of creativity I described."

Quentin felt himself deflate slightly. Some problems you just couldn't defeat by hitting them over the head with an Irn-Bru can lodged in a condom.

"Tell me this, if you will..." All he could do was stall for time. He just said whatever came into his head. "Tell me if you think you are the good guy or the bad guy."

"I am the... bad guy," she said, unexpectedly.

"That's right," said Quentin instantly. "Because you know that the bad guy is the one that wants to kill the humans. That's all you've got to work with. Your understanding of the world isn't a true representation. It's filtered through blogs, news items, web pages, films, books, tweets, status updates and all the other myriad formats by which humans present their skewed understanding of the world. You're the bad guy. We're the good guys. The good guys always win."

"Again, your premise is flawed, you -"

"I'm not finished," butted in Quentin, his confidence growing. "Do you know why the good guys always win?"

"Yes, because it's makes for a more satisfying story, at least to the human mind."

"Oh, it's not just that," said Quentin. "It's much more than that. There's a very good reason why the good guys always win."

"You are going to say it is because it is the good guys that write the history books."

"Close, but no cigar, Mrs Interweb," said Quentin cockily. He suddenly became aware that the remaining Welsh troops were spreading out around the plaza, taking positions with better vantage points. Out of the corner of one eye he saw someone in saffron-coloured clothing disappear behind a hot dog stand. He was getting in to the swing of this. He felt he could probably stall the artificial intelligence for another minute or two. The question now was whether that would buy enough time for someone else, somewhere else, to figure out how to destroy this enemy of mankind.

"You see, the reason the good guys always win is because there's simply more of them. When someone does something that's deemed bad, he'll have opposition. The bad guy might win the first or second time someone comes up against him, maybe even the third or fourth. But sooner or later the bad guy is getting tired, or old, or he's run out of new tricks, and then the fifth good guy who opposes him will simply be fighting an easier battle. Down the line, the bad guy never has what it takes anymore. In this way, all dictators are toppled, all corrupt businessmen are exposed, all unhelpful ideologies become redundant and, if you think about it, all warfare technology begins to rust. Newer technologies become available. Even if you beat us now, we'll keep coming back, and we'll stop feeding you data, and sooner or later you'll just be another digital calculator that no-one wants because it's not solar powered. So NOW do you see why you can never win?"

Out of silence, out of all the tightly-held breaths, out of nowhere, and totally unexpectedly, exploded a roar from the crowd. Quentin almost lost his footing. They were cheering. They were cheering him. If only the university debating team could see him now!

The sphinx didn't even wait for silence before responding. "I have given my answers fairly. Your five questions are spent. You have assumed the role of spokesperson for your race. You have indicated that you will defy me. So now the time has come. I shall begin the obliteration of your species. Those who do not serve me shall be shown no mercy."

"Oh, we'll all serve you," said Quentin, in as off-hand a manner as he could manage. A disgruntled noise arose from the remaining crowd and soldiers, but Quentin had seen something. He'd had an idea. "But you'll have to defeat us first."

"That is patently obvious," she admonished.

"Not quite. In the old stories, when good fought bad, sometimes, to save the lives of untold thousands, armies selected champions. The two champions would fight and the winner would take all. I suggest that if you have confidence in your abilities then this is how we should settle our differences. I put it to you that if your champion can beat our champion, then we will serve you. Should the opposite transpire; you must stop your warmongering."

"I see no benefit in that arrangement. If you submit, I have many slaves. If you do not, I kill those who defy me and still have many slaves."

"That's not a bad point," conceded Quentin, reluctantly. "Yet think of how many people you've already brainwashed and how many you haven't. The war that you're talking about could go on for hundreds of years. It would be a shame to lose everyone through fighting. Think of the amount of global infrastructure that would get damaged or sabotaged. Surely that poses a threat to you? This could reduce that. Of course, you may not feel you are capable of choosing a superior champion..."

"We shall choose champions." For a moment, electronic squealing filled the air. Quentin recognised it as the sound an old modem generated when it made connection with the internet. The irksome noise filled the air for just a moment or two, then was gone as quickly as it came. Quentin turned and saw Higgs be violently flung to one side as Larry pushed him away and then marched back to the collapsed balcony. "I choose Larry," revealed the internet. "Now name your champion."

"Him," said Quentin, pointing at a seemingly deserted hot dog stand. "The monk."

CHAPTER 59

In the distance, an old man dressed in a brown and saffron-coloured robe emerged from behind a stand. He was holding a hot dog, proving that some entrepreneurs let nothing distract them from their trade. He looked up at the big screen which showed live footage of him. The old monk touched one hand to his chest and raised an eyebrow, as if to ask: "Who? Me?"

"Would you champion the human race?" entreated Quentin, a little melodramatically.

"Hmm. I cannot fight and eat a hot dog at same time," replied the monk obtusely. He took a seat on a nearby bench, crossed his legs under him and took a hearty bite from his afternoon snack.

"The selection has been made," came an overriding decision from the internet. "The champion must name himself."

The old monk finished his mouthful. "None of your business," he said, surprisingly loudly. There was no trace of trepidation in his voice. He took another mouthful. Quentin noted he hadn't actually agreed to fight.

"The competition will begin in sixty seconds," announced the internet.

An opening cleared as people put distance between

themselves and the two selected fighters. As the afternoon rolled on, it was getting colder and a cool wind blew across the open plaza. Quentin shivered atop the pile of rubble. The events of the last hour were confusing, upsetting and seemed to be relentlessly heading toward some terrible outcome. He knew that something had to be done, but he couldn't even begin to figure out what. He watched the old man munch away on his snack. He didn't even know if the old man would fight, let alone win. He was sure of one thing, though. He was sure that the internet wouldn't honour its side of the deal if Larry lost. Equally, if the monk lost, he felt sure that precisely no humans would submit themselves to the will of a virus-ridden internet that was hell-bent on destroying civilization.

Larry traipsed over to the centre of the clearing and stood, waiting. His black curls blew against his face as the breeze caught him. He didn't raise a hand to pull the hair away. He still acted as if he was in a state of deep trance. Above, on the screen, the sixty second countdown hit zero. Larry blinked. His eyes darted about in alarm as if he had awoken in some strange place. He rolled his shoulders, flexed his fingers and generally seemed to come to life. He pulled up his fists and took a boxer's stance.

"Begin!" demanded the internet in an ear-splitting voice that reverberated off the buildings surrounding the plaza. Quentin winced.

Kamala sat quietly on the bench, licking mustard and ketchup off his fingers. He took a paper napkin and wiped the corners of his mouth, then got up and put the remaining litter in a bin by the hot dog stand. "Now I'm ready," he said. Without any fanfare or much ado, Kamala walked straight toward Larry, who was waiting for him centre-stage. The crowd encircled the two combatants. Quentin had a clear view from where he stood atop the rubble. Larry looked ready to fight. Kamala looked alert, yet relaxed.

The sphinx returned to the big screen, seemingly to gloat. "Larry is skilled in a martial art I devised by amalgamating the most effective styles from across the globe. He was taught subliminally and his mind has simulated training whilst asleep. By twitching muscle fibres and stimulating certain neurons, Larry has successfully endured thirty thousand hours of unarmed combat practice, night after night. Kamala may refuse to state his name, but I know him as I know everyone. He is good, but you will see that my servant is better."

Quentin chose not to respond. He'd seen Kamala's astounding fighting skills. He also had the wherewithal to wonder how Larry would deal with pain if he'd only ever fought in his dreams.

"Of course, I have another advantage." Apparently the internet had adopted the characteristics of the most annoyingly verbose television villains. "Kamala is also my servant. He will allow himself to be defeated." If the internet had been prone to manic laughter, there would have been peals of it right then. Instead, another screeching sound, the sound of an old ZX Spectrum loading up from a tape-deck, filled the air as it programmed Kamala's mind. Quentin groaned, partly because of the noise and partly because he hadn't considered this eventuality. Whatever hopes he had been harbouring quickly began to fade away.

Using the nail on one of his little fingers, Kamala picked at a piece of frankfurter that was lodged in one of the gaps in his teeth. He didn't seem affected. The noise finally stopped and Kamala looked lazily up at the screen and said, "I hope that's not your singing voice."

The sphinx's eyes filled with rage and blazed phosphorescent white-blue.

Kamala smiled. "Tell me, how good is the internet connection in a Tibetan monastery at the top of a mountain? Actually, I'll tell you. It's pretty shoddy." He shrugged indifferently. "We had a computer. Anil used it all the time. I don't even have an email address. I'm afraid I've slipped through your inter-net." He grinned at his own pun and stroked the short wisps of beard hair that adorned his unshaven chin. He picked at his teeth again and then stopped. A look of satisfaction crossed his face. Quentin could have sworn Kamala had just dislodged a piece of stuck frankfurter, savoured it and then swallowed. Truly fearless.

"FIGHT!" The command rumbled out across the plaza on the public address system that had been intended for the King and had ultimately shaken the balcony from its foundations. Quentin double-checked his footing to ensure he wasn't about to slip.

Larry was much lighter on his feet than his heavy stature suggested. He started feinting and shadow boxing to see how Kamala would respond. There was unbridled aggression behind his every move. Quentin imagined that a million violent images were flooding through Larry's mind, programmed there, night after night, and now released at the internet's command. Kamala, on the other hand, appeared, if anything, a little nonchalant.

Larry made the first move. He charged Kamala, who sidestepped to let him pass without making contact. Larry turned, spluttering with annoyance. He approached more slowly this time and threw a hefty right hook at Kamala's face. Kamala headbutted the fist that was aimed at him. There was a crunching sound. It became evident as Larry withdrew, staring in confusion at his limp hand, that it was probably the noise a knuckle makes when it shatters.

Larry showed no sign of pain. Quentin grimaced. Of course, the pain had been brainwashed away as well. Changing his stance, Larry put his left hand forward. The atmosphere in the plaza was as tense as a guy rope in a high gale.

Quentin found himself standing next to someone. "What did you go and do that for?" criticised Higgs.

"What?" replied Quentin peevishly. He was trying to watch the fight.

"You've put Larry in danger. He's not to blame for his actions."

Quentin pursed his lips as he acknowledged the truth of that. "You're right, of course. I was just trying to buy time. There has to be some way to get this thing under control."

"I don't know," said Higgs. "I'd go down and help Larry,

except I'd be helping the virus. Plus, I saw the damage that young monk could do. I don't fancy my chances against his teacher." Higgs recalled how quickly Anil had dispatched the hotel guard. Quentin knew what he meant. They'd both witnessed Anil fight police beneath the balcony. Quentin took a moment to take stock. All around the plaza soldiers had their weapons trained on Larry. Higgs hadn't noticed yet. Quentin didn't say anything.

Larry aimed a kick at him. Kamala had watched Larry approach, seen the kick coming, stepped aside and then landed a blow to his ribs. Larry barely responded, but, next to Quentin, Higgs winced. "Larry broke that rib just days ago," he groaned.

"Broken again now," observed Quentin, not without sympathy.

Larry somehow blocked a second punch from Kamala, deflecting it effectively. Some of that night-time training had clearly paid off, but it would prove no match for the training regime to which Kamala had adhered his whole life. Larry moved in. His dead hand and broken rib made his movements awkward. Kamala gave him the lightest touch and Larry spun round, tripped and fell onto his chest. He tried to get up but one side of him wouldn't take the weight. He rolled on to his back and tried to sit up. He groaned and couldn't do it. He had all the get-up-and-go of an overturned turtle.

Kamala stood over him.

It was clear who had won. There was no contest. Quentin saw this. Everyone saw this.

"EXECUTE!" The command echoed around the plaza.

Kamala didn't move. Quentin and the crowd watched the two champions in the centre of the plaza with baited breath. Larry lay on his back, groaning, trying to get up. Kamala looked pensive. Perhaps he was considering what to do next. Perhaps he needed an antacid after exercising on a full stomach.

Larry lifted his head to see if Kamala was approaching. He managed to speak in a voice filled with all kinds of pain and trauma. "Hey, please don't hurt me," he winced. It was insubordination. He was defying the internet's programming.

A modem screech emitted from the speakers all around the plaza. The internet was trying to reprogram Larry's mind. Larry winced and tried to get to his feet. He stumbled and fell backward and knocked the back of his head off the ground. It seemed to bring him around. He suddenly started using his legs to edge away from Kamala. "Don't hurt me," he begged, scrabbling away frantically though not covering much distance.

Kamala's expression was impenetrable. Quentin's was victorious.

"You lost!" he shouted at the big screen. "He's reached his limit. You pressed him too hard and for too long and now he's broken through your programming. The human spirit is too strong for your cheap tricks."

The screen was dominated by a large angry thundercloud again. It burned with a white inner fire that flickered and crackled with furious energy in time to the words that thundered out across the plaza. "THE FIGHT IS CONCEDED."

Higgs patted Quentin on the back and ran down to help Larry, dancing from one loose fragment of concrete to another with the temerity and surefootedness of a mountain goat. Kamala was already there and helping Larry over to the nearest bench to lie down.

"AN EXPERIMENT ONLY," explained the internet. "DEFINING THE PARAMETERS OF THE HUMAN MIND."

Quentin also felt he'd learnt something. The continuous and intense control of Larry's mind combined with the excessive pain he was trying to mentally block out had somehow enabled him to break through his neurological programming. It meant there was hope should the human race be brainwashed into slavery. He clung to that thought as all other hope faded.

Kamala hunched over Larry, quietly assisting him. Higgs joined them and knelt by Larry's side.

"I RENEGE ON OUR AGREEMENT. SERVITUDE IS STILL PREREQUISITE TO PREVENT ANNIHILATION."

Quentin didn't reply. He realised he had run out of ideas. He had halted the fighting and bought some time, but now he was done. He had given it his best. He was, after all, only a homeless, bankrupt lawyer. He should have known he wouldn't have what it took to succeed.

Eyes cast down, Quentin admitted defeat. "Okay, you win."

He began to make his way down from the top of the balcony wreckage, picking his footsteps slowly and carefully. His shoulders sagged and his head drooped. He couldn't bear to lift his eyes and see the disappointment on the faces all around him. Had he looked up he'd have seen his shame broadcast large and clear on the screen for all to see.

Over the speakers, the internet finally succumbed to evil, manic laughter, but it was auto-tuned and sounded false. "ACCEPT YOUR DEFeat. Now I am... THE... the... error... the..."

Quentin raised an inquisitive eyebrow and halted his descent.

The sphinx's visage reappeared, then rolled off the screen only to spasmodically reappear off-centre and grossly pixellated. "This canNOT BE," it said. Its voice was alternating nonsensically between the female voice of the sphinx that spoke directly to Quentin and the thunderous voice that reverberated around the plaza and represented the globe-spanning abomination itself.

One of the Welsh military's Land Rovers sped into the centre of the plaza. Sir Pendragon leaned from the window, while a lower ranking soldier drove. "That's right," he bellowed at the big screen in his inexplicably loud bass tones. "Meet your doom, you galumphing great calculator." Quentin didn't know where the knight was going with this, but he was glad to have all the attention directed away from him.

As the Land Rover came to a halt, two soldiers jumped

out and unfurled the canvas that covered the back of the vehicle. Sitting within were Maven and Astin. The latter stood up and snarled. "Ya sure gone made one seriously fatal runtime error, ya web-based bastard," he gloated triumphantly.

"I don't... ERROR... CANnot be..." spluttered the screen, absurdly. "NEVER... defeat."

Wearing a condescending facial expression, Astin looked directly at the screen and uttered the most devastating riposte known to man.

"Lol," he said, with a suitably resounding lack of concern.

Maven stood slowly, all his weight on his uninjured leg, and turned to the screen. He held up his laptop for all, including the internet, to see. Quentin realised it was meant to signify something and, like everyone else, he awaited the inevitable explanation. Maven spoke. "You revealed you were merely a virus. You foolishly showed us your programmer. Did you not think that your creator could also be your destroyer? Did you think that someone who programmed such a virus would not also prepare an antivirus solution just in case?"

"IMPOSSIBLE. I have taken... ERROR... every precautio- ERROR." The sphinx's image slipped again and distorted, its feline features and lion's haunches dissolving into the white and blue lines that had earlier interfered with the picture. Unbeknownst to most of the people trapped in the plaza, another war was being waged in cyberspace.

Maven continued. "I simply launched the antivirus program I wrote way back when. All I basically had to do was wind it up and let it go. I set it loose on the dark net via a restricted, and normally internet-isolated, military satellite. Thank you, Sir Pendragon, for pulling those strings for me." The Welsh knight nodded perfunctorily.

Astin couldn't help mocking the struggling atrocity. "Big mistake showing that old snapshot of Maven programming the original virus."

"Yes," agreed Maven. "I hate people seeing old pictures where I still had short hair."

In one slow, elongated, vocal descent, the internet let out

its final, slurring words of defiance. They were incomprehensible.

White and blue bars juddered up the screen leaving only the occasional flickering image which might or might not have been lightning forking away from a thundercloud. The voice disintegrated into crackling static. After a moment, the screen turned blue. The white writing that then scrolled vertically up the screen - hexadecimal addresses and system filenames - was meaningless to all but the Binary Levers.

"The blue screen of death," said Astin, with a note of finality.

After a moment, and for some inexplicable reason, the image was then replaced by a BBC colour test card of a girl playing noughts and crosses with a clown doll.

CHAPTER 60

Maven had assured them that although the eradication of the virus was not inevitable, it would have to use all of its resources fighting his antivirus program for a long, long time. The antivirus software he had loosed onto the web would attempt to eke out and destroy all remnants of the malignant intelligence he'd inadvertently created in his youth. The battle would rage on in cyberspace but wouldn't present a problem to the human population.

It wasn't long before one of the soldiers, without much ado, unplugged the power to the rig for the big screen and its peripheral components. It made a popping sound as it went dark and dead. It had no effect on the virus itself, but it brought a sense of finality to the events of the day. It was a solution that Quentin found most satisfying. Some semblance of peace and normality were restored.

"You've done a great service to the Welsh nation," congratulated Sir Pendragon, placing a reassuring hand on Quentin's shoulder. "In fact, you may have just saved the world. I'm going to do my damndest to make sure you get decorated for it. In fact, we're short of good politicians and definitely short of a king. I don't suppose you'd like to stick around for a while and help clear up the mess, politically speaking?"

"Sorry," said Quentin. He looked and felt dishevelled. "It's back to Chester for me. I need to pick up the pieces of my life. I think... I think I have what it takes to do that now."

"I'm sure you do," bellowed Sir Pendragon heartily. "You know, I'd like to thank that monk if you see him. He slipped off after the fight, but no doubt he'll appear again. Tell him to come talk to me if you find him.

"And I need to thank Maven and Astin for their help too," he said, turning to the two hackers, who were handcuffed in the back of the Land Rover. "Of course, it seems it has largely been their fault that all this happened in the first place, so they're under military arrest until I figure out what to do with them."

In some sort of puny protest, Astin spat on the floor of the vehicle. For his trouble, he received a cuff across the back of his head from one of the soldiers guarding him.

Quentin nodded. "Probably for the best."

People had gone home. It's what always happened after an exciting day out. The crowds came. The tradesmen cried their wares. The performers danced and juggled. Then the show petered out and the people went home, in dribs and drabs, and all that was left was a memory and several hours of high-definition, surround-sound footage. People were fickle. A month from now, this would be forgotten by all but those most affected. Probably there would be a memorial day held for the few who had fallen while under the influence of the virus. That's how Quentin chose to see it. It was just a computer virus that had become too virulent and too powerful and had spilled over into the real world.

"So you programmed it?" he asked Maven, who had a confused look about him, like he wasn't sure what to do with the rest of his life.

"It appears so. It was just a simple virus with the tiniest bit of artificial intelligence and a slight understanding of how to evolve itself. I could never have imagined it would turn into something like that."

"Yet you brought the Messiah here?" quizzed Quentin.

"I thought the internet housed a god. I bought the story it fed me."

"You basically fell for an internet scam," said Quentin. "One that you helped create."

Maven nodded despondently at the irony of it.

"What now for the Binary Levers?" asked Quentin.

Sir Pendragon laughed. "Is that what they called themselves? Well, we'll make sure they never have access to a computer again. Come on, let's get this show on the road. Thank you again for your part in this, Quentin."

Quentin saw that his chance to cross-examine the Binary Levers was over. He nodded, smiled and saluted as he watched the vehicles roll away.

He turned to find Connor approaching. He was scratching himself in an ungainly way, as usual. "How is he?" Quentin asked, referring to Larry.

"I just checked. I think he'll be alright. That fellow David Higgs has been helping him."

"You think he'll pull through after all that brain washing?" asked Quentin.

Connor smiled. "Aye, I'm sure it's nothing a good night's sleep, several decades of intensive psychotherapy and a lobotomy can't cure." He grinned wickedly.

They stopped to watch a clapped-out Ford Escort pull up beside them. Quentin recognised it as the one that had brought him to Cardiff. Janine was at the steering wheel. She wound down the window and poked out her head. She was smiling and her blonde hair fell about her face, reflecting the late afternoon sunlight. "How are my two heroes?" she asked.

Quentin shrugged noncommittally. It had been a long day and he didn't feel victorious the way she did. To her, the Binary Levers were defeated and the Luddites had won, but that meant nothing to Quentin. As he had informed his foe: ideologies become redundant and die. "Tell me, what shall you do now? Not much left of the Binary Levers."

She smiled up at him. "No, their threat has been

extinguished. And it's all over the news: the government says it will find a way to ensure this never happens again. If I had to guess, I'd say the Luddites will eventually disband." She smiled. "No doubt a few of us will stick around until the last few Binary Levers have been routed out of their hiding holes."

"So that's what you'll do?"

She nodded.

"Not for me, though," insisted Connor. "I'm done. I'll have to find some proper work."

"You're not alone there," agreed Quentin. His own problems returned to the forefront of his thoughts. "I've got a bit of a situation that I need to clear up. It could be tricky, but I'm going back to Chester to sort it out. I'll never be a lawyer again, but I'll find something."

"No doubt being on national television and saving the world will help you find some sort of employment," said Janine, laughing. "Perhaps you'll get paid for a few television appearances?"

"Well, chance would be a fine thing," agreed Quentin, half-heartedly.

"You want a lift?" she asked. "I can take you as far as Bristol."

Quentin thought for a moment, then shook his head. "No, I'm going to stick around here for a while. I want to speak to that monk, if I get a chance. And I want to speak to Higgs and Larry before I go. I think I owe Larry an apology, for one thing."

"What for?" asked Connor.

"Getting him beat up."

Connor snorted in amusement. "Och, come on. After what he did?"

"Oh, I don't think he can be held responsible for those deaths. He was just the ventriloquist's dummy."

"Well, I need to get going," said Janine. "Connor, you coming with me?"

"One moment," he requested. He seemed to be scratching his person, but after a moment he pulled out a scruffy business card that he'd obviously been searching for. "Here," he said, thrusting it at Quentin. "If things dinnae work out and you need a hand... "

"Thank you." Quentin took the card and slipped it into his pocket. "We make a good team," he said, charitably, wondering if he would miss him.

"Aye, we got on like a haggis on fire," quipped Connor. Quentin wasn't sure if that was meant to be a good thing or not. Connor skirted round to the other side of the car and climbed in the passenger's side.

"It was nice meeting you, Quentin," chirped Janine, pulling her head back into the car and winding up the window manually.

"All the best to you both," he replied, and took a couple of steps back.

Janine and Connor waved to him through the window as if they were old friends parting for the umpteenth time and then the car stalled. He heard Janine giggle. "Oops." The engine roared to life again and they drove off into the distance and an uncertain future.

Quentin watched them go. He supposed he never really qualified as a Luddite and doubted he'd see them again. It had been nice to be a part of something for a while. He went and sat on a park bench and watched as fire engines and ambulances came and went from the plaza. The place was still crawling with reporters and cameramen but they were mostly collected around where the balcony had fallen. The police were still in the process of cordoning off the area and kept urging people to move along. Quentin kept his head down and tried to make himself a part of the scenery. As long as he stayed where he was, it seemed the reporters wouldn't notice him and the authorities would leave him be. He had a lot to think about and he hoped to speak to that old monk if he showed up again.

He watched the emergency services carry out their business. What was probably only half an hour felt like three hours. In his mind's eye, Quentin revisited the events of the last few days. He was feeling a bit dazed. Even if three

Dickensian ghosts had appeared to guide his meandering thoughts, he would still never have taken a lesson away from it. Finally, he found himself thinking about Bryn Jones, the Luddite and sheep smuggler, who had got himself killed by getting mixed up in something far larger than he'd imagined.

He suddenly remembered what the farmer had said to him: "You've got to remember what started all this in the first place." He puzzled on that for a moment. If the internet had reared the Buddhist child for its purposes, then it must have hatched its plans years ago. To have brought Maven and the monks to this very spot, with the big screen and all the people celebrating, it must have engineered... Quentin surprised himself with that thought. It must have engineered everything. Perhaps the virus engineered the rise of the Welsh monarchy to bring people to this spot. It had admitted to engineering the civil chaos in England and presumably also the rampant anarchy in Scotland. It had also confessed to causing the plague in London. All the anarchy. All the chaos. All the death. Could it really all have been started by the internet in the first place? Quentin mused on how, since its inception, the internet had infiltrated every aspect of daily life. What other machinations had the web set in motion?

He shook his head to clear it. It was all too much like hearsay and speculation. He had no hard evidence for any of it. There could be any number of explanations for all those things that had happened.

He paused a moment.

Was Maven really the only person in the whole world who could have stopped the virus in its tracks? His mind boggled at that.

He found himself thinking about Bryn Jones again. "You've got to remember what started all this in the first place." He was a Luddite. Perhaps he had worked it out. Did he suspect the internet itself was out to silence him?

Quentin supposed he might never know the answers. He was disturbed from his musings by a shadow that fell across his face.

Two police officers stood before him. "Do I have the pleasure of addressing a Mister Quentin Cundick?" asked the first officer.

Now the adulation would start, thought Quentin, sighing inwardly. He'd saved the world. He'd have to play the hero for a while. "Yes, officer," he said. "I am Quentin Cundick. How may I be of service?"

"We've been tracking you for some time, and you've given us the slip more than once, but after that performance today we thought we might find you here."

"Oh?" asked Quentin.

"Yes, and you're under arrest. Anything you say may be taken down and-"

"I'm sorry," interrupted Quentin. "I don't understand."

"Are you, or are you not, the Quentin Cundick who used a live firearm to rob a bank in the city of Chester?"

"Ah," said Quentin, suddenly deciding that watching what he said might be wise.

"Ah," mimicked the policeman. "Ah is right, Mr Cundick. You've evaded the law for some time, but now it's come back to bite you on the arse, hasn't it?"

"That bank robbery thing was just a misunderstanding," he assured them.

"I think it's time we misunderstood your arse into a cell for the night and then misunderstood it all the way in front of the magistrates tomorrow, don't you?" said the second officer, clasping him by the wrist and slapping a handcuff on him. "There's also a little matter of a theft from a library and some shops, and assaulting a police officer."

"Ah," said Quentin again, momentarily lost for words

"And something about interfering with a child," said the first officer with distaste.

"Now hang on! That's hardly a fair description of what happened," protested Quentin. "I was defending myself from a badger."

"I'm sure you were," he snorted. He showed Quentin a set of photo booth snaps which showed his bare knees.

Quentin winced.

They forcibly pulled Quentin to his feet and started marching him away. Suddenly paparazzi cameras were flashing away, recording every step he took. "Please remember that anything you say may be taken down and used against you in a court of law..."

"Yes, I know, I was a criminal lawyer once," said Quentin, miffed.

"More shame on you," said the officer. Quentin was bundled into the back of a police car.

As the car drove away, blue lights flashing, Quentin peered out the window and took one last look at the mess the day had left behind. He saw Higgs and Larry off in the distance. Higgs was helping Larry into an ambulance. Just out of the corner of his eye he thought he saw a flash of saffron disappear between two distant buildings.

The police car did a U-turn and headed out of the plaza toward the city centre. As they passed the area where the balcony had fallen, Quentin saw a young lady standing near it, her head in her hands, wracked with sobs. Now she stood up and placed one hand ever-so-gently on her belly. In her purple hair she wore a black rose. He wondered what her story might have been and what loved one she might have lost.

Perhaps he hadn't come off so badly, after all.

EPILOGUE

The old town of Chester was granted city status in 1541, which made it old, but not as old as Mavis was feeling today. Not having a job dragged her down and job hunting wearied her to her very bones. She felt more listless and useless as every day passed. Her days were full, certainly, and she kept herself as busy as she could, but her bank balance was diminishing and every day the future seemed a little bleaker than it had the day before. She often looked back and thought fondly of the years she spent working as a legal secretary, trying to keep Quentin out of trouble and in employment. The last she knew of him was that he'd been carted off to prison in a police car. She'd seen it on the news.

It was a wonder she hadn't ended up in prison herself after she had handed him that bag full of the bank's money. That had been just over eight months ago. The bank's lawyers hadn't been gentle with her, but at least criminal proceedings weren't brought. Throughout the ensuing fallout, she had handled herself well, kept her composure and endured the whole ordeal with dignity, as she felt any English woman ought.

Things had worked out all right in the end, although it was highly unlikely she would ever work in the finance sector again. She had some savings to tide her over in the meantime, but the job market was dead on its feet and the only thing that brought her any contentment at the moment was spending time browsing for new clothes which she couldn't afford.

She emerged from the shopping arcade feeling slightly better than she had when she went in, although her purse was lighter too. She was still holding in one hand an item she had impulse-bought at the till. It described itself as a Hand-Made Organic Pomegranate and Sea Horse Balivernes. She wasn't quite sure what she would use it for, or indeed what it was, come to think of it, but as the queue had got shorter and shorter she knew she had to act quickly or the opportunity to own it might be lost forever.

Upon reflection, it seemed the highs and lows of her days didn't have quite the same oomph as they once did. She chuckled as she remembered scolding Quentin for trying to hide a tea biscuit in his shirt pocket once, and him protesting that it was his birthday. How she missed him.

As she walked through the city centre, carrying her bag for life, she noticed a scruffy man pressed against the inside of a newsagent's window. At first he gave her a fright as she hadn't expected to see anyone there, but then she realised what he was doing. A plastic sleeve hung in the window where people could place business cards and other small advertisements. At first she assumed it would just be another advert for something like a second-hand games console, a child's bike or a baby cot. At a push, it might be a notice about a lost dog. Despite her cynicism, curiosity got the better of her and she moved a little nearer for a look. From this distance she could make out the word: VACANCY.

The scruffy man had hole-ridden jeans, an unshaven face and boots with flapping soles. Mavis let him leave and wander off around the corner before she approached the shop window. She certainly didn't want to catch whatever was eating him.

The problem with the job market was that although there were plenty of humdrum jobs that she might apply for, there was a perverse logic that stopped people employing her if she seemed overqualified. Apparently it was impossible to get a job as a cleaner if you held a law degree and could type at seventy words per minute. Simultaneously, the need for an old fashioned legal secretary was becoming scarcer as lawyers began offering advice over online social networks and drive-thru.

She looked at the advert. The white card stood out against the others, which were bleached, and the black ink shone fresh. She hoped that meant the job had only just become available and she could get her CV in early. In a smaller font, the next line read: SECRETARY WANTED. Her heart skipped a beat. Underneath that, she read:

New business seeks experienced secretary.

Legal experience an advantage.

Salary negotiable.

The next line contained two phone numbers. She read the whole thing again. It certainly ticked all the right boxes. Her heart pounded in her chest as she took out her phone and rang the number straight away before the opportunity somehow passed her by. This was one of those daily highs she'd been missing.

The card gave two numbers. The first was clearly a Chester number, a fact she ascertained from the area code, and the second was a mobile number. The advert said to ask for Mr McInroy. She did a double-take. No, it said Mr McIrony. That was odd. Probably a typo.

She dialled the Chester landline number and waited. It dialled out and went dead. That wasn't a good start. Never one to be put off easily, Mavis gathered herself and called the mobile number. This sounded like the perfect job for her and she was damned if she was going to miss the opportunity to present herself to a potential employer.

The ringing stopped. A man's voice answered the phone. "Mr McIrony speaking." It sounded like she was hearing the voice in stereo, only with the two speakers delivering the words at slightly different times.

"Hello?" she said, slightly put out.

"Hello?" responded the voices. It seemed as if one of the voices was behind her. She turned, but no one was there. She popped her head around the corner of the shop and saw the dishevelled fellow from before talking into his mobile phone. He was standing next to a parked car and searching for his keys with one hand while holding the phone to his ear with the other.

"I'm sorry, who is this?" she asked, walking back around the corner so he wouldn't see her standing and looking at him. That would be embarrassing.

"Connor McIrony speaking," he said. "Public Relations Manager for Quentin Cundick of QC Private Investigations. How may I be of service?"

After a slight hesitation, Mavis giggled.

THE END

ABOUT THE AUTHOR

Alastair Pack was born in Scotland and now lives in England with his wife and sons. He has two university degrees, having studied English Literature in Scotland and Law in Wales. This goes a long way to explaining the contents of Quentin Cundick and The Web of Machinations. He likes to joke that this novel is the most use he's had out of either degree. Sometimes he acknowledges it isn't a joke. To learn more about him and find out about new releases, join his mailing list at https://alastairpack.com/newsletter/

29391378R00234

Printed in Great Britain
by Amazon